TOUGH Love

BOOK 2

SPECIAL COVER EDITION

DIANNA ROMAN

Published by Wild One Press
Cover design by Stephanie Henigin & Dianna Roman

Interior Cover Model: David Carrion
Photographer: Rafa Catala
Interior sketch: Christopher Jensen by David Farquhar
Illustrations by Stephanie Henigin

ISBN: 978-1-959553-99-1 (ebook)
ISBN: 979-8-9853313-9-4 (Trade Paperback)
ISBN: 978-1-959553-98-4 (Special Cover Edition Paperback)

Also available in Audiobook

Visit the author at www.diannaroman.com

and

TOUGH Love

I used to think I didn't know who I was,
but now I know I'm me.
I'm me because of him.
He can have however much of me he wants.

CONTENT ADVISORY

This book contains adult language, explicit consensual sexual content, discussions of homophobia, and discussions on loss of a loved one.

DEDICATION

to Christie—

for your big heart, appreciation of love stories,

and making my book funnier

than I ever could have on my own

PROLOGUE

Graham

My twin sister is a sadist. That's all there is to it.

Maxie never misses an opportunity to torture me over the fact that I've been married twice. That means I had two weddings, which means I had two bouts of choosing caterers. Summary: sampling her caterer's food is the last freaking thing I want to be doing right now, but she's my sister, and she's happy.

Still, I wish someone could explain to me why she can't pick out her own damn food. It's not like she gives a shit about my opinion…on anything. Ever.

"I still don't understand why I have to be here. How the hell am I supposed to know what you two want to eat at your wedding?"

"It's a family affair, Graham Cracker. I want family input because unlike you, I'm not a grumpy anti-social hermit who only cares about holing up in his cabin, and I'm only getting married once, so I want to make sure everyone enjoys it," she tells me, dropping a dollop of tzatziki onto her plate.

My fists clench on the table, pinning her smug profile as she ignores my reaction like always. "Thank you, Maxine, for reminding me for the thousandth time that I've been married more than once. How could I ever forget it with you around? And giving up my evening no matter how I choose to spend it to watch you stuff your face with the rest of our family doesn't seem very uncaring or anti-social to me."

Why don't I feel better after getting that out?

Maxie's good at reducing me to a petulant child. If she had any clue of the sacrifices I've made for her, I bet she'd wipe that smirk off her face, but I sure as shit am not going to tell her.

Telling everyone about sacrifices defies the purpose of doing the right thing. You don't do the right thing for attention. You just do it because it's right, even if you're paid back with harassment every day of your life by your own flesh and blood.

"So, after I pick out what I want to eat, I'm done with this wedding bullshit?"

Maxie lets out a sigh, her gaze never leaving the Greek salad she's portioning onto her plate. "No, dumbass. I'll give you the menu list we decide on. Then it'll be your job to make sure everything is right on the day of the wedding, that all the plates are clean, and the seating arrangements are set. And if the Andropolises run out of something or have a crisis, you'll be in charge of making the decision of what food to replace it with and how to snuff out the fires. Can you handle that?"

"My job is to stop food emergencies? Wow. I feel so important. Am I going to get blamed if anyone gets food poisoning or chokes on a chicken leg?"

Picking up a platter, she drops two filo dough-wrapped appetizers on my plate because although she's an obnoxious boil on my ass, she cares about me in her own messed up way. "It's Greek food. They rarely do chicken legs," she informs me. "You're supposed to be the big foodie of the family. Why do you think I asked you to oversee the catering?"

Grabbing a thick slice of bread, her backhanded compliment is appeasing enough for me to drop our squabble. I sit back in my chair when she returns to chattering with her fiancé, Veronique. Except now I can feel Damiano Andropolis' bicep brushing up against mine again—or *Dami*, whatever the hell playboy-sounding name they call him. *Day-mee*. It sounds like a pet name like *sweetie* or *baby,* not something you call an employee.

At least he has the build for hard labor. He's got an inch on me and probably twenty pounds. Whether or not he's ever done any strenuous physical labor remains to be seen. Lucky me, I'll get to find out tomorrow, since my brother made the genius decision to hire his boyfriend's young cousin to come work for us. For now, my assessment is limited to sound, sight, and touch as we sit sandwiched together at this table. I could really do without the touching part.

The heat of his thigh is seeping through my jeans, making my blood stir. Every time I try to squirm to break the contact for a second, we end up squished back together, making it feel like I'm purposely writhing against him. I already shifted over as far as I could when he checked me in the ribs earlier. I don't know what it is, but something about him agitates me even when we're feet apart.

Maybe it's his stupid cheeky smile, or his bubbly demeanor, or the way I caught him staring at me all the time when we re-bricked the patio wall here at his family's restaurant last summer. He makes me uncomfortable, and I don't get uncomfortable. But what can I say?

I'm sure as shit not going to admit some college kid has my pulse kicking so hard, I want to get away from him every time I see him. Maxie and my brother, Aiden, would both laugh my ass into the next decade.

Why the hell did Aiden have to hire him of all people to work for us? I know we need help now that Dad's retiring and our older brother, Skyler, will be taking over the office side of things, but I assumed we'd hire somebody who—oh, I don't know—fucking knows something about masonry.

Straight out of college. A city kid. Twenty bucks says he doesn't even own a pair of work boots.

"So, boss!" Dami chirps with that annoying zeal of his. "What time do you want me there tomorrow?"

"Five a.m."

"Five in the morning?"

His widened blue eyes say that early hour is a rarity for him. And so, it begins. Give me strength.

"Yeah. There a problem with that?"

"No. That's just when I come home sometimes," he says with a laugh, his nimble fingers making himself up a pita.

There's not a callous in sight on those pretty hands of his. This kid is in for a rude awakening. No doubt that muscle tone of his was all acquired in a gym rather than from a lick of real work. I am not spending my time on the Hodges job training some newbie or worse, listening to him whine at every turn and not carry his weight.

"You show up drunk or hung over, you're gone. I don't put up with people who aren't fit for work. That's a safety hazard."

"I won't. I'll be on-time," he says, unphased by my stern warning.

That means he's either blowing smoke up my ass, or for some reason my no-nonsense attitude that got me barred from dealing with our crappier suppliers doesn't cow him. Who in their right mind doesn't have a modicum of apprehension for their new boss? I knew there was something wrong with him.

"What should I bring with me?" he asks as though my face says I look like I want to talk.

"Wear old clothes that you can work in. I'm not listening to you cry that you ruined some designer outfit. No tennis shoes. Dress in work boots with a steel toe. If you don't have any, get some by the end of the week. We'll give you gloves, but if you lose them then the next pair is on you. And bring a lunch and plenty of water. There's no plumbing or electricity out there. I'm not driving all the way back into town to take you to lunch every day. We eat on-site and get back to work as soon as we're done."

Good. That seems to have burst his bubble. Except, I can feel those big starry eyes on me—the same curious eyes that were so unnerving they made me smash my thumb last summer when we were building the patio wall.

Freaking Aiden is going to owe me big time for this. And what the hell was with that warning he gave me yesterday when I overheard him and Johnny talking about Dami being gay? I wasn't the one blabbing about people's secrets. After all these years, does he seriously think I would hold someone's personal preferences against them? If he only knew.

My family has no clue about the things that go on inside my head. To be fair, lately I don't either. Last month, I couldn't stop gawking at the two clean cut businessmen at Olympus Bar and Grille when I went out to dinner with Aiden. My heartrate was hammering so hard, I cut out of there and drove around with my truck windows down for an hour before I went home. What is wrong with me?

The longer I'm away from Jen this time around, the more potent the thoughts get. She needs to figure out whatever she's figuring because I'm only human, not a cactus. And this freaking kid that looks way too old to only be twenty-three needs to stop smelling like concentrated shower gel. I want to ask him if he hung on a clothesline in a mountain glen.

Glancing over, his wary expression tugs at my stupid nurturing heart. I catch Aiden shooting me a questioning look as though to ask if I hurt boy wonder's feelings already.

Fucking-A.

Doesn't anyone have thick skin anymore? All I did was answer his question.

Sighing, I return my attention to Dami, only to find him studying me. His bright smile is gone. His expression is so forlorn my stomach dips. He's a complete stranger. Why am I concerned about whatever that look is on his face?

"What?" I let out more impatiently than I mean to.

He glances at Aiden and then back to me. "He told you. Didn't he?"

"Told me what?"

He scans the table, his gaze stopping on his parents on the far side of the room. Leaning into me, his breath ghosts my ear, sending a shiver all the way down my spine. "That I'm gay."

The flutter in my chest at his proximity gives me a weird sense of paralysis, locking up my lungs as a rush of shivers run all the way down my arms. What the hell is that about?

I like men. Always have. Like them in the sense that I appreciate looking at them, but that's where it stopped. You don't do more than looking when you spend all your younger years combatting all the crap people talk about your brother and sister behind their backs. And you don't do more than looking when you trade virginities with and then marry your high school sweetheart.

Since Jen left last year though, I've been doing a lot more than looking. I've been feeling…things—things I certainly shouldn't feel if I'm waiting for my ex-wife to change her mind and come back.

It's never made any sense to me. I love Jen. I was married. I'm still supposed to be married. I made my choice about who my person was—made a promise in front of her and God and our families. Done deal. Search over. I'm not supposed to want anyone else. So, how in the hell can I get hot and bothered for anyone other than her? And why is it happening more frequently the longer she's gone?

Maybe it means if I hadn't been married, I might have…I don't know. Fuck.

It doesn't matter. I'm thirty years old. What the hell does a thirty-year-old who's only been with one person his entire life know about being bisexual?

Christ, Graham. Get your shit together.

I turn my palms up, not daring to move any other part of my body. "Yeah. He told me. What about it?"

Dami's tongue crests his lips, wetting them. I watch it more intently than I should. I can't help it. It's transfixing and slightly erotic, slipping over that mouth of his. It occurs to me now—that's the issue with my discomfort. There's something highly erotic about everything this kid does, and a guy who's stupidly pining for his ex-wife to come back shouldn't be noticing how erotic some twenty-three year old's mannerisms are.

Pursing his lips together, it almost looks like he's trying to appear tough for a second, but he just can't quite pull it off. Sure, that jaw of his is square and rugged, but his flawless olive skin doesn't scream intimidating.

"Um. Mr. Brandt, I really want this job. I promise, I'll work hard for you. I want to learn a new trade and be good at it, but I have to say, if you're going to hold what you know against me or treat me unfairly because of it, then you don't deserve to have me as an employee."

What the…

A puff of air gusts out of my mouth, watching his jaw set. His throat undulates as he holds my gaze with those chalky blue eyes that now show me a flicker of tenacity in their depths.

The kid's got grit. It's wavering from the look of his fingers fidgeting with the tablecloth, but that took balls, nonetheless. I've never been in a situation where I've seen a man stand up for his sexuality before. Usually, I'm the one standing up for people. Seeing it coming from this unworldly kid who's depending on me for a job is way sexier than it has any right to be.

I can't be fucking friendly with this kid. There's no way, not when he makes my palms sweat and my nuts tingle, but I sure as hell am not going to make him worry that his new boss is some kind of bigot. He can just think what everyone else thinks—that I'm a grumpy asshole.

"Calm down, kid. You asked me a question, so I answered you like I'd answer anyone. I don't care who or what you do on your own time. I like Johnny, but I don't care how related you are to him. You make your own way. I just wanted you to know there's no special treatment."

He nods, the corner of his mouth ticking up. Nobody should be allowed to look that good. "I don't want special treatment. You can work me over as hard as you want."

Fuuuck.

Looking back at my plate, I pinch my eyes shut and take in a slow breath as the innuendo of his words flit around inside my head. I wouldn't even know what to do with a man if presented the opportunity. How can the mention of working him over hard make my cock swell?

"Wh-whatever. Just…don't be late."

"I won't."

Aaand…he's freaking staring at me again. I can feel it.

What is it with this kid? What's so damn interesting about me? Does he have some obsession with people in positions of authority? The term boss is practically a joke. I've never been anybody's boss with the exception of overseeing some contractors. If he's trying to kiss my ass, he's going about it all the wrong way.

"So…" he hedges in that thick sultry sounding whisper of his. "We're good then. Right?"

Exhaling, I glance at his parents who are starting to serve another round of selections. Aiden said Dami's folks don't know about his preferences. I'm no one to him. I shouldn't have as much empathy for his situation as I do, but the part of me that's always wondered what my life might have been like if I'd fallen for a John instead of a Jen in high school does. Be patient, Aiden said the other day.

I can be patient. It doesn't mean I have to be his guidance counselor or BFF.

"Yeah. We're good," I whisper back.

His soft breath of relief brings me more joy than it should, making my heart feel lighter than it has in years. Usually, when I try to do something for my family, I end up miserable and berated for it. Why are my effortless sentiments to this kid so appreciated?

Something brushes the fabric of my jeans underneath the table. Fingers rest over the place on my thigh above my knee, and squeeze. A jolt of high-charged static races up my leg and splits off, shooting through every limb in my body.

"Thanks," he says, leaning in so close again I can feel the heat of his breath on my neck. "I really appreciate it."

My heart is flapping faster than hummingbird wings. Its source—that hand on my leg. Even as he withdraws it, the current in my veins is pulsing so much blood to my heart, I can't steady my breathing. What the hell is happening?

I manage to swallow at the dryness is my throat. The tension in my boxer briefs tells me I know exactly what's happening.

Holy shit. It's never hit like that before. What did Dami do to me?

"Hey, boss," he whispers again, rubbing his hand across the back of my shoulder blade as I force slow breaths in and out through my lips, eyes locked on my plate. "Are you okay? You don't look so good."

"Graham?" Aiden's voice breaks through the haze of unbridled lust taking over my brain. "Everything alright?"

The lock on my muscles releases, allowing me to move again. Pushing off the floor, I shove my chair back and spring up. At least I have the wherewithal to lean forward like I have a gut ache, clutching the hem of my shirt enough to distract from the imprint at the front of my jeans.

"Yeah. Fine! Fine. I just…I ate some bad lunch. I…I've got to go."

The inquiries from my family are an incomprehensible buzz around me as I practically scramble to the door. Maybe I'm imagining things, but I swear Dami's gaze is on my retreating back. Just the thought of it sends a shiver down my spine to my nuts.

This is ludicrous. I'm reacting like a horny teenager. The terrifying part is that I don't ever remember being this overwhelmed by arousal from an innocent touch to my leg and a few hot breaths at my ear in my life. It's not possible for a person to elicit that effect in someone. I've just been alone too long.

I need to talk to Jen, and I need to stay as far away from Damiano Andropolis as possible. In the formula for getting my life back in order, he's trouble, nothing but trouble.

CHAPTER 1

People who say high school is the best four years of your life obviously didn't go to college for five. If there's one thing my higher education taught me, it's that I had been living under a rock my entire life—a rock called Olympus, Wisconsin. It hit me a couple months ago after graduation, when I was lying in bed, Ma and Pop's TV blaring down the hallway, while I tried to silently jerk off without any lube because I don't have a dime to my name. Talk about a come to Jesus moment.

Okay, so actually, there was no coming. I was too depressed about being back under my parents' roof at the age of twenty-three. No more college parties around every corner, no more hooking up several times a week, no sea of eligible gay men, no sexual freedom, a bank account controlled by my mother, and no job prospects. Apparently, employers don't eagerly seek a recent college grad with a degree in general studies whose longest resume entry is as a dishwasher in his parents' restaurant. That moment of blue-ball clarity sure put things into perspective.

It's why I'm so grateful to be sitting at this table with the Brandt family tonight as they sample our menu for Maxine's wedding. I still can't believe Aiden invited me to join them. I mean, the guy just offered me a job with their brick masonry business last week. Now, he got me out of bussing tables and is treating me like an adult. The man is *hella* cool in my book. My cousin Johnny was lucky to snag him.

I flash Johnny a smile where he's perched on Aiden's lap. I owe him just as much. To think, if I hadn't ventured to that gay speed-dating event downtown last month determined to find a flesh and blood partner for the evening rather than my hand, I never would have run into and inadvertently outed myself to him.

Not my finest hour. Definitely not a smart thing to do in Olympus when I still haven't come out to Ma and Pop and don't want them to hear it from anyone else. Yet, it was probably the best mistake I ever made.

Johnny let me move into his apartment and hooked me up with this new job. If he ever needs a kidney, I will give him all three of mine.

"Are you ready for your first day?" Johnny asks.

It's still surreal to see him getting personal with a man in front of our family. The way Ma and Pop don't even bat an eye when they see the two of them together gives me hope that I can bite the bullet and spill my guts one of these days. For now, I need to focus on the positive. Baby steps. Operation first-adult-job-ever.

"Heck, yeah! I can't wait to get started." Shifting my attention to Aiden, I add, "Thanks again for taking me on. I really appreciate it. I won't let you guys down."

Beside me, the intoxicating, solid body that I do not mind *at all* being pressed up against at this tightly packed table shifts as Aiden's brother Graham grunts. "You'll regret that soon enough."

One of the happy bubbles inside me pops. Will I hate the work? I don't understand how that could be possible after spending most of my employed life scrubbing soggy food particles off kitchenware.

"Ignore him," Aiden says. "Graham's going to take you out to work at the old Hodges place with him tomorrow. If he gives you any shit, just remember I have seniority so you can give me a call."

Fifty more happy bubbles balloon in my sternum. I'll be working with *Graham*…the hottest Brandt brother…all by myself? Oh…my Gosh!

Aiden with his big, beefy frame, boyish smile, and rugged looks is hands down a ten, but Graham… Graham is hands and feet and tongue, and knock-me-the-frick-down-and-do-me-right-now a twelve.

The man is six feet of lithe, sculpted, tatted, sun-kissed muscle, wild sandy hair, and a matching goatee that I want to drag over every inch of my body like a feather duster. I have just hit the good-fortune jackpot. My new job already has great benefits—hundred proof eye candy.

Nudging his side with my elbow, I shoot him a chipper ice breaker. I've never actually gotten to speak to him before, only drooled from afar. "What do you say, boss? You going to show me the ropes?"

His frame tenses, those captivating mythical sea-themed tattoos on his forearm go taut as he grips his fork. Eyes never leaving his plate, he mutters, "*I* need a fucking rope."

Geesh. Someone's having a bad day.

Hm. It's probably hard to be that sexy. I bet he gets hit on every waking hour.

I wish I could snap a picture of him to send to my buddy Dante. He'll freak when he hears I finally got up close and personal with my number-one fantasy. Okay, so our jean-covered thighs brushing isn't exactly up close and personal, but the dude is straight, and grumpy, and way too old for me, so this occurrence is pretty much as close as I'll ever get.

Uhn.

How can even the back of his neck be sexy—the way those long locks of hair tickle the base of his head as he talks to his sister, Maxie and her fiancé, Veronique. It takes effort to pull my gaze away to locate Ma and Pop. They nearly busted me gawking last year, when I was home for summer break, and the Brandts rebuilt the patio wall behind our restaurant, Tapas. I had never looked forward to getting to work early before until those three days that Graham Brandt was laboring under the hot sun, sweat-slickened skin shining like a god's.

Mamma passes me a tight-lipped smile as she whirs by to refill drinks. I can see it in her chestnut eyes, that ever-present worry. It's been my caretaker since childhood, almost like she's two entities, my mother and a concern as big as the planet.

She's still not happy about me moving out, but I could tell she realized I'm too old for her to object. It helped that Johnny said he needed someone to watch over his apartment above his photography studio now that he stays at Aiden's place most of the time. Good play, Johnny.

Pop is quipping some joke to Graham's parents, dazzling them with his wiry humor, completely oblivious to me as usual, which is totally fine by me. Sometimes I wish him and Mamma could balance out their level of attentiveness for me.

Mamma heads back to the kitchen, so I sneak another peek at my new boss. Oh, crap. Busted!

I swallow against the thickness in my throat. Holy shit. His eyes are bluer than arctic ice and do all kinds of things to my pulse. I seriously need to get it together. I'm going to have to work with this man without sporting wood.

"So, boss! What time do you want me there tomorrow?"

"Five a.m.," he says without missing a beat.

"Five…in the morning?"

"Yeah. There a problem with that?" he challenges, quirking a brow.

Whoa. He's actually serious? I'll have to get up at like four a.m. for that. Who does that? Maybe this is like an initiation or something. I bet we go in at like nine or ten the next day.

"No," I answer airily. "That's just when I come home sometimes," I quip with a grin.

Apparently, that was the wrong thing to say because he sucks in a breath through his nostrils, his lips forming a thin line. "You show up drunk or hung over, you're gone. I don't put up with people who aren't fit for work. That's a safety hazard."

"I won't. I'll be on-time."

I don't want to lose this job before it even starts. This is my chance to earn a paycheck that I can actually see and get out from under Ma and Pop's rule. There's no way I'll find another job that pays like this. Hotty McHot-Tempered needs to know I was just joking. I can get up when the world is still sleeping. How hard can it be?

Forging ahead, I address his profile, while he looks to be practically glaring at his plate. "What should I bring with me?"

Without turning his head, he rattles off a stream of orders like a drill instructor. "Wear old clothes that you can work in. I'm not listening to you cry that you ruined some designer outfit. *No* tennis shoes. Dress in *work boots* with a *steel toe*. If you don't have any, get some by the end of the week. We'll give you gloves, but if you lose them then the next pair is on you. And bring a lunch and plenty of water. There's no plumbing or electricity out there. I'm not driving all the way back into town to take you to lunch every day. We eat on-site and get back to work as soon as we're done."

Wow.

Okay, number-one: that was hot. Is bossy a kink of mine? Phew.

Number-two: crap. I think he hates me.

All I can do is gape at him because aside from it being really difficult to not look at all that sex appeal, I'm at a loss for words. I'm a happy, easy-going guy. People love my personality. I never have problems getting anyone to warm up to me. Graham Brandt, however, appears to be immune to my positive attitude, my most powerful attribute. If I can't use that, how am I going to impress him at a job I know nothing about? I am so screwed and not in the way I want to be.

Turning his head, he catches me watching him again, which does not help the happy bubble that has slid up into my throat and mutated into a nervous bubble. His gaze flicks to the end of the table, and he frowns even more severely. Maybe it's not me he's mad at.

I follow his line of sight to Aiden and catch his brother giving him a slight shake of his head. Johnny's gaze darts worriedly from Graham to me, his features a mask of guilt.

What is that all about?

Graham sighs and looks back to me, the corner of his mouth forced up in a begrudging smile like he just threw in the towel on an invisible battle. I'm getting the impression they all know a secret that I don't. What am I missing? I don't…

Oh, wait.

No.

Oh, my gosh.

That…explains everything. The gruff behavior. The clipped commands. The reason my sunshine is being blocked out by Mr. Super Sexy Face. My secret is no longer a secret. My stomach churns.

Damn it, Johnny.

I don't care if he told Aiden, but clearly, Aiden told Graham, and clearly, Graham does not approve. His eyes scan my face, his scowl an unavoidable neon sign.

"What?" he huffs.

Glancing at Aiden and Johnny, their sheepish expressions confirm my suspicions. This wouldn't be the first job I had where someone didn't approve of my sexuality. My part-time jobs at college and during summers when I tried to break away from Tapas exposed me to occasional bigotry.

Meeting Graham's perturbed gaze, the words fall from my lips sadly, watching pieces of the fantasy I've built up of this man crumble before my eyes. "He told you. Didn't he?"

His brows knit like I'm speaking in riddles. "Told me what?"

Either I'm wrong or he's playing ignorant. Scanning the room, I spot Mamma by the cash register immersed in the night's invoices. Pop is shuffling more dishes back to the kitchen.

Leaning in, I whisper, "That…I'm gay."

I wait for a reaction—denial, confirmation, disgust, anything, but Graham just sits there like a statue, staring at his food. His throat undulates. I know he heard me. My stomach sinks lower as the silence stretches.

I can handle close-minded people. I ran into my fair share when I lived out and proud at college, but I'm a fool for putting so much stake in this job without considering the possibility I could be working with one. Just because Aiden is bisexual and Maxine is a lesbian, doesn't mean their brother is cozy with their sexuality. Stupid me for assuming it was a given.

His hands shift, palms turning up on the table. His gaze slides to mine, and he shrugs. "Yeah. He told me," he murmurs with a bit less bite than before, but certainly not any warmer. "What about it?"

I can't get a read on him. I neither expect nor want him to hop up and blow a party bugle, but he's leaning pretty far from congenial.

Dante's always telling me I'm a pushover, that I need to stick up for myself more. Graham's not my parents. If I'm serious about making it out in the world on my own, I'm going to have to stand up for what I believe in. The life I picture for myself certainly does not include having a boss that turns his nose up at my sexuality.

Wetting my lips, I purse them as Graham's brows pinch together again like he's getting impatient. Sucking in a shaky breath, it's time to test out my spine. I can do this. I have to do this.

"Um, Mr. Brandt, I really want this job. I promise, I'll work hard for you. I want to learn a new trade and be good at it, but I have to say, if you're going to hold what you know against me or treat me unfairly because of it, then you don't deserve to have me as an employee."

Damn. Is this what being an adult feels like? If so, being an adult equals sweaty nuts.

Covertly, I blow out a slow breath, forcing myself to hold his gaze. He lets out a puff of air like I just knocked the wind out of him. Is that a good sign? A bad sign? His frowny face is almost gone. Honestly, he looks a bit shocked. Can he not handle people talking back to him? Did this job opportunity just crash and burn before it even began?

How am I going to pay Johnny rent and save up enough money to leave Olympus, if I have to keep relying on Mama to pay my bills? Maybe Johnny will help me out, while I look for another job.

As much as my dreams look prolonged, judging by Graham's silence, I don't care. This is one thing I've hidden long enough. I'm going to have to face it someday, or rather the world is going to have to face the real me.

Graham's throat undulates again, and the harsh lines around his mouth smooth a bit. "Calm down, kid," his gruff voice says softly. "You asked me a question, so I answered you like I'd answer anyone. I don't care who or what you do on your own time. I like Johnny, but I don't care how related you are to him. You make your own way. I just wanted you to know there's no special treatment."

Air floods back into my lungs. "I don't want special treatment. You can work me over as hard as you want."

I don't know why his eyes dart back to his plate. I smiled and everything when I said that. Now they're pinched closed, and he's sucking in a slow breath like he's trying to calm himself from a meltdown.

"Wh-whatever," he grumbles. "Just…don't be late."

"I won't."

Fiddling with my pita, I sneak a few glances. I'd always imagined if I ever got the chance to talk to him, we'd share either some witty or smoldering conversation. Okay, the smoldering conversation fantasy was quite a stretch, but a boy can dream. His silence and unsettled reaction have me wondering if he meant what he said about my little truth bomb.

Leaning close, I whisper near his ear, "So, we're good then. Right?"

His eyes scan the restaurant, tracking my parents' movements. Is he actually looking out for me? That's…pretty freaking cool of him.

"Yeah. We're good."

He probably has no idea how much those three words mean to me. It sets my entire body at ease. He's only the second person in Olympus after Johnny that I've come out to. A straight guy probably wouldn't understand the anxious relief swirling in my chest over this occasion. My skin tingles all the way down to my fingertips at what I just accomplished. I have the overwhelming urge to hug him for just listening and not making a spectacle of who I really am.

Reaching under the table, I give his leg a little squeeze right above his knee and lean in while tracking Ma and Pop. "Thanks," I whisper. "I really appreciate it."

I didn't expect a response, a nod seems like it would be appropriate to at least acknowledge me, except Graham looks like he's in a trance, fists clenched on either side of his plate. I swear he's vibrating, his body shuddering in tiny little tremors. His face kind of looks like Dante's did right before he passed out on graduation night, all slack-jawed and confused.

Crap. Is he sick? Does he have old guy health problems?

"Hey, boss? Are you okay?" I rub my hand in between his shoulder blades like Mamma does to me whenever I'm not feeling well. His body quivers under my touch. "You don't look so good."

"Graham?" Aiden calls, his face pinched in concern. "Everything alright?"

Graham's back muscles flex under my hand. Like someone flipped a switch, he snaps out of his paralysis and jumps to his feet.

"Yeah. Fine!" he barks, glancing toward Aiden but like he's seeing through him, finagling himself away from his chair. "Fine. I just…I ate some bad lunch. I…I've got to go," he stammers over his shoulder to Maxie and books it for the door.

"Graham? Where are you going? You didn't even eat anything!" Maxie hollers.

Shoulders hunched, clutching his stomach, he throws a single wave without looking back, then shoves through the doors like a broken version of the strong, indestructible man I've discerned him to be. Weird.

"What's up with Graham Cracker?" Maxie asks me.

"Um, not sure. He seemed fine one minute then…just got real quiet. Is he sick?"

She flips one of her long brown braids over her shoulder and rolls her rich brown eyes. "Probably sick of being my wedding bitch is all. Weddings are a sore subject with that one."

"Oh?"

"Yeah. Best not to bring it up, or he'll bite your head off and pout the entire day. I'm the happy twin. Graham's the broody one." Loading up a pita she adds conspiratorially, "That's code for giant man-child who can't handle his feelings."

"Ah." I nod and chuckle, kind of wishing I could see the two of them have another verbal face off like they did last summer on the patio job.

She kept calling him Graham-a-lamma-ding-dong, which only made me wonder about *his*…Graham-a-lamma-ding-dong. Okay. Maybe that's a bad idea. I really need to stop obsessing over straight Graham-a-lamma-ding-dongs.

Maxie returns to conversing with Veronique and Mr. and Mrs. Brandt. The family's concern over Graham's abrupt departure seemingly forgotten, something that wouldn't happen with my family.

The lure of being a guest at the table is suddenly gone now that Graham isn't here. Excusing myself to Aiden and the rest of the Brandts, I make my way to the kitchen. The dishes aren't going to wash themselves, and I can't up and leave them when I haven't officially started my new job yet.

Turning the radio on, I get the water running and start unloading bus bins. When I'm elbow deep in soapy water, shifting my hips to the beat, the clip of Mama's heels cuts through the music. She smiles, depositing another bin of dishes on the stainless-steel counter.

"What's got you so happy?" she asks in her Italian lilt.

"Just excited about my new job tomorrow."

The instant dejection that pollutes her expression makes the smile fall off my face. Quitting my full-time hours at Tapas feels like I'm betraying my parents. They've run the restaurant since they got married. The unspoken message, *this will all be yours one day*, is like an arranged marriage I neither want nor can escape. My guilt and sense of obligation have me adding, "Are you sure that you and Papa don't mind me quitting the restaurant?"

"Dami, sweet boy. You can't be a dishwasher forever. I know this, but are you sure brick masonry is the right kind of work for you? I imagine it will be very physical labor and dangerous. You could hurt your back lifting all those bricks, have something fall on you, or get injured using tools you don't know how to use."

Grinning, I flex my bicep as Pop comes in with another basin full of dishes. "Ma, bricks aren't any heavier than a tub full of dishes. Look at these arms. I can handle physical labor, and I'll learn all the other stuff."

"Ha!" Pop barks, setting the dish bin down. Grabbing Mama around the waist, he presses a playful kiss to her cheek. Judging by the way she yelps and jumps, he gave her one of his signature ass pinches. "Don't worry, mi amor. He has to get up on time to get there first before he can get hurt."

I should be used to their pessimism by now, but it still stings every time I hear them doubt me. Just once, I'd like them to say they think I can handle something or at least not make some comment about why they think I can't.

I'm going to show them. This time will be different. They didn't help me get this job with the Brandts. I did that on my own. Well, okay, with a lot of begging for Johnny to put in a good word for me with Aiden, but that doesn't matter. It's going to work out. I can feel it. It has to. I need to pay my own way and keep a roof over my head that isn't there because of my parents.

"I can get up on time," I assure Pop. "I unpacked my alarm clock this morning."

"Did you pack your mama in a box and set her on your nightstand?" Pop jokes, patting me on the cheek and hustling off deeper into the kitchen with a laugh.

Frowning after him for his lack of faith, I find a severe look on Mama's face. "I'll get up, Ma. I'm an adult. I got up for all my classes at college, and I made it to work on time for the last few jobs I had."

"Dami, those jobs were in the afternoons, and you only stayed at each of them for a matter of weeks. When you were in school, I had to call you to make sure you were awake to get to your classes."

"Well, I could have gotten up on time, you just always called before my alarm clock went off," I point out, but her expression makes her doubts evident.

Patting my hand, she kisses my cheek and heads to the cooler. "It's okay. I'll call you in the morning anyway just in case."

"Are you going to hire another dishwasher?"

"No." She waves a dismissive hand and retrieves a brown paper bag from the cooler, bringing it over to me. "Your father and I can manage, but you can still help some nights, can't you?" She rolls past the question like she always does. Sometimes I wonder if she does it to distract me. "Here. I packed you a lunch for tomorrow."

Is she serious? And my cousin Johnny used to think his mother wouldn't take *no* for an answer. My throat closes up, knowing the bonds of this place will still be shackling me. Mama is not ruining this for me. I love her, but I am officially breaking up with Tapas.

"Mama, I'll be working long hours. I might be too tired after work to do a dinner shift."

Shoot. There she goes with her hand gestures.

"You see? I knew it. It will be too much for you. Why don't you tell Aiden you changed your mind. It's not too late. He'll understand. I'm sure he was just being polite giving you the job and doesn't really need the help."

Something sharp twists in my chest. Graham made a similar claim, assuming Aiden only gave me the job because of Johnny. It's not entirely false, but I'd like to think I have a little potential.

"*Polite?* You mean…you think he's just doing me a favor because he knows us?"

"Dami, what do you know about brick masonry or construction work?" Before I can answer, she clucks her tongue and cups my jaw. "Nothing. It's a specialty profession where you have to have very particular skills."

"Yeah, but Aiden said it's an entry-level position, that they're willing to train me. I can do it, Ma. I'm willing to learn. Give me a chance," I beg, grasping her hand, hating that I've cornered myself into asking permission I shouldn't need. Butterflies quiver in my belly, imagining my hopes dying in front of me with one swift decision from her, because as much as I'd want to, my devotion prevents me from disobeying. "Please, I want to try this."

I'm twenty-three years old, and I still do everything my parents ask me. None of the guys in college had this problem. I had a life there. I got to think for myself for the first time. It was a little overwhelming in the beginning trying to figure out my class schedule and how to work the laundromat machines down the road from the apartment I shared with Dante, but mostly, I felt like I'd been let out of a cage I didn't know I'd been in my entire life. The fear of failing was exhilarating because it was something that was mine.

"Eh, let him go," Pop grunts walking back toward us. "Dami," he adds, narrowing his gaze on something behind me, "put the dessert plates back on the top shelf."

Grimacing, I glance at the rickety shelf that always wobbles when someone slams the kitchen door. It's going to collapse one day, so I avoid stacking anything on it in spite of Pop's insistence. I'll probably get blamed for that too when it happens, but I learned long ago there's no use in arguing with my parents over anything. "Sure, Pop."

When he leaves, the worry lines by Mamma's eyes streak a new wave of panic through my chest. Respect is such a curse.

"They're counting on me to be there tomorrow, Ma. I can't let them down," I blurt on a rush of breath. "I don't want them to think I'm lazy."

She exhales, her lips pressing together. "No, of course not."

My entire body relaxes at her concession as she disinfects the bus bins. "That younger brother, Graham," she says absently. "He didn't look very well. I can imagine he'll need all the help he can get, if he's under the weather." Clucking her tongue she shakes her head, stacking the empty bins to the side. "Such a handsome man. It's a shame he seems so severe. I bet he would turn all the girls' heads, if he smiled."

And a certain boy's, I think to myself, carting the dishes to the sink to hide my blush. One day. I'll tell her one day, but there's no way I was coming out to my parents as their grown, dishwashing son who still lived under their roof. I'm supposed to carry on their name. I can wait a little longer to add my sexual preference to the list of ways in which I've disappointed them.

"How is Angelica?" she asks, the question making me stiffen as I pick up the sprayer.

"Um, good. They gave her a big fancy office and everything, I guess. I bet she'll be managing that company in no time."

"Is she seeing anyone?"

While my oldest friend and fake childhood sweetheart is the last thing I want to discuss with Mama, hope blooms inside me. This is the first time she's ever spoken of the possibility of Angelica seeing someone else. Maybe my claims that we're no longer an item, albeit a fake item, have finally been accepted.

"Not sure. I think she's focusing on her job right now." Reassuringly, I add, "I'm sure she'll meet someone though. Milwaukee's a big city, and she's a great girl."

Frowning, she studies me. I fight to hold the casual smile on my face, my hands trembling beneath the dishwater.

"Hm. I suppose," she says sadly but then smiles wistfully. "And I suppose you'll be meeting a new girl any day now. The next thing you know, you'll both be starting your own families."

The sound I produce is supposed to be a laugh, but I'm not sure you could call it that. "Yeah. Maybe?"

When she heads back out to the dining room, I realize I'm holding my breath. How did I get myself into this situation?

I wish I'd just come out to her when I was a teenager like Johnny did to his parents, not that he had smooth sailing afterward. It's about so much more than who I'm attracted to though. Every ounce of my compliance is a lead weight around my ankles, chaining me to the role of submissive child.

Enough of that, I chide myself. I'm headed in the right direction.

Thinking of my bedroom in Johnny's apartment, my sketch pads and pencils set up on the small desk there, I'm reminded that half the battle has already been won. Tomorrow is the beginning of the rest of my new life. The endless possibilities have my body buzzing again.

I'm so grateful I'm an optimist. Who wants to waste time being miserable when you can always focus on something positive? Speaking of miserable, Mama was right about one thing—Graham Brandt is definitely the most miserable looking person I've ever seen.

Geez, he looked like he hated me there at first. What was with the mad dash out of the restaurant?

Hm. Maybe he can't handle ethnic food.

Guess I'll cross drizzling tzatziki over my chest for him to lick up off my fantasy list. It's okay. I've got others, plenty of others. That man has no idea the things we've done in my mind since I first laid eyes on him last summer.

Okay, so Mama was right about two things.

His smile *can* turn heads. I caught him laughing at something Aiden said last summer, and I was a goner. It is a crying shame he's not gay, but that's for the best. As long as I don't look at his face or his body, I can put my fantasies to bed and focus on learning the job. I am going to be the best employee that grumpy man has ever had. I love my life.

CHAPTER 2

Graham

"I hate my life." My rusty voice pierces through the chuffing sounds coming from the coffee maker as I pour the steaming liquid into my mug through half-lidded eyes.

This kid is going to be the worst employee we've ever had. I can feel it in my tired achy bones.

A freaking college kid. Aiden probably did this on purpose just to screw with me. Happy people suck. They're so damn smug they think throwing joy at others will make it rub off. Well, I've got news for Aiden. Boy Wonder's inexhaustible zeal is not going to rub off on me.

My cock twitches against my underwear at my choice of words. I press the heel of my palm to it to get it to go down.

Yeah. Think about *rubbing* one more time after last night, Graham. That'll freaking help the problem you've got down there.

Padding out to the porch swing, I close my eyes and let the rocking soothe me. It reminds me of my days on a ship, when my life had order.

Getting up at four a.m. never bothered me in the Navy and not even when I moved back home to help with the business after Dad's heart attack, but I've never been up half the night with a hard-on before, a freaking hard-on over a twenty-three-year-old man. Because that's what happened. Isn't it?

You either tell it like it is, or you're a liar. I don't have the capacity or patience for lies after living one my entire married life.

Till death do us part. Did either of us ever mean it?

My phone buzzes on the porch side table. A blip of hope unfurls in my chest. With any luck Aiden's calling off the Hodges job for today or phoning to tell me the kid chickened out. The name on the screen makes my heart skip. Luck is not in the cards for me today.

"Jen?" I answer. "Everything alright?"

"Yeah." Her airy chuckle comes across the line. "I should ask you the same thing, calling me three times in the middle of the night. Sorry that I couldn't call you back until now. I'm on midnight shifts this week. I'm on my last break though. What's up? Is something wrong?"

A wash of heat creeps up my neck. Did I really call her three times after I left Tapas? How pathetic does that look? That damn kid got me so frazzled.

"Nothing. I…everything's fine. I just…um, I thought maybe we could get dinner some night this week."

"Oh. Uh. Sure," she says, making me shrink at the surprise in her voice. Asking the woman that you spent your entire life with to meet you for dinner shouldn't elicit that kind of response. It's a sad reminder of how far apart we've fallen. "Um, let's see," she mumbles in thought. "I'm off Thursday and Friday. Oh, but Friday, David and I are meeting some friends of his from work."

"You're still dating *him*?"

The silence that follows has me shifting in the swing. Why in the hell can't I ever have a filter?

"Yes," she finally answers, patiently, as though it's common knowledge.

I don't know how I'm supposed to react over my ex-wife dating other people. Where is the rule book on that? We've been divorced twice now, so a realistic part of me says my turn is over, and I should be supportive. I've loved her since we were fifteen years old. How can I want anything other than for her to be happy? That part of me, however, says I'm the one who's supposed to be making her happy.

"So, um, how's Thursday?" she ventures. "Is your family doing something?"

Pinching my eyes shut, I curse myself for poor planning. This just gets better and better. I never had to plan how to deliver a conversation to Jen when we were married. Ever since divorce number-one though, my tongue feels like it's in a knot. Of course, she assumes we'd be eating with my family like we did practically once a week for the last decade.

"Uh, no. I thought we could eat here…and talk."

The uncomfortable silence settles in again, the silence I didn't notice before the first divorce and regret not probing about prior to the second. Why does this have to be so difficult? You get married, and that's it. If there's a problem, you work it out. You don't end up back at square one, trying to ask your wife out on a first date.

"Graham, is everything alright?"

"Yeah. Everything's fine."

She's across town, living in her own house, dating another man, and my dick was spearing my mattress last night because some kid whispered his hot breath into my ear, squeezed my leg like I was his hero, and pulled this sexy as fuck move by telling me to piss off if I wasn't cool with him being gay even though I could tell he was nervous as hell. Damn it. It's still turning me on. Everything is not fine. Everything is totally fucked.

"Are you sick? Is it Mom or Dad?"

"What?" I sit up and piece together her train of thought, which makes my gut twist for worrying her. "No! Nobody's sick or hurt or…everybody's fine."

"Oh, thank God," she lets out on a rush of breath. "You scared me."

Her relief stings. The depth of which she still loves my family is just another reminder of the void in my life. My person, the one who's supposed to get those terrifying phone calls about sick loved ones in the middle of the night, won't be next to me in bed for those moments, rousing me to help me cope with the situation.

"Sorry," I murmur, running my hand over my face. Pushing off the swing, I dig for courage. Time to pull off the bandage. "I wanted to talk about us."

More silence. Seriously, this is getting old.

"*Us?*"

"Yeah."

"What about…*us*?"

Now it's my turn to delay. Aiden and Maxie always say I speak without thinking. It seems dishonest to calculate what you want to say. Facades aren't going to make Jen and I work, or any marriage for that matter, so I release the spring trap on the truth contained tightly in my chest.

"We need to figure this out, Jen. It's been long enough. We…we've got to do something."

"Graham," Jen's tender voice mixes with the scrape of chair legs and a heavy sigh. "Sweetie, there is no us anymore…not like there used to be."

As her words clamp around my heart, her shuddered breath adds another slice of pain. I've failed. I know it. She's not going to budge this time.

"Graham, we're divorced. There's no more *us* to talk about."

"We've been divorced before," I jest without feeling a drop of amusement.

"Yeah," she lets out on a puff of breath, "and look how it ended up. We can't keep doing this…to each other or your family."

My family. Doesn't she understand part of why I'm fighting this battle is for my family? Who wants to see their thirty-year-old son twice divorced? I should have given my parents grandkids by now. "I think they'd rather see us together than apart."

The exhaustion in her breath weighs on my hopes, exacerbating the panic in my stomach. What the hell do I do if she doesn't come back this time? Where do I go from here? Who's going to take care of her car and make sure she eats well? Who's going to comfort her when her mother falls off the wagon and screws with her life again?

Years ago, I had a plan. It was hand-crafted for me by the example in my household. Get married, have kids, take them to family functions, barbecues, and holiday events. I'm the responsible one out of my siblings, the one who solved all his own problems.

No money for college? I joined the Navy.

Dad got sick? I left the Navy to help my siblings run the family business.

Even when I was younger, I held my own. I never made my parents worry by coming home from school crying like Maxie used to whenever someone made a comment about her outspokenness of her sexual preferences. They told her to keep being vocal, as she should have, but what did they tell me? Dad took me aside and told me to take care of her bullies, so I did. Despite what Maxie thinks, Dad didn't even need to ask me.

When I met the new girl, whose mom showed up drunk at school, I took care of her too. I knew what it was like to have a family that didn't fit in with the majority. That's how Jen and I clicked.

Mom and Dad loved her from the first time I brought her home. I was the guy who had no problem making the fairytale of childhood sweethearts play out. I never imagined any other path. I always did what I was supposed to do, worked hard, bought a house, provided. Then I had to announce my divorce and suddenly *I* was the kid who made my parents worry. Two years later, I had them worrying again—me, their rock steady child.

I'm sick of looking broken, sick of Mom asking about Jen and me, sick of Maxie giving me shit, sick of the smart ass remarks at the bar about my family and failed marriage, sick of wondering if I'll give Dad grandkids before his next heart attack. I'm supposed to be halfway through the race, not back at the starting line with my head a mess over some curiosity I never explored and have no idea how to navigate. Is this a mid-life crisis?

"Graham," Jen's voice cuts through my thoughts. "I have to get back. I'll stop by Thursday night, okay? We can talk then."

Her coddling tone isn't inspiring. I sense the drop of a gavel, the start of a countdown to the final nail in the coffin of our association.

"Alright. I'll be home by five."

Home. What a joke. I can't even trust my vocabulary anymore. She probably doesn't think of our house as *home* any longer.

"Alright," she concurs. "Hey, have a good week. Okay?"

"Yeah. You too," I tell her, hating that it's a reminder of the polite throw away comments we've become accustomed to for too many years now.

"And Graham?"

"Yeah?"

"You're going to be alright. Okay? Don't worry."

"Of course."

Clicking the "end call" button, my gut feels like someone made a hard pass at it with a thirty-pound medicine ball. Something tells me nothing is going to be alright, not now, not ever again.

CHAPTER 3

"Ugh. Stop!"

The harsh commotion pulling me from my deep slumber turns into a chipper jingle coming from my nightstand. Forcing my eyelids open, the blurry glow from my alarm clock comes into focus.

3:45 a.m.

What is happening? Palming my cell phone on the second attempt, I bring it to my ear, which is all the energy I can muster.

"Hello?" I croak, my vocal cords still as asleep as the rest of my body.

"*Buongiorno, tesoro*," Mama's voice coos over the line.

I whimper. It is too early for speaking or listening in any language. "Ma? Wh-what…*why*…"

"Are you awake?"

"No," I groan, checking the clock again. "I have another half an hour."

"You said you have to be there at five," she says defensively.

"Make it stop," I whisper into my pillow.

Dang it. I was in the middle of an epic dream. Vincent Stoller, the god of pop music, was giving me a lap dance, wearing nothing but his guitar. Idly stroking my morning erection, I can tell by the rigidity, it was shaping up to be one heck of a performance. At the sound of Mama's voice, I release my grip at the speed of light like a deviant that's just been found out. I don't even live under her roof anymore, and I still can't touch my cock.

"But you need to shower and eat breakfast. You can't go to work on an empty stomach," she jabbers.

"I showered last night," I rasp, sitting up.

My eyes won't open. How can she sound so lucid this early?

"Well, your blood sugar will drop if you wait until lunch to eat," she continues. "You don't know when you might get a break, and make sure you take a thermos of water. It's still been very warm out for September weather. You don't want to get dehydrated."

"Ma, I'm up. Okay? I'm up," I assure her as I stumble toward the bathroom. "I'll be fine."

Her silence is indicative that she's plotting her next detail to fret over. I need to distract her stat.

"Uh, could you pick me up some steel-toe work boots today from out of my account? I need them for my job."

"Of course. I'll go before we open Tapas."

"Thanks."

"You can pick them up at Tapas after work and tell me how your first day went."

My forehead makes a *thunk* sound as I lean my head on the bathroom door. Wonderful. That means I'll be pulling a dishwashing shift at the restaurant. All it will take is a while-you're-here-comment, and my sense of obligation will serve me up like a sacrificial offering. I didn't even make it through my first day with Brandt and Sons and she's already roped me back into Tapas' kitchen.

"Gotta go make some coffee, Ma. I'll talk to you later."

I've never been big on coffee, but I have a feeling I'm going to need all the coffee, every day of my life for the foreseeable future.

My heart does an anxious jig in my chest as I tug open the door to the Brandt warehouse. A dusty scent invades my senses. It smells like a gravel driveway after a rain with undertones of fuel and oil. My tennis shoes squeak against the concrete floor as I pass by the window of what looks to be the office. I don't see Skyler, the oldest Brandt sibling, the one Aiden told me handles all the administrative tasks, including the most important one—my paychecks.

Industrial lights cast a glow over pallets of bricks and bags of mortar mix up ahead deeper in the warehouse. A big shiny blue rig with the Brandt logo on the door is parked in the center of the building, a trailer with some kind of construction vehicle on it attached to the truck.

Wow. Will I get to drive either of those?

My face hurts from the size of my smile, possibility fizzing inside me like champagne. I'm part of something important for the first time in my life. I'm going to get to build things. I'm going to have an actual career, not just some part-time job for extra cash at college, not working for my parents like an indentured servant.

Rounding the corner past the office, I follow the sound of voices. Skyler's holding a clipboard, hand on his hip, looking to be giving orders. Aiden, Maxie, and Graham are leaning against the trailer, their expressions a mix between bemused and annoyed.

Aiden unfolds his large muscular frame and throws me a nod. Twirling one of her long brown braids, Maxie smiles and waves, then elbows Graham in the stomach. "Told you he'd show up. Hi, Dami!"

"Hey, Maxie. Morning guys."

Graham doesn't turn around to acknowledge me, but I don't get to give it much thought when Skyler extends his hand for me to shake.

"Dami, welcome aboard. Glad to have you with us. I've got some paperwork in the office I need to give you, and then Graham's going to take you out to the old Hodges place outside of town. It's been abandoned for years. Some company bought it and wants it restored. You guys'll be doing a complete rebuild from the ground up, so you'll get to see the entire process from start to finish. Don't be afraid to ask questions. We took most of the supplies out there last week, and Graham leveled the ground, so you guys are all set up and ready to go."

"Okay, sounds great," I enthuse to which Graham lets out a sigh and mutters something.

"Aiden and Max," Skyler continues, "make sure you check your measurements on those windows at the Bickman job, and remember they asked for a four-inch offset around the doorways."

"Skyler, we got it," Aiden cuts him off at the same time Graham mutters, "It's like being in the fucking Navy all over again."

"What?" Skyler huffs emphatically. "I'm just doing my job. Dad put me in charge when he retired. I want to make sure you guys know what you're doing."

"We've known what we've been doing for the last decade and a half, Sky," Aiden says patiently.

"In all fairness, he was asleep for most of it," Maxie murmurs.

"I have kids. You try operating on three hours of sleep," Skyler snaps at Maxie, then directs his attention back to Aiden. "I know you know what you're doing, but people can get complacent when they've been doing things for a while. It doesn't hurt to go over a few details."

Maxie places her fist over her mouth and makes a walkie-talkie noise. "Kkkh. Planet Micro Manager to Sky Captain Control Freak. Abort! Abort!"

Skyler's face goes red as his siblings all snicker. My pulse stutters at the sight of Graham's mouth curving into a sheepish grin, his vivid blue eyes crinkling at the corners. Can you say too freaking beautiful?

His gaze clashes with mine, and every happy line on his face falters, slipping into a mask of stern displeasure.

Shoot. Busted again.

It's been three months since someone besides myself has made me come. I really need to get laid. That's the only way my dick will forget that this man isn't an option.

I'm not sure what's up with the weight on my heart though every time he gives me one of those broody looks like he can't stand the sight of me. Maybe it's human nature to crave approval. That has to be it. Why else would it physically pain me to not be in his good graces?

CHAPTER 4

Graham

I need to get laid. That has to be the only explanation for these damn flashes of heat venting through my body every time this kid looks at me like a popsicle that needs licking. Do men go through something like menopause? I mean, it has the word *men* in it. It's not completely far-fetched.

It's been a little over a year since Jen and I split this time, and we weren't exactly hot and bothered the last few months we were together. I don't understand how my body thinks it needs some attention now that she's gone but didn't have the urge when she was around.

Is my dick like an ungrateful person who only appreciates something once they no longer have it? Regardless, it needs to get the memo that the childhood itch I never scratched is not a possibility. I married the love of my life. I'm going to do whatever I can to marry her again. End of story. Third times a charm. Right?

Maxie punches me in the chest as Dami heads back toward us from the office with his paperwork. "Be nice, Graham Cracker," she warns.

I resist the urge to rub the place where her sharp knuckles connected. "Try listening to your own advice."

"For you? Never." She saunters off to the truck she and Aiden take to their work sites.

I'm aware of how juvenile the unspoken agreement is that she and I never ride in the same vehicle and only work on the same job sites when absolutely necessary. The bee up her ass over me will outlive us all, so I can live with juvenile to keep the peace for everyone.

My skin goes taut. Another wave of heat assaults me.

Damn it. He's staring at me again. I can feel it.

Turning my head, I'm met with that annoyingly exuberant smile. Jesus, his skin is like a damn baby's all radiant and smooth-looking.

Who has hair like that? Dusky black, fluffy, and swept back toward his head in a natural arc. He should be a shampoo spokesman not a laborer.

I am *not* checking him out, I reassure myself, as I size up his work clothes. A white t-shirt with some long-haired, shirtless pop star on it with the name Vincent Stoller scrolled in glittery letters. Pfft. Old Vinny's going to look like a garage band singer by the end of the day. Who wears white when working with mortar?

Don't even get me started on the backpack slung over his shoulder. Does he have homework or is he planning on sitting on his ass, taking notes while I do all the grunt work? Traveling down, I hate that I notice the way his jeans fit snugly to his hips and probably means they hug that pert ass of his, or maybe I hate that it's forcing me to imagine his pert ass, or maybe I just really hate that I once noticed he has an insanely pert ass.

And wouldn't you know? Tennis shoes. Fucking white tennis shoes.

Cocking a brow at him is the only warning I give. Someone can't follow orders already.

"My mom's picking me up some boots today," he gets out in a rush.

His mommy. Figures.

Grunting, I wrench open the door to the truck and bound up into the seat. Boy Wonder blinks at me from the warehouse floor. "You coming? Daylight's burning."

Heading down the state route that leads out of town, I try to focus on the lush Wisconsin countryside and the way the soft morning glow is waking up the vivid colors of the September greenery on the canopy of white oak and pine trees. A red tail hawk swoops across the road as I take another sip of my coffee. Sounds relaxing, right?

Wrong!

Do I have something on my face? Seriously, has this kid never seen a blonde man before? Tattoos? What? What the fuck is so interesting about my profile?

"You need something?" I ask without turning my head.

"Huh?"

"You've been eyeballing me since you got in the truck. You got something to say just spit it out."

"Sorry." He laughs, shifting in his seat. "Just…my mom was right. Your face *can* turn heads."

What the… My mug freezes halfway to my mouth. Did I just get hit on by a guy? By…Damiano Andropolis?

"What?" I practically croak.

"Well, my mom said your *smile* would probably turn heads, but even without the smile, you're a good-looking guy. I bet you get that all the time though."

No. I get that none of the time with the exception of a few hey-hand-somes from the women at Schmitty's bar this past year. I certainly never got it from another man…or man-child.

I turn his head? Jesus…does he really think I'm attractive? Like as in he's attracted to me?

Fuck. Focus, Graham.

"What…uh, what do you know about brick masonry?" I stammer, anything to get the topic of conversation off me and this weird static charged air in the cab of the truck.

"Um, nothing?" He chuckles. "I mean, I know you use mortar to stack the bricks together, right? I'm sure I'll catch on quick."

Cradling my mug back in the cup holder, I let out a slow breath. "Did you take any mathematics in college?"

"Just a basic course to meet my requirement. It was an arts degree, so I didn't really need any math."

"What was your major?"

"Um, general studies," he says, but adds brightly, "It turns out you actually don't have to pick a major. You can just leave your options open."

Luckily, I've driven this road hundreds of times, so I miss nothing when I pinch my eyes closed for a second to process his delusional optimism.

"Wait. Aiden said you're twenty-three. Wouldn't you have been twenty-one or twenty-two when you finished a four-year degree after high school? What have you been doing the past year?"

"I just graduated in June. I…went to culinary school before I started my bachelor's degree."

"Really?" Why is there a little firework going off in my chest? I do not care if I have any interests in common with him. So, what if he likes to cook? Lots of people do. "Then why aren't you cooking in your parents' restaurant or being a chef somewhere?"

"Um," he hums, chewing on his lower lip. "It didn't work out for me?"

Does he have to answer everything as a question? He sounds like this nervous guy in my old unit who was afraid to have an opinion.

"Didn't work out how? Was it too expensive?"

"Uh, no. Ma and Pop covered everything, but…well, I kind of started a little fire…accidentally, and it was sort of unspoken that the instructors didn't really think I was a good fit," he says, rubbing his wrist anxiously.

Great. I'm working with an undeclared pyro whose mommy buys his shoes. Fuck my life.

"So, if your parents paid for everything, is this your first job?"

God, I can't even imagine not starting a career until the age of twenty-three. I was going to job sites with my dad and grandpa when I was eight years old and worked for them every free minute I had since I was fourteen.

How cushy would it have been to get a free ride to college without lifting a finger? Even if I hadn't heard my parents discussing college tuition woes when Skyler started at university, I still would have joined the Navy. Someone clearly didn't instill the lesson of self-reliance into this kid that I learned from my parents.

"No, I've had other jobs. I've washed dishes in my parents' restaurant since I was in high school, and I had a few part-time jobs when I was at college. Barista," he starts rattling off. "I was a cashier at the campus cafeteria for a few weeks."

"A few weeks?"

"Um, the whole lunch credit thing was a bit complicated. Like you had to look up everyone's information, if they didn't have their campus ID, and run this report after every shift in time before the caf manager had to set up for dinner. It was…you had to be fast, and I guess I wasn't very fast." He looks out the window, chewing on his lip again. "Um, I worked at the fitness center downtown last summer for a little bit, but…I guess it wasn't really my scene, so I went back to washing dishes at Tapas the rest of the summer."

Smearing my hand down my face, I bite my tongue. This just gets better and better. He can't even keep a job a teenager could do. What in the hell was Aiden thinking?

Deciding that I'd rather be ogled than hear any more disturbing biographical disasters about Dami Boy Wonder, the rest of the drive is silent. When I park at the old Hodges homestead, my phone chirps the message alert.

> **THOR:** Four more months of this shit, and I'm done. You
> need a banged-up sea dog on your staff?

Chuckling at my old crew member's message, a wash of comfort swaths me. Thor Breckenridge was my best mate in the Navy and probably the best friend I've ever had besides Jen. It was a hell of a lot easier to make friends in the Navy than in Olympus, and I'm grateful his has lasted after I got out. I send him a reply, not feeling eager to start masonry 101 with my apprentice.

> **ME:** Had you pegged for a lifer. Not going for Master
> Chief of the Navy?
> **THOR:** No way. The recruits get younger and dumber,
> while I get older and…well, just fucking old.

ME: Tell me about it. Training a new guy today. Fresh out
of college.
THOR: Ooh, shit. Bet he knows everything. You might
want to take notes.
ME: If only. Gotta go. He's waiting for me to inspire him.

And sure as shit, Dami *is* waiting for me, still sitting in his seat with
that stupid smile on his face. I gesture with my phone. "Sorry. Old Navy
buddy."

"You were in the Navy?"

"Yup."

"That's so cool. Is that what all the tats are from?" he asks, nodding
to the inked sleeves on my forearms.

My skin prickles, hearing his perusal of my body isn't just limited to
my face. I could elaborate on my ink, but I get the impression the more I
divulge, the more questions he'll ask, the more talking he'll do, the more
I'll have to hear that voice that's increasingly making my nuts draw
up tight.

"Something like that. Come on. Let's get to it."

Apparently, avoiding speaking to Dami is not an option. After I gave
him a rundown of the layout plan for the rebuild, I started simple—level-
ing off one of the few existing walls that were salvageable. My definition
of *simple*, however, isn't the same as his. Lesson learned.

"I thought you said it was already level because we did that thing
with the string," Dami says, pointing to the level line that took ten minutes longer to set up than if I'd been doing it myself.

Never in all the years I've worked this job have I had to explain it to
anyone. Again, Aiden. What the fuck were you thinking?

Motioning to the corner joint I started off the old wall as a demonstration, I force patience into my tone. "It's not just about if it's level. We
need to make sure it's plumb too."

His nose scrunches up. "Make sure it's what?"

"*Plumb*." I gesture to the rows of brick courses I started, feeling like
a circus monkey without its cymbals. Clearly, his vocabulary of construction terms isn't as extensive as mine, so I clarify, "*Plumb*—up and
down."

"*Plum?* Like the fruit?"

"No. *Plumb* with a *B*."

Brows pinched, he blinks for a moment, mouth agape. "*Blum?*"

"Jesus, fuck," I mutter under my breath and pinch the bridge of my
nose. Watch. I'll get blamed for him not knowing shit when he goes on a
job with Aiden. "No! *Plumb* with a *P* in the beginning and a *B* at the end.
It means you don't want the wall to lean one way or the other. It needs to
be straight up and down."

"Oh, okay."

I shouldn't give two shits that his voice has lost some of its optimism. He's the one who signed up for this gig. So, why is my stomach squirming in sympathy? I never claimed to be good at teaching people things.

"Look," I preface, snagging his attention, those unnaturally marbled, blue eyes of his sending a zing down my spine. "Do you remember how I mixed up the mortar?"

"Yeah."

"Okay. Well, go mix up another batch over there, and I'll get you started on the south wall when you're ready."

"Alright."

Four days. I just need to get through four days of this, and figure out where I went wrong with Jen, then everything will be fine.

CHAPTER 5

"Are you mad at me?" I hedge, as Graham grumbles on all fours, flinging mortar onto the tarp he wrenched out of his truck after that wheelbarrow took a nosedive in the wrong direction. I swear I aimed for the mortar board.

Pausing his cursing under his breath, cheeks red, he snarls, "What?"

"You…seem kind of mad…like more mad than a normal person would be about someone spilling mortar."

"It's job training, kid. I'm not here to hold your hand and throw out gold stars every time you half ass something."

Gold stars? Wow. Do I seem that fickle? Man, he's hard core.

I know I should be focusing on how to defuse him, but instead I'm transfixed by the image of him prowling around on all fours, scooping the mortar off the grass. What would that sight look like on a bed, and is he even capable of whispering sweet nothings?

"What?" He growls again, stirring a tingle in my belly. "What's that look for?"

"Nothing, just…I guess I thought there'd be a little TLC with it being my first day and all."

He answers with a snort, moving with the spry strength of a leopard. "TLC, huh? Does this face say tender to you?"

It says I want it to throw me down and do me. Probably not the answer he's looking for. Swallowing the glob of lust in my throat, I shrug. "Not exactly."

"I'm showing you as much love as is appropriate for any new hire, and as for the *care* part, I care about the job and getting you to do it right. Does that meet all your expectations?"

"Yeah, I just assumed the love would be the hey-welcome-aboard-new-guy kind," I joke on a nervous laugh, but it falls flat judging by the glower he flashes me. Gosh, that is so sexy I almost want to cause more trouble.

"It's called tough love, sweetheart. There isn't any other kind."

My brain and my cock have a quick fantasy over the word *sweetheart* before I snap myself back to the cold reality of the snarling man at my feet. Geez, he's uptight, and I thought I was the one who needed to get laid.

"Where's your hard hat?" he snaps.

"Over there," I gesture to where I set it on the trailer.

"Lot of good it's going to do your head, sitting over there."

Glancing up at the morning sun in the cloudless sky, I can't for the life of me see the purpose of wearing that uncomfortable thing that digs into my scalp. "What could possibly fall on my head? There's no roof on this thing yet. Just a few old walls that aren't any taller than I am."

"It's an OSHA requirement. Just do it."

Osha must be a picky woman, but I comply. I think I've poked the bear enough today, and it's not even lunch time yet.

Since Graham refused my help in cleaning up my mess, I have an idle moment. My parents have trained me to not insist on making myself useful. It's best to just stay out of the way sometimes.

Wiping the perspiration from my forehead with my t-shirt, I tug it over my head, then grab my hard hat and toss the shirt on the trailer. Mom wasn't kidding. It's still scorching out.

Maybe Dante will still have his pool open at his house for his birthday party. I cannot wait. It's probably the only party I'll get to go to until Christmas. No way am I not getting laid there. Two more weeks. I can hold out for two more weeks.

"What the hell are you doing?" Graham barks.

I stop in my tracks and glance around on instinct because I'm certainly doing nothing wrong, but it's only me and Graham, so that question was for me.

"Getting my hard hat."

"Yeah, but where the hell is your shirt?"

"I threw it on the trailer."

"Well, put it back on."

"But…it's hot. I'm all sweaty." I demonstrate by grazing my finger through a droplet that's running down between my pecs.

Graham's eyes pinch closed. His chest rises and falls in the silence. Aiden said they don't have a uniform policy. What is the deal?

"Then rip your sleeves off," he says through his teeth, not even opening his eyes. "We wear clothes here."

"Is that one of *Osha's* rules too?"

Scowling at me, he takes a second to answer. "Yes."

Geesh. What do I know? Shrugging, I reclaim my shirt and tug it back over my head. Looking to Graham's t-shirt as a guide was a bad idea. I can see one of his flat brown nipples through the sleeve openings where he clearly tore his sleeves off at some point.

Gripping a handful of shirt at my shoulder, I yank on my sleeve, but nothing happens. Grunting, I try again, but someone took their stitch job serious when they made this.

"It won't work," I grit out, trying to pull my sleeve at different angles. "All it's doing is stretching out my neckline. How do *you* do it?"

Graham sighs and stomps over. I hear a *click* noise, and the next thing I see is him raising a pocketknife.

I flinch because angry-man-with-a-knife doesn't sound like a safe combo. He must sense my concern as he grips my sleeve.

"I'm not going to cut you. Just hold still."

I don't even have time to decide if I trust him. His blade tears through the fabric and then a sharp point glances my shoulder.

"Ouch!" I yelp, a sting erupting at the top of my bicep.

"Shit," Graham mutters.

"Hey! You said you wouldn't cut me!"

"I didn't do it on purpose!"

Graham presses the dangling sleeve which is now half cut off to the nick mark on my arm. When he pulls it back after a few seconds a crimson line of blood droplets emerge. Grimacing, he licks his thumb and presses it to the cut.

I don't know what's more captivating—the look of genuine compassion on his face, like there's another side of him other than the gruffness I've seen, or the press of his wet flesh to mine.

His gaze collides with mine. Mixed with the overpowering masculine scent that is uniquely Graham, my head spins. Can a person actually suck you into a vortex? Is this what a crush feels like?

Frowning, he shatters the moment, slicing through the rest of my sleeve. His rough grip on my other shoulder spins me around, and in two seconds my other sleeve is gone.

"Here," he says, tossing the fabric at my chest. Turning on his heel, he pockets his knife and stomps off.

He's well out of range by the time I squeak out past my trembling lips, "Thank you."

CHAPTER 6

Graham

It's Wednesday and by some miracle, Dami still thinks he wants to be a brick mason, and I haven't lost my shit. Seeing him doze off on the ride to work the last two mornings tells me he's struggling to get up, but he's arrived at the warehouse on time every day. Half of me admires his punctuality, while the other half wants to take joy in his misery.

The conflicting feelings are making me feel like Dr. Jekyll and Mr. Hyde, or maybe just one of them. Which one was the asshole? Well, there's normal asshole-me, then there's bigger asshole-me who keeps snapping at everything he does.

I tried keeping him at a distance the last two days, making him pick up all the old bricks I tore down last week and throw them in the dumpster. That worked out well until he got stung by a wasp, and I had to see that sad little grimace on his face and the way he bites his lip.

I should have been proud of him for not complaining. Instead, I went off on a tangent about him not wearing his safety glasses. In my defense, that was shortly after I had to sit through another lunch break of him staring at me while he doodled in some notebook like the giant kid he is.

And for the record, it was funny, *not cute*, that he showed up with a cooler for his lunch the last two days after frowning at his slimy, wilted sandwich he left cooking on the dash of the truck Monday in a paper grocery bag. Extremely funny. Thor thought so when I texted him. That validates my behavior. Right?

Fine.

It's possible that I may be taking out some of my frustrations over Jen on him, but the fact that I'm frustrated over meeting Jen tomorrow night only freaks me out more. There was nothing promising about her words when we talked Sunday. She said *I* was going to be okay, not *we're* going to be okay. Typical, Jen. She's been my biggest champion my entire life.

When I wanted to join the Navy, she backed me up a hundred percent. It was good for both of us. It got her away from her mom's toxic behavior, got us out of Olympus, and let me stand on my own two feet to provide for us. Maybe I shouldn't have asked her to wait to have kids because after my enlistment when I brought it up, then she was the one who wanted to wait.

Fair is fair. What could I say?

I just wish I could figure out what made it start to go wrong. If I knew, it'd be like a crack in a wall. I could find a way to fix it. The more I analyze it, I worry there were thousands of tiny cracks I never saw and never will, which means I'm fucked.

"Do you only listen to oldies music?" Dami's voice interrupts my thoughts.

Glancing at the radio, I catch the bars of REO Speedwagon's "Take It On The Run".

"The radio's broken. It's stuck on that station," I lie, which has nothing to do with catching him shaking his ass to some pop music he was streaming on his phone yesterday, after which I insisted my seniority meant that I was in charge of the music. "And that's not oldies. Fifties and sixties music are oldies."

"Well, I never heard it before, and it's kind of depressing and about being in pain."

"No. It's about love. Ninety percent of songs are about love, and love is painful."

"No, it's not." He chuckles. "Love should be happy and hopeful."

"You know a lot about love, do you?" I retort, guiding the other end of the level line. "Have you ever even been in love?"

I can guess his response by the way he does that nose-scrunching thing whenever he stops to think. To my surprise though, he shrugs.

"Sure. Lots of times. Raoul. Ethan. Cameron," he rattles off.

I'd considered naming a son Cameron if I ever had one. I never realized how little I cared for that name until now or the other ones. I cast Dami a dubious look in response to his list.

"What?"

"That's a lot of love for such a young person."

Laughing, he shrugs. "I'm a lovable guy. I want a lasting love someday, but I just moved out of my parents' house. There's no way I'm settling down yet after having to hide everything from them. I've got lots of lost time to make up for. That's what our twenties are for. Right?"

"Yeah. *That* sounds like the road to true love." Adding another dollop to his course of bricks, I correct him, "Use more mortar. That's not thick enough."

"I'm betting lots of roads to true love have been paved with one-night-stands. I'll get there…someday, maybe when I'm older like ten years from now."

Judging by the look of concentration on his face as he swipes away the excess mud, I can tell that wasn't a dig. Great. It still means I'm fucking old.

"I have a plan, you know?" he adds.

"A *love plan?*"

"Well, yeah. Kind of."

"This should be good."

"Step-one was finishing school and moving out. Step-two is building my career, so I don't have to rely on anyone. See? I'm halfway there."

His beaming smile is so assured, I can't hold back a scoff. "It's your first week. I wouldn't call it a career yet."

I solemnly swore to not engage with this kid, but he's certainly more entertaining than the scrape and slather sounds of the mud against the bricks. When he saunters back with another armload of bricks, my curiosity gets the better of me.

"Is there a step-three to this diabolical plan?"

"Yeah. Step-three, I'll meet a handsome financially sound guy, but I'll have made enough money I won't have to depend on him. He'll respect me, you know?"

Try as I may, I can't find much fault in his plan because it sounds similar to what mine was at only eighteen with the exception of the financially sound partner or the guy part. I wouldn't have imagined a kid who has "lost time to make up for" would want to settle down. Hell, he could be me, if he wanted—

"And we'll get married, and have three kids," he adds, derailing my entire train of thought.

My hand freezes mid-air with the brick I just took from him. His words make the weight heavier.

He wants kids.

At twenty-three, he's on step-two of a three-step plan that leads to happily ever after and three children. I'm a thirty-year-old childless divorcé whose ex squeezed him in for a dinner date on a night she wasn't busy with her boyfriend. The sense of kinship over him sharing the plan I once had is officially dead.

"What? You don't want kids?" he asks, studying my face, which probably looks as bitter as I feel.

How can it hurt to lose something you never had?

I have to clear my throat as I rise and dust my hands off on my jeans. "I'm divorced. It doesn't matter what I want anymore."

As I walk away, I can't help but wonder if it ever really did. You can make all the plans you want, but no one's guaranteed a fucking fairytale.

CHAPTER 7

I should really be finishing that sketch I'm doing of Dante for his birthday, but I need something more enthralling to keep my eyes open than the roommate I listened to snoring for four semesters. Scratching out the fine hairs of Graham's goatee on my sketchpad, I use my thumb to add in a bit more shading.

It's the first night this week I didn't have to wash dishes at Tapas, so I refuse to go to bed at eight o'clock even though I need it. No wonder Graham's in such good shape. Brickwork is no joke.

As more of his face takes form on the paper, I can't help but feel I pegged him wrong. I thought he was just grumpy all the time, but the face looking back at me seems troubled, pained even, and maybe a bit vulnerable.

It's all in the eyes. I could stare at those eyes all day, tell them jokes until they light up and crinkle at the corners. Put a flicker of hope in them that it does matter what he wants, even if he is divorced.

Ugh. What am I saying?

Stupid crush. Stupid untouched cock in my pants, making me think silly things about a straight man that hates me.

Ironically though, this might be my best work yet. Maybe it's just my best subject. Johnny wouldn't like the sound of that, especially considering most of my drawings are of his former models whose pictures I "borrowed" out of the file cabinets in his studio.

My phone pings, so I tuck my pencil into the spiral binding of my sketchpad. My group chat with Angelica and Dante is lit up.

> **DANTE:** You two still making it to my party?
> **ANGELICA:** Might have to miss for a work thing, but Dami, if our mothers ask, I'm meeting you there.
> **DANTE:** LAME!

ME: You will be missed, Ang. I'll run defense if needed,
per usual.
DANTE: Didn't you two "break up" ages ago?
ANGELICA: It's complicated.
ME: Yeah. She caught me with another man while she
was hitting on her girlfriend.

At least this is one crowd I can joke with about the sad lies of my life. Except staring at the glow of my phone, it's not as funny now as I hear Johnny and Aiden in Johnny's old room, moving out the last of Johnny's stuff.

I know I told Graham that our twenties are for sowing our wild oats, but what if it takes all of my twenties to fess up to my parents? It's freaking exhausting pretending to be someone else.

DANTE: Speaking of work, how's the brick business?
ME: #mybosshatesme
DANTE: #angerbang
ME: #notgonnahappen #waytoostraight
DANTE: Says the man with a fake ex-girlfriend

Ouch. Hashtag reality check.

Johnny and Aiden's voices grow louder, so I toss my phone to flip my sketchpad closed. I know Aiden is cool, but I'm not about to let him catch me drawing his little brother. Hashtag stalker.

"Hey, I think that's it," Johnny says, carting a laundry bag under one arm and a box labelled *Sexy Underwear* under the other.

Aiden emerges from Johnny's room behind him with a stack of boxes three-high. "You sure you don't mind having the place to yourself?" he asks.

"Nah. I'm happy for you guys. You deserve some privacy."

Johnny shoots Aiden a heart-eyed smile that is still a bit foreign for me to see on his face. If I'm lucky, that'll be me when I'm older. I'm still in awe to know it's possible for a boy from Olympus.

"Um, so we're leaving the swing bed," Johnny says, referencing his crazy ass platform bed that hangs from his ceiling. "Too complicated to take down, but uh, feel free to use it or pitch it. Whatever your heart's content. Just, um, be warned it feels extra swingy when you've been drinking."

"Alright. Thanks."

"But it's fun for…*other* activities, sometimes dangerous, but also fun."

"Um, okay."

"Right, well. I mean, it's not like I won't see you thirty-seven more times this week at the restaurant, but I guess this is kind of a goodbye."

Smiling, I hop off the couch and pat him on the back. That's as close to hugging as he gets with anyone but Aiden, yet I know him well enough to see he's getting sentimental.

"Oh, um, thanks," he says awkwardly at my miniscule show of affection. Glancing around his apartment, he looks a bit melancholy.

"You gonna be alright, baby? We don't have to take this stuff?" Aiden murmurs to him.

"No. Paradise awaits me with the best man, just, you know—memories. Photographer here. I mean, this is where we first…" He doesn't finish the sentence, but judging by their heated looks, I can fill in the blanks. Clearing his throat, Johnny smiles at me. "Well, she's all yours. Once again, have fun cocking it up."

Chuckling, I hold the door for them. It was the same choice phrase he left me with when I came out to him at that speed dating event months ago—*go forth and cock it up.*

As quiet settles over the room when they depart, it occurs to me that I very well can cock it up in here now whenever I want. I seriously have my own place all to myself for the first time in my life.

I must be overworked because even the thought of rubbing one out is exhausting. Maybe being an adult is being so sleep-deprived you prefer to finish sketching a broody, handsome face over touching your own dick.

I'll hit the dating apps tomorrow. That'll take care of this unhealthy crush.

CHAPTER 8

Graham

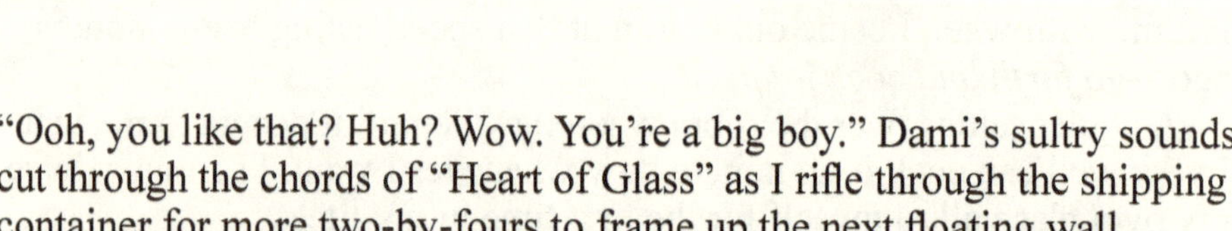

"Ooh, you like that? Huh? Wow. You're a big boy." Dami's sultry sounds cut through the chords of "Heart of Glass" as I rifle through the shipping container for more two-by-fours to frame up the next floating wall.

Is he fucking serious? I thought I told him to stay off that damn phone earlier. What part of don't check dating apps on the clock didn't he understand? I told him to take a break, but I'll be damned if I'm going to stand here listening to the sound effects of him finding his next one-night-stand.

Kicking one of the old wooden chairs we keep for lunch breaks out of my way, I stride out of the shipping container with purpose. "I thought I told you to stay off that damn phone while you're—Jesus Christ!" Sheer terror catapults my heart into my throat. I scramble back so fast, my ass collides with the side of the shipping container. "What the fuck is that?"

Dami spins around with a satanic ball of tabby fur cradled in his arms, flashing me his signature million-dollar smile. "It's a cat," he laughs. "You want to pet him?"

"No! Where did you get it, and why the hell are you holding it?"

"I found him by the wood line," he says, gesturing over his shoulder. "I think he's hungry."

Holy shit. He's getting closer. My lungs seize. My belly churns on a wave of nausea. Thank God, my legs are working. Stumbling over the circular saw, I save my footing and leap onto the break chair.

"Stay there! Don't come any closer!"

"What? He's sweet. I swear," Dami says, scratching the mongrel's ears, obliterating any misguided fantasy I had about his hands.

"There is nothing sweet about a soul-sucking grimalkin."

"A what?"

"A grimalkin," I wheeze, every one of my limbs trembling. This chair better not pick today to break. "Supernatural beings. Witches used to keep them."

"You cannot be serious. It's just a cat," he laughs, hoisting it up to rub his cheek against it.

"Oh, God! Stop that! Put it down!"

Realization finally hits his face as he eyes me up and down. "How can you be afraid of a cat? It's adorable."

He holds it out as though a closer look will get me to believe his heinous falsehood. Its creepy eyes bore into my soul, so naturally I lift and angle my knee to protect my nuts.

"They're toxic! Have you ever heard of Cat Scratch Fever? It almost killed me. They have filthy little daggers in their litter diggers, and on top of that, they make unnatural sounds."

On cue, the venomous flea bag's ears go back, and it lets out an unholy guttural howl.

"Calm down! You're scaring it!"

The yowling goes up a pitch. I can't take it anymore. I've got seconds before that thing strikes my jugular, and I'm stuck out here with no one but Smiles McPerky Butt to relay life-saving directions to paramedics.

Waving my arms to make myself look bigger, I emphasize, "See! Did that sound adorable to you? Oh, Christ!"

Dami fumbles as it scrambles like a cracked out Tasmanian Devil, bursting from his arms. I wince, and brace myself, but fortunately it barrels off toward the woods.

"Ouch!" Dami howls, clutching his chest, where I can only imagine the Dark Lord of Pets just infected him with its kitty-cooties.

"Look! I told you! Don't screw with nature!"

"I wasn't screwing with it. I was petting it."

"Yeah? Well, no more interacting with varmints. Get back to work. I see you with another cat on the job site, you're done."

"Is that an *Osha* rule too?"

Panting, I hold his confused, pouty gaze. Fuck it. It's not like I have any dignity left after screeching on top of a chair. "Yes!"

"Geez." He folds his arms. "*Osha* sounds like a jerk."

"That's because it's not run by five-year-olds who get distracted by shiny objects."

He can look as dejected as he wants. I don't care. Truly, I don't. If this is how my day is going, I can only imagine how tonight will turn out.

CHAPTER 9

Graham

Jen pops her car into park in the driveway and throws me a smile where I wait on the porch. Butterflies are good. Right?

I can't remember the last time she gave me butterflies. At the lawyer's office maybe? The last few times we had sex?

Fuck. Maybe they're not butterflies. Maybe they're drunk June bugs, pinging around my stomach like pinballs. I'm just nervous because I still don't have a plan. Stupid Dami, distracting me all week.

"Hey, there," she calls, the breeze catching her shoulder-length blonde hair as she makes her way up the steps.

"Hey."

Opening my arms, she steps into them, wrapping hers around me. Hugging her used to feel natural, comforting, like coming home. There's a rigidity now and a foreignness. Parts of it still feel right and warm, but it's the comfort of a memory rather than a sense of completion. When did that happen? Are we that broken?

"The place looks nice," she says, glancing at the yard.

"I need to mow. I went fishing last weekend and let it get away from me."

Lifting her eyebrows, she rocks back on her heels, tucking her hands into her jean pockets. "Ah, your love affair with the fish continues." She grins, but quickly schools her features. "Sorry, bad joke."

Smiling, I gesture to the swing. "It's okay. I know you were never a fan of fishing. I didn't mind."

"No! I liked it," she exclaims taking a seat next to me. "Just maybe... once every few months?" she tapers off, and I can't help but crack up at the abject guilt written all over her face.

"Stop it," she scolds, swatting my arm with the back of her hand.

As our laughter peters out, I think of all the times she politely declined to go with me on the boat and usually brought a towel to sunbathe when I fished on the dock rather than participate. It made me restless that she didn't join in like I had to cut it short because she was waiting on me.

"You hungry? Dinner'll be done in about fifteen."

"I'm good." She smiles, tucking a strand of hair behind her ear. Does she know she looks thinner? Should I not let it bother me? Maybe she wanted to be thinner. "What did you make?"

"Uh. Baked breakfast casserole. Bacon, sausage, bell peppers, and onions over cheesy hashbrowns."

"Really? Wow. Not what I'd have guessed from the guy who refuses to eat meals out of order."

"I do not!"

"Yes, you do," she laughs.

"No, but if you eat eggs for breakfast, why would you want eggs for dinner? And if you eat a waffle for dinner, you just limited your choices for breakfast the next day, and so on. It's a precarious cycle." I shut my trap when I realize she's staring at me, eyes dancing with mirth. "Whatever," I chuckle, shaking my head. "You said…you said that you were on midnights again, so I figured this is when you eat breakfast."

I feel her gaze on me as I stare out at the woods beyond our vast yard where we've hosted countless gatherings of my family, my face heating. Why is this so difficult and yet like nothing at all has changed?

Her hand closes over mine and squeezes. Encompassing her grip, my fingertips graze the indentation on her ring finger.

"Thank you. That was very thoughtful."

"My middle name," I murmur, rolling my eyes.

"Mm. It is, and I've still never told your secret."

I let out a breathless laugh at her age-old compliment but am met with a challenging smirk. I always loved that smirk. It says *go on, defy me*. As much as Jen could roll with the punches and be a vulnerable mess in the face of her mother's disasters, she could stick it to me when I was being impossible, and hold me up when I wouldn't let anyone else in.

Like a cloud dissipating to let the sun through, it all makes perfect sense now as I roam my gaze over her face—the face of my best friend fifteen years in the making. We were just two vulnerable kids who threw on a mask of invincibility together. We made each other better…until we didn't, I guess.

"So…what did you want to talk about?" she hedges.

And there it is. Any grasp I had on calm is shattered now that we have to get to it. It wasn't much of a grasp after the last few weeks of my restlessness spiraling out of control. Sucking in a breath, I don't think I can get any words out the way my chest is seizing up, but finally something tumbles free.

"I know you said…it was you and not me, but it takes two. There's got to be something else," I babble as she releases my hand to clasp hers together in her lap. "I don't care what it is. I just…I need to know. You can tell me."

Chewing on her lip and squinting out at the setting sun, her silence has my muscles bracing for impact. No matter how bad the complaint, this is what I need. This woman sitting right here—the other half to the only life I've ever known. If I have to gut myself open to keep her, I'll survive.

"Are you just…not attracted to me anymore?" I venture. "Was it… was it the sex?"

My stomach folds in on itself at the suggestion. She once told me it didn't feel like I was connected when we made love, like I was focused more on concentrating than enjoying it. It's definitely the last thing I want to discuss, but maybe if anyone can help me figure out how to get over it, Jen can.

"Graham, I'm sorry I ever mentioned anything about the sex."

"No. It's alright. If that's the problem, we need to talk about it."

I don't want to talk about it. I don't fucking want to talk about it.

Her green eyes are pained, grimacing, she squeezes my hand again. I'm starting to think that's not as reassuring a gesture as I initially thought.

"You tried," she intones sympathetically. "I know you did. I could tell. It just…it didn't feel like the way two people who are in love are supposed to feel, and even when you did try to initiate after the first divorce, it…it felt…forced."

Now I'm the one with the urge to pull my hand away. What the fuck does that mean? I have to force myself to keep it still because every cowardly fiber in my body knows she's telling the truth.

I'm not good at sex. Never have been. As long as she made enough sounds for the both of us, I figured I was doing a good enough job. I'd get off, but the older I got, the more it felt like a struggle. Who in God's name would ever tell that to their wife? The best I figured was that I was an asexual who fell in love with a woman.

"I…I'm sorry."

"Don't be." She squeezes my hand. I can feel her long audible breath dust the warm skin of my forearm. "I love you, Graham. I'll always be attracted to you, and I'll always love you, but at some point, I just…I started to realize that maybe we just loved each other and weren't *in love* with each other."

"And that's not enough?"

"I don't know. Maybe…for some people. I guess that's why I said it was me, not you because…God, I feel like shit for saying this, but…for me, it's not. And it was fucking terrifying walking away from being loved. Listen to me. I probably sound like I'm not making any sense."

"No. It's…let it out. Was it…was it because I asked about kids? I feel like you asked for the divorce not long after I brought it up."

A puff of breath leaves her lips. "It felt like that would have just been a bandage to mask what was missing between us. I don't doubt for a moment that you would be a terrific father. I just didn't want to be two parents who loved their kids." Shaking her head, a self-deprecating laugh leaves her lips. "That sounds so selfish."

Putting my arm around her, I give her shoulders a squeeze. There are only so many things a man can hear. "There's not a selfish bone in your body, Jen. The shit you've gone through taking care of your mom, supporting me to join the Navy, putting up with the squabbles between me and Maxie…"

"I wanted to go. I'm glad we moved away."

Pursing my lips, my heart sinks. "Is that when it all fell apart?"

"What?" Her brows pinch together.

"When we moved back after my dad had the heart attack?"

"Graham, no!" Her eyes go round. "Is that what you think?"

"We…were happy in Virginia. When we moved back you had to deal with your mom again, and all of my family's overwhelming chaos."

"She'll always be my mom. I learned how to distance myself when I need to, how to not make her problems about me. I have you to thank for that." She grips my knee. "I love your family. You did the right thing coming back to help them, as long as you're happy. I was more worried about you being disappointed about it than me."

"They're my family. It's my job to take care of them."

"No. *A job* is your *job*. Do you love brick masonry?"

How did this become a topic of conversation? Can't the fucking oven timer go off when a guy needs it to?

Schooling my features, I try to give the question a moment of honest thought for Jen's sake. I don't hate it. I'm good at it. Really fucking good, if I were bragging. Aiden's told me countless times I'm the best out of all of us and that he's grateful I moved back home.

My thoughts drift to a fluffy, black-haired kid with a stupid smile. Why is my blood warming when I have my arm around my wife…or ex-wife? Fuck. Yeah, I hate my job for reasons that have nothing to do with my job.

"Love is a strong word," I let out on an exhausted breath. I'm suddenly ready to close my eyes for a week and bury my head under the covers. "What does this have to do with us?"

"Graham, you do things for everyone else, never yourself. The fishing? Why do you think I never complained about that? It's the only thing you've ever done because it was something you were really passionate about. You get this glimmer in your eyes when you get your tackle together." She laughs, eyes crinkling at the corners.

"I do not. What…why… What are you getting at? You want me to look at you the way I look at fishing tackle?" I joke, hoping she'll see how far off topic we've gotten.

Why the fuck is she looking at me like that? The corner of her mouth ticks up, but it looks anything but happy. "Yeah."

"O-kay. I…I can try…"

"You asked me a question," she cuts me off. "But I want you to ask yourself the same question."

"What?"

"If *you're* really attracted to *me*."

A glass of cold water couldn't have shocked me more. When I realize I've stared with my mouth gaping open for probably too long, I blurt out without any finesse, "You're beautiful. I've always thought so."

It's the truth. I'm not lying, so why is her mouth turned down into a sad little frown. It's the same kind my nieces and nephews get when they get told they can't have something they want.

"What?" I ask her probing gaze. "You are."

"Yeah, but…do you ever want to tear my clothes off?"

"What?" I bark out a laugh. "What the hell kind of question is that?"

Sighing, she looks out at the yard, shaking her head. "Nothing. Nevermind."

Damn it. I'm losing her. Giving her shoulder a squeeze before I pull my hand away, I wish like hell there was someone who could just fix this for both of us.

"No. Hey, I asked you to say whatever you wanted. I…I don't think I'm…" Running my palm down my mouth, I fight to not squirm. Christ on a cracker, I can't believe I'm about to voice this aloud. "I think maybe I've just never really been a sexual person."

Fuck. I'm practically panting, it's so damn hard to breathe. I never thought in a million years this would come up or be a problem, while at the same time I think it was always a secret worry in the back of my mind. Why can't I be normal? Why can't we both go back to being ignorant and just enough?

Her fucking hand squeezes my knee again. I want to laugh deliriously at the symbolism of it. It's both a punishment and reward for my honesty, a consolation prize for what's coming, and comfort bred of former bonds.

"I'm sorry," I rasp pathetically. "I don't know what's wrong with me."

"Nothing, Graham. There's nothing wrong with you," Jen's voice soothes but does little to quell the heavy weight of shame in my veins. I'll never be able to give her what she needs, and the worst part is she isn't mad about it.

Her audible breath warns me, it's time. Whatever she's about to say next are the words I'll remember forever—the final composition of we're done.

"Did you ever think…that maybe…you might be attracted to men?"

Every sound stops along with my pulse. For a second, I scramble to decide if she asked the question or if it was an utterance I've long ago buried in the deepest recesses of my brain. My skin is melting off my face, my palms sweating.

Breathe, Graham. Jesus Christ, breathe. Say something!

Self-preservation kicks a puff of air out of my lungs. "What? You think I'm bisexual?"

A second could have passed or an entire minute. Regardless, the silence is too much. As stiff as my neck is, I manage to turn my head.

Nothing ever looked as foreboding as the pitying expression on her face. "No, Graham," she says as though speaking to a child who doesn't understand. "I think…maybe you're gay."

I don't know why judgement is the first thing I search for in her eyes rather than hurt before I sputter and tear my gaze away. I should be laughing or offended she knows so little about me or denying it and reassuring her doubts. I do none of those things.

Time and sound speed back up even though I'm frozen. My heartbeat is in my eardrums. My mouth goes dry, and the odd sensation of being bare ass naked overtakes me. All of a sudden, I have the overwhelming urge to cry. I never fucking cry.

I don't need a stopwatch to tell me too much time has passed without me admitting or refuting her assumption. Sometimes nothing says everything.

When I face Jen, a puff of air chokes out at the understanding smile on her face. Shaking my head, all I know is that I need to reassure her I meant every promise and intention I ever had where she was concerned.

"I never—"

"I know," she whispers, squeezing my hand.

"I…I wouldn't have ever…"

"I know."

Her thumb rubs gentle circles over the top of my hand, an understanding so deep in her eyes I could drown in it. Holy fuck. This actually just happened.

Dropping my face in my hands, I have to rest my elbows on my knees to hold my head up. Somewhere a buzzing sound is going off. Dinner? I could care less. Blowing out a breath, I try to understand how I feel.

Relieved? Why do I feel relieved? This is horrible. Telling your ex that you might be gay doesn't get her back, but that ship has sailed. Hasn't it? Is that why I was so desperate for her to come back? So, I could hide behind her like a coward while she was quietly miserable? I'm too old to be gay.

At some point, I acknowledge the hand rubbing my back. Freaking Jen. This David guy better fucking deserve her.

"How long have you…thought that?"

"I don't know." She shrugs. "I never had an ah-ha moment. It was little things over the years." When I just stare guiltily for the crime I've inadvertently committed in my head, she elaborates. "I realized, not once in fifteen years did you ever comment on another woman's looks, not anyone we saw or even a celebrity. All men do that."

The unspoken words *straight men* are implied, making me blush. I'm not straight, I realize with more clarity, deciding now is not the time to wrap my head around it.

"I was proud you were perfect," she continues, smiling cheekily. "Then I wondered if maybe you were too perfect. You…never had a problem, agreeing or disagreeing with me over actors I found attractive. I…blame that stupid football coach sometimes," she adds, frowning as she glances at me.

My stomach knots at the mention of bitter memories. I can still hear that asshole shouting at our team in the locker room, doling out the words *pansies* and *faggots* like they were candy at a fucking parade.

"Coach Rutledge?" I interject. "What the hell would he have to do with anything?"

"All that crap with you and Maxie when you were kids," she challenges. "It bothered you more than you admitted, Graham. I knew it then but didn't understand why until years later."

I refuse to let some bigoted high school coach be the reason I didn't know up from down my entire life. Testily, I reply, "I can think for myself. You were it for me back then, I promise. I just…I don't know. I…I wondered…about *the other*…sometimes, but I figured it was just confusion, or maybe I was trying to understand Aiden and Maxie. I'm sorry."

"Graham, you don't have to take any blame. I'm just as much to blame. The whole sex thing and how intimacy should feel…I didn't know any better for a long time. Hell, neither of us did." She smiles, bumping my shoulder with hers. "We were just kids, and we never had a basis for comparison."

My face heats, finding the hole in her logic. At some point, she figured it out while I kept on going like an ostrich with its head in the sand.

"Yeah, but we're not kids anymore, Jen."

"Well, nobody tells us how to figure everything out. Luckily, it's not a race."

Once again, I'm off the hook for a lifetime of hiding and confusion or rather hiding from my confusion. In spite of the rawness of the moment, there's a sense of peace in the silence as the swing rocks. Whether she got it moving or I did, I haven't the foggiest. Maybe it's gratitude, soothing the storm inside me. She doesn't hate me. We'll never be husband and wife again, but she doesn't hate me.

"You okay?" she asks, after a while.

"Fuck if I know," I get out on an exhausted laugh.

Turning her body toward mine, her leg bent on the swing, she drapes her arm behind me. "I don't regret anything. You know?"

It's so bittersweet, saying goodbye to your past, especially the best part of it. Settling my hand on her knee, I return her smile. "Me neither."

She drops her head on my shoulder, and we just stay like that, swinging, staring out at the place we called home for a while. I don't know what I'll remember about this day twenty years from now, but this is my favorite part.

"So…I have to ask…" Jen's voice slips through the silence after we watch the sun set.

"Hm?"

"What are you into?"

"What?" I scoff, hoping she doesn't mean what I think she does.

Damn it. That smirk on her face says that's exactly where she's going with this.

"Like the big muscular kind or the sassy nerdy type like Johnny?" she expounds.

Fuck me. Pinching my eyes closed, I take a moment to reclaim the modicum of calm I'd barely touched.

"Jen, this is my favorite spot to not think about complicated or awkward shit. You didn't get it in either of the divorces. Please at least leave me this swing."

Her amusement tickles my neck. Turning her head, she rests it back on my shoulder.

"Alright. Too much. I get it. Just…you can talk to me. Okay? If you ever need to. I'll try to help if I can."

"Thanks." No way is that ever happening, I don't add. A change of subject is in order to put this to bed. "How, uh, what's new with you?"

"Hm," she hums. "Well, I got a cat."

Is she serious? She couldn't have opened with that? I'd have known in an instant my crap shoot idea of salvaging something was toast, and we could have avoided the whole who are you attracted to can of worms.

"I need a beer."

After packing up overcooked casserole for Jen when we both agreed to forgo dinner, we parted with a hug and cheek kisses. Ironic we ended just as we started, our exchange as innocent as fifteen-year-olds.

Now it's just me, my swing, and beer number-two with beer number-three standing at the ready.

"A fucking cat," I mutter at the lip of the bottle.

I have the sneaking suspicion she just ruined my swing because all I can think about is complicated and awkward shit. Like what is my type…of man?

Fluffy black hair, a bright smile, foolishly optimistic marbled blue eyes, glowing skin, muscular arms clutching a furry, orange, spawn of Satan—no. There is no way the first man I'm accepting that I'm attracted to is a perky-butted, cat-loving, dishwasher.

This is *his* fault. This whole fucking thing is his fault.

CHAPTER IO

"Is it safe for him to drive like that?" I ask Maxie as Graham pitches his lunchbox in the cab of the truck and all but snarls getting in the driver's seat.

"Meh," Maxie haws, her bottom lip pressed into the top one. "Considering in another life he was an old woman who wrote the fifty-five to stay alive speed limit rhyme, I think it's safe to say that the only thing at risk is the steering wheel from his death grip."

I try to laugh in solidarity, but the way Graham marched in late without saying a word to anyone tells me his pot is already boiling. "Does this have anything to do with the cat I found at the job site yesterday? He was pretty upset about that."

"You found a cat out there?" she chortles. "Oh, my God! That's great! He got scratched once when we were kids and has been a giant baby about them ever since. How bad did he freak out? Did he run into anything when he fled for his life?"

"Um, no. He hopped up onto a chair, and then it ran away because it was scared."

"Ah, damn it." She sighs, walking with me around to the passenger side of the truck.

I'm starting to think Maxie is the last person I should ask for Graham-related advice.

"Today, Junior!" Graham's voice barks through the open window.

"Coming boss!"

Maxie punches me in the shoulder and whispers, "Get video next time."

Five hours later, my hypothesis still stands correct. Someone's extra crabby today.

After a silent commute, answering my attempts at pleasantries with a series of grunts, and the embarrassing moment when he caught me working on that sketch of him at lunch, I have been banished to the far side of the building. Everything has a silver-lining though. I don't know what he was thinking after he gaped at my sketchpad and stalked away in silence, but I'm definitely going to heed the warning he left me with when he instructed me to tackle this wall all by myself—*don't fuck it up.*

I'm five courses in—still not sure why he doesn't just call them rows—minus the base course he started for me, and I must say…well, it looks like a wall. See? I knew I could do this.

One week down and I've already got the hang of it, working unsupervised. Graham might hate me, but clearly, he trusts my skills, or he wouldn't have tasked me with this.

Now all I have to do is make it through next week without starving so I can use what little cash I have left for fuel to get to work. Maybe it's defiance or ingratitude, but I refuse to ask Mama to give me money for rations. I'm determined to hold out for my first paycheck from Brandt and Sons.

Stupid bi-weekly pay schedule. Who can budget like that?

Feathering another line of mortar the way Graham taught me, I run some calculations. Math isn't my strong suit, but I should have enough to pay Johnny some rent, buy groceries, and get the drawing table I've had my sights on at the art store downtown.

Johnny was right. That swing bed of his takes some getting used to, but if I sell my bed and use his since I have no idea how to dismantle his contraption, then I can make my old room an art studio. Maybe one day I can design brick houses for people.

Crap. That probably requires math. Well, I guess I could—

"What in God's holy name are you doing?" Graham's voice booms from the corner of the building.

Oh, shoot. Did I play my music too loud on my phone? He's weird about his old man music. Is the mortar too runny?

"Uh, I was just finishing off this course." I silence my phone and gesture with the trowel to my handiwork.

"Look at your level line!" He points to the string I double-checked that's still pulled tight.

"It's level. I checked it twice."

"Are you fucking kidding me?" he mutters, stomping over to where my courses meet the existing wall. "Here!" He points to the seam in between the courses of the other wall at the joint with his trowel then runs the tip of it to one of my seams. "Does it look like you levelled it three courses ago?"

I have to squint to see the flaw. My mortar seams do look a tad bit lower than the seams on the existing wall.

"No!" he continues. "It looks like you were in *La La Land*. It's a quarter inch off."

I gasp as he starts plucking bricks off my last course in quick succession, scraping the mortar off each of them, and flinging the mud back onto the mortar board. My achievement is being hastily dismantled before my eyes.

"And look at this!" He gestures to my seams again. "You didn't even use enough mud! It's not fucking super glue, Dami. Damn it! You've got to lay it thicker than that or it'll crack. I fucking told you this a dozen times. What the hell were you doing when you were watching me all week? Dreaming about your freaking dating apps? Or what your mommy packed you for lunch?"

Ouch. Gosh.

Okay. To be fair, I may have thought about those things, but the way he said them makes me sound childish and irresponsible. I *was* paying attention…or at least, I thought I was. Judging by the increasing pile of discarded bricks as he dismantles the last two hours of my efforts, apparently, I'm delusional.

"I…I'm sorry. I'm really sorry."

Glowering at me, cheeks reddened, I swallow against the lump this new level of Grumpy Graham creates in my throat. Super Duper Grumpy Graham isn't as hot just…scary, but more so depressing. I let him down.

"*Sorry* doesn't cut it in the real world, kid. If you didn't know what the hell you were doing, you should have said something. You know what? Scratch that. Why the hell did you even think you could do this job? A freaking dishwasher," he mumbles under his breath.

The volume of his words doesn't lessen their impact. They pummel me to the core of my soul, quite aptly like a ton of bricks.

Numbly, I start stacking the discarded bricks back onto the pallet. I can't fuck that up, at least.

Graham's right. It's just like every other job I've had, culinary school, and even college.

Dante helped me with more papers than I care to admit. Luckily, my math instructor was gay and hot. Shameless flirting for a passing grade wasn't exactly selling my soul, but I have to wonder if I really earned that C grade.

There's a reason Ma and Pop don't let me work in the kitchen, but now I'm starting to think washing dishes is just the one thing they *let* me do because they know their kid needs to do something. Can I even do that right? Pop's always rearranging dishes after I stack them after all.

I think my plan might need to be adjusted. Either I'll need to find a guy who won't mind me having to depend on him the rest of my life, move back in and live with Ma and Pop forever, or hope there's some low-paying mindless job I can't screw up too badly so that I can give every cent of my earnings from it to Johnny for housing me at a reduced rent price.

Poor Graham. I bet he regrets the day I set foot on this place.

CHAPTER II

Graham

I think I'd rather eat broken glass than make this walk of shame. Shoving open the warehouse door, I curse Skyler for making us come in on a Sunday over his worry about the weather turning and Maxie being gone on her honeymoon soon. Overtime usually doesn't bother me, but there's nothing else left to curse after all the wallowing that I did yesterday.

Man, I'm a dickhead.

So, the kid didn't figure out the job I've been doing most of my life in one week. Way to snap his fluffy head off.

Can you say sexual preference frustrated? Thanks for that, Jen. Have a nice life with your evil furball while I'm stuck here with a cock conundrum the size of California.

I am not looking forward to seeing those sad puppy dog eyes when I round this corner. Fuck. He looked so damn crushed Friday after I finally got over my tirade.

In my defense, I didn't expect to see his hands working an incredible likeness of me at lunch. If his hands can do *that,* why is he wasting them on hard labor? My God, it was so precise and…intimate. The longer I stood there gaping at it, the more naked I felt.

Then I had to walk around the corner of the building later and find him wiggling his ass to that sexed-up pop music he listens to. The way his shirt sleeves were all jaggedly cut off and the stubble he's growing like he's trying to be a mini-me should not have been fucking adorable… or flattering…or oddly attractive.

What is wrong with me? My blood went hot, and I saw red.

That's what homophobes do. I can't be a homophobe. I'd gouge eyes out if anyone ever said shit about Maxie or Aiden and damn near have. Am I a *me-aphobe*?

No. I gave in. I decided that yesterday somewhere between the fifth small mouth bass I caught and the case of *Rolling Rock* I downed on the dock.

Men…do…*something* for me. I'm fucking exhausted over denying it. What the hell I'm supposed to do with that information at the age of thirty, I have no fucking clue. All I do know is that if I have a type, it can't be some *sunshiney* kid that I have zero in common with. I mean, what the hell would he want with someone like me? I'm basically a crotchety old virgin with a bad attitude.

Three pairs of narrowed eyes and crossed arms greet me when I round the corner into the warehouse bay. Yeah. One. Two. Three.

Where the fuck is Dami? Did they not call him in for the over-time?

Or…did something happen to him? My pulse takes off like a mustang at the thought.

"What's going on?" I ask my siblings who look like they've just come from a murder but haven't gotten the bloodthirstiness out of their systems.

"Hey, asshole," Maxie snarks.

Skyler just shakes his head and walks back to the office, where he does whatever the hell it is he does these days. Aiden's perpetually serene face has transformed into a junkyard dog's.

Okay. Was there a family cookout I missed? Mom's birthday? No. That was in February. More of Maxie's wedding bullshit?

"What?" I challenge, head pounding from my self-medication.

"Way to go, man," Aiden says, eerily.

"Way to go *what?*"

"Pfft. Like you don't already know," this from Maxie. "Don't hear you asking where your sidekick is."

"Wh-where is he? Is he late?"

"He quit," Aiden's perturbed words hit me like a punch.

"Quit? Are you shitting me?"

"Does he look like he's shitting you, Graham Cracker?" Maxie's rhetorical is adorned with a sneer.

"Not now, Max," I snap. I need answers. Dami never said shit to me Friday. It was a quiet ride back to the warehouse after work, but he could have mentioned it. "What the hell happened?"

Aiden unfolds his arms and settles his hands on his hips. Judging by his bad cop stance, I'm not going to like the sound of this.

"He called me yesterday and said he didn't think he was the right man for the job, that we should fill the opening with somebody who has *more skills,* so they don't *slow you down.*"

A choking noise passes through my lips. No way. He had to have dimed me out for Friday's mind snap and my dickery all week. That's what young people do, blame everyone else.

"That's it? You didn't try to talk him out of it? I mean, he didn't explain what about the job was a problem?"

Aiden gives me a hard stare as if to say *I* was the problem. I knew it. Here it comes.

"I tried to talk him out of it. I asked him to give it more time. Told him we were happy to train him, and that he'd improve and feel more confident the longer he was here, but he seemed to have his mind made up. The only other thing he said was to tell you he was sorry."

"Sorry? What the hell for? For quitting?"

Aiden's brows furrow as he studies me. Why is my gut squirmy?

"He wouldn't say. Just kept telling me to apologize for letting you down."

He's sorry he let me down? Seriously?

Oh, that's cute. Playing the whole guilt angle. Not falling for it.

He can church it up however he wants, but the bottom line is he couldn't handle a little ass chewing so he gave up. It's just like the rest of his resume. He's a quitter. He could have at least had the decency to tell me, not run to my big brother. How do you work with a guy all week and then abandon him?

Maxie's and Aiden's stink eyes pin me. Yeah, I know what they're thinking. Graham the Crabass strikes again.

Throwing my hands up, I spin on my heel toward my work truck. "The kid wants to quit, that's his choice," I yell over my shoulder, leaving nothing for debate.

Because there is nothing for debate. He freaking quit on me. He drew a picture of me that looked like he could see into my soul and then fucking quit like I was one of his one-night stands.

CHAPTER 12

Graham

You know who's *not* a quitter? Me, because apparently an eleven-hour workday isn't long enough to stop thinking about how pissed off I am that Dami tucked tail and ran.

How can a guy ruin a work site in the course of a week? I like working alone, but all I thought about today was how quiet it was without Dami there. Maybe it's because that stupid cat showed up looking for him. Even it looked at me like I'm a bastard when I screamed at it that he wasn't there as I took sanctuary in the bed of my truck.

"Freaking up and leave without a damn word," I mutter at a traffic light, headed in the complete opposite direction from my house.

Dami's little *SMART* car wasn't parked at Tapas, so that can only mean two things. One—he's selling oranges out of a grocery cart in some alley, or two—he's sitting on his perky ass at home, thumbs-deep in dating apps. I officially hate oranges, and when I finally get to his apartment, I'm going to kick said perky ass.

Sighing at the gridlock ahead of me, my reality occurs to me. I'm tracking down a kid that drives a fucking *Matchbox* car, speaks in hashtags, and spreads mortar like whitewash.

Then what the hell are you doing, Graham, a voice inside my head asks. Ugh.

Maybe I refuse to feel responsible for the demise of his ridiculous three-step plan. Maybe I'd at least have liked a chance to apologize. Maybe I let my personal conflicts get in the way of being patient with him and showing him how to do the job. Maybe I'd have liked to see him use the same spine he had when he told me I didn't deserve to work with him if I couldn't accept his sexuality. Where is *that* kid? And seriously, why are his parents letting him wash dishes or work for me when he can draw like freaking DaVinci?

My phone pings. If it's more cat GIFs from Maxie, I'm throwing my phone out the window.

THOR: How's your apprentice treating you?

Wonderful. Like I need another reminder.

ME: He up and quit on me.

THOR: Nice! Guess you dodged that bullet.

Swallowing against the tightness in my throat, I can't share his enthusiasm. *I* was the bullet.

Despite his lack of knowledge, Dami was a hard worker. The only thing he complained about was being sweaty, and I even freaked out on him about that because I couldn't stand what the sight of his glistening, naked torso did to me.

Looking at Thor's contact picture on my phone, I'm reminded of how many times I silently admired his larger-than-life physique. Is that why I was drawn to befriend him in the Navy? He made it no secret that he was bisexual, no matter how much crap the other guys gave him. Granted, he was the biggest motherfucker in our unit, and nobody dared mess with him.

As the light turns green, I tremble. Am I barreling toward Damiano Andropolis' apartment because he quit or because I want him more than I've known it was possible to want another human being?

Ten aggravating minutes later, I push through the back door of Johnny's studio that leads to the apartment stairs. The sound of a familiar laugh coming from inside the studio shoots a tingle down my spine, stopping me in my tracks.

"Yeah. Just like that. Hold it. Perfect!" Johnny's voice cheers from inside.

Making my way past his office, I head to the studio. The main lights up front are off, the blinds on the windows, closed. Only the glow of backdrop lights is casting a beam across the floor in front of me. The click of a camera mingles with the sound of a giggle.

My nuts clench. I know that giggle. Why the fuck is Dami giggling when I've been pulling my hair out all day?

"Come on, Dami. Hold still. You're the one who begged me to do this," Johnny says.

Another giggle. "I'm trying, but it tickles."

What the ever-loving fuck are two grown-ass cousins talking about tickling for? And why do I want to rip Johnny's arms off and shove his glasses down his throat? Passing the office wall, the studio comes fully into view.

What are…

Holy shiiit.

My eyes are flooded by the sight of six feet of glowing skin, sprawled out on a furry blanket that's draped over a chaise lounge. Correction—six feet of glowing skin, minus the perky ass covered by one black man-bikini.

Johnny's camera flashes a few more times, each click sending a pulse of heated blood to my cock as I stare at that luminous smile, Dami's chin nestled on the crook of his arm like some lover just left him sated.

"Graham?" he calls, meeting my gaze. "What are you doing here?"

I might have walked in here because he quit, but I'm not leaving until he comes back because I'm a hundred percent certain I just realized my type.

CHAPTER 13

Wow. He's the last person I expected to see.

Crap. Did he need his gloves back? Was there some paperwork I needed to sign?

"Graham!" Johnny startles. "I didn't hear you come in. To what do we owe the pleasure?"

Are…Graham's nostrils flaring?

Eyes locked on me, his voice comes out eerily low and gravelly. "What the hell are you doing?"

Before I can come up with a reply, Johnny babbles nervously, "Um, we're starting a portfolio for Dami. I'm going to put some feelers out for him."

Graham doesn't even glance at Johnny. His steely gaze bores into me with a clear message—he has a bone to pick. Great. Just when I was starting to feel optimistic again.

Drawing my legs up, I rise to my feet. Graham tracks my every move, making my skin prickle. It's still totally unfair that man is straight, even if he hates me.

"In his underwear?" Graham accuses, sparing a heated glance at Johnny.

"Um, all models do it. Not that I was comfortable with the idea," Johnny sputters. "Eh heh. This just…this just looks worse than it is. I mean, we're related, but I don't drive that bridge. I see stuff like this all the time. You probably don't get much exposure to male models in Olympus, so I can see how—"

"I need to speak with Dami," Graham interjects.

"Oh, um. Sure. I mean, we're done, so—"

"*Alone*," Graham adds, making me swallow a lump in my throat.

"Uh, right." Johnny glances from Graham to me and mouths, are you alright? I give him a clipped nod. The only thing Graham will hurt is my feelings, but it's safe to say he accomplished that already on Friday.

"Okay, well, um, then I'm…I'm going to go. Mm-kay? I told Aiden this'd only take about an hour anyway, so…um. Yeah. Are you two sure you're okay here? Feels a little tense in here."

"Fine," Graham grits, clenching and unclenching his fists.

Gosh. Maybe he's looking to hurt more than my pride.

"Right." Johnny laughs nervously. "Big boys we all are. Silly question."

Johnny makes haste leaving the room. A few awkward seconds later, I hear the back door close. As soon as it slams shut, Graham stalks forward.

"What the hell are you doing?"

Man, he looks practically deranged. Shifting, the fur blanket draped over the back of the chaise lounge tickles the bare skin on the back of my thighs just below my speedo. "Modeling, clearly."

"You quit on me out of the blue to become a model?"

"I was no good at laying bricks. You said so yourself."

"So, you're just giving up again like all those other jobs you had? How about sticking it out until you get better at it? Did you ever think of that?"

"You said they'd solve global warming before I ever figured out how to mix mortar."

"So, you're going to take your clothes off for money now?"

"What's wrong with that? I'm not good at anything else, but I'm young. I've got a decent body. I might as well use it."

Is he…grinding his teeth together? What is his deal? Why is he even here?

"You're not quitting. Get your clothes on." Grabbing my jeans I discarded earlier, he tosses them at me.

Shoot. Did his brother not give him the message?

"I called Aiden. I already quit, and you can't tell me if I can quit or not. You'll be better off anyway without me there screwing stuff up and annoying you."

Sighing, he waves a hand in the air and starts pacing back and forth. "You didn't screw up. You're still learning. There's a difference. Everyone's allowed to make mistakes. I'm not going to be the reason you sell half naked pictures of yourself."

I thought I couldn't feel any worse, but the idea of Graham pitying me makes my stomach churn. I don't want to be his charity case. Setting my jeans down on the chaise, I straighten my posture.

"Is that what this is? I'm not coming back because you feel guilty. Me quitting had nothing to do with you. You didn't say anything that wasn't true. I get it. I'm just not good at stuff, but I've got no problem taking my clothes off. I'm half Greek, half Italian, so it's like in my genes to be half-naked. Johnny's a great photographer. He was a big deal before he moved back home, so if I'm going to do modeling, he's definitely someone I can trust to do things right. His pictures are tasteful."

"You want to be on a billboard in your underwear for everyone to see you? How is that tasteful?" His voices pitches even though my words were meant to soothe. Snatching up my t-shirt, he shoves it at my chest. "Cover up, for God's sake. Will you?"

I can handle being ashamed of myself from time to time, but not by someone else for things that aren't shameful. This is getting out of hand, even for Graham.

"No!" I snap, tossing my shirt to the floor. "You don't get to tell me what to do, and so what if I end up on a billboard. I'd be lucky to. You're not my parents to judge me. What do you care?"

"Would you just get some damn clothes on?" He snags up my jeans again and presses them to my chest. "I didn't come here to argue with you!"

"Well, it seems like it! Quit shoving stuff at me! What is your problem?"

"*You're* my problem! You're so freaking difficult and don't listen to a damn thing!"

"Oh, my gosh!" I wrench the jeans out of his grip, letting them fall to the floor. "This is so stupid. I'm not your problem anymore. That's what I'm trying to tell you. I left so you don't have to be pissed off all the time."

Throwing his arms out wide, he spares me a crazed look. "Well, it didn't work! I'm still pissed off! Now would you put some fucking pants on?"

"Geez! I'm just going upstairs. It's not like I'm going to walk around town in my underwear."

Swooping down, he scoops up my jeans again and thrusts them at my chest. "Just put them on, and then we can talk about work."

It hits me that he's barely looked directly at me since he walked into the studio. This isn't a shirt violation of an *Osha* rule.

"*What* is your problem with my pants? Maybe I don't want to work with someone who freaks out when he sees a gay guy in his underwear!"

That got his attention.

"I'm *not* freaking out!"

"Yes, you are. You can't even look at me like I'm going to rub my gayness all over you!"

"Oh, my God. Would you knock it off?" He grips both sides of his head and pinches his eyes closed. Further proof, I'm right. That is such a disappointment.

"No! I told you before I started, I don't want to work with someone like that. I'm fine with who I am. And I'm fine being the guy who doesn't know how to do things. I can do some modeling until I figure something else out. I can't screw that up. I mean, how hard is it to take your clothes off. Right?"

"Dami…" he pants.

"No. I'm serious. There's a lot of gays in the modeling world. It'll be good for me. I don't know what your issue is with gay people, but honestly, thank you for trying to teach me a new profession. I didn't mean to waste your time by sucking at it. I really wanted to be so good for you. I wanted to work so hard you never thought about hiring anyone else ever again. I'm sorry all I ever do is screw things up. I'm just…I'm hopeless."

Rough hands grip the sides of my face. Oh, crap! He's coming at me!

I don't have time to *Google* search how to fight an angry brick layer while wearing only underwear. My hands go instinctively to his shoulders to stop him. He steps into my space, backing me up against the chaise and…

Oh, my gosh!

The feather duster is on my mouth!

His lips slam hard against mine, devouring in sloppy, urgent brushes, raking that sandy goatee across the skin around my mouth.

Is my speedo cutting off circulation to my brain? Is this really happening?

Tearing my head back an inch, I gasp for air. "Wh-why…are you kissing me?"

Graham's stormy sapphires blink at me as though he's coming back from an out-of-body experience. His Adam's Apple bobs, his breath heavy against my bruised lips.

"I…you…you wouldn't shut up."

"If I talk some more, will you do it again?"

Because let's face it, I am not going to die saying I was kissed by Graham Brandt and didn't even participate. That's like a month-long spank bank deposit.

His face crumples in confusion like he's trying to decide if I'm making fun of him. One thing I am good at is getting it on, and there's finally a hot guy in front of me initiating. I lift my hand to the back of his neck and tug.

He flinches when my lips dust over his, so I send out a welcoming committee, flicking the tip of my tongue across the seam of his mouth. He groans and sucks my lower lip in between his.

Mm. Yes!

He tastes like anger and that sweet tea he drinks at work. Like in that movie with the girl with the ruby slippers, my brain chants, I don't care if he's straight, I don't care if he's straight, because his straight tongue sweeping over and around mine feels like a whole lot of perfect.

He smells like the woods, dipped in honey. His hot breath and *grunty* noises are the only meal I want to eat for the rest of the year.

Moaning, I wrap a leg around his thigh, threading my fingers through his wild hair. My libido didn't plan very well because I topple over backward, losing my grip on my fantasy-come-to-life.

"Fuck," Graham utters, hands frozen in mid-air where they were cupping my face just a second ago.

Scrambling to my feet, I smooth my hands down his arms. No harm, no foul, but he goes rigid. Panting, he blinks down at my now two-sizes-too-small speedo and then at a very delicious bulge in his jeans.

"Fuck," he curses again.

Two *fucks* in a row can't be good, not even from Graham. I watch helplessly, unsure of what to do.

He digs his fingers into his hair and starts to back away, stammering, "I…sorry. I…I'm sorry. I don't…uh."

He doesn't even finish a sentence, just turns away like he's back to being afraid to look at me. Crap. Is this what a gay freak out looks like?

"Graham, it's okay."

Still gripping his head, he starts toward the door, staggering like he's drunk.

"Where are you going?"

He stops and turns his head a fraction, but not enough to see me. "I…I've got to go. I…I'll see you tomorrow."

He'll *see me tomorrow?*

Where? Clothed? Unclothed? Dami needs details!

Adjusting my speedo, I know I should probably stop to consider that I just kissed my straight, ex-boss, but I gather up my clothes. I don't know if I'll see him tomorrow, but I sure as heck will see him when I get out my lube and close my eyes upstairs in about five minutes.

CHAPTER 14

Graham

Somehow, I've made it to Olympus Avenue even though I'm shaking like a cow in a slaughterhouse. I kissed Dami. I *kissed* him.

Me.

I did it first.

Kisses aren't supposed to feel like that. Does he lace his lips with drugs?

Smashing my thumb on the ignore call button again, I watch as Aiden's name goes dark on my phone screen. I can't even speak right now.

Am I having a heart attack?

Did my kiss do to him what his did to me?

God, his dick was hard. It was hard *for me*. Those little black underwear should be illegal. I actually wanted to tug them off. But then what? What the fuck happens then?

Damn it, Aiden!

Swiping my screen, I hit the speaker function to stop my phone from blowing up.

"What?" I bark, unable to say anything more than one syllable. Am I even headed in the right direction?

"Graham, where are you?"

"On my way home."

"Johnny said you showed up at the studio to talk to Dami. Everything alright?"

No! Nothing is alright. I just molested him in his teeny-weeny bikini.

"Yeah. Fine. Everything…fine."

Am I having a stroke now on top of the heart attack? I've lost the ability to use verbs.

"I think you're breaking up. Did you get him to come back to work?"

"Yeah. Fine. Tomorrow." *Damn it, Graham. Use a verb!* "He'll be there."

"Oh, good. That's great. I'm glad to hear it."

"Yeah. Great. Okay. Bye!"

I finally take a breath when I hang up on him. *Great? Fine?* What the fuck am I saying?

I don't remember a damn thing that was said in the last half hour except for all the awful stuff Dami was blathering about himself. All I recall is that I couldn't take one more second of hearing him disparage himself because of me being an asshole, so…I kissed him.

Naturally.

Fuck me.

Pulling over into a parking lot, I scowl at the sign on the building— *Olympus Senior Center*. The universe has a sick way of pointing out that I'm losing my faculties and just kissed a baby. With shaky fingers, I bring up Dami's contact info and punch out a text message.

ME: Are you coming to work tomorrow?

And because I'm a cowardly little bitch, I add, *Aiden wants to know*.

I wait a solid five minutes before I give up and head down the road. I can only imagine the inquisition at the warehouse in the morning if a certain clown car doesn't show up. It'll be roast Graham part-two. A chime from my phone has me swerving.

DAMI: Are you going to kiss me again?

What does that even mean? Is he trying to make this more difficult for me? Does he want me to kiss him again? The thought brings on a new round of palpitations.

ME: No.

A piece of me dies with the finality of my response, producing an ache in my chest. I want to kiss him again even if it would kill me.

It takes twenty minutes to get to my place from the edge of downtown. Undoubtedly, however, this was the longest twenty minutes of my life.

Did he fall asleep before he could answer? Is he shaking his ass to Vincent Stoller songs and didn't hear my message?

I can't deal with this many what-ifs. What if he doesn't answer? What if he shows up tomorrow? What if my family finds out I attacked the help with my face?

Jamming my truck into park in my driveway, I palm my phone and head for the house. I need to clean my fish tank and do laundry. I don't have time to—

The alert sound from my phone makes my arm muscle react like it was electrocuted. I juggle the device, nearly dropping it.

DAMI: I guess.

"*I guess?* What the hell is that supposed to mean?"

Is he getting cocky on me? Pouting after what a jerk I was? Or is he bummed I said *no?*

"*I guess?*"

Five hours later, *I guess* I'm not getting any damn sleep tonight.

CHAPTER 15

Should I say something? He looks kind of rough today. The shards of morning light peeking through the trees as we drive to the work site create a kaleidoscope effect over Graham's haggard, chiseled face. Even disgruntled and exhausted though, he's still the most handsome man I've ever seen.

Crap. I'm staring again.

Not going to piss him off today.

Redirecting my gaze to my window, I watch the woods, the leaves just starting to show their fall colors. I actually had to grab a sweatshirt this morning with the late summer heat finally becoming just a memory.

Graham clears his throat, but I force myself not to look. What that man does for a flannel shirt is criminal. I would be the first in line with handcuffs. Shoot. Wrong image to plant in my imagination. Shuddering, I finger my lips, savoring the memory of his beard brushing against my face.

Ugh. I *will* get off again with another human being sometime this century.

"Uh, morning," he rumbles.

We didn't trade a single word back at the warehouse. Granted, the welcome back I received from his brothers and sister kept me occupied, but I figured he'd opted for a vow of silence.

"Morning," I return.

"Thanks for…showing up."

"Thanks for taking me back. I wasn't sure if you really meant it yesterday…especially after…um, well, you know. I…I'm kind of confused actually," I stammer on a nervous laugh. "But what else is new. Right?"

He grimaces at my joke. Note to self—stop trying to be funny.

Running his hand down those lips that I now want to think of as my property, his eyes scan the October horizon as we pull into the work site. He pops the truck into park and rests his hands on the steering wheel, staring out the window.

"I, uh, want to apologize for my behavior last week. I've been… going through some personal issues, not that that's any excuse, but that didn't exactly help my state of mind."

"It's alright," I assure him.

"No. It's not." He shakes his head and runs a hand through his mane. "I wasn't very patient with you. You came here knowing nothing, relying on me to teach you, and I only did the bare minimum. I didn't give you a fair chance. It takes a while to learn all this shit, so my impatience was completely unrealistic. I'll, uh, I'll be happy to show you everything there is to know about brick masonry, if you really want to learn it."

His words are like sunshine on my soul or rather the gesture alone. "Yeah. I'd love that."

Eyes darting to me, the corner of his mouth jerks up for a second. Hitching his thumb over his shoulder, he says, "Good. Um, should we… get to it?"

"Yeah. Sure."

I hop out of the truck, taking that as my cue he's not ready to discuss last night. It's okay. I can be patient. I've got the patience of a saint.

He takes me back to the wall I fudged on Friday and goes through Mortar 101 with me from the beginning. Unlike last week, there's no bite to his tone. His voice is soft and patient, and to my surprise he rewards any small achievement with praise.

Yeah. Good job. Just like that. That's perfect.

Each utterance makes my heart do a flip like I'm a puppy and Graham is petting me. Man, I could get used to this Graham.

Speaking of things that I could get used to… It's barely been an hour since we got here. Apparently, I'm not a saint. Patience is for people who knit or those monks that vow to never speak.

"So, not to ruin my first day back on the job, but, um, can you tell me why you kissed me yesterday?"

For a second, I think he's going to lock up and storm off, judging by the way he flinches and stands up from his crouched position next to me. As he fingers his goatee, I wait patiently, idly jabbing at the mortar pile with my trowel.

"You…wouldn't stop talking. You were driving me crazy."

"You kiss everyone who won't stop talking?"

His scoff sounds more amused than those I've heard before as he shoves his hands in his pockets and cranes his neck back to look up at the sky. "I…didn't like all the stupid shit you were saying about your-self. You're not hopeless or annoying or…whatever else you said."

"But you said I should have never applied for this job."

Shaking his head, he grips the back of his neck and stares at the place between his feet and mine. "I was wrong and pissed off. I didn't mean it. You're a hard worker, and you've actually caught on pretty quickly."

"Really?"

"Yeah."

"Oh."

As his compliments burst inside me like little fireworks, the realization that I got a pity kiss fizzles them. He knows I'm gay. Maybe he's not confused about his sexuality like I assumed yesterday. Johnny said he was married to his ex for a long time. Maybe he thought the way to reassure a gay guy was by kissing him.

Shifting gears, I segue as a last-ditch effort for answers. "I was just surprised about the kiss. I thought you were straight."

"I…thought so too."

Hello! Was *not* expecting that.

The trowel falls from my hand and clatters onto the mortar board. Peering up at him, I make to ask a meaningful follow-up, but all I get out is, "Um…"

"I…well, I've always been…straight. I don't go around kissing guys."

"You've never kissed a guy before?"

"No."

I know this is a window to ask other questions, but I'm stuck on the fact that I was the first man Graham ever kissed. Biting the inside of my cheek, so I don't scare him off with the smile that's threatening to over-take my face, I rise to my feet.

"So…are you thinking about dating men now?"

"No," he snorts. "I don't know. I mean, no. How would I…I don't even know how to…how…" Rubbing his forehead he lets out a huge breath. "Forget it."

"No. You can tell me."

"I…wouldn't even know what to do and at my age, that's…it's too embarrassing. It's not worth the trouble."

Worth the trouble? Is he serious?

"So, just because you're old you aren't allowed to have what you want?" I counter, which finally earns me some eye contact, except it's in the form of a glare. "*I* didn't say you were old. *You* did."

Kicking at a fossilized glob of mortar, his lips move, but only take and release audible little puffs of air for a beat. "I'm too old to try to figure out how to…how to be with a man. Okay? So, I'll just be a fucking hermit like Maxie says."

Watching the way his broad shoulders hunch underneath his black and gray flannel shirt, it occurs to me the one thing he didn't say. He said nothing about being bisexual.

Wow. He's doing a full switch. No wonder he's so tensed up. I try to picture him in thirty years and imagine a still handsome version of him as an old man. To think of him spending thirty years alone seems like a waste of an attractive man.

"That's so sad."

Graham scoffs. "Orphans and starving children are sad. Abused puppies are sad. The state of my dick isn't sad."

"No." I laugh, happy to hear his sarcasm again. "I just mean, you could live to be like ninety. That's like forty more years of no sex. What if you get lonely?"

"Sixty years," he mutters, "and…I won't."

"What if you get horny?"

"I won't."

Well, now he's lying. There is no way I could go sixty days without being horny. His gaze connects with mine. I think my lower lip will permanently be stuck in a depressed pout over his situation. He grimaces at it and gestures to the mortar board.

"Why don't you, uh, worry about the mortar instead of my dick?"

"How can I not worry about your dick?" I exclaim.

He snorts again, and this time there's laugh lines by his eyes, but I didn't even mean for that to be amusing. "Because you don't even know my dick. Ugh," he grumbles, crouching down to revive our mud with his trowel. "Listen to me. You've got me talking like you do now."

"Like *I* do? What's that supposed to mean?"

"Like all…sexual innuendo and shit."

"I do not." I snicker.

"Whatever. Come on. Stir this, or it's going to set. You need to keep mixing it so there's air in it."

As I watch him explain about how the sand in the mortar reacts, I realize it's just one of many things he's taught me. He might not be the most eloquent person, but neither am I. And he might not know anything about gay sex, but he's in his element out here.

I've heard Aiden talking to Johnny several times about how they give Graham all the jobs that call for complicated or intricate brick designs because he's a natural, an artisan at his craft. I really am learning from the best.

I know they're paying me, and I'll be making a crap-ton of money on overtime every week with the eleven-hour days they work during the good weather season, but it doesn't seem fair. I wish I could give back more than just shadowing Graham on the job site. All I can do for now is reassure him.

"You know, you shouldn't let it overwhelm you. Two men being together isn't any more difficult than a man and a woman being together. It's not complicated."

His cheeks turn red as he scrapes up the excess mud oozing out of the seam when I place my next brick. "Maybe not for you."

I didn't think of it that way. I've known I was gay my entire life, but Graham? Poor Graham still has to go through all those awkward and yet wonderful discoveries that took me all of high school and college to acquire. I mean, I'm practically an expert at gay intimacy compared to—

Oh, my gosh! I'm an expert!

"Put it this way," he says, when he catches me gaping. "If I didn't learn how to ride a bike by now, I'm sure as shit a lost cause."

"You're right."

Rolling his eyes, he scoffs. "Thanks for sparing my feelings."

Aw, Sensitive Graham! How cute is that?

Smirking, I can't hold back my chuckle. "No. I don't mean about the *lost cause* part. I meant about it not being complicated for me. I've got skills!"

He shoots me a look like I'm wearing that speedo on my head. "While your sexual self-confidence is awe-inspiring, you're bragging to the wrong person."

"No! I'm not." I laugh, grinning from ear to ear. "That's just it. Don't you see? You're absolutely the *right* person."

"You lost me."

"*I mean*, I'm stuck back in Olympus trying to get work experience and save money to move away while the gay community here is *population two*, to which we're both related. That equals zero sexy times for this guy," I expound, pointing to my chest with my thumbs.

Squinting, his face scrunches up. "What the fuck kind of math are they teaching these days?"

"The best kind! Meanwhile, you're…*you* with your…*dilemma* and no one to help you out with it, so…"

"So…"

"Sooo…" Rising, I extend my arms out wide. "*I'm* your guy! It's perfect!"

Graham blinks at me, looking wary. His throat undulates as all the muscles in his face go slack. I'm too excited to hold back. This is probably the best idea I've ever had.

"I could show you things just like you've been showing me!"

"*Show me…things?* What kind of *things?*"

"Like…practice. Whatever you want. Kissing, touching, asking me questions, exploring to see what you're comfortable with so you don't feel like you have to live the rest of your life in the hermit closet."

"What?" He snorts. "Like…gay sex education?"

Man, if they'd only taught that in school. Laughing, I agree. "Yeah. I guess."

Grabbing more bricks, his brows pinch together. "Are you…hitting on me or making fun of me?"

"Neither. I swear! Well, I mean, I *can* hit on you, if you want."

"No! No." He holds one of the bricks up. "That's fine. Just…why would you offer to do that?"

"I know what it's like to not be able to be who you want."

The way he looks at me, I swear some sad understanding passes between us. I can't imagine what he's gone through bearing the weight of his untapped feelings all on his own.

The mood suddenly feels a bit too heavy, so I make an effort to lighten it by adding, "And you're hot, and messing around feels good, so it's not exactly like it'd be a hardship. We both get what we need and keep it between us."

Dang. Did I just make him blush? The only time I was ever with a virgin was in high school, but I didn't take much notice in the guy's reactions because I was a virgin too and worried about my own behavior. Virgins are officially hot.

Closing the distance between us, I lower my voice. Clearly, the man is in a fragile state. "I mean it, Graham. Use me. Do whatever you want."

His face blooms even brighter. "Do you always talk like that?"

"Like what?" I honestly can't remember the question once I get a hit of his sweet woody scent.

I'm mesmerized by the allure of discovering if his flannel feels as soft as it looks and if his chest is as solid underneath as I imagine. Sliding my hands up over his chest pockets, I should probably focus on his face.

His eyes are hooded, staring at my mouth. I can feel his breath panting between his parted lips. He's not pulling away, not flinching this time. He's still standing here. Maybe he does want to be my student as much as I want him to be.

I lean in a little closer to let him know I'm open for whatever, murmuring encouragingly, "You're a good kisser by the way."

His disbelieving breath ghosts my upper lip, and then I feel fingers on my hip, the barest of contact. Yes! Class is in session!

Brushing my lips against his, I close my eyes. It seems appropriate for a guy like Graham. What am I saying? I've never met a guy like Graham. I've never put much emphasis on or stock in kissing. Kissing wasn't a big part of fooling around in college. Flirty pecks between friends, sure. Drunken sloppy ones at parties, of course, but chaste, cautious kisses? I'm not about to admit this part of my lesson plan is new to me. It certainly doesn't make it less enjoyable, especially when his lips begin to part and brush, part and brush, hesitantly in return.

I can feel him trembling underneath my touch, even beneath the layers of his shirts. Soothing, I run my palms down his arms, mapping the curve of every muscle there that I've only seen but never touched.

Definitely the best idea I've ever had. I'm a freaking hero, and I'm loving my reward.

Cresting his lips, his taste draws me deeper. Uhn. How can someone who looks so prickly be the flavor of sweet desires?

Maybe it's the strangled little whimpers he's making as his other hand clutches and unclutches my other hip or how his tongue seems caught in a dance of wanting to dive deeper and uncertainty. Whatever it is, I have the best boss on the planet.

Wait. My *boss*. He's my boss again.

Crap.

"No," I practically groan, pulling back. "Stop."

His feather duster plants another kiss on the corner of my mouth before his head jolts back. "S-sorry. I thought…"

"No! No. It's cool. That was *fire*," I laugh breathlessly. "Just…maybe not here? You know? Like I should probably *work* at *work*. I don't want to be *that guy*—the one that messes around to move up."

Chuffing, he runs his hand over his mouth like he's hiding what we just did. "Don't worry. There's no room for promotion here. I've been this unimportant for ten years, but…um, yeah. You're right."

"Cool. So…after work?"

He blinks, his eyes going wide as he returns his gaze to mine. "You… really want to…do this?"

"Yeah. I was serious. I'm you're man, Graham. I'll show you the way."

Those blushes will never get old. Sigh. Or maybe they will. I mean, I'm probably such a good teacher that he'll have forgotten how to blush by the end of the week.

"I…I'll probably be bad at…everything."

"Practice makes perfect." I shrug, wriggling my brows and swat his arm. "Come on. You can trust me. What are the odds you'll find some other guy around here you can trust to show you the ropes without half of Olympus finding out?"

Peering off, chewing his lip, I can tell he's thinking about it.

"Nothing crazy. I swear," I reassure. "I'm not a kinky freak. We'll only do whatever you want."

Rubbing his eyes, he lets out a lungful of air. "This is crazy."

"Uh, if by crazy you mean brilliant, okay."

Snickering, he shakes his head. "Can we at least…"

"What?"

"Could we…go to my place, so we don't run into Johnny or Aiden?"

"Sure." The twinge I get is silly. I'm probably the first person he came out to. He's like day-one gay here, so my reflex shouldn't be to cringe at his priority to hide this deal from anyone. I mean, I basically suggested I wouldn't tell anyone.

Smiling, I cup his cheeks, delighting in the surprise on his face when I plant a quick kiss on those lips that are going to save me from my dry spell. "Alright, now show me how to lay this corner joint," I exclaim enthusiastically, motioning to the bricks. "Most motivated employee ever!"

CHAPTER 16

Graham

Did I really agree to sex education from Damiano Andropolis? What does that entail?

Should I shave? Do I need to hydrate and stretch? Am I ready for this?

I've only acknowledged that I'm gay like seventy-two hours ago. What the hell am I doing? He really thinks my kisses are *fire?*

Jesus, listen to me. Now he's got me using his punk ass adjectives.

Oh, God. The *Matchbox* car just pulled into the driveway. He's here.

"I can't do this. I can't do this."

Shit. What do I do?

Whirling around in my living room, I don't even know what to assess for situational awareness. Dinner is on the stove. I showered. My clothes are clean. I brushed my teeth. Is that enough?

Do I look alright? Should I have bought him flowers? A fucking candy bar? Is he going to want to have sex tonight? The knock on the door sends me jumping an inch off the floor.

Okay. First thing's first. Don't have a heart attack.

My cheeks puff on a gust of breath, and I open the door. Dami's face beams back at me. His fluffy hair is damp but still looks perfect and swept back the way it always does. He's in a black leather jacket, jeans, and a gray t-shirt. At least I don't have to worry I underdressed in my jeans…and matching gray t-shirt. Fuck, we look stupid. This is so awkward already.

"Hey!" he calls. "It's beautiful out here."

"Uh, thanks." Do I compliment him? Is this like a date? "Um, you look…clean."

Chuckling, he eyes me up and down shamelessly, rocking back on his heels with his hands tucked into his back pockets. Apparently, he's not nervous.

What's with that bookbag? Does he take the thing everywhere with him? Is my picture still in there?

"So do you," he says then plants a kiss on my cheek and steps inside.

Wow. Why is that more embarrassing than recovering from a kiss on the mouth. It was sweet…just like him.

When I close the door, I find his eyes lit up looking at my fish tank. "Wow! This is freaking awesome," he gasps.

Pride swells in my chest for his appreciation of my saltwater aquarium. It took my years to perfect everything, keeping track of pH levels in my *Fish Files* notebook.

Shit. My *Fish Files* are on full display on the side table, complete with a fish drawing on the cover that I did, which compares with the artistic skills of my five-year-old nephews. Sidestepping Dami as he gapes at the aquarium, I swipe up the notebook. Stuffing it inside the table drawer, I clear my throat.

"Um, did you eat yet?"

He looks through the open floor plan to the kitchen and shrugs. "I can always eat. Can I help?"

Not lazy, I muse. Not lazy at all. What else did I misjudge about him while I had my head up my ass?

After he loses his jacket and backpack, I check on the chicken cordon bleu I have cooking in the oven. Pulling the bacon-wrapped mozzarella balls that I prepped earlier out of the fridge, I set the tray on the counter and tell him he can fry them up if he wants, while I gather ingredients for salads.

Alright. This isn't so bad.

As long as we're cooking or eating, we're not *sex-edding*. However, with Dami's presence in my house, my cock says it wants the accelerated course. Luckily, my virgin brain is still somehow manning the wheel of control.

When I return to the counter with the lettuce and vegetables, Dami's chewing his lip, staring at the frying pan like it's the Boogie Man. The burner's not on, and he hasn't touched a thing I left for him to cook.

His wary expression turns to me. "So…I'm not very good at frying things."

"Oh. Well, for those you can just dump enough oil in to cover the bottom of the frying pan and set the burner to low," I tell him, gesturing with my chin to the jug of cooking oil I left out.

Rubbing his wrist, he grimaces at the bottle. "Um, ye-ah, about that. Okay, so when I say I'm not very good at frying things, I mean I'm like really, really not good at it."

"It's alright. I promise I'll eat them." I laugh.

Did he just…whimper? Wow. I think he's scared.

"You must have learned something in culinary school," I wonder aloud.

"That incident I told you about…with the fire…it may have involved a fryer…and a trip to the emergency room." Releasing his wrist he rotates his arm, holding it out to me. "I can't grow hair right here any-more."

Not that Dami has much arm hair, but there's a noticeable bare patch on half of his left forearm where the skin is a shade darker. Damn. That had to have hurt.

"I hate grease," he whispers almost like he's talking without realizing it.

Seeing him without confidence on top of being terrified sends a wave of protectiveness through me, which is silly. I mean, it's just a frying pan, but then again, I'm afraid of cats—totally a more rational fear—but I'm not going to judge him. Maybe my sympathy stems from the whole age gap thing, like I have to look out for him because he's younger and less worldly.

"Alright. It's really not that bad. Here. I can show you a trick. Take a little bit of water and dump it in with the oil. That'll keep it from pop-ping and splattering you."

"Even with the bacon?"

"Yeah, even with the bacon, and you can put that lid over it in case you're still worried."

"Okay. Thanks." The corner of his mouth ticks up, erasing the trau-ma from his face. Why does it make me feel like a king that I assuaged his fear?

"I don't get why you quit culinary school. So, there was a fryer inci-dent. Wasn't it their job to teach you?"

"It was pretty fast-paced. All the other students were like super chefs already, I swear. They'd all been cooking at one place or another before they started. I was the slow kid who was always lagging behind."

"You didn't learn anything from your parents?"

He shrugs, peeking hesitantly under the frying pan lid. "I sliced my finger a few times and burned some things. After a while it just seemed easier for my parents to do the cooking. I mean, they already knew how, so I was just in the way and slowing them down."

I suddenly regret asking because it's becoming apparent that no one's taken the time to show him anything. Just like I didn't.

Dami discusses his three-month stint at culinary school while we work, which should be mundane banter to pass the time, but it exposes deeper valleys of his life. Without him saying so point blank, I glean that he doesn't cook anything at Tapas because he's never been given the op-portunity. His parents don't sound like they have much faith in him, but he's got this ho-hum attitude like they know best, or maybe he doesn't even realize it's okay to stick up for himself sometimes.

We eat over surprisingly companionable conversation. He asks me about the Navy. I tell him a few stories about missions I was on and about Thor, which he finds to be a hilarious name. He tells me about his recent family trip to Greece. Unlike Johnny's parents, his alternate their summer vacations every year between Greece and Italy. His mother's Italian and his father's Greek. Something I realize I knew already, but never paid much attention to.

The interesting part? He speaks both Greek and Italian. The guy's freaking multi-lingual and thinks he doesn't have any skills. I feel like I barely know English most days aside from my sailor vocabulary.

I've lingered over my empty plate as long as I can. Now that dinner is over, my anxiety has come back a knocking. I should just tell him to forget it. I know he meant well, but I mean, who agrees to love lessons? I really have lost my mind.

Getting up, I gather my plate and silverware. I hear the faucet running and find Dami adding dish soap to the sink.

"What are you doing?"

"Washing the dishes."

"Why?"

"Well, that's what I do," he says, chuckling over his shoulder. "You invited me over and made dinner. I don't mind."

There's something innately wrong about how natural the gesture seems to be for him. I don't think I've ever met anyone as effortlessly good as Dami. I'm both touched and angry on his behalf at the same time. How many people haven't taken him seriously because of it?

"Not here," I caution, shutting off the faucet. "I'll get them later."

"Oh, okay." He dries his hands, and I realize I've just shortened the fuse on the inevitable conversation as he stuffs his hands in his pockets and smiles at me. "So, how do you want to do this?"

Fuck. Here we go.

"Dami, maybe this was a bad idea."

"You changed your mind? Did you have a gay freak out?"

"What? No! I…still gay," I babble, raising my hand like I'm taking an oath. I still can't believe I'm voicing that aloud. It feels strange, but also…right?

"Oh. Well, is it me?" He grimaces. "You're just not attracted to me?"

"No. No, I didn't say that."

"Is it my face?" He points to said face. "Or maybe my body? Do you prefer bigger guys or twinks?"

"What?"

"Because I get it. If you don't feel it for a person, you just don't feel it."

For crying out loud. This is why I can't do this. I don't even know what to say when he speaks so openly like that. Why does he make it look so easy?

"I…I feel it. Okay? You're…attractive."

"Yeah?" He grins.

Great. Did I just flirt with a man for the first time? *Not* helping my nerves.

Boring the heels of my palms into my eyes, I grunt like I'm constipated. "Yeah. Whatever. I just…I *told* you—I don't know how to do this. I've been with one person my entire life. I haven't flirted in fifteen years."

My face heats behind my hands, hearing his amused sounds. Sighing, I lean my ass against the fridge door. I created this mess.

"*That's* the problem?" he asks. "Well, we don't need to flirt. We made a deal, so we're good."

Fingers wrap over mine and tug my hands away from my face. The laughter is gone from his eyes, replaced by tenderness. "Why don't we come up with a safe word," he suggests. "If you don't like something, just say your word, and we'll stop and try something else or quit entirely."

"A *safe word?* Like kinky people do?"

"No." He lets out on a snort. "Like *respectful* people do. Geesh. You're uptight. I bet you don't role play either."

Role play? Holy crap. What have I gotten myself into?

"Fuck," I mutter. "What am I doing?" I start to shift away in case he gets any ideas about whipping me or…

"Graham, wait! Come on. I was teasing," he laughs, holding out a hand for me to stop.

His foot snags on one of the chair legs as he cracks up at my expense. I'm glad one of us is enjoying my humiliation.

Collecting himself he sighs and steps in front of me. "Okay, our safe word is *chair*."

"*Chair?*"

"Yeah." He chuckles, motioning to the one he just ran into. "It was your comfort item of choice with that cat the other day."

"You're hysterical."

Smiling, he ignores my embarrassment and runs his fingers up and into the back of my hair. Every inch of my skin prickles with gooseflesh, while he seems completely calm and content, eyes roaming over me like I'm dessert.

"What, uh, what do you…want me to—"

"Whatever you want." He shrugs like this is the simplest thing in the world.

"Right," I agree, even though I have no clue what I'm agreeing to.

Grabbing my hands, Dami places them on his hips. "Why don't we start with what you do know—kissing."

"Yeah. S-sure."

The temperature goes up about ten degrees between us as I stare at his eager mouth. It's a turn on that it looks eager, but I'm still getting used to the fact that he's only the second person I've ever kissed in my life, and the little fact that he's a man or rather that I like the fact that he's a man. He's being incredibly patient and generous considering how I treated him last week on the job. I know I'm not being timed, but I can tell I'm the one holding up the show.

Nodding, I murmur like a navigation system, "Okay. Gonna kiss you."

Ghosting my mouth against his, his lips are as soft as I remember. I never paid much attention to things like noses brushing noses, breath mingling with breath, but I am now, and it only heightens the thrill rushing through me.

The tip of that bold tongue of his touches my lips. It's like a button because instinctively I open, wanting every taste he's willing to give me, willing to take. It feels like I'll float away if I don't hold onto something, so I tighten my grip on his hips, ignoring the needy noises my throat is producing. This is…so incredible. Is it just him, or was I missing out because I married the wrong gender?

Inching forward, Dami's chest bumps into mine, pressing my back against the fridge. He's clinging to me as though my kisses are a lifeline, and fuck, am I supposed to love it this much?

His moan vibrates in my mouth. I can feel it all the way down to my toes as we sweep and explore each other's mouths like we're painting a canvas with our tongues. Groaning, he leans into me.

I never knew weight could be so exhilarating, except…some of it is hard, *extremely* hard. Every inch of his arousal is pressed right up next to mine. I need to quit referring to him as a kid. The iron bar pressing into me is all man. Then…he rotates his hips in a sensuous grind. My cock throbs, pummeling sparks of heat up my shaft, my pulse kicking up to dangerous levels.

Breaking away, I pant, unsure why it comes out like an accusation, "You're hard."

"I've been hard since you kissed me yesterday," he clarifies, peppering the side of my mouth.

I made him hard for that long? It's like finding out I have a bizarre superpower.

"Really?"

"Well, no. Not exactly."

Why the hell is he chuckling? Pushing him away an inch is enough to break his mouth from my face.

"You don't have to lie to me. If you're not into this, or I'm doing something wrong…"

"No. I *was* hard, I just…took care of it after you left. That's all I meant."

"You…"

"I…jerked off." He shrugs like admitting why is no big deal.

"Because of me kissing you?"

"Well, yeah. You came in all hot and heavy and were like *I'm so mad at you. Roar!* It was freaking hot as hell." He grins, running his hands up and down my arms.

And damn me, if I'm not cracking up too now because somehow, despite all my concerns, we're doing this and having an actual conversation. He's easy to talk to. He makes me want to laugh more than anyone I've ever met.

"*Fire? Roar?* Do you have anything besides four-letter words to describe me?"

"Hm," he purrs, chewing his lip. God, why does that do it for me? "Sexy, mean, salty… Nope!"

When he dives for my mouth again, I don't care if he can't spell or thinks OSHA is a person. All I can focus on is how good his kisses taste, how perfect every touch of his feels. His fingers breech the hem of my shirt, grazing the skin of my flank. I don't know who groans louder. How can I want more when this is already sensory overload?

I settle for gripping his hips like they're a stress ball. His little gyrations are getting more force behind them. I always thought denim was thick, protective, good for keeping the flesh safe on a worksite. No matter the thread count of our fabric, our jeans are doing nothing to prevent me from feeling the head of his cock, rubbing against mine.

Coming up for air, his forehead has a sheen of sweat as I rest mine against his to glance down at the erotic pelvic dance between us. It's obscene, but it's sexy because it's obscene. Who am I?

The terrified part of me says I'm Graham, the straight son of Bob and Marge Brandt, married to Jennifer Brandt, my wife. An overruling part says I haven't been a husband in a long time and that this is what I've been waiting for my whole life as Dami's lips draw a trail down the side of my neck.

"Touch me," he pants. "If you want to, touch me."

Swallowing against the thrill of the permission that I craved and yet hoped he wouldn't give, I run my fingers through his hair, possibly my body's way of letting him know he can live at my neck. So fucking soft and fluffy. Weird kink discovery.

My other hand plays copycat, sneaking under the back of his shirt like a pickpocket. Dami's lips move to my collarbone and suck, making me officially a dead man.

Since when is my collarbone an erogenous zone? Moaning like I'm in agony, which isn't far from the truth, I drop my face to his shoulder, reveling in the feel of his flesh under my touch and his hot breath on my body. His pulse is a living thing against my lips. It's accelerated pace is because of his reaction to *me*. I can't not pay that phenomenon tribute. Like someone will cut it off if they find out, the tip of my tongue hesitantly takes a swipe of salty, pleasantly musky Dami skin.

He groans against my cheek, fucking groans. Something deviant tells me to be a good student, so I lick again. If his groans are gold stars, I want to paint the fucking sky.

My waistband jostles, releasing pressure. I feel fingers. *Mother effing love of hell!* His hand is around my cock.

I'm just as shocked as him when I find my hand, gripped tightly over his wrist, preventing him from his next move. Do we go this far? How many firsts are acceptable in one week?

He's gone rigid, muscles locked up as he stares at me. That concerned look on his face mixed with the passion I stirred in his eyes is all it takes to make my decision. He's not going to push me, but he wants me as much as I want him. Gripping the back of his neck, I recapture his lips. My hips buck into his grip like a stallion that's been held back too long, fifteen years too long.

"I've wanted you since I saw you last summer," Dami murmurs. "I couldn't take my eyes off you."

"You still can't," I tease like a confident man even as my hand trembles when I graze it over the outline of his arousal.

"Oh, ye-ah," he moans, thrusting into my palm, all the while working my cock better than I ever have.

His pumps and twists build a rampant need, wrapping around my spine, collecting in my balls. It's like every bit of arousal I've ever had in my life compounded into this one moment. The headiness of it slams me, making my head light. Swaying, I release his neck and halt his wrist one more time. He's just too much.

"What's wrong?" He breathes. "Chair?"

Him and his safe word. I need a safe word for making out? How sad is that?

"No. I…I'm going to come."

Scoffing, he smiles. "Then come."

"In *your hand?*"

"Unless you want to come in my mouth?" he teases, stroking my shaft again and flicking the seam of my lips with his tongue.

The visual…the freaking visual of that tongue where his hand is? I can't. Before I can say a word, I pulse in his grip and erupt all over his fingers with a stifled cry.

Gripping a fistful of his shirt, my eyes slam shut, my head *thunking* back against the fridge. Relief and ecstasy ripple shudders through me as my cock twitches in Dami's grip. The sound of his pleased gasp, followed by a needy groan doesn't help matters. It's like a sexy applause for my embarrassing performance. With lazy strokes, he drives me through the waves, peppering kisses all over my neck and face as though he's rewarding me for losing it.

My God, what was that? Five minutes of petting? My freaking toes are tingling.

I don't know how I avoided this my entire life, but now that I've experienced it, I have a feeling it'll be my undoing. Dami's school of love is addictive, and I've only taken my first hit.

CHAPTER 17

So, that was…nice. Super nice. Better than nice actually.

Shifting my junk inside my jeans, I wonder if I have time to rub one out before Graham returns from the bathroom. Maybe I need a better lesson plan or a syllabus. Point number-one: make sure the other guy comes too.

The floor in the hallway creaks. Graham inches back into the kitchen, a sheepish look on his face as he rubs his freshly washed hands on the legs of his jeans. Okay. I can be strong if I get to see that look for suffering. The guy is so damn cute when he's vulnerable. It makes me want to find a cat so I can rescue him from a chair.

Running a hand through the hair that I had the time of my life messing up, he shoves the other one in his pocket and ducks his chin. "Um, so…you were okay with that?"

The poor fella. We have got to get him out of that hermit closet.

"Yeah. Didn't I sound *okay?*"

He makes no sound other than the gust of air I hear push out of his nostrils. Biting his lip, he glances around the room like a stranger in a strange place. Shoot. I'm not being a very good teacher.

"Were you?" I inquire.

"Yeah. Yeah, of course. I…I agreed to it."

Ouch. Compliance does not equal enjoyment. "Wow. What a compliment. Guess I need to work on my skills."

"It…you were fine. Good. Great. Just…I'm processing."

Ah. Okay. I can live with that. I need to remember literally everything is his first rodeo, while it's my…hm. I don't even know how many rodeos I've had. Is that bad?

"Right!" I chirp. "Process. Yeah. That's good. Definitely, you should process."

Joining in his survey of his house, I realize I have two options. One—I could initiate round-two to take care of my problem, but I don't want to be pushy and maul him. Two—I can hop in my car, rush home, and take care of business before I have to get to Tapas.

Time is precious, and only one of those ends in certainty. I imagine *processing* is probably something he meant he should do alone. Stepping forward, I give him my best smile and a peck on the cheek.

"So, I should go. I need to get to the restaurant for the after-dinner shift."

"Really? After working all day?"

"Yeah. It's no big deal. I'll sleep on the weekend," I joke, but he frowns. "I won't slack off at work. I promise. I've been pulling nights there almost every day since I started and still haven't fallen asleep on you yet," I reassure him, but it doesn't seem to help either. I guess I'll just have to prove it to him tomorrow. I need to buy more coffee. "Well, I'll see you in the morning then?"

"Uh, yeah." He says, making his way to the door with me. "Yeah. S-see you in the morning."

His hand pauses on the doorknob. I wait for him to open it, so I can get past and speed home to knock one out, but when I look up, he's leaning in.

Oh. A goodbye kiss. Huh. Not used to those. Heh. It's like an apple for the teacher, I guess.

I take my payment and leave him with a smile, trying to walk normal to my car with the extra weight in my jeans. Better luck tomorrow.

CHAPTER 18

Dani

It turns out, my luck sucks. Tuesday night, Graham cooked me dinner again. Steak with twice-baked potatoes. Delicious. Dessert was delicious too—making out on his couch, followed by another hand job.

Except…it was a one-sided hand job.

His efforts improved since Monday but entailed him teasing the crap out of my cock. I even wore thin workout shorts, but his sporadic little squeezes and grazes weren't quite enough to do the trick.

Ugh.

At this rate, I'm going to sprain my wrist. I went from jerking myself off to having to jerk off two people. My great idea backfired.

There's a feather in my cap, seeing that little smirk he's been wearing all day and those bashful glances he's shooting me, but pride does nothing for my problem. He staggered out of the living room as soon as he shot, disappearing into his bathroom again to clean up.

Does he have an issue with fluids, or is it just virgin jitters? I mean, at some point, I was hoping my penis would be touched by another human being. Shouldn't hands-on lessons be…I don't know…hands-on?

I went home stabbing my steering wheel again. Do you know how difficult it is to turn when there's a rudder jamming the wheel? I could get in an accident. Death by boner. I wonder if *Osha* would think that's a hazard?

I'm starting to sympathize with my former instructors. Did they have this much difficulty figuring out lesson plans? Where do I go from here? Do I come over tonight and let him fuck me?

I highly doubt he's ready for that. I could demonstrate the art of oral, but I haven't even gotten his cock to make an appearance yet. I should have asked for introductions on the first day of class.

It is extremely difficult to figure out what to do with someone who doesn't initiate. I'm also sure there's supposed to be some kind of balance here, some slowly progressive order in which gay thirty-year-old virgins should proceed. Unfortunately, *slowly progressive* is *not* where my libido is at after three months of abstinence.

Ugh. I am the worst teacher ever. One more thing I suck at.

I need to figure out something though, because I refuse to be responsible for scaring a man back into the closet with my horniness. Honestly, I don't even know why I'm considering going to his place. It's like a twenty-minute drive. I'm not sure I have enough gas to make it to work and out there until I get my paycheck Friday afternoon. My new-found stubbornness refuses to let me ask Mama for gas money out of my account.

Cleaning off the mortar board with a bucket of water from the portable tank we have on the site, I finish wrapping up for the day. I still can't believe I'm building a house.

"You about ready to go?" Graham asks, coming up beside me.

"Yeah."

"What's up?" he asks.

I realize I'm gawking at our handiwork again. The front of the house has taken shape. Wide stairs lead to a sizeable, covered porch, supported by pillars that Graham made erecting look like child's play.

"Nothing, just admiring your work. It's really starting to look like a house."

Bumping my shoulder with his, he smirks. "*Our* work, and yeah. I guess, but that was the point. Right?"

Heading back to the warehouse, the cab of the truck is filled with a weighted silence. I love how I'm starting to notice when he gets a heated look in his eyes. He *wants* to explore. I can see it, but alas, my protégé isn't ready for the advanced methods I desperately long to use.

The best option is to take a teacher's institute the rest of the week and hold off for this weekend. Maybe if I get some of my sexual frustration out of my system at Dante's party, I'll be able to withstand the gingerly pace Graham needs and be the self-controlled teacher he deserves.

"I was going to make lasagna tonight…if…you wanted to stop by," he says, adorably obvious.

Crap. My wrist throbs in protest already. "I, uh, have some things to do tonight actually, so I can't, but thanks for the dinner invite."

"Oh. Alright."

The disappointment in his voice makes my stomach flip. Just a week ago, he couldn't wait to get away from me.

"I need to try to take my bed apart so I can turn my old room into kind of an art room. I've been wanting to do it, since Johnny moved out permanently, but with work and shifts at Tapas, I haven't had much time yet."

"Johnny officially moved in with Aiden?"

"Y-yeah." How did he not know this? Is he shocked by it? "Pretty cool. Right?" I venture.

"Uh, yeah. Yeah, I had no idea. I mean, I knew he spent a lot of time over there."

"Yeah. He was pretty much never at the apartment anyway, so… Well, now I guess it's all mine."

"An art room, huh? That's cool. I'm glad you'll have a dedicated space."

"Well, I've got to figure out how to take the bed apart first," I say on a laugh.

After a pause, he adds, "I could help, if you want."

"Oh, you don't have to do that. I'm sure I can figure it out, but I have to figure out some way to get it downstairs and to the resale shop, so… okay. Maybe I didn't actually think this through."

Crap. Why is adulting so complicated?

Snickering, Graham pulls into the warehouse lot next to my *SMART* car. "Let me go home and shower, and then I'll be over. Do you like pizza?"

Pizza? Why is he talking about pizza? "Uh…yeah. Who doesn't?"

"Aiden. Something about garlic."

"Huh. That's weird."

"Yeah. Well, I'll grab some tools, and we can load your bed up in my truck and drop it off at the resale shop tomorrow. Sound good?"

"S-sure."

"You don't sound sure," he teases.

Um. Probably because he's coming over to my apartment. Probably because he's going out of his way to help me. And probably because I have no idea why that's making my insides all nice and toasty.

Am I supposed to like my student this much? This is not helping my locked-down libido problem.

CHAPTER 19

Graham

You'd think no one ever bought the guy a pizza before the way Dami's entire face lit up when I walked in. He really needs to start upping his standards, if he's planning on finding some established rich guy who will respect and want to marry him. For now, pizza and a little manual labor is the least I can do for what I owe him. I tell the part of my brain that says, *he touched your dick and you're bringing him pizza*, to shut the hell up.

I never imagined myself being in a situation like this. After two days of Dami giving me the best two orgasms of my life, however, I'm starting to wonder what caliber of student I am.

I know he sounded excited about our arrangement, and that he said he enjoyed himself, but did he really enjoy himself? After a failed fifteen-year relationship, I may be a bit insecure when it comes to pleasuring someone else. It didn't escape my notice that he didn't get off.

I don't know how to contribute or if I should. All I have to go off of is the crazy urge running through me to devour him anyway I can. He whispered for me to touch him both times, but where, how, and for how long? I couldn't bring myself to ask those embarrassing questions, and thinking wasn't easy to do while he was making me lose my mind.

Then there's the awkward moment afterward when he leaves. Kissing him goodbye seems…right, instinctual even, but he looks shocked when I do it. I don't get it. We've kissed plenty by now, and he's had my dick in his hand. Doesn't that at least merit a goodbye kiss?

While I lack the mental tools and the talent for his lessons, at least I had the foresight to bring my toolbox with me for Operation Art Room. Closing the pizza box, he dusts the crumbs off his hands and leads me into his bedroom or *former* bedroom, I guess. It doesn't matter, it smells like him—that sweet, musky Dami scent. Like a predator, after one whiff, I know he's lived in here. My cock thickens in my jeans the more of it I breathe in.

This was probably a terrible idea. Alone in a room with Dami and a bed, I have no idea how I'm supposed to concentrate.

I help him upend his mattress and prop it against the wall. When I explain the different types of screwdrivers, I try to not think about how exhilarated it makes me feel to have his rapt attention. I give him a set of screwdrivers to start on one side, while I start on the other. A task this simple should not make a guy look as proud of himself as Dami does, but I find myself smiling with him over his achievement as the edge of the frame comes off on his side.

Dragging the headboard away from the window, something jams into my hip. I turn around and pick up a stack of papers I must have bumped off a desk in the corner of the room. Nothing could have prepared me for what I'm seeing.

Finite lines, expert shading, living, breathing life on crisp, heavy white sketch paper. A man in his underwear, hunched over like that statue, *The Thinker*.

Mesmerized, I card through the stack slowly. Each image is more breathtaking than the next. I never knew body hair could be so captivating or sexy, but Dami's detail is so impeccable, I find myself drawing the pad of my finger across a sketch to appease my mind that I can't actually feel the texture of it. The rendering is just that lifelike.

"Oh, sorry about those. I don't really have anywhere to put them yet," he rushes, coming over to retrieve the drawings from me, but I can't seem to relinquish them just yet. "Um, you…probably don't want to look at those. I know they're a bit much, all the nudity, but I like to practice the human form. I sneak pictures from Johnny's filing cabinets from his model-shooting days and practice drawing them."

"Dami, these are incredible. Why the hell aren't you doing this for a living?"

He makes an incredulous sound. "Yeah, sure. Twenty bucks a pop won't pay the bills."

"Twenty bucks? Why would you only sell them for twenty dollars?"

"Well, that's what I charged a few people in college who asked me to draw stuff for them."

Frowning, I carefully set the drawings back on the desk. "Those were college kids on a budget, taking advantage of your talent."

"They weren't taking advantage. I was happy to do it for them. It's fun. It's just a hobby."

"Did you take any art classes in school?"

"A couple." He shrugs, helping me move the desk so we can continue dismantling his bed.

"Do your parents know you draw?"

"Yeah. Sure. They have me draw on the specials board at the restaurant once a week." Fidgeting, he adds, "But they don't know about this stuff, so…maybe don't mention it to anyone?"

Shaking my head, I have to school my features. How come no one ever noticed his talent and encouraged him? How many people treated him the way that I did?

"I won't," I mutter, even though keeping something this phenomenal a secret seems like a crime.

Dropping to a knee to dismantle the rest of his bedframe, he joins me on the floor. I find myself staring at his fingers as he works a bolt loose. I can't let it go. Pulling my phone out, I shoot my mom a text.

> **ME:** What's the name of that online store where you sell
> your sewing stuff?
>
> **MOM:** *Etsy.*

I thank her and go to pocket my device, but it pings again.

> **MOM:** I saw Jen yesterday. She said you guys had dinner
> last week. Glad to hear that things are going well with
> the two of you.

Fuck.

I know Jen wouldn't encourage my mother, especially after our bizarre confessional last week, but the mere mention of a shared dinner is enough to give my mother hope. I no longer want her to have hope. I can't ever visit her without her asking about Jen. I'm not looking forward to telling her it's finally and officially over once and for all.

> **ME:** She's doing well. Working midnights. Talk to you
> later.

My phone chimes again. Damn it.

Now is not the time for idle chit chat with my mother. Jolting, I realize somehow, I've come to think of my moments with Dami as precious time that shouldn't be squandered. How did that happen?

> **MOM:** We're cooking out tomorrow at five.

Crap. One of the regular family cookouts. What if Dami wants to hang out tomorrow? Every fiber in my being decides he's a priority over family dinner. I can't invite him to my parents' house. Well, technically, I could, but how awkward would that look and be? It shouldn't be any more awkward than when they invite Jen, but I didn't look at Jen like I wanted to tear her clothes off, now did I?

Right. Scratch inviting Dami.

> **ME:** Going to have to miss this one. Have some errands
> to take care of.

Putting my phone on silent, I shove it into my pocket and return my attention to the object of my increasing desire. What started as solely a physical attraction is becoming…more. What started as lessons are becoming a need, a bone ravaging need that I still don't know how to navigate.

All I know is, watching Dami's nimble fingers work the bolt on the bed frame, there isn't a part of him I don't crave to touch twenty-four hours a day. There isn't a secret of his that I don't long to learn. There isn't a sound or word he says that I don't wish I could hear. What part of this education is that?

"Everything alright?" He asks, quirking his brows.

"Yeah. My mom sells some of her sewing online on a site called *Etsy*. I was just messaging her to get the name of it for you. People sell all kinds of crazy shit on there. You should post your drawings for sale on it. I bet you'd do well."

"With drawings by a guy people don't even know? I doubt it," he scoffs. "And I'd have to ship them, so after the shipping costs cut into the twenty bucks, I really wouldn't be making any money."

Where are his big dreams when they have to do with his confidence? Grumbling, I whip my phone out and bring up the website. Punching in a search for artwork, I find some sketch work and show Dami the prices the artists are charging. He gapes, jaw slack. I gape at his slack jaw, remembering how it felt underneath my fingertips.

"That guy is asking for over a hundred bucks for some of those!" he declares.

Shrugging, I tuck the phone back into my pocket. "And yours are better, so imagine what you'd get."

"No way." He shakes his head. "Nobody knows who I am, and I'm not even that good."

"I don't know who in the hell that guy was, so who cares." I gesture to my phone. "You *are* good. Phenomenal, actually. You're talented, Dami. You have no idea what a gift you have."

My little speech came out heated and passionate, but the little smile he gets on his face as he stares at me, absorbing my compliment, stirs a different kind of passion inside me. Cupping his jaw, I glide my thumb across it and lean in. It's just a touch on the cheek. Surely, that's not too much overstepping after what we've done already.

"I mean it," I add softly, but my gaze snares on the way his tongue darts out to wet his lips.

"Yeah?" he asks, all breathy, sounding drugged.

It pulls me in closer. Is he giving me a green light? How can he want *me?*

Do I care why right now?

"Yeah," I breath into his mouth, sealing his with mine.

It's a tender and delicate kiss. A shiver runs up my spine from the intimacy of it.

And then…he tackles me to the floor.

"Ouch!" I wince, digging a screwdriver out from under my ass.

"Sorry." He chuckles. "You can't say things like that and look at a guy like that and not expect to get tackled."

"Oh, yeah? I'll have to try it more often." My breath hitches as soon as the words leave my mouth. I don't know where my boldness came from, but it might have to do with how good his weight feels on top of me.

Moaning, he grips my shoulder and digs a hand into my hair as he invades my mouth. Tender and delicate have just gone out the window as his tongue battles with mine. We feel so connected like this, chest to chest. I can feel every rise and fall of his breath when his stomach expands against mine. Shaking, my hand slides from the small of his back, downward as he starts to grind against me.

That pressure, the friction. I don't want to wear jeans anymore. They feel too much like a barrier. Denim is safe, but I don't want to be safe around him.

Gripping a handful of that ass I have obsessed over one too many times, he groans at my touch. Fuck. It feels as perky as it looks. I sync in time with his movements, helping him thrust against me.

"Pants," he blurts. "Undo your pants."

Complying, my breath hitches, wondering what will come next. His hand bumps into mine as I undo my fly. He's undoing his jeans too.

In a flurry of movements, he pulls himself out and then me. I'm transfixed by the sight of his bare cock an inch away from mine. I take in everything, the way his is the barest shade darker, a fraction longer, and the slightest bit thinner than mine. The domed head, glistens with precum.

It's just a cock. I've seen a cock before. I see one every time I take a leak, but I can't tear my eyes away from it until he draws his palm up to his mouth and licks. He laps it in a slow, dirty motion, painting his skin with saliva.

"Oh, my God," I rasp as he wraps it around the both of us, pressing heated flesh against heated flesh.

I never imagined two cocks could fit together due to their anatomical shape. Dami is a fucking puzzle master, locking us together and pumping as he thrusts into his grip. His pants of breath hit mine between kisses. I could die on his floor right now, and that would be fine by me.

Groaning like he's in pain, he grumbles, "My wrist," and releases us.

I feel the loss immediately. Is it strenuous to jerk two cocks? I have no idea, but—wait.

Why is he sliding down? Oh, fuck.

Air hits my stomach where he wrenched my sweatshirt up higher. His lips dance below my belly button. His breath tickles my happy trail. Is he… Should I let him? I…

"Oh, holy uhn—" I freaking bellow, watching the tip of his tongue flick up the slit of my cockhead.

He closes his eyes and makes this savory sound that turns my balls into granite. "Mm. So good," he whispers, diving down and capturing the head of my cock between his lips.

"Dami, fuuuck," I whisper like I work in a naughty library.

His wet heat slides down, engulfing me. I'm a babbling fool, gaping at his fluffy head bobbing as he repeats the action, and repeats it, each descent encasing me tighter. Oh, hell. Was that his tongue?

"Uhn! Sh-shit!"

I'm no longer librarian-volume. I'm full-fledged, swearing sailor as his tongue swirls and laps while his mouth hugs my cock to the depths of his throat. Gritting my teeth like I'm wrestling a grizzly bear, I try to stave off that knowing tingle threatening to burst up my shaft. He was right. He does have skills.

Gripping his hair, my hips jerk against my will. My other hand is tracing any part of his face with my fingertips that I can reach, scrawling cryptic script on his skin with the message *thank you, you're amazing, don't ever stop.*

Something creaks in the other room, followed by a *slam. Voices.* I hear voices.

Holyfuckingshit! Aiden and Johnny!

"Hello?" my brother's deep voice calls, ripping me out of my euphoria as I jerk Dami's head off my cock.

"Ah," he winces, gripping his jaw as I barrel roll to my side and shove my dick back into my jeans. "Crap," I hear him curse, followed by the sound of his own zipper.

Fuck. Fuck. Fuck!

"I thought you said Johnny moved out?" I whisper accusingly.

God, look at him wiping his mouth. *I* did that to his mouth. His lips look like they got stung by a damn bee.

"He did!" Hunching over, he tugs his sweatshirt over the bulge in his pants. "Uh, in here!" he calls.

Is he insane? We don't want them in here. I shouldn't even be here.

"Hey, Dami! Oh! Graham! I thought that was your truck downstairs. What are you two up to?"

"Building a spaceship. What does it look like?" I grunt, my back to him as I chuck my tools back into my toolbox.

"Ooh, opting for the swing bed, I see," Johnny's voice floats into the room.

The swing bed? How could I forget? I only saw it once, when I came over for drinks with Aiden and Johnny and needed to use the bathroom. The thought of my big brother screwing his boyfriend on a bed that's a swing is an image that will forever scar my mind. It's only now that I put two and two together. *Dami* will be using the swing bed.

I can't handle that image while my cock is still covered in his slobber. How did this happen again? I received more sexual favors that I didn't reciprocate. Does he like steering the ship? What does he really want out of these lessons anyway? I certainly can't think with a clear head about it while my brother and Johnny are in the room.

"Glad to see you two working together," Aiden adds.

"Yeah," Dami replies. "Graham was a big help. I'd probably still be wrestling my mattress if he hadn't come over."

"Ah, you should have called me. I'd have helped you," my brother says.

Before I can tell my mouth what a bad idea it is, I blurt out, "He didn't need your help. He had mine."

And now they're all looking at me. Perfect.

"So, I'll help you load this up tomorrow. Okay?" I tell Dami, standing with my toolbox strategically placed in front of my crotch.

"Um…s-sure. Okay. You're leaving?"

"Y-yeah. I…I've gotta get home and…feed my fish."

Aiden looks at me like I've sprouted piggy tails. Screw him. He isn't hiding a hard-on from our one and only employee. He didn't just get a text from Mom asking about his ex-wife, and he's known with certainty which ways his dick has swung for years. None of this is easy for me.

"Thanks for the pizza," Dami calls as I shoulder past our two spectators.

"Pizza party?" Aiden murmurs. I shoot him a look, but he adds, "Wow, he must be a better worker than you said, if you're springing for pizza."

"Why wouldn't he be? He learned from the best," I retort, resorting to childish digs in an attempt at nonchalance.

"Oh, yeah? That's great, then we can send him out on his own sooner than I thought."

That has me faltering at the apartment door. Aiden can't just take him away like that. He's a person, damn it, not cattle.

What am I saying? Of course, Aiden or Skyler can send him on another job. He's our freaking employee, our employee whose mouth I just had my cock inside.

"Yeah, but…after the Hodges job. Right? I mean, we're still not done yet."

"Mm. Yeah. Sure, if you need him longer."

Nodding, I leave. I do need Dami. Just not in a way I can tell anyone.

CHAPTER 20

I can't even follow through on a teacher's institute day. One minute Graham was complimenting me so hard last night, my head was spinning, the next my mouth was wrapped around his gorgeous cock.

At least he seemed to enjoy the lesson on oral gratification while it lasted. Way to ruin it, Johnny and Aiden.

I'll never know if he would have reciprocated. I don't know if I'm agitated over that or the way he scrambled to close up shop when we were intruded upon by two people who already know I'm gay. I know this is all new to him, but I'm the last person who needs a reminder that the way I am can't be seen in Olympus. It's not good for my confidence. How can I work up the nerve to tell my parents when I'm spending time with a guy who is terrified of who he is?

Ugh.

It's not my job to help him come out. I'm just here to help him explore, I remind myself. Except I don't know how much more my gas tank, or my libido, can handle driving out to his house just to get one of us off.

"Um. I have to wash dishes at the restaurant tonight," I inform Graham in response to his dinner invitation at his place as we pack up for the day.

"Again? How long are you going to go on working all these hours? That can't be good for you."

"Well, I can't exactly tell my parents *no*. I hinted around a few times that they need to find a new dishwasher, but my mom's good at changing the subject."

Slamming the tailgate of his truck, my heart stutters at the look of concern on his face. "Can't you just tell her you want to quit, that you can't work two jobs?"

Gosh. This is so embarrassing. Why did I open my big mouth?

"I tried, but she said that meant this job was too much for me."

"Is she…controlling?"

"No. I don't know.," I stammer. "Not in a bad way. It's more like over-protective, I think."

"What do you mean? She thinks you'll get hurt out here?"

Ha! If he only knew. "She always thinks I'll get hurt."

As my face heats for speaking something that feels like betrayal about my mother, Graham just blinks at me in confusion, waiting for further explanation.

Damn it. No way out of it now.

"I…had an older brother."

"*Had?*"

"*Stefano*. I was two and he was five. We were crossing the street. My mom was holding me, and Stefano got away from her and ran in front of a car."

I hate that I just made his beautiful face look like it lost all its glow. Watching his squint lines sag, I swallow against the nausea in my belly.

"Dami, I'm so sorry," he whispers.

Shrugging to lessen the impact for him, I can at least try to paint more of a picture. "I don't remember him that much, and I don't remember the accident. I'm sorry he died, especially like that. I'd like to have had a brother, growing up, but sometimes I've felt mad at him for dying or maybe my mom for how she handled it." Running my hand through my hair, I tremble at the shiver running up my spine. "That sounds so awful. I just…she used to talk about him a lot when I was little, and how she lost him and didn't want to lose me, and if I said I didn't like something, she'd say how Stefano probably would have liked the chance to like or dislike it. I know she didn't mean to make me feel guilty, that she just missed him, and it was part of her heartbreak, but it…it just felt like this extra pressure on me to be perfect and never disappoint her. She and my dad used to fight about it a lot, but I think he just gave up at some point."

Now Graham is full-on gaping at me like I debuted a horror film. Wow. I'm a terrific storyteller.

"Sorry," I rush out. "I didn't mean to get all depressing."

Inching forward, I swear his nostrils are flaring as he squeezes my shoulder. "You don't have to fill anybody's shoes but your own."

"Yeah. I know. Just…easier said than done."

His mouth flickers up at the corner in what I imagine is empathy. Now that the memories of Stefano and my childhood are out of my system, my stomach flips for a different reason. I've never really talked about that to anyone before. I certainly never imagined telling Graham, or that he'd react with supportive wisdom.

Nodding toward the cab of the truck, he heads to the driver's side. I get in and try to figure out how I can dispel the awkward silence, but he does it for me.

"So, how about I come help you wash dishes and afterward you come by, and we'll watch a movie or something?"

Oh, no. No more lessons tonight. My hand and my balls can't take it.

"Just to hang out," he blurts. "Not a…lesson or anything."

Oh. He wants to…hang out? With me?

"Uh, s-sure. That sounds…oh. Wait."

"What?"

Fantastic. Like I haven't humiliated myself enough for one day.

"Well, eh heh, this is kind of embarrassing, but I'm a bit low on gas. I think I have enough to get to work tomorrow until I get paid, but I don't know about driving all the way out to your place again and back."

His forehead creases into that sexy stern expression of his. "Don't your parents pay you for working?"

"They do," I enthuse optimistically and fiddle with the lock mechanism. "Um, just I don't exactly get a paycheck. My mom says she puts money in an account for me, and when I need something, I ask her. She either gives me some cash or just buys what I need."

Okay, now he looks pissed. Shoot. I really need to stop talking. He's going to go back to thinking I'm a helpless idiot. Not that I care. I mean, why would I care?

"I know that probably makes me sound irresponsible. It's just…easier to let her handle it than ask for her to turn it over to me. So, technically, I have money, but I kind of made this promise to myself to not have to ask her for anything anymore. I know that sounds stupid. I'm being stupid. I'll just shut up."

Ugh. Kill me now. He's gawking at me like I sprouted a unicorn horn.

"It's not stupid," he finally says all low and sincere. "A man needs to make his own way."

Why did that just give me more shivers?

"So, how about this?" he prefaces, clearing his throat. "I'll follow you to your place. We'll load up your bed, drop it off at the resale shop, and then we can drive to Tapas together."

"You…still want to hang out?"

Starting the truck, he shrugs as he looks out over the dash. "Yeah, and if you want to grab some stuff, you can crash on my couch, and we can just ride to the site together in the morning. We don't need to go to the warehouse. I'll text Aiden that we're both just going to head straight to the site tomorrow."

No way! He did not! Slumber party at Graham's? I'm sold.

"Yeah. Okay!"

The teacher's institute is officially over. My student is eager to learn if he's inviting me over for slumber parties.

CHAPTER 21

That was…weird. Having Graham in my dish haven felt like that dream where you're naked. Not the good kind of naked dream, the kind where you're naked like at a family function or something and someone you're crushing on is in the same room.

Instead of staring out the window above the sink at him like I did last summer, he was next to me. Elbows were bumped. Smiles were exchanged. Kisses were wanted. Man, I'm really starting to develop a kissing kink.

It might have something to do with the way he bragged to my mother about what an excellent worker I am, what an asset I am to the Brandt business, and how he hopes she finds a new dishwasher soon because they're so happy to have her "talented" son working for them. Talk about foreplay.

I don't know whose jaw hit the floor longer, Mama's or mine. It was bittersweet to see the reflective expression on her face. When she shooed us from the kitchen only halfway through the dishes, insisting that one of the servers could help her finish up later, I was about to ask her if she'd been abducted by aliens.

The couch dips next to me. Graham settles in, holding his plate in one hand, a fork in the other.

"What'd you find?" he asks, nodding at the TV with his chin, taking a bite of the cannoli my mother sent with us.

"Aquaman?"

"Let me guess, you've got a thing for Jason Momoa?"

"Who doesn't?" I swallow, watching his tongue peek out to lap a bit of filling from the corner of his mouth.

I do have a *thing*, but it's for the freshly showered man in sweatpants sitting next to me. Graham rocks the shit out of sweatpants. I barely made it through the risotto Mamma sent with us. I couldn't take my eyes off the way the gray fabric hugs his sinewy thighs and lays just right over the part of him I want my mouth on again.

Who am I kidding? I don't just want it in my mouth, I want it everywhere.

Except I think when he proposed a slumber party, he really did mean a G-rated slumber party. My hormones let me hear what I wanted.

No lessons tonight. Right. I can do this.

"Man, your mom can cook," he hums around another bite.

"Rub it in."

"That wasn't a dig at you."

"I *know*."

Casually, he angles his head without looking at me. "I could teach you, if you want."

"To cook?"

"Yeah. Why not?"

"So, I can go work at Tapas, 'cause it kind of sounded tonight like you were spearheading a campaign to get me let go," I venture.

He smirks, and I file away how cool it is that his ears get red when he's embarrassed. "I didn't say anything that wasn't true."

"Thanks for that by the way," I murmur, tucking my knees up to my chest. I have to force myself for the first time in my life to focus on Jason Momoa.

From my peripheral, Graham shrugs. "Well, if you ever want to learn how to make anything. It's not a problem. Then you can impress that rich husband of yours someday."

I bark out a very unsexy awkward laugh. "Right."

The whole rich husband dream makes me squirmy for the rest of the movie as we sit in silence. I'm starting to want part-three of my plan sooner than I thought. Maybe it's all these make out sessions lately and the fact that they're making me hornier than a jock at a sorority instead of cooling my urges like I hoped they would.

If Graham doesn't want to take his "final exam" with me, I can get some extra credit in at Dante's party this weekend to reset my battery. Maybe now that I've got a good, steady job, I *should* start looking for my Mr. Right instead of wasting my time on Mr. Right Nows. Well, after I get tested again next week if I get lucky at the party, and after Graham's lessons are over, of course. I can't leave the guy hanging after all. A deal's a deal.

Glancing over at the sound of steady breathing, I take in my sleepy student who seems to have dozed off. Here I thought something aquatic would catch his interest due to his love of water, and fish, and mythology-themed tattoos.

Arms folded across his chest, slouched down, legs open wide, head angled toward me with his lips barely parted, he is a sight to behold when he's asleep. Every fiber in my being wants to wake him up by crawling onto his lap right now.

Maybe I don't need a rich guy. I could find somebody who's just really good at a blue-collar job he loves like Graham is. Somebody who knows how to cook like Graham does. A sandy blonde maybe? I didn't realize how much I like that hair color or facial hair.

Uhn.

Yeah. A feather duster is a must.

And I suppose, my forever guy could be kind of growly, as long as he believes in me and isn't afraid of my mother. What else?

Sweatpants.

Yeah. He definitely needs to rock sweatpants as good as the man next to me.

CHAPTER 22

Graham

"This was a horrible idea," I mutter to my bedroom ceiling.

How in the hell am I supposed to go back to sleep when the person I can't stop thinking about is sleeping in the other room? I wish he hadn't woken me up. At least passed out on the couch, I had a reprieve from all the thoughts running through my brain.

I want to go in there and tell him he's so much more than second place to a memory of the son his parents lost. I want to hold him and kiss him until he divulges every suppressed dream he's ever had, so I can learn them and find a way to make them come true. I want him to tell me this thing between us is more than lessons, and that his heart is nose-diving into something just as deep as mine is.

Fuck. No way am I getting back to sleep.

Whipping the covers off, I decide on a glass of water. That's a plausible excuse to creep past the couch and into the kitchen. I contemplated cleaning all the crap out of the spare room that Jen and I used for an office and making it a bedroom but held off in case she decided to come back. Now I'm kicking myself for not doing so after my impulsive sleep over invite to Dami.

At my doorway, I hesitate, listening for sounds of life. Snoring, maybe the mumbling of steamy dreams about me, something to let me know what he's doing.

The house is still except for an odd sound. There it is again.

And again—a *schick, schick* noise like wet meat slapping together when I marinate steaks.

"Oh, yeah." Dami's breathy voice takes my gaze to the couch.

One of his hands is suspended in the air, holding his phone aloft, the glow casting down.

Schick, schick, schick.

I hear panting as I inch closer like a moth to that phone light. What is he looking at?

Is that…that Vin Stoller singer he likes? The guy's practically naked in that music video he's watching without the sound on.

Why is there no sound? Where the hell is that noise coming from?

"Yeah, Vin. Yeah. Just like that," Dami moans all breathy.

Schick, schick, schick.

Oh, my God! Is he…

"What the fuck?" I snap, my eyes snaring on the slick, hard cock in his grip as I step up to the back of the couch.

"Oh, crap!" He flinches, dropping his phone on his chest and snapping his fist around the head of his cock.

"What the fuck are you doing?"

I have no idea why I'm angry whispering. It's my house. No one else is here, but it feels like I intruded on a private moment, and yet I'm pissed that it didn't involve me.

Dami looks down at his dick like he just realized he has one and then holds up that obscene music video. Vin is grinding his barely covered ass against a drum set. "Um. Paying tribute to Vincent Stoller," he says innocently.

"On *my couch?*"

Why does he look like he doesn't understand how fucked up this ordeal is?

"Do you want me to go in the bathroom?"

"No! I want you to *not* jerk off on my couch!"

His face scrunches up. "But…I've jerked *you* off on this couch."

Truth. He has. Fuck.

"That's…that's different!"

More frowning. How does he not get that this is…unfair?

"I'm confused," he says. "Does it matter whose dick is in my hand? Are there couch-dick rules?"

Holy shit. He still has it in his hand. It's *glistening*. I can see it *glistening!*

"Just…put it away!"

"What?" he asks all clueless.

"Put your dick away!"

"But I'm still hard," he whines, glancing down at said dick.

"You're always hard," I snarl, stabbing my eyes with my fingertips.

"It's not *my* fault!"

"It's not *mine* either, apparently!"

Gasping, he beams up at me. What the fuck is so amusing?

"Are you…jealous?"

"Of your dick?" I snort. "No! Why would I be?"

"No. Of Vin," he says, shaking that stupid video at me. "Because that's seriously cute. No one's ever been jealous over me before."

Jesus. I *am* jealous. My face feels like it's about to burst into flames.

"I'm not fucking *cute* just…don't come all over my couch!"

Spinning on my heel, I stomp back toward my room but only get half-way there. It's slower and softer than before, but I hear it.

Schick…schick.

Is he fucking kidding me? It's only been like ten seconds.

"Oh, my God!" I growl at my ceiling. "I can *hear* you jerking off!"

"Ugh! Well, someone has to! At least I'm not afraid to touch my dick."

My feet pound the floor before I can even think, stopping on his side of the couch. "What the hell is that supposed to mean?"

"Nothing," he says all casual, snapping his sleep pants up over his cock.

"No. You said it for a reason, tough guy. What the hell do you mean *I'm afraid?*"

I am. I'm totally afraid to touch his cock. He has the sex drive of a freaking jack rabbit, and I don't know what the fuck I'm doing. So, why am I talking?

Squirming, he adds, "Just that…I mean, I know we didn't like make a lesson plan or anything, but don't you know it's the polite thing to do to make sure your partner comes too? I've been blue balling it all week and having to jerk off when I get home."

I take a few gulps of air imagining the visual he just jammed into my head. Him going home after being with *me*. Him needing relief after being with *me*.

"You've been jerking off all week?"

"Well, yeah. Seriously, can you *please* just let me finish, or go somewhere you can't hear me, if you have a problem with this?"

No way am I going back to my room, knowing he's out here jerking off because of our lessons. Shoving at his knee, I grunt. "Move over."

He gapes at me. A second later he scrambles to sit up, flinging his legs over the edge of the couch and grins like a kid that inherited a candy store.

I have a feeling my candy store is only stocked with black licorice and his grin is premature, but I take a knee on the couch next to him, my heart running wild as I close my eyes and lean in for his mouth.

He's still panting from working himself up, making my cock thicken even more. With the darkness, maybe I can find courage and release the untrained urges he stirs in me. With the darkness, I won't have to see how bad I screw this up.

Licking his needy little whimpers inside his mouth, I run my hand down the soft fabric of his t-shirt, covering the hard plain of his stomach. His fingers dive into my hair, making me preen knowing such talent is touching me. The heat seeping through his thin sleep pants at the juncture of his thigh meets my fingertips, promising his declaration of *fire* if I venture further.

Trembling with need and nerves, I divert my palm to the hardness behind the fabric, pulling a moan from his throat. I want more of those moans. Grazing my thumb over the domed head of his cock, I put the shape and feel to memory. I file it under delightful things I'll remember till I die.

With his hands shifting and pawing across my shoulders, gripping my arms like he's begging for a salvation only I can give him, my nerves die away. He wants me. It's that simple. I can do this.

Squeezing, I slide my grip up and down his fabric-covered shaft. His hips jerk in an erotic invitation, a desperate plea for more.

"Oh! Yeah," he rasps, against my lips, blooming an aching need through my entire body.

Swallowing his words, I don't even think, just act. Guiding his shoulders, I lower myself on top of him and tug the waistband of his pants down, marveling at the glory of every brush of his flesh. His fingertips skim the top of my ass and yank my pants down over my hips.

The air kisses my flesh on one side, but Dami's hot, slickened arousal connects with mine on the other. It's like being addicted to drowning, aching for breath but unable to tear my mouth from his for air as his cock grinds up against mine.

Fuck. He feels so good underneath me, his breath on me, his pants and whimpers in my eardrums. An errant thought tells me to be mad at Aiden for not letting me know how good this feels. I have a brother who could have told me about these secret pleasures, if only I'd asked.

Remembering my training through the fog of lust, I reach between us and wrap my hand around our cocks. A shudder racks me at the overwhelming euphoria of holding us both in my grip. It's so intimate, so private, so trusting that another man is letting me manhandle his body with mine. And then I stroke.

"Oh, my gosh," Dami wheezes. "Oh, yeah."

Peppering my jaw, he works his way up my neck, licking beneath my ear. I can feel his heartbeat in his cock and where my lips ravage his jugular, feeding off his noises. Gripping his hair, I angle his mouth back to mine, the full-bodied connection bursts an eerie sense of power through me I'm scared that I enjoy. It feels like I own him, like I'm controlling him.

After three failed performances, I remind my aching balls it's my mission in life to make Dami come first. Undulating my hips, I quicken my pumping, and snake my free hand up his shirt, gliding it over his ribcage. When I get to his chest, my fingertip grazes his nipple. He groans and arches into my hand. Biting my cheek to stave off the urge to come, I circle his nipple with my fingertip, producing a whimper.

"Uhn, Graham. Yes!"

"You like that?" I whisper at his ear because I truly want to know.

Flicking the pad of my finger over the hardening nub, he writhes again against the backdrop of the *schick, schick* sounds I'm now conducting.

"Yeah! Heck, yeah," he pants, rocking into my grip, his slick heat, sliding through my grip.

His fingers knead and dig into my ass, adding more pressure to each of my grinds against his pelvis, each thrust into my grip. Every time his balls slap against mine a shiver shoots up my spine. I must look like an animal, rutting against him like this, but I don't care.

Clamping his nipple between my thumb and index finger, I can't explain why, but I fulfill the urge I have to lick his ear. His cry gives me both a start and a thrill as he clutches my ass and arches off the couch. Why the hell didn't he tell me about that move during the first lesson?

I do it again, and another time on his other nipple. Head thrown back, neck straining, he lets out this guttural sound as his taut body arcs into mine. Holy hell. I could watch that all night.

Clamp. Lick. Moan.

Clamp. Lick. Moan.

I can't get enough of his reactions. My balls are screaming to release.

"Fuck me, please," he moans against my ear. "Need you to fuck me."

Every piston inside me locks up. I blink, staring at his drugged-up expression. Heavy lids, panting, ravaged lips.

"What?" he rasps, chest heaving.

I don't know if he even realizes what he said, but the plea is written all over his blissed-out face. No one's ever begged me to fuck them before like I'd be putting them out of misery. My body is telling me to fire the gun and save him from the need I helped to stoke, but my heart cripples in on itself, crashing into my stomach.

I *do* want to fuck him, but I don't want it to be because of a lesson. Somewhere along the way, something changed. Sketches, smiles, his giant optimistic attitude and selflessness—I can't pinpoint the one thing that got me. Whatever it was deserves more than rutting him into my couch in a primal exchange of meaningless orgasms. *This*…as good as it feels is just us using each other.

Even if I hadn't just reunited with my conscience, I wasn't able to give Jen what she needed in fifteen years, why would I be able to give him what he needs after one week? He'd probably have to guide my dick and draw me an instruction manual. That's not the way I want him to remember it because, yeah, I absolutely want him to remember it. Maybe he can sow oats, but I'm learning I can't. I mustn't be wired the same way.

"What's wrong?"

"We should stop. We…we need to stop this," I babble, sitting back on my haunches.

The bewilderment on his face is too much. I focus on tucking myself away, so I don't have to feel the sting of his disappointment.

"O-okay. Okay," he repeats, still sounding sex winded. "Are you alright?"

"Yeah. Just…I think I've had enough lessons."

I *haven't*. I want *all* the lessons, but I want to be his only student ever. I know we have no foundation for me to ask that of him, so the best I can do is quit using him even if what he wants is for me to use him.

"Oh. S-sure. Okay," he stammers, sounding anything but sure as he covers himself up.

Standing, I run my hands through my hair, discovering what a mess he made of it. "I…sorry. I'm sorry. I just…I don't think I need any more lessons."

Sitting up, he gives me one of his easy smiles. "Nothing to be sorry for."

"You're…we're cool?"

Cool? Listen to me. I'm such a chump.

"Of course," he replies, so effortlessly it stings.

I have no clue what else you're supposed to say after derailing an emission, so I just nod. "Good. Um, okay. Goodnight."

"Goodnight," he parrots, knees tucked up to his chest, gaze still on me.

This time I close my bedroom door to resist temptation. It's a good thing that I stopped when I did.

Fuck me, please. Need you to fuck me.

The words echo inside my skull. I'm starting to think I should work for Dami instead of the other way around because I realize that I'd do anything he asked of me. Now I just need to figure out how to do it well in case I'm lucky enough for him to ask me again.

CHAPTER 23

Hard hat. Check.

Shirt on. Check.

Not jerking off on Graham's couch anymore. Check.

The thing about Graham's freak out last night, I understood it. To a degree. He's a newbie at this.

There's that saying *you can't teach old dogs new tricks.* I mean, if he wanted to get technical, I'd be happy to let him know I was really, really, *really* enjoying his tricks on the couch. I just need to accept that I'll never get to see him finish one.

It's not my fault he wore sweatpants. Stupid aphrodisiac apparel.

Ugh, but it is totally my fault that my sexed-up brain blurted out what Graham in sweatpants made me want Graham to do to me.

His face, I'll never forget that look on it. Fear, abject horror. I probably scarred him for life.

The thing I don't get? He's all super casual today. Not that I was looking forward to awkward, but what does it mean? I need a *Snapple* bottle cap to tell me my future because I can't figure out this business-as-usual attitude and those polite little smiles.

When he tells me that we're wrapping up early for today to swing by a carpentry business to pick up the interior plans for the kitchen, I all but melt in relief. I am two hours away from cashing my first Brandt and Sons paycheck, which means I am no more than four hours away from hitting the road to Dante's birthday bash.

Hello, orgasms!

We pull up to McDunough Designs on the east side of town. Going over my party packing list in my head, I don't realize Graham is standing outside my door until he says something.

"You want to come in?"

"Oh. Yeah, sure. Sorry, I didn't think you needed me."

He opens the truck door for me. No guy has ever done that for me, and I certainly wouldn't expect my boss to do so.

"We collaborate with these guys sometimes. You might as well meet them in case you ever have to pick up plans someday. They used to build furniture and cabinets but branched off into interior design a few years ago," he explains walking up to the artfully weathered barn that's clearly been updated into a commercial building.

Wow. Two gentleman points to Graham. He's holding the door for me again.

I think Maxie has it all wrong. She said she calls him Graham Cracker because he's so easy to fluster, falling apart like his food namesake, but I think he's more of a Teddy Graham, cute and extremely edible.

Crap. Stop it, Dami. Remember the plan. Operation Orgasm tonight.

Walking up to the empty counter, Graham leans on a forearm and dings the bell. Jutting out one of his narrow hips, his jeans hug his ass.

Man, the guy even leans sexy. That is so not fair. I had my chance to explore all that, and I blew it. Is he ever going to date a man, I wonder? Will the guy be patient with him? Will they know he's only crunchy on the outside, but sweet under all those tough layers?

A devastatingly handsome man with dark slicked-back hair and a face that says *pissed off* is his single expression comes out of the office. White dress shirt, gray slacks, a fancy watch—he screams *Wallstreet*, not *Midwest carpenter*.

A second later a big, bearded guy in a red flannel shirt walks around the corner but stops short when he sees the other guy. "Oh, you got it, boss?"

Fancy Slacks scowls at him, or maybe that's just his natural reaction to everything. Geesh. I don't think I'll be stopping here like ever again.

"Somebody has to," Fancy Slacks growls then turns his attention to us. His cold gaze pauses on me for a millisecond, giving me an icy chill. He must deem me unimportant because he looks to Graham, extending a hand. "Will McDunough. How can I help you?"

"Where's Donny?" Graham asks.

Folding his arms, Will replies flatly, "On a leave of absence."

"Dami?" a familiar voice calls from my left.

When I look up, the big, burly lumberjack guy is still standing further down the long counter, but he's facing me now. He looks really… Oh, no way.

"Brennan?" I call, my throat closing up when he smiles at my recollection.

Crap. Not only can I feel Graham eyeballing me, but so is Captain Anger Management.

"Long time no see," Brennan calls. "How are you?"

Crap. Crap. Crap.

Flashing a polite smile to Graham and Will to excuse myself, I make my way to the end of the counter before Brennan can get any ideas about coming over.

The thing about hooking up with people on dating apps when you're home from college for the summer is that you shouldn't have to see them again unless you swipe them on the app. This is so awkward.

Brennan is a super nice guy. Like *the* nicest, but he's not my type, and I have lots of types. There was that instant chemistry of knowing we both wanted to get laid when we hooked up last summer, but the second time? I shouldn't have done a repeat, but there weren't many options within driving radius on the *Man About Town* app.

"Good," I reply quietly to set the volume when I reach the end of the counter. "I didn't know you worked here."

"Yeah, for a few years now."

Cringing internally, I force myself to ask. "Do you…live in Olympus?"

"Yeah. I moved here a few years ago to take care of my grandmother. When she passed away, I'd kind of fallen in love with the place by then."

I remember him saying something about that when we met, but not that he was from Olympus. What are the odds?

"Oh, that's right. I'm sorry, but I'm glad you're happy here." While all my engines are primed for sexy times at Dante's party tonight, I don't really want to risk Brennan seeking out meet-up number-three. He had this hopeful, longing look in his eyes the last time we parted. Best to stick to safe topics. "So, uh, how do you like working here?"

Running a hand over his beard, he chuckles sardonically and glances over at Will like he's seeing if the coast is clear. "Well, aside from the new boss hating me and thinking I'm his personal whipping boy, it's pretty cool."

I catch said-boss shooting Brennan a look that would fry eggs, and then he growls, "Brennan, if you're about done flirting, maybe you could get back to all that work we're behind on."

My face goes red, catching the curious expression on Graham's face. How freaking bold of that guy to assume I'm gay *or* flirting.

To Brennan's credit, he doesn't fluster. He may have been shy when our clothes were off, but he had a jolly wit while they were on. Straightening up, he wields it at Will with a high-wattage grin. "Almost."

Whoa. Graham looks pissed. Will looks like he wants to murder both of us. I may be promiscuous, but that's not information I want spread around to the Brandts' work contacts.

"Sorry about that," Brennan whispers. "I didn't mean to embarrass you. He's straight and an asshole to boot. Doesn't like fat people either," he adds, patting his belly. "I couldn't resist."

"It's alright." I laugh, feeling sympathy course through me. Brennan certainly doesn't deserve all that.

"Dami," Graham calls, rolling blueprints up in his hand. "You ready?"

At least my boss isn't a huge dick, and his broody was sexy-broody, not scary-broody. Poor Brennan.

"Yeah. Coming," I call. Turning back to Brennan, I throw him a nod. "Good seeing you."

"You too. Message me sometime, if...you're bored."

Ouch. What a depressing pick-up line.

I shrug. "Sure. Maybe for like a coffee some morning, if you need to get out of the house," I suggest, hoping he'll read the G-rated subtext.

"Yeah," he agrees, but I can tell he got the message.

"Brennan!" Will barks, his expression resembling a warrior prepared for medieval combat. "My office. Now!"

Brennan pinches his eyes closed and sighs, but then gives me a nod and turns away to meet his doom. Dang. I am so glad I didn't apply here, and now I feel like I actually should buy Brennan that coffee just for putting up with the boss from hell.

Back in the truck, Graham heads toward the warehouse. I fidget in my seat, feeling like I've done something wrong, but he says nothing.

"So, that McDonough guy seemed intense," I venture.

Graham's brows quirk thoughtfully. "Yeah, certainly not as easy-going as his brother, Donny. Guess he just moved back to help the family business. I don't think he's too thrilled with the prospect."

"Well, it shows."

"So, how do you know that worker you were talking to?"

"Brennan? Um, well, funny story actually. He and I hooked up a couple times last summer on a dating app, but I haven't seen him since. I didn't even know he was from here." I'm not sure why I feel guilty. Graham knows I sow oats, and it's not like we're dating. It's not like we're even having lessons anymore. He made sure of that last night. To lighten the subject, I add, "So, it looks like the gay population of Olympus is up to five now. A few more and we might get our own population sign."

Okay. I thought that was kind of funny, but he's not laughing. Is the gay population back to four, I want to ask.

He breaks the silence with, "Are you...going to see him again then?"

"Ah, no. He was nice and all, but he didn't really do it for me."

"What didn't do it for you?"

"Well, I kind of got the impression he wanted me to *top*, and I just wasn't feeling it with him."

"*Top?*"

I blink at him a few times to see if he's serious. When he finally glances over, I want to snatch him up and tuck him in my pocket so I can keep him safe. Poor Graham. I had so much to teach him. Maybe even though he doesn't want hands-on anymore, I can at least pass on my knowledge.

Studiously, I explain, "So, *topping* is when you penetrate a guy. You're *the giver*. If you're *bottoming*, it means you're *the receiver*."

"Oh," he lets out on a cough and proceeds to act like he has something in his throat, even giving his chest a pounding.

Red ears, Teddy Graham. I see the reddened ears, I don't say, biting back a smile.

"S-so…he wanted you to…*top him?*"

"Yeah."

"And you…you're not into that?"

"I am. I mean, I've done it a few times before, but I just didn't get the vibe I needed from him to do it."

"*Vibe?* What kind of vibe?"

"Like when I've done it before, it felt like this really intimate, special thing. I mean, someone's trusting you with their body, so it felt… *off* when I did it casually. I know some people feel the same way about bottoming, but for me, topping feels like I'm taking more than when I'm bottoming. I think like maybe if it was my forever guy, I'd feel different, but Brennan felt just like an acquaintance, so I wasn't feeling it. I don't know if that explains it. It's just a personal preference thing. Everybody's different, and both ways are nice."

"No, it, uh…yeah. Makes sense."

When we walk out of the warehouse office fifteen minutes later with our paychecks, my eyes bug at the amount on the paper. My chest is glowing with pride. Not only is the amount more than I thought, but it is a representation of my sweat, sore muscles, exhaustion, and learning curve. I can't wipe the grin off my face.

Graham shoulder-bumps me, smirking at the stupid expression on my face. "Big plans this weekend, *Money Bags?*"

"Yeah." I laugh at being busted, mooning over my first fortune that I didn't have to get from my mother. "I'm going to my friend Dante's for the weekend."

"Who the fuck is Dante?" he snaps.

That…was weird.

Clearing his throat, he adds, "You never mentioned him before."

"Oh. He's my old roommate from college. He's having a big party at his house in Bartlett."

"Oh." He nods, shoving a hand in his pocket as we exit the warehouse.

"What are *you* doing?" I ask, returning his shoulder-check.

"No plans. Probably just go fishing off my dock." Scratching his feather duster, he speaks to the ground rather than me, "You can, uh, come with if you want. I could pick you up in the morning."

Fishing? He wants to take me fishing? Why do I have the feeling he doesn't take many people fishing with him? I am almost sorry I'm going to get laid tonight instead. What is wrong with me?

"Thanks, but I'm probably staying in Bartlett tonight. I won't want to drive after drinking."

He nods, kicking a few rocks where we stop between our vehicles in the parking lot.

"Must be a good friend if you'd drive all the way to Bartlett," he muses, leaning on his truck.

"Yeah. We're pretty tight. It's going to be epic. His dad basically gives him free rein over this mansion. He does these parties a few times a year. He gets a DJ and everything. I danced till I dropped last time."

"Sounds cool."

He doesn't sound like he thinks it's all that cool, but I think it'd be super cool to see Graham at one of Dante's parties. Maybe he could let loose in an atmosphere like that and shed some of his inhibitions. Brick masonry is basically his life. The fishing thing is cool, but how is he ever going to find himself just going to job sites and out to the lake by his house?

Now there's an idea. The only gay people Graham has ever been around that I know of are his family. It would do him good to socialize with non-relatives in the gay community. He's certainly not going to get that here unless he calls up Brennan.

Ew. I don't like that idea. Graham deserves better than my sloppy seconds and one lone gay friend in Olympus. Besides, he could still use supervision. If he goes with me, I'll be there on-hand to answer questions. It'll be like a field trip.

Heh! Maybe I'm not such a crap teacher after all.

"You could come with me if you want."

"*Me?* To some kid's birthday party?"

Geesh. How young does he think I am? "He's not a kid. He's a computer engineer who works for *BarTech,* and he invites people of all ages to his parties. *Lots of gays,*" I emphasize, nudging his shoulder. "It'd be good for you. You could mingle."

Scoffing, he cards his fingers through his hair. "That doesn't sound like my scene."

"What? The *gay part*?" I ask, my stomach squirming.

"No. The dancing and mingling and lots of strangers part."

"Oh, come on. Live a little. Then you can go back to being boring and anti-social if you hate it."

Pursing his lips, his eyes crinkle at the corners, absorbing my low blow. He is totally not boring, but the man needs a shove.

"Okay. Fine."

"Really?"

"Sure."

Yes! Graham is officially stepping into my world. It's a sign he's still comfortable with his sexuality. He may not want my lessons anymore, but there's a comfort in knowing he's still on the same team as me. I mean, who knows? If I don't find my forever guy, I could live with helping Graham out now and then once he finds his stride.

CHAPTER 24

Graham

Why the fuck does he need a body-sized duffel bag? And I thought *the bookbag* was too much. What am I getting myself into?

"Are you staying the night or a month?" I ask, opening the tailgate of my truck for him. At least he gave up insisting we could take his *Matchbox* car.

"It's supplies," he says, laughing as he hoists the load into the truck.

"Anything illegal in there?"

"In which country?"

Jesus. I'm going to a freaking college kid's party with…basically, a college kid. Infatuation makes people stupid.

A half hour down the road, Dami pulls his phone out of his backpack. Yeah. He brought the backpack too. Does he ever go anywhere without that thing?

He starts slapping my arm, making me swerve. "No way! Oh, my gosh!" he squawks.

"What?"

"I sold three drawings!" He angles the phone toward me, showing me his earnings. "*Three!* Holy cow! Can you believe that?"

"Yeah, actually, I can. See? I told you."

I never knew another person's smile could fill up the empty parts of you with sunshine. He's practically bouncing in his seat. The disbelief on his face has me shaking my head. Maybe he'll never know how great he is, but the ache inside me to be able to be there to remind him expands in my chest. I was just accepting that my body wanted men. I never expected that would turn into my soul wanting one in particular. Once again, something else I don't know if I can give him.

How would I tell my family who've seen me married to a woman all my life, that now I want a man? Mom and Dad are some of the easiest going people I know, but how do you do it, shatter the mold you presented to the world? It was different for Aiden and Maxie. They were much younger when they did it. They weren't previously married to a different gender. They haven't spent the last ten years hearing all the homophobic slurs I hear at local bars, because as ignorant as those people are, they're also cowards who won't say things to someone's face.

When Thor and I would go out in the Navy, I'd hear it all the time. I don't know if people assumed because Thor was this big buff dude, he couldn't be bisexual or what. He'd shrug it off and refuse to let me get in a fight over it, so we didn't end up in the brig. Part of me thinks I'd fight the world for Dami, but sickeningly I think a bigger part of me knows that's just a hero's dream. Could I actually live it, or would it pilfer all the joy out of being together?

Glancing over at a rustling noise, I catch Dami pulling his sketchpad out of his bookbag and chuckle. "You worried you need to replenish your stock?"

Blushing he grins at me. "Maybe?"

"What are you going to draw?"

"It's probably not a good time to draw. If you hit any bumps, my lines'll be messy. I could draw you again for practice."

"Oh, so it's okay to hit a bump and draw a hooked nose as long as it's just mine. I see how you are."

"I was just going to practice," he says, chuckling and flipping the pad open to a clean page.

I like the thought of his eyes and thoughts on me. I'll try any tactic that keeps his mind focused on me instead of the snake pit of gay men that we're barreling down the highway toward.

Shrugging, I add casually, "Go ahead. I don't mind."

"Yeah?"

"Sure. I'll even sit still."

His snicker gives me goosebumps. I imagine he's the kind of person who could even wake up laughing. What would it be like to witness that every morning? Blue-eyed joy and perfection.

Two hours later, we pull into the northern city of Bartlett. As I read street signs to guide me through the directions I memorized, Dami sits up and tucks his pencil back into his backpack.

"All done," he declares, turning his sketchpad toward me.

I expected it would be some boring picture of my profile while I was driving, boring but impeccably drawn, of course. Darting my head from the road to the sketch and back several times so I don't kill us, his creation is nothing short of mesmerizing. The sketch is of me looking at him with a little smile on my face. The only way he could have done that is if his mind is somewhat photographic. His talent doesn't cease to amaze me. Plus, that smirk in my depiction makes me wonder if that's how he sees me. It's been the running theme amongst my family that I'm moody. I certainly see happiness when I look at Dami, and the thought that it's reciprocal is a balm on my soul.

We're spending the night together somewhere. I don't know how much physical happiness I can give him in one evening given the fact that I didn't get to look up gay sex techniques I planned to *Google* search after last night's fiasco. I can only hope there's a part of him that will hold out for an old, inexperienced man with good intentions and no idea how to make them happen.

"Don't sell that one," I murmur before I can think better of it.

"No way. I'm keeping it."

My breath catches at his quick reply. His face blooms, and then he clears his throat and tucks his sketchpad away. Maybe all hope isn't lost.

I can hear the bass thumping from Dante's backyard all the way to where we parked on the front lawn. This is going to be a blast.

Graham looks wary, glancing up at all the lit-up windows of the massive house. Tucking his hands into his pockets, he blows out a breath and positions himself between me and the walk up leading to the front door as I collect my backpack.

"Hey, hold up," I tell him, heading to the back of his truck. "I need to grab my duffel bag."

Frowning, he comes over and unlocks the truck bed cover so he can let down the tailgate. The glow of interior lighting in the house casts shadows across his black corduroy button-up. The top two buttons are undone, showing his white thermal shirt underneath. I know it's a bit *nipply* out tonight—seriously, I can see my nipples poking the snug t-shirt I wore—but he's going to sweat his ass off in all those layers once we get to dancing.

"Are we staying here? I thought we'd go to a hotel or something?"

"Yes and no. It's a camping party."

"A what?"

What's with that look? Did I not mention this to him? I thought I did.

"A camping party," I clarify. "Dante's one rule is that no one sleeps in the guest rooms, so he doesn't have to worry about the house getting trashed."

"Are you fucking kidding me?"

"No. Everybody does it." Sprinting the few paces to the fence gate of the giant backyard, I swing it open to reveal what I knew would be plenty of partygoers already set up on the lawn. "See. There're tents all over the backyard."

Geesh. His face looks like a bulldog's right now.

"I'm *not* fucking sleeping in a tent."

"But you're like an outdoorsman. You're in nature all the time."

"Yeah, and I'm thirty years old. Do you know what happens when a thirty-year old sleeps on the hard ground?"

Is this a trick question? My assumption is that he just falls asleep like everyone else.

Graham lets out a long breath and burrows his fingers into his eyes. "Nevermind," he grumbles, wrenching his Navy logo-adorned gym bag out of his truck.

Rushing back over, I hoist my duffel over my other shoulder. "It's okay. I brought sleeping bags and pillows. They're soft."

"Good. I can bury my head under them when I try to go to sleep, listening to drunk people all around me."

Is he serious? Did this man never party in his life?

"Oh, my gosh. You have so many issues."

Leading my grumpy plus-one into the backyard, we stop briefly when I find Dante. He could have done a better job of not giving me that shit-eating grin when he put two and two together about who Graham is. I didn't even kiss and tell, so it's not like he knows Graham is getting lessons from me. *Was*…getting lessons. Right. Operation Orgasm is in effect.

First, I need to get our happy home set up for the evening, so Graham has a safe place to crash once he lets loose. I find a spot a further away from most of the other tents to give Graham the anti-social space he seems insistent upon.

I don't get that. It's a party. How do you avoid people at a party? Why did he come?

After I poke myself in the eye with one of the tent braces and collapse the canopy on my head, Graham finally quits pouting and steps in to help. He's a freaking boy scout, a sexy ass boy scout. I try to shove the vision of him hunting down a squirrel and roasting it over a fire for me from my mind. I mean, who even eats squirrels? That's just the weirdest sexual fantasy ever.

Ten minutes later, the tent is set up and all our gear is inside. Graham goes all military on me, sprawling out both of our sleeping bags and pillows next to each other, perfectly lined up, and even smooths out the wrinkles. Do I need to add anal retentive to my kink list?

"I'm really glad you came," I tell him, but when the silence between us stirs that heat inside of me, I know it's time to get my head in the game.

Graham came to explore his first gay social outing, not for me to ogle him until I want to beg for more lessons. There are plenty of other tents here, plenty of dark corners, plenty of rooms in the house Dante wouldn't mind if his best friend used just long enough for me to take care of some overdue business before I turn in with my former protégé for a night's sleep.

The way I see it, this operation has two parts.

One—hang with Graham long enough to get him to loosen up, so he can go off and have fun. Maybe he'll find some older gay who builds things and hates cats. Schmoozing will help him see he's not alone in this.

Two—discreetly take care of sexy times so I'm good to go until Mr. Forever comes along or…in case Graham decides to resume lessons again someday.

Grabbing his hand, I start toward the back patio where the strobe lights are blazoning a trail of electric light. "Come on. Let's go dance."

"I'm not a good dancer."

He resists the tug I give him, so I try again. "It's fine. No one's going to judge you here."

He starts moving, but grumbles, "I'm not into this new poppy shit."

The DJ is playing "Can't Get You Out of My Head". That's like one of the founding songs of pop music. He's such a character.

"What are you talking about? It's Kylie Minogue. This is old. You should know it."

I get a look for that. If he doesn't like being called old, he should stop acting like he's old. We reach the edge of the patio. It feels like I'm pulling dead weight, but I get Graham's feet to step onto the concrete. As usual, I'll have to be the initiator.

Draping my arms over his shoulders, I start getting down, throwing out head nods to people I recognize. Except, I notice a few amused and curious looks cast my way. Graham's barely moving. His hips are shifting back and forth, but I wouldn't call it dancing. A mother swaying her hips when she holds a baby has more moves than him. His shoulders are tense underneath my forearms.

Wow. Look at that face. Staring down at our feet like he's solving equations, his mouth is set in a tight grimace. No wonder everyone's sending me sympathetic looks.

"Dude, it's like dancing with a robot," I joke. "People will think I'm horrible company."

"I told you I can't dance," he seethes, glancing around.

"It's fine. Just relax a little. Enjoy yourself."

Sighing, he rolls his shoulders and gives me a tight smile. I shift, forcing him to turn on occasion so we don't look like we're at a junior high dance. Someone bumps into my shoulder.

"Hey, Dami! What's up?" some guy named Noah or Trevor who flirted me up during the last party beams, one hand draped across his partner's chest.

"Hey, how's it going?" I throw him a chin-nod. He gives me a definite once-over that looks promising. I'll have to put him on tonight's options list.

"Save me a dance, will you?" he asks as Graham and I shift away for more room.

"Yeah. Sure." Smiling at Graham, I motion over my shoulder. "See. Everyone's friendly here."

"Yeah, clearly," he grunts.

Laughing, I hip-check him and tug a lock of his hair. "They are. Just chill out. It's Friday. Come on. You worked all week. Let it all go."

Nodding, he rests one hand on my hip, but his attention's not on me. His eyes scan the other guests suspiciously. His touch has all the heat of a coroner performing an autopsy. His robotic hip-shifting doesn't improve. In fact, it gets worse. He looks positively miserable.

"Are you even trying to have fun?" I query.

"Yeah."

"Because it doesn't look like it. You didn't have to come, you know."

Nostrils flaring, he stops moving all together. "This was your idea. I could be at home on my couch right now."

Ouch. Geesh. No lessons. No dancing. No fun. I give up.

"Fine. Do you want to leave?"

"No," he heaves, gripping his neck, eyes darting everywhere. "Just… have fun. I'll…I'll go mingle." He flashes me a smile, but it seems forced.

"You're sure?"

"Yeah. Go dance your ass off. It's just not my thing."

"I can go mingle with you if you want," I offer.

"No. I don't need a babysitter. Enjoy the party. I'll go find a beer."

"Alright. Good. Mix it up. Make some friends," I suggest. "I'll see you later?"

"Yeah. Later." He smiles, giving my shoulder a squeeze.

Good. Crisis averted. See. I knew he could do this. It kind of feels like I just let a puppy out of a moving car, but that's probably only because he looks so wary. It'll be good for him. A hundred percent.

Now, if I hurry up with part-two of this operation, I might have time to try for another dance with Graham after he's loosened up a bit. I bet he has all kinds of questions by the end of the night. This is going to make for great conversation on the job site next week. I can feel it. I seriously have the best ideas.

CHAPTER 26

Graham

Now I understand the phrase odd duck. I am definitely the odd duck at this party. Dami was right. There're people of all ages here, even some I heard a guy refer to as sexy silver foxes. I wouldn't go that far, but maybe gray hair just isn't my thing yet.

Part of me feels liberated like I'm walking for the first time on the planet I was meant to inhabit. Another part of me says this is all wrong because aside from not being a people person, the only one I want to talk to is out dancing his ass off on the patio with everyone but me.

I can dance, for the record. Pop music just isn't in my bones. Freaking college kid's party. I have it bad if I let him drag me here.

Like an old creepy veteran, I've circled the perimeter three times, idly checking for threats because it seemed like the only natural thing for me to do at a place where I have no idea how to fit in. Whatever Dante's dad does sure as hell pays more than building brick buildings. The place has to be on at least twenty acres of wooded property. A Wisconsin mansion in the woods. How the hell can I compete with that? Dami's probably lived more than I ever have if he's been to parties like this before.

One look at the way that guy on the dance floor eyed him up and down and I felt like a shrimp next to a piranha. That look said that guy knows what to do and is willing to do it. I am so out of my element.

All I can do is occupy myself while Dami has his fun and get myself in a better mood before I link back up with him. Maybe we can just be weird friends who messed around once. Clearly, we're not on the same wavelength if this is the kind of entertainment he enjoys. I'd never be able to make him happy.

Grabbing another beer from an ice trough, I make my way to some open patio chairs around a free-standing fire pit close to the back of the house. Two shirtless guys sprint past me, laughing. One catches up to the other and pinches his ass. They laugh some more and toss their arms across each other's backs. Like I could ever do that with Dami in Olympus. Who was I kidding? I mean, his parents don't even know he's gay yet. What would we have left? Holing up in my house every night? Plus, he'd probably be jerking off on my couch all the time since I'm too old to keep up with his sexual prowess.

Right. Back to square-one. *Just fucking drink, Graham.*

Settling into one of the padded patio chairs, I give a nod to two guys occupying the chairs to my right. They're clothed and calm-looking, staring at the fire. My kind of people, mellow.

The younger one reaches his hand behind the older one's neck and whispers something. Fuck. Now they're kissing. Getting up, I scan the back of the house for another place to sit and drink.

"You don't have to go on account of us," the older man says, his salt and pepper hair, glinting in the firelight.

"Yeah, it was just a love peck. I promise we're not going to give you a show," the younger guy with spiky hair adds.

"Sorry," I say, casually reclaiming my seat. "I just didn't want to intrude."

The older guy smiles thoughtfully. "Not big on PDA, are you? We aren't either. That's why we're the boring couple who sits by the fire pit."

"Uh, no. Guess I'm not."

"Hardin," the older guy says, extending his hand.

"Patrick," the younger one adds, smiling and tilting his chin.

As I introduce myself, my eyes track Hardin's hand as he rests it on Patrick's leg above his knee. What an unlikely couple.

Hardin's all buttoned up in a sweater vest, a freaking sweater vest. Patrick with his spiky black hair and baggy jeans looks like a groupie for a rock band. The obvious age-gap takes a backseat to their contrasting appearances. I thought Dami and I were too displaced in years, but these two clearly have us beat in more ways than one.

"You a friend of Dante's?" Patrick asks.

"No. Uh, my…" What is Dami? My friend? My former make-out partner? My sex-ed teacher? "My friend is," I supply. "I'm just along for the ride."

"Looks like you fell off the ride," Patrick says, chuckling.

Blushing, I'm grateful for the cover of darkness and the orange glow from the fire. "Yeah. This isn't really my thing. Dami's off dancing. I didn't want to spoil his fun."

"Oh, you know Dami?" Hardin perks up.

How the fuck does he know Dami or how well, I should say? "Yeah. We work together."

"Really? I work with Dante. What do you two do?"

"I'm a brick mason. Dami just started a few weeks ago."

"Oh, what a fantastic trade to be in. They don't build things like they used to," Hardin expounds, turning to Patrick. "See, brick is still in fashion."

Patrick snorts and squeezes Hardin's hand. "Just because I looked at *one* pre-fab doesn't mean I don't want a house that's built to last."

Smirking at me, Hardin rolls his eyes. "Kids."

Fucking fantastic. I just got accepted into the silver fox club. As Dami might say, that is so not cool. While I'm grateful to have found some easy conversation while Dami's busy shaking his ass, that is not a title I want just yet. I'd like to think I have a few more years of being, I don't know, more eligible. What am I saying? First, I need to figure out how to be eligible.

"So, how did you two meet?" I can't keep from asking. I'm sure it's an interesting story.

"Well, it's not a very interesting story," Patrick chimes. "He needed a mover after he got divorced, and I worked for the moving company he called."

"And he took *forever*," Hardin adds with what I assume is false annoyance.

"Hey! You liked the way I carefully placed each of those boxes down in your apartment. I was just trying to be helpful when I stuck around to suggest how you should set up the place."

Hardin barks out a laugh. "He means he was trying to get me to look at his ass every time he bent over and get me to picture what he'd look like on all of my furniture."

Whoa. I get a visual in my head of how their courtship played out. It's…actually kind of amusing, and I find myself chuckling along with them as they banter playfully. They make it look so effortless, and on top of that, they look genuinely smitten with each other.

"How long have you been together?" I ask, remembering they said something about building a house.

"Five years," Patrick supplies. He leans back and stretches coyly, glancing at Hardin. "Yup. I ended up in that apartment after we'd been dating about a year, but now we're building a house, so we'll get to re-enact out meet-cute."

"Congratulations," I offer, imagining the house Dami and I are building, but in my mind, it's furnished, and we're in it. How crazy is that? I've only really known him a matter of weeks. I must sound like a damn stalker.

Speaking of stalking, I scan the crowd on the dancing area for my *friend*. Bodies are moving in liquid motions that I could never perform. The strobe lights flicker off bare chests. Is going shirtless recommended at a gay dance party? Because half of the people out there seem to have forgotten it's like only fifty degrees out tonight.

Finally, I find Dami's fluffy hair and that snug ass pink t-shirt he wore. Pink. Who in the hell knew a guy could make a pink t-shirt look hot? I'm so fucked if he turns me on even when he's wearing flamingo. You can see his damn nipples poking through that thing. Did he buy it when he was in high school?

Hardin asks something, but it's just a background noise to the thumping of the pop music as I watch that guy from earlier who bumped into Dami, snake his hands around Dami's waist. Way low around Dami's waist. My stomach twists in on itself, watching Dami smile at him, slinking an arm over the guy's shoulder the way he did to me just two hours ago.

"Graham?" Patrick calls.

"Sorry, what?"

"We just asked if you had a special someone," Hardin amends.

Clearing my throat to get it to work right again after it closed up watching that horrid dance show, I reply, "Um. No. Twice divorced to the same woman."

Fuck it. What does it matter at this point if anyone here knows? These two guys have been pretty cool to me, but I'll probably be voted off Gay Island from that confession.

"Wow. You must have really loved her," Patrick gapes.

"Yeah. I did, or I do. It's…it's complicated."

When I glance back over at Dami, his partner's hands are on his ass. They're on Dami's perky ass, hips grinding together. Gripping the armrests of my chair, I suppress a growl. My brain says that's *my perky ass*.

Forcing my gaze away, I breathe in through my nose and focus on the fire. This is torture. What was the point in accepting that I'm attracted to men, if the one I'm most attracted to would rather sow wild oats than put up with my lackluster bedroom confidence? Granted, I'm the one who pumped the brakes, but he certainly hasn't even flirted with me since then. I had hope for a second when he said he wouldn't sell that sketch he did of me in the truck, but now that his ass is being tenderized by another dude's hands, hope has freaking fled Gay Island.

"Does…complicated have to do with somebody on the dance floor?" Hardin ventures.

My head starts to shift instinctively both craving and fearing another view of Dami and his partner. I stop myself and flick my gaze to the friendly couple for a second. "Maybe. I don't know. I…I'm new at this," I confess and find myself scoffing. "I don't think I have as much to offer as the competition."

"Oh, I doubt that," Hardin soothes.

My smile this time is genuine. Dami was right. There are nice people here. "That's generous of you to say, but I'm afraid it's the truth."

Patrick leans forward, resting his elbows on his knees, his expression turning serious for the first time since he introduced himself. "No way, man. Don't be like that. I'd just figured out I was bi when I met Hardin. I didn't know what in the hell I was doing, but as soon as I saw him, I knew I wanted him. Sure, I was scared, but if you find something you know will make you happy, you've at least got to go for it, otherwise you'll never know if you missed your opportunity."

It's shocking that wisdom comes from the younger half of this couple. Hardin gives Patrick this heart-eyed expression that says without a doubt, he's happy Patrick made that effort for them. Watching them kiss again, I no longer feel like an intruder now that they've shared a piece of their story but rather a witness to something beautiful and maybe even sacred.

I might never know why I wasn't able to feel this way about Jen, or why after what's basically a blink in time, I feel it for a man who seems like he'd be the least appropriate for me, but maybe Patrick's right. I've spent my entire adult life doubting what I wanted. There's no doubt what I want now. I just need to figure out how to stop doubting myself before he slips through my fingers.

First thing's first. I need to get over there before that asshole's hands violate any more of my favorite perky ass.

CHAPTER 27

Part-two of Operation Orgasm isn't going as I planned. After Graham stomped off, I didn't foresee running into Dante again so soon. We must have shot the shit for almost an hour.

He's my best friend. It's his birthday, and I haven't seen him since graduation. It would have been rude to dodge him to get laid, I remind my libido.

It was a sweet bonus that he loved the sketch I did of him. I now have six custom requests after he showed my drawing to everyone within hearing distance. I'm going to need my wrist stamina more than ever.

Like a good former teacher, I had to at least attempt to look for Graham after that. I have no clue what he was up to. I couldn't find him anywhere. I checked the truck three times, the house, and the backyard. It wasn't until a half hour ago when I finally spotted him by one of the fire pits, but he's talking with Hardin and Patrick Gentry, so I'm comforted by knowing he's in good hands.

In the last thirty minutes, I've been offered a blow job, a hand job, dinner, and even a threesome. My luck is fire tonight. Except…I have no interest in any of those propositions.

Hand Job guy was good-looking, but I just…I don't know. I happened to glance over at Graham and remembered our hand jobs, and the prospect kind of turned me off.

It's weird. I almost felt guilty like I should save hand jobs for Graham. Ha! That's so ridiculous.

It's why I finally shook off my funk and pressed on when Trevor-slash-Noah asked me to dance. I probably should ask him his name again.

He's definitely easy on the eyes. Great body. Close-cut, curly brown hair. A smile that speaks of illicit things. Yeah. He's absolutely down for what I need. A bit handsy on the ass grabbing, but I just want to get laid, not marry the guy.

There's just one problem. I've been hard for the last two weeks straight. What is up with my dick tonight?

I'm barely at half-mast even with Trevor-slash-Noah's grinding and grabbing. Are my interests changing? Doesn't he like kissing?

A hand clamps down on my shoulder and tugs. A shot of heat floods my belly. Finally, my body is reacting the way it should to a willing male. Trevor-slash-Noah looks past my shoulder, and I realize there's three hands on me. The two on my ass haven't moved. The third one is a new addition.

"Dami," a deep voice sets my pulse to a purr.

Unfastening myself from my dance partner, I turn around to find Graham. If I could only buy one word to describe him, it would be haggard. His face looks like someone set their phaser to stun, and he took a direct hit.

"Hey, is something wrong?"

His gaze flickers to Trevor-slash-Noah who's still trying to hump my hip. Geesh, can't the guy wait two minutes for me to talk to my friend?

Looking back to me, mouth still hanging open like he forgot the ability to speak, Graham swallows then slings his arm over my shoulder. "I drank too much," he says pulling me with him as he starts walking off the patio.

Oh, crap. That explains what he was doing the last two hours.

"Hey! Where you going?" Trevor-slash-Noah calls.

"I'll be right back," I reply, slinking my arm around Graham's waist.

His gait seems normal as I steer us toward the tent. "Are you going to be sick?" I ask, but he just shakes his head, focused on the ground in front of us like he's dazed.

I get the tent unzipped and follow him inside. Once he's settled on his ass on his sleeping bag, I work on his boots.

"How much did you drink?"

His gaze darts back and forth between my face and where I'm undoing his laces. "Three beers. Maybe four." He shrugs.

Tossing his boots aside, I recollect that's about the same as I had, and I've only got a minor buzz going.

"And you're drunk?"

"No. I'm just...tired," he says on a sigh, running his hand down his face. "I didn't want to be out there anymore."

Shoot. Here I thought he'd finally gotten the hang of mingling.

"Did you have a bad time?"

"No," he adds thoughtfully. "I met this couple, Hardin and Patrick?"

"Yeah. They're super cool."

"Yeah. They are." Finally, a smile. Nodding to the tent door, he adds, "Who was your friend?"

"Uh. Trevor, I think. Or Noah," I correct with a laugh. "I can't remember. It was kind of loud."

Grimacing, he flips his sleeping bag open and lies down. The party lights cast just enough of a glow to give the tent a soft amber hue, making him appear warm in the shadows. I fidget as he unbuttons his corduroy, stripping down to just his thermal shirt. He's serious about settling in for the night, apparently.

It's only ten o'clock. There is way more time for party favors to be had out there for one sex-deprived apprentice mason.

What to do? What to do?

He's always going on about how old he is, and he did fall asleep during that movie the other night. I bet he passes out in like ten minutes. I could totally go back out and see if I can muster some *feels* for Trevor-slash-Noah or someone else and then creep back in without waking him up.

As long as I get out of here and stop ogling how inviting Graham looks all nestled in this tent, I can make that happen. I *have to* make that happen.

Seriously, this crush and its powerful mating lure are going to kill me. Does the guy shower in soulmate pheromones? Because he's making it difficult to leave the homey ambiance that he gives this tent.

"So…you're good?" I force myself to ask. "Not sick or anything?"

"No." He smiles, tucking his hands behind his head. "Just a long day."

Perfect. Great. There's my green light.

Rip off the bandage, Dami. Get back out there, far away from one-sided releases that are giving you tendonitis.

"Alright!" I chirp, turning toward the tent flap. "Well, goodnight!"

"Where are you going?"

Crap. Crap. Crap.

"Back to the party," I let out casually.

Frowning, he sits up. "You're going to leave me here?" The way he asks, you'd think I left him to be mauled by alley cats.

"You said you were fine."

"Yeah, but…aren't you tired? It's late."

"No."

"Well," he sputters, glancing at the tent wall, "*why* are you going back out there?"

Dang it. Do we really have to do this? Maybe it's best not to lie.

"Um, because I'm young. I have needs."

"*Needs?*"

"Needs that *need* to be *satisfied*."

Is he just going to gape at me all night like I've got an STD? So… awkward.

Okay, I'm just going to go. He can't be afraid of the dark. He'll be fine. I certainly can't suffer through lying awake next to him on a bed of blankets and not want to touch him. This is for the best for both of us. Pivoting, I make to exit, but I never stop spinning.

Hands latch onto my shoulders, whirling me around in a complete circle until Graham and I have changed positions. A hard body tackles me to the tent floor in a move so hot and swift it ought to be in a Kama Sutra book, but my one non-horny brain cell says, *danger!*

So, I yelp, "Whoa! What are you doing?"

"Satisfying your needy ass," he rasps, crushing his mouth over mine.

Hands cradling my face, every inch of Graham pressing me into the ground as his tongue carves around mine, I let out an embarrassing moan. Why does he always have to feel so good?

My horny brain cells jolt to life and call an urgent meeting. Not that I mind as my cock thickens in my jeans, but *what* is he doing?

Pushing at his shoulders, I manage to break this super-hot kiss. His lust-hazed eyes focus on mine.

"What?" he rasps.

"I thought you said we were done with lessons."

Frowning, he glances at my lips. "I…changed my mind, and…clearly you need…*something*."

This could either be a really good thing or a really bad thing, I muse as his thumb strokes my jaw. Does he feel obligated to satisfy me?

"You don't have to do this because of what I said."

"I don't mind. You can get what you need from me."

Shoot. While a big part of me is celebrating him re-enrolling in the *Damiano School of Love*, the twenty-three-year-old-sore-wrist part of me reminds me I will likely be left sexually frustrated again.

"I don't mean to sound ungrateful," I preface, "but I'd really like more than a hand job while I have this weekend away from home."

Judging by the way his breath hitches and his jaw falls open, he got the message. I knew it. He's still shocked by the idea of touching a man beyond kissing and petting.

"I didn't mean I expected *you* to," I clarify delicately. "I'm just saying, I can get that here from someone who's comfortable with it and not feel bad about it afterward like I corrupted a confused man. You need time to ease into things. I get it. I just…kind of need to take care of something while I have the chance."

His mouth forms a thin line, nostrils flaring. "Are you done?"

Geesh. No need for him to look all pissy. I thought I presented that delicately.

"I…yeah. That's pretty much the gist of it."

Yikes. He's getting up. Why do I have that tossing-a-puppy-out-of-a-car feeling again? The loss of his weight on me snuffs out the warmth in my belly.

Whoa. What is he…

Air hits my stomach as he tugs my shirt up and settles on his knees between my legs. He's staring at my lower half like he's trying to decipher a code.

Did I push him too far? Is he going to cut out my kidney with his pocketknife?

"What…what are you doing?"

Licking his lips, he keeps his gaze locked on my pelvis. "Thinking."

"Thinking about what?"

"About what to do with your cock."

About what to do with my… Oh. My gosh!

The feather duster has landed!

His lips brush the skin below my belly button. The coarse hair of his goatee tickling my sensitive skin sends little bursts of static jolting to my nuts. His fingertips skirt underneath the waistband of my underwear as his mouth maps a trail across the flesh just above my jeans.

His fingertips skirt underneath the waistband of my underwear as his mouth maps a trail across the flesh just above my jeans.

Groaning in relief, I shiver at every brush of his fingertips between my skin and the elastic as his hot breath ghosts my navel. Is this really happening?

"Take them off," I plead, fumbling with the button of my pants.

Knocking my hand away, he grumps, "Why are you always in a hurry?"

"Because I'm always horny."

Scoffing, he sits up and reaches for my fly with a little smirk on his face. "Slow down, sweetheart."

Sweetheart? He keeps adding to my kink list.

Huffing, I clench my teeth and let my head fall back on the pillow, willing my body to be still. That proves difficult when the feather duster revisits my waistline, while Graham gets last place in the speed race at pulling off pants.

I have no idea how far he's planning to go, but my shirt is half-ridden up, cutting off circulation to my chest. I've had this thing since high school, but my assets look good in snug.

Flamingo pink. Hello, Ma and Pop. Red flag!

I tug it over my head in my impatience as Graham works my jeans off my feet like he's unwrapping a virgin. Can you die from blue balls?

His mouth returns to my stomach, and my breath catches. His fingertips have just breached the elastic of my underwear again and are tugging.

Yes! Oh, yes!

It's go-time!

His kisses blaze a trail down my pelvic bone as the air hits my junk, my painfully hard cock bobbing free. The fabric slides down as I lift my ass. Every brush of it against my leg hairs sends a wave of gooseflesh across my skin as Graham tugs my underwear down past my feet.

I've been naked so many times before with guys, but this is different. We can't even see each other clearly, but I've never felt more exposed. Why does it feel like my first time?

Trembling, I take in the sight of Graham sitting back on his haunches, gazing down at me like I'm a natural wonder. Is he afraid? Is he going to chicken out again?

"Touch me," I whisper. "Please."

Chest rising and falling, his gaze flickers to mine, and he swallows. For a second, I think I've lost him, and it feels like a part of me dies inside, but then his hands move.

Gently, he glides his palms up my thighs. The way he shudders just as hard as I do is a heady thing. Leaning down, his lips touch my thigh and slowly work their way up to the juncture of my hip. It's all I can do to lie still.

His left hand takes a detour. My breath catches in my throat as his fingertips stroke softly up my shaft. Oh, yeah. He's the best student ever!

The feather duster moves, tickling my sensitive juncture, until I feel his hot breath on my cock, making me whimper. Through the shadows, his face is tense with concentration as he hovers there an inch away.

Do it, Graham. You've got this, I shout in my head.

His breath moves away back to my juncture, planting more kisses. Ugh. I'm going to explode from lack of fulfillment.

"Graham," I whine, dropping my head back on the pillow. "You're so mean."

Something hot and wet flicks the slit of my cockhead. My shaft spasms, and I hiss, "Yesss!"

My neck is cramping, popping my head back up again to witness. He hesitates just for a second, and then I watch in awe as his lips part and capture the head of my cock.

Groaning, I drop my skull again and bask in the sensation of every muscle in my body turning to hot butter. His tongue does this little swirl around my tip, and then his heat envelopes me, taking me in halfway.

"Oh, my gosh," I wheeze, diving my fingers into his hair.

He lets out a muffled grunt at my touch, so I stroke his scalp encouragingly. His technique is slow and worshipful even if a bit sloppy.

My hips rock in anticipation. I can't hold back anymore. Graham Brandt's mouth is around my cock. How in the hell could anyone hold back?

Two big palms grip my hips and hold. My body wants to rut into his unchartered territory, but his hold is solid, preventing me from moving things along.

Damn him. How does he keep ahold of his control?

"You're killing me," I groan. "You're going to kill me with my cock."

He pops off with a sordid wet sound. "You don't like it?"

"No. I like it! I like it a lot! I just…like it so much I want more."

"*More?* I just had your whole cock in my mouth. I can't do more if there's no more cock to suck."

Gasping, my mouth falls open. *Hello. Rude!*

"Are you saying I have a small cock?"

"No! What the…" His face scrunches up, and then he sighs. "Why don't you just let me finish? Maybe that's the problem."

"Yes, *please! Finish.*"

I don't care if he's scowling. Seriously, the man is going to give me a medical condition. How much teasing can a guy take?

I'll give him credit though, he drops the argument and dives right back in. Except, it's more wicked little licks and slow draws. He did say he changed his mind about lessons. Maybe now is a good time to throw out a helpful pointer.

Clearing my throat, I stroke his hair and whisper, "And…I won't complain if you go a teensy bit faster."

CHAPTER 28

Graham

Is he kidding me with this shit? Can't a guy have a second of peace to concentrate on his first blowjob?

"Well, now you're lying!" I snarl. "You always complain."

I can just imagine the weak denial that's about to tumble out of his abashed face. As he sucks in a breath to argue with me, I drop my head back down.

"I do *nooot!*" he wails.

Holy shit. I think his cock just hit my tonsils, but at least that shut him up. Suppressing a cough, I suck harder, still astounded by the feel of his slippery, velvet girth on my tongue. It's nothing like I expected. Each slide, each swirl, makes me want to give him more, to take more of his earthy scent and salty taste. I was enjoying savoring the moment, attempting to drive him wild. Wild turned into obnoxiously needy, so this works too.

Now he's groaning his head off. His hips are fighting to buck against my hands like he's losing his mind. With each dirty slick sound of my mouth, each *whimpery* noise from his throat, I feel like a starving animal, feeding before winter.

I want to ask him if he's forgotten about his dance partner now, if he wants to devour me the way I want to devour him. Stroking his thighs, I can't touch enough of him. His hips start to do some of the work, fucking my mouth.

My face is burning at the concept of it, but my dick is harder than *Rebar*. He *wants* my mouth. He actually likes what *I'm* doing.

Slowing to catch my breath, I can feel my jaw tensing. This is so much harder than it looks, but I don't want to fail.

Dami draws his knees up. His feet scoot closer to his ass. I shift my stance, licking another pass around the circumference of his head.

Something brushes my knee, so I shift again to let him get comfortable, but his forearm stays pressed against my knee. Glancing down, his hand almost looks like it's…

Releasing him from my mouth, I whisper, "What are you doing?"

"Nothing," he replies brightly, squeezing my thigh.

Maybe he had an itch. *Way to ruin the mood, Graham.*

Running my hand up his chest, I pepper a few kisses to his stomach because I can't resist the feel of his abs flexing underneath my lips. Flicking his slit like I'm some kind of pro now, I take him in again, groaning at the return of his hot flesh to my mouth. It's so surreal that it feels like it belongs there.

I hear a *slurp* sound that doesn't sound like mine. Dami's elbow presses against my kneecap again. His hand is back down by his ass. I can't see his fingers.

Holy fuck.

"Are you…fingering your ass?"

"No?" he says, even as I watch the erotic sight of him removing a finger from his hole.

"You were! I just saw you."

"So? Don't worry about it. Keep going. You're doing great!"

"Apparently not, if you're doing that!"

"No. It just makes it feel even better," he soothes, rubbing my forearm.

I know when I'm being coddled. This is exactly what I was worried about. My skills mustn't be as good as I thought.

"Well, it's distracting!"

"Then don't look."

Is he for real? "It's hard not to when my face is inches away!"

Scoffing, his lower lip pouts. "Why are you yelling at me?"

"I'm not yelling."

"Well, you're getting mad, and you shouldn't be. I'm just trying to help you get me off."

"I don't need your help."

Glancing down at his hole, I try to consider the prospect. How far in do I go in? Will I hurt him? When I look back up at him, his eyebrows raise.

"Did you want to do it for me?" he asks hopefully.

"Put my finger in your ass?"

"Have you ever done it to yourself?"

I'm embarrassed at how loud I sputter. I must sound like such a prude compared to him. "No."

"Really? Never?"

My cock was hard a minute ago, but the in-depth discussion of all the things I haven't done is taking care of the fear I had of shooting too soon. Gripping my head, I pinch my eyes closed. "Can we stop talking please?"

When I open my eyes, Dami smiles and waggles his brows. "*I* know how you can stop talking."

"Oh, my God. You don't deserve a blow job."

There's only one way to stop his incorrigible words, so I take him in again, hoping the conversation will disappear like a favorite sock in the washing machine. He moans, setting some of my nerves at ease.

Son of a bitch, his arm just bumped into my knee again. Popping up, I heave out a breath. "Really?" I arch a brow, tilting my chin down to where I can tell his finger has once again disappeared. "Am I that bad at this?"

"No. It's got nothing to do with you," he pants.

"It sure doesn't seem that way."

"It just…feels so good that it makes me want to…touch my prostate."

Hearing him grunt like that and seeing him writhe on his digit, has my nuts fluttering again. It's a bizarre sensation coupled with the butterflies in my belly. Licking my lips, I have to force my gaze away from the sight to his eyes again.

"Can you just stop?"

"It's my body! I can do what I want with it," he says all breathy as hell.

Unfuckingbelievable. Does he take hormones or something? How can I keep up with that shit?

"Well, how am I supposed to finger you if your finger's already in there?" I scathe.

Said finger withdraws with a dirty little *squelch* noise. Dami's brows hike. His expression goes all repentant at the concession I just insinuated.

"Oh. Well, you don't have to."

Now he gets humble. "Apparently, I do," I grouse, lowering my head and swallowing the lump in my throat.

I can't concentrate on pleasuring him at two points. That's way too advanced for me, so I kiss the skin around his cock and glide my hand over the curve of his ass. Inching closer to where his cheeks part, I graze my finger delicately through his channel.

I'm touching his ass…like really his ass. I can't believe I'm about to do this. I can't believe I actually want to. I want to hear him grunt like that again but because of *me* and *my* finger.

Circling the rippled pucker, I shudder, feeling it pulse against the pad of my finger as I nervously run my other hand over his nipple. I can feel him watching me as always. Holding my breath, I press at his entrance and feel him tense under my touch.

"Wait! Lube!" he blurts, making me nearly have a heart attack.

Fuck. I didn't even think about that. His slick sound from earlier explains what he was doing with his finger. He was so needy, he probably resorted to slobbering it up.

"I don't have any," I tell him, feeling stupid for even saying it aloud. Why would I have any? Glancing around the tent, I spot his backpack and remember the *schick* sounds he was making on my couch. "Do you have some in your sex backpack?"

"It's not a sex backpack."

The way he protests tells me that's highly bullshit. I snatch it out of his grip and dump it on the tent floor. By the power of *Grayskull* an entire pharmacy's worth of condoms tumbles out along with a giant bottle of lube and…holy shit, a long, green, silicone dildo.

"How much sex were you planning on having this weekend?"

"The box was open! It just looks worse than it is."

Eyeballing the rubber dick, I shoot him a dubious look. Yeah, let's refute that, Dami, I want to tell him.

Instead of looking sheepish, he actually smiles at me. Fuck. There go the eyebrows. That's always the sign of one of his bad ideas.

"You could use *that* instead of your finger," he suggests.

I can't believe I'm crazy about him. Batshit crazy apparently, because I still want to silence him until he's a puddle of moans and panting, so I can see if he gets that bewildered little smile on his face afterward the way he does when I compliment him.

Grabbing the dick, I toss it at the tent wall, so it won't break my concentration by being in my line of sight. He gasps like it's a family heirloom, but I cover his mouth with mine before he can make me lose my nerve with more bad advice. This is the one thing I think I'm good at, so I kiss him until he sounds senseless. Feeling for his family-sized bottle of lube, I flick open the lid and let it douse my fingers, then skirt my hand back to where he insisted that he needs it.

As long as he's not narrating, I can do this. I fucking build buildings all day. I can stick my finger in a horny guy's ass.

Stroking the length of his seam, I graze over his pucker each time I pass. Saying *hello*. Getting acquainted. It's the least I can do before I go pillaging it.

"Are you going to put it in?" Dami whispers against my ear as I kiss his neck.

"I'm working up to it. Relax."

Graze. Hello. Circle, circle. Graze.

He moans, sounding desperate. "Put it in. Put it in. Please. Please. Please."

"Yeah!" a voice outside yells, "Put it in!"

My head pops up so fast, a pain shoots up my neck. "Shut the hell up!" I yell to the wall of the tent.

Two laughing shadows pass by outside. *Memorable*. I wanted the next round of intimacy with Dami to be memorable, so he'd never forget it and want more of me. This is not the type of memorable I had in mind. Digging my fingertips into my eyes, I growl out my frustrations, until I realize what I just did.

"Ah, fuck!"

"What?" Dami asks, sitting up.

Gripping the bottom of my undershirt, I swipe the fabric over the eye I just touched with my finger—the finger I just had pressed to Dami's asshole.

"Am I going get pink eye now?" I wet the hem of my shirt with my mouth and swipe it over my eyelid.

"This is *so* sexy," Dami drawls, sighing and flopping back down on his pillow.

"Yeah? Well, so is pink eye! I was in the Navy, communal living! Have you ever seen a pink eye outbreak? It's like a zombie apocalypse!"

"I'm never going to come," he grumbles, throwing his arm over his uncontaminated eyes.

I just potentially infected my vision with his butt particles, and he's more worried about getting off? That. Is. It!

I don't think. I act.

He lets out a long, breathy groan, his hips arching off the ground as his asshole clenches around my finger. My finger…I freaking stuffed it in to the first knuckle. What the hell is wrong with me?

"Shit! Are you okay?" I freeze, not daring to move and risk hurting him.

"Ye-ah!" he lets out like he just came. "Oh! Thank you!"

Holy hell. His jaw goes slack, a haze taking over his eyes as he blinks at me like I'm a damn superhero. Yes. More of that. I want more of those expressions and sounds.

Bending down, I take him into my mouth. Carefully, I back off from the intense, hot grip he has on my finger and then retrace my path.

Glancing up, it is a sight to behold seeing his head thrown back. He's moaning like he's dying in the best way possible. Gasping, his eyes meet mine, and he plunges his fingers in my hair.

"Graham, oh, my gosh. Oh, my gosh," he pants, cheeks flushed.

I feel like a god at a circuit board. My controls are his cock in my mouth and the way I glide my finger in and out of his snug grip. I pass over a spongey impression and flinch when his entire body jolts.

"Oh! *Oh, my gosh!*"

I want to laugh at all the different ways he can emphasize *oh, my gosh.* Clearly, I've found a spot he likes, and he's treating me to his favorite catch phrase. Growling like a freaking cave man, I set to work faster and harder, determined to oh-my-gosh him until he sees stars.

His cries grow louder. His hips buck and twitch more jerkily. He's snarled my hair into fifty-seven knots, but I don't care. I reach down and have to pinch the head of my cock through my jeans to keep from going over the edge at the sight of his unraveling.

"Graham!" he keens, clenching around my finger. "C-come. Gonna come!"

I can feel him harden and twitch it my mouth. I know it's better if I stay, and I don't want him thinking I'm a snob about fluids. A second later he pulses against my tongue—hot, creamy, and salty. I freeze. I have a second to decide if I want to release his load and all my saliva somewhere.

I swallow and shudder, not at the taste or the sensation, but rather over the realization that I just consumed a part of him. I drink him down again along with the echoes of his high-pitched moans, grazing my finger over that spot inside him that tipped him over the edge. He's freaking beautiful, looking down at me, panting with passion-drunk eyes.

Releasing him and withdrawing, I sit up and wipe my chin. Discreetly, I press the heel of my other hand to my cock. Patrick was right. If you want something, go after it. The way Dami's looking at me brings me peace. I think I finally passed the test I needed to keep him.

Panting, he gets to his knees, and I realize I'm still fully clothed while he's bare ass naked. It's no matter. As rock hard as I am, I'll pass up relief just to get to stare at him like this.

He shuffles forward. I wonder if he's about to kiss me. Latching onto my shoulders, he shoves his knee against the inside of mine and tackles me onto the sleeping bag.

I land with a grunt as his mouth comes down on mine. Chuckling, he comes up and beams at me like he just sold a hundred drawings. I grin back, skimming my fingertips over the smooth skin of his ass.

"You were holding out on me," he teases, reaching for the button of my jeans.

Catching his wrist, I want him to know it's not all about sex, that he can just lay back and enjoy his moment. "You don't have to. I owed you."

Frowning, he props up on his elbows. *Shit. Did I say the wrong thing?*

"Can we stop with the you-don't-have-to comments? I think we're both past that."

My heart unfolds in my chest, setting that desperate fear of losing him free. Cupping his jaw, I draw his mouth down to mine and whisper, "Yeah. Yeah, we are."

CHAPTER 29

Graham lets me take over pulling down his pants. Operation Orgasm officially took a turn. I'm still trembling, my prostate still pulsing. Was not expecting that. I am going to blow this man's mind now in return for his efforts.

Yanking his shirt up over his head, I get a wicked idea when it catches on his elbows. Sliding down his gorgeous, tatted body, I draw my tongue through the seam of his ass with lightning speed. He lets out a stilted cry, hips bucking up so violently it looks like I electrocuted him.

"What the fuck?" he gasps, peeking out at me from under the neck hole of his shirt.

"You don't like it?" I chuckle, dipping my head again to place a kiss on the curve of his ass as I massage his other cheek.

"I…you could have warned me."

"Okay," I preface with a smirk and settle onto my stomach between his muscular thighs. "Graham, I'm going to lick your rim."

Scoffing, his scowl is the last thing I see before I divert my gaze and deliver on my announcement. His pucker twitches. His cheeks clench around my tongue and then relax from his body's natural reflex to seek pleasure. Yup. My boss likes my tongue.

"Yes," I whisper, getting a hit of pure concentrated Graham. "You taste so good."

He sputters and then lets out a breath. His thighs sway out a fraction, inviting me back. Burying my face, I wrap my hand around his shaft while I get to teasing and lapping.

He's panting like he ran ten flights of stairs. The guy is fit as a fiddle, so those breaths are giving me a big head. I can barely contain my smile, knowing he's enjoying my treatment. Running my palm up his thigh, I whisper, "Legs up."

He blinks at me and swallows, but then complies. Getting to my knees, I flash him a smile and then take him into my mouth.

"Aw, God," he groans, fisting my hair. Then he adds a moan when I stroke his pucker. "Dami, Jesus."

When I flick open the bottle of lube, I feel him flinch. Glancing up, his eyes meet mine, but he doesn't say a word. The fact that he trusts me makes me lightheaded. I give him a tender smile, letting him know his pleasure is my priority.

Taking him to the back of my throat, I graze his seam, lathering it up just so he can experience the slick feel of contact there.

He alternates between muffled curses and my name, hips twitching like he can barely hold back. Pressing the tip of my finger to his entrance, he stiffens for a second then lets out a deep breath. That's my cue.

Pressing gently, I pass the initial resistance of his tight ring as I move my mouth to his balls and lathe their circumference. His stuttered breath makes me self-conscious. I hope it's out of pleasure, rather than nerves. I've always thought I was a considerate lover, but I've never been so cognizant of or concerned about my partner's pleasure as I am for Graham. It has less to do with his lack of experience and more to do with the fact that he's special.

He's the first guy to believe in so many aspects of me and my life. I think I'll forever remember him as the first lover of my adulthood. All the others were just meaningless romps of my youth in comparison.

His throaty moan raises in pitch. I feel his channel relax around me as I pump into it in slow thrusts, searching for his P-spot. I had to find mine on my own when I was in high school, wrestling around on my bed like a contortionist. It's not lost on me that I'm the first person ever to touch this guarded man in such an intimate place.

"Sh-sh-sh-shit, Dami!" he stutters, shuddering on an arch, throwing his head back, when I graze what I was looking for.

"Good?" I venture, moving my mouth back to his cock.

"My p-prostate?" he asks.

"Yeah," I say between flicks of his head with my tongue. "It likes me."

He lets out a snort, but it gets cut off when I take him to the back of my throat. Recently, I was starting to question if all my fooling around in the past would make me less desirable to someone like Graham who has traditional beliefs. Feeling his hips start to rock into my hand and then up into my mouth, I'm grateful my experience is paying off.

Watching his abs flex, hearing his strained cries, feeling him clench around my finger as he pulses in my mouth, I don't think I've ever enjoyed fooling around this much. Gasping, he cries out my name. A tingle runs up my spine and I moan around my swallows at the soothing heat in my veins from witnessing his undoing because of me.

Releasing him, I take a moment to appreciate his rising chest in the amber light. The bass of the music outside mimics what looks to be the rapid thump of his heartbeat as he closes his eyes and lets his arms splay out to his sides like a gloriously sexy sacrifice. I'm in such awe of all his body parts that I even check out his hands, reminding me of his cleanliness concerns.

Scanning the tent floor, I spot the pack of baby wipes I packed and grab us a few. He glances at all the stuff he upended from my bag and flashes me an I-told-you-so look but doesn't complain that I came prepared. Panting, I flop down on my sleeping bag beside him and make to shift, when I realize my head has landed on his arm. He bends his elbow, draping his arm around my shoulder, so I stay put.

Contentment washes over me lying here with him, staring up through the ceiling screen at the stars. What could have been a disaster shaped up to be one of the most perfect nights of my life. I'm definitely adding camping to the list of things I'll do with my forever guy. I wonder if this special moment will make all other camping events seem incomparable.

Graham squeezes my arm and rolls his head to look at me. "Satisfied?" he asks.

"Yeah. Definitely." I chuckle. "How about you?"

Another blush. He's so damn cute. That'll never get old, and here I always thought I preferred experienced and confident.

"I was satisfied that you were satisfied," he replies.

Well, dang. Ten points for the perfect answer. Craning my neck, I give him what I intended as a quick kiss for that thoughtful remark, but he cups my jaw. I give in easily to his slow, sweet kisses, which seem a lot like post-coital snogging. College guys weren't big on sentimental petting afterward, so this is new for the teacher, but…nice, really nice. It seems both fitting and contrasting of Graham, the tender side I've seen and the gruff one the rest of his little world assumes.

When it ends, our gazes get snared in an awkward silence. His eyes dart nervously across my face, and he wets his lips. "If you…need *anything* when we get back home, I can…" When he ends with a shrug, I find myself smiling.

My student has just enrolled long-term. "Are you…offering?"

"I'm not exactly getting nothing out of it," he says, shifting and glancing up at the skylight.

Snagging my underwear, I chuckle and slide them on, rolling onto my side with my back to him. I don't want him to see how I can't stop smiling at the prospect.

"Alright," I throw out casually, pulling my sleeping bag flap over me.

He rustles behind me, a signature shift of him reclaiming his drawers. He's a foot away when he settles back onto his bag, but his heat and presence give me sensations of coming home.

He shifts again, bringing his warmth closer. Skin brushes my bare side, a solid arm wrapping over my ribcage. Sucking in a quiet breath, my heart does a jig when his chest presses to my back. My stomach flip-flops, and I have to force myself to swallow against the lump in my throat, a giant ball of being the recipient of his affection lodged there.

So, Graham is a cuddler? Wow.

Inching back artfully, I settle snugger against the inviting heat of his bare skin. His feather duster rests against the back of my neck, giving me gooseflesh.

When we both sigh at the same time, I feel my cheeks heat and eyes go wide. This feels like forever-guy activities. Suddenly, forever-guy sounds like a threat that would shatter this perfect bubble I'm living in inside Graham's arms. Maybe forever-guy can wait until whenever Graham gets sick of me. I've got plenty of time.

Reaching to interlace our fingers, I'm not even sure why I'm doing it or why my hand is trembling, but I'm grateful for the absolute silence between us and the way his fingers freely curl around mine. My eyes get heavy all of a sudden, swathed in this fulfilling sensation of completion and safety. Spooning is going to the top of my kink list, right below Graham's kisses.

Yeah. Forever can wait.

CHAPTER 30

Graham

"What are you up to today?" Dami asks over the rim of the carry-out coffee we got at the diner we stopped at for breakfast as we make our way down the road.

It's surreal to have a normal conversation with him after last night, but it was the same at breakfast. It was the same every day at work after the nights we messed around last week. He never makes it awkward. It just feels like it's a normal day. Make out with Dami and carry on. Well, it's a new-normal kind of day, I guess. I'm still baffled by how right it feels.

"I need to mow my lawn," I reply, wondering if he has much more interesting things to do.

"With that big tractor of yours?" he asks like he's talking about a *Porsche*.

"It's not that big."

"Can I run it? I could cut the grass for you."

"No," I say without hesitation, imagining my tractor sinking into the lake as Dami bails off it.

"You don't trust me?"

I definitely don't trust him with my baby and feel awful for it when I catch the look of hurt on his face. "I didn't say that."

"You don't. Do you? Come on!" he coos. "I'll be really careful. You can show me what to do."

"Do you have a tractor obsession?"

"I've never driven one. I've always wanted to. My uncle in Greece has a little one for their farm, but he's never let me drive it."

Well, that settles that.

Two hours later, the morning sun has nipped the chill from the air as I go over the controls on my tractor. Dami watches attentively, standing next to my seat on the platform with his ass leaning up against the fender.

I make two passes around the house and shed because, while I want to have faith in him, I wouldn't trust any first-timer to not hit one of my buildings with the wide mower attachment I use to cover my three acres of yard. Lining the tractor up for the next pass that will put Dami on a safe path far enough away from the house, I kill the PTO shaft on the mower and pop the tractor clutch into neutral.

"Alright. Your turn," I inform him.

Before I can make to get up and finagle trading places with him in the cramped space, he slides onto my lap. Gripping the steering wheel, his ass shifts against my thighs when he looks down at his foot to locate the clutch pedal.

Not what I was expecting.

I glance around my yard, which is silly. There's no one out here to see us. We're surrounded by woods even all the way down to my dock.

His weight doesn't feel as heavy as I would expect the feel of a grown man sitting in my lap. It feels…nice having him close and connected to me. It also feels safer than if I had to stand against the fender and lean over to help him with the controls, so I settle back and slink my arm around his waist. I've got to make sure he doesn't slide off if he lurches us forward after all.

The sheer glee rolling off him as he navigates the tractor is infectious. He's positively brimming with joy, a big cheeky grin on his face that I catch sight of each time he glances back to check the mower deck. I can't keep from chuckling at his excitement or his pride over this simple accomplishment. It's a privilege to be a spectator to both.

At some point, I realize my thumb is rubbing the fabric of his sweatshirt over his stomach, my other hand, doing the same to his thigh. The unconscious petting surprises me. I've never been a person who can't stop touching his partner the way Johnny and Aiden do.

Partner.

Is Dami my partner? I don't think screwing around equals *partner* to him, but the guy is fucking sitting on my lap while we cut my grass. That seems partner-like to me. I told him I changed my mind about quitting lessons last night though.

Fuck. Why did I have to say that?

For all I know, he probably thinks that's all that last night was, but it felt like more than a lesson to me. Okay, so I learned a few things, namely, how little credit I previously gave the amount of pleasure you can give and receive from anal stimulation.

When Dami finishes cutting the grass, I direct him back to the shed. My breath only catches for a second when he stops the tractor a foot away from my workbench. Killing the engine, he twists around on my lap and grins at me. "I did it. That was awesome!"

"You did, and you didn't destroy anything. I'm impressed."

"Hey! Don't be too impressed, or I'll be offended," he says, elbowing me in the stomach.

"I'm not. You're a natural operator, even if your driving made your passes look like the shape of one of those fun slides at a water park."

Squinting, he glances over my shoulder out at the yard. The way his smile falls makes me sorry for teasing him. He turns back to me though and laughs. "I'm an artist. What do you expect? At least your yard doesn't look boring now."

A month ago, I might have let the wavy lines on my lawn bother me. I laugh with him though for the simple fact I know I now prefer having his mark on my lawn rather than the perfect yard. Hell, maybe I won't cut it again for two weeks just so I can look at it longer and think of him.

"So, what are we doing now?" he asks.

A giddy sensation makes my heart flip, realizing he wants to spend more time with me. "I don't know. What did you have in mind?"

"Weren't you going fishing today?"

"I was, but I don't have to."

"Well, don't blow it off because of me. Can I come?"

Can he come? Yes, he *can* when I work him over with my mouth, I don't say.

Clearing my throat, I shift my legs. "Yeah, sure. As soon as you get your boney ass off my lap."

The little tease does this gyration, grinding against my junk before he laughs and gets up. I want to tell him, screw fishing and to do it again, but don't know how to say that without it sounding like I'm asking for more lessons.

We gather my tackle and an extra pole and head down to the dock after packing up some sandwiches in a cooler. It's a crime learning that he's never been fishing before. I show him how to cast until he looks like he has it down enough to not send the line sailing into a tree.

He casts and then drops down into the extra lawn chair I keep on the dock. No one's hardly ever sat in it but Jen with the exception of my dad and Aiden on occasion. My good mood plummets. There's no way this will be enjoyable to a vivacious twenty-three-year-old who goes to camping parties at mansions. Why in the hell did I have to mention fishing?

"What do we do now?" Dami asks after wolfing down his sandwiches, staring at his line in the water with a frown.

"What do you mean what do we do?"

"To catch the fish."

"You're doing it. This is it." I laugh.

"But…"

"But what?"

"But it's so…"

Great. Here it comes.

I didn't expect him to like everything I do, especially since I'm a man of limited tastes, but the disappointment I anticipate stings. I have little to offer, so it's only a matter of time before he grows tired of my luke-warm lifestyle. I just hoped it wouldn't be so soon.

"Boring?" I venture, remembering the way Jen used to sigh all the time in that very spot

"No. Peaceful," he says wistfully. "I thought it'd be more adventurous and physically demanding like all Bear Grylls."

"What did you think, we were going to pull a shark out of the lake?"

"No." He laughs.

I can't help but notice how his eyes never leave his line like a devoted angler. Warmth spreads in my chest not because I'm watching another fisherman potentially being born but because it's Dami. I wouldn't have expected him to be the type who could sit still and enjoy simple things. He never ceases to amaze me.

A while later, I glance over and find his head tilted up to the sun, eyes closed with a tranquil smile on his face. He hasn't said a word in thirty minutes and looks just as happy not catching fish as he was for me when I reeled one in.

His body jerks and his eyes flicker open. "Ooh! I got one!" he cries. "I think I got one!"

It's all I can do to keep from laughing at his excitement as I coach him on reeling it in. If this fish gets off his line before he gets it out of the water, I'll dive in and murder it. I'm so far into *partner territory* for him there's no turning back.

CHAPTER 31

Fishing is a freaking blast. Okay, well, it's not really *a blast*. All you do is sit here like you're meditating, communing with nature, but then *bam!* I have a freaking bite!

I'm doing my best to listen to Graham's calm, soothing voice, telling me when to reel and when to tilt my pole, but I just caught my first fish. I feel like a freaking gladiator.

Geesh. Do I have a thing for bloodlust?

Ew. It better not be bloody. That'd be so sad.

"You're doing fine. Just like that. Not too slow. It'll get off the hook," he croons.

I shiver, imagining that tone and those words in my ear in the bedroom. My ass is still humming just from sitting on his lap. Maybe it's from the vibrations of the tractor, but still. Graham has a nice lap.

He lets out a gasp. I squint at the water, wondering if he can see my fish yet. Is it a whopper?

The sound of Graham's feet shuffling backward on the dock draw my eyes away from my line. His face is stricken with terror, his mouth gasping for air. Is he having a heart attack?

"Graham? What is it?"

Pointing toward the woods behind me, he sputters, "Ch-ch-chair!"

Turning my head, I spot a mangy black cat sauntering onto the dock, its attentive green eyes locked on the bait by Graham's chair. Oh, no.

"It's just a cat," I rationalize, torn between checking on him and the sight of catching my first fish.

The cat lets out a squeaky meow, the kind that reverberate when they're hunting a bird. Graham makes a terrified wailing noise that doesn't sound human and scrambles back farther, toppling over his chair.

It's like slow-motion as he yelps, and his feet fly up in the air. A second later his back hits the water, sending a spray over the dock as he disappears under the surface.

"Graham!" I call out, dropping my pole on the dock.

His head re-emerges along with his flailing arms. Gasping, he flounders and goes under again.

Can he swim? He was in the Navy, but his boots are probably weighing him down. How deep is the lake?

My stomach feels like its bottom dropped out. I can't breathe, but panic has me moving, pitching myself off the dock. When I resurface after my plummet, Graham's head is above water. Coughing, he looks at me like I'm a stranger.

"Are you okay?" I ask, gripping a hand under his arm to support him.

"No! Kevin chased me off the damn dock!"

"Kevin?"

Pursing his lips, he swipes his hair out of his face. "That little bastard that always comes after my bait. I keep a spray bottle full of water by my chair for when he comes around, but you distracted me with your fish."

Trying not to snicker, I glance at the dock. There's no sight of *Kevin*, and…crap. My pole is also missing.

Dang it. I must have had a big one if the fish pulled it into the water. Now is probably not the time to tell Graham I lost his gear.

"Kevin, huh?" I muse. "Yeah, he looked pretty dangerous."

"Go ahead. Laugh it up."

"No," I chuckle, totally sounding like I'm mocking him. "I'm not laughing about the cat phobia. I just think it's cute you named your fear."

Frowning, he glances at where I'm bracing his arm. "What are you doing?"

Letting go, I shrug. "I didn't know if you were alright."

"Did you jump in to save me?"

"Well, from the water, not Kevin, but I think he's gone if you want to get out now."

I follow him, and we muck our way up the bank. I catch him glancing around for my pole and pretend to be interested in the scenery when he looks at me. Sighing, he starts back toward the house, our wet clothes making squishy noises in time with our steps.

Seeing the turn in his mood pains me, not just emotionally but physically. I hadn't planned on him wanting to spend the day with me. Truth be told I think I kind of pestered him into it. I didn't mean for that to happen. It's just that I was having so much fun that the thought of going home never crossed my mind. Now though, seeing him gloomy, I have the feeling there won't be any more hanging out tonight or lessons. The thought of having to part from his company causes an ache inside me.

A hundred percent, I was looking forward to more lessons, but I'm starting to crave being in his presence even if it's just mowing grass or sitting on his dock. Graham Brandt is becoming addictive in every aspect.

We make it back to the house and stop on his porch. Just when I'm about to ask him for a towel I can sit on in his truck for when he drives me home, he informs me, "You…can strip out of those wet clothes out here and hit the shower if you want. I'll throw them in the washing machine for you."

My pulse kicks at the possibility of a shared shower but judging by the way he's rubbing the back of his neck, I'm skeptical that's what he's insinuating. I smell like the lake and not in a good way, so I nod.

"Yeah, sure. That'd be great."

It's difficult to strip sopping clothes off in a sexy way. My attempt to do so is wasted though. When I finally get my sweatshirt over my head, the door to the house swings shut on a barefoot Graham in only his jeans.

Yup. No lessons tonight, if he's back to avoiding looking at me when I'm in my underwear.

When I get out of the shower, I pause at the bathroom door to wipe the smile off my face. I smell like Graham's shower gel from head to toe. I am officially in love with myself. Getting ready to strut my stuff in this towel, I wrench open the door, but stop short.

"Hey," I chirp, coming face-to-face with Graham.

How long has he been standing out here? I can't decide if it's hot or concerning.

"Hey. Uh, here's a t-shirt and some sleep pants."

"Oh, thanks." So much for working it in this towel. Wait a minute. Sleep pants? "Did you…want me to spend the night?"

"Oh, I…" he glances down the hall, where I can hear the washing machine running. Crap. Right. I'm an idiot. These are just temporary until he can scuttle me home in my clean clothes.

To my surprise though, he says, "Sure. You can if you want. I can make dinner and give you a lift home in the morning."

For the record, the word *lift* is the least flirtatious word in the English language, but I'm such a sucker. I don't care if the rest of the evening only entails dinner. This crush on my student is starting to consume me. "Yeah. That sounds good."

Three hours later, I'm sitting on Graham's couch violating one of his spoons with my tongue, sucking on it like a freaking pacifier even though the ice cream on it is long gone. Freshly showered, he's wearing sweatpants again. Gray sweatpants. I was not warned there would be sweatpants.

Yawning, he stretches his arms above his head, forcing his t-shirt to ride up over his taut stomach. I might actually die if he doesn't touch me.

"You sick of Kate and Leo?" he asks, smirking at me.

"Hm?" I hum, tearing my eyes away from his bulge.

"You picked it," he adds, gesturing to the TV where *Titanic* is playing.

"Mm," I concur around the spoon.

Snickering, he adds, "Like that ice cream, do you?"

"Mmhm."

Geesh. I sound like an imbecile. I don't even know what he asked me, but I'll agree with anything at this point.

Glancing at the clock, he scrubs his hand over his face. "Well, I think I'm going to turn in. You need anything?"

You, I want to shout. What has he done to me?

"Uh, uh," I blather around the spoon that should be a hot, hard Graham Brandt cock instead.

Mouth quirking, he hesitates for second, making my hopes rise. "Well, um, goodnight."

"Night."

Now, I'm so depressed I need more ice cream. He said when we got back, if I *needed anything* he could take care of it. Am I supposed to beg for it? I thought I'd established that I always need it, especially if it's from him.

Twisting so I can peer over the back of the couch, I want to weep, watching that perfect gray cotton-covered ass walk away from me. If I call out, will he think I'm *too* needy? Do guys have a decrease in sex drive once they hit thirty? Or is this just a shy Graham move? Did he change his mind again? I don't want to ruin this perfect weekend by making demands.

Ugh. This is torture.

More lessons were supposed to mean *more lessons*. This need for him is starting to scare me. What if I can't turn it off?

Flopping down on the couch, I abandon my ice cream bowl on the coffee table along with my willpower and stroke myself through the sleep pants. I can't help it with visions of Graham's sweatpants-swaddled sugar plums dancing in my head. The memory of his breathy cries last night loop in my head.

To heck with it. He won't hear me with *Titanic* playing in the background.

Digging out my phone and lube from my backpack, I pull up my *Spankbank* playlist and select a Vin Stoller video. I seriously don't need inspiration right now, but it seems wrong to think about your host while you rub one out.

I finger my hole for a few minutes and then coat my shaft. I only get two strokes in when the floor creaks behind the couch.

"Are you freaking jerking off on my couch again?" Graham's voice seethes.

Sitting up, I find him a foot away…in those damn pants. Not helping. "Do you want me to go in the bathroom?"

"What the fuck?" he sputters. "We just…last night."

"Yeah, and it was great. I just…"

"You what?"

"You…" My eyes snag on the erotic way the frumpy gray fabric hugs his every curve. "You're wearing sweatpants," I murmur, feeling drugged. "*Gray* sweatpants."

"Yeah? So?"

"I couldn't stop thinking about them." My voice sounds robotic as I give myself an idle stroke. Wow. Do I have a sex problem?

"Is *he* wearing sweatpants?" Graham asks, pointing to my phone.

"Huh? Who Vin Stoller? No. It just seemed like it would be rude to jerk off to the person whose house you're staying at."

He blinks a few times like my logic makes no sense. Great. I've finally pushed him over the edge.

Now he's moving. He's…coming around to my side of the couch. Oh, boy. Is he going to toss my horny ass outside?

Taking a knee next to me, his expression all stormy, he cups my face and crashes his mouth onto mine. I moan so loud I should be embarrassed and drop my phone. Vin Stoller, who?

"I told you I'd take care of your…needs," he rasps angrily, coming up for air only long enough to lay me back on the couch.

Mouth back on mine, his hand snakes between us and opens the gates to *Sweatpants Town.* Oh, sweet baby, Jesus. Yes! I'm going to buy every postcard in that village.

His hips start frotting into me, gliding our cocks together. He's hard as iron, making me feel redeemed. I'm so grateful, I have the urge to apologize for starting without him.

"Sweatpants are my weakness," I explain between kisses.

"Yeah?" he purrs, nipping my bottom lip.

"Yeah."

"I have *a lot* of sweatpants," he rumbles, moving his lips to my neck as his hips work against mine.

When his hand grips an entire palmful of my ass, I lose what's left of my mind. "Graham, fuck me. Please!"

He goes utterly still along with my heartbeat. No! Dang it! I did it again! I need a freaking *sex muzzle* for my mouth around him.

Lifting his head, he stares down at me. Swallowing at the sudden dryness in my throat, I grip his arms tighter, bracing myself for his freak out.

"Sorry," I blurt. "I didn't—"

"How?" he rasps.

Whoa. *How?* Did he just say…*how?*

Oh…*my* gosh!

I have never moved so fast in my life, practically shoving him off me. I scramble onto my knees and yank the sleep pants the rest of the way down my ass, assuming a position over the back of the couch. And then…I wait.

Crap. Did I rush too fast?

Slowly, he shifts behind me, settling his knees on the cushion between my spread legs. When his hands glide over my hips, I tremble. Graham Brandt is going to fuck me. I really might actually die.

His fingers graze across my ass cheek down to my seam. I feel one trail up the path between my cheeks, stopping on my rim.

"Is that…lube?" he asks, gliding his finger back and forth over my slickened entrance. "Did you…"

Glancing back, my face heats. I seriously do have a sex problem or at least a Graham problem. I smile and lift my brows. "Um. You're welcome?"

He scoffs and shakes his head then resumes tracing the circumference of my rim. When he slips his finger inside, I collapse my weight on the couch and groan.

"Oh, yeah."

How is his finger better than any other finger I've felt? Rocking back shamelessly onto him, I moan each time he strokes my prostate. His warmth comes closer. He's pressing kisses down the length of my spine.

It's too much, this sensation of being both worshipped and pleasured. I am not going to blow this when I finally have my chance to have Graham inside me.

"Now, please. Now!" I beg.

His finger disappears. I hear his hand rustling in my backpack as he leans toward the end of the couch. I will feel embarrassed later at the realization it really is a sex backpack. His hands return to my hips, the distinctive cool foil of a condom wrapper between his fingers kisses my skin.

What is he doing? Why isn't he putting it on?

"I can't."

The whispered words assault me. Did he really just say that?

"What?" I ask, looking over my shoulder at his conflicted face.

"This is wrong," he says gravelly.

No. No, no, no. I'm going to die.

Collapsing, I press my mouth against the cushion to suppress my groan. I was so close. The couch rocks as he stands. I want to cry.

A hand clutches my bicep and tugs.

"Come on," he whispers.

Rising to my knees, I pull my pants up and gape at him. "What? Where?"

"You're sleeping in my room," he informs me, snagging up my book-bag. Taking my hand, he practically drags me there since I'm so befuddled, I can't comprehend anything.

If he thinks having sex with me or men is wrong, why is he taking me to his bedroom?

"Why?" I blurt.

"So, I can make sure you call out the right name when you come."

CHAPTER 32

Graham

Closing the door to my room, my heart threatens to hammer its way out of my chest. I should have never walked back into the hallway to put his clothes in the dryer. Now look what I got myself into. I didn't even get to look up gay porn yet.

Taking a deep breath, I make my way over to Dami who has gone unnervingly silent. Have I shocked the shit out of him? He begged me to fuck him not two minutes ago. Maybe he's not as confident as he lets on. That thought actually settles my nerves as I run my fingers through his hair, leaning in to kiss him.

"I'm confused," he says. "Are we still having sex?"

A puff of breath leaves my lungs. What did he think, that I brought him in here to make him jerk himself off in my bed?

"Dami, I'm not fucking you over my couch like two horny teenagers."

"Oh." He chuckles, bringing his hands slowly up to my chest, much less eager beaver than in the living room.

Why is this suddenly awkward? Is it just me, or did I kill the mood by insisting on the change of scenery?

I've only had sex with one person in my entire life. This is a momentous occasion for me that seems more worthy than bending him over the back of a piece of furniture. Not that the image of that will ever leave my mind. The way he scrambled to present himself, was almost as big of a turn on as the way he jumped into the lake thinking he needed to save me after that bastard cat ruined his first fishing trip. I don't even care that he lost my fishing pole.

When our mouths connect, some of the trepidation dissipates. His kisses can make me forget almost anything. I'm not sure who moved first, but when the back of his legs hit my bed, my pulse kicks. The Eagle has landed. We're that much closer to this happening.

I can feel the arousal dripping off him by the way he trembles when I help him lose his shirt and he helps me with mine. As he drops his pants and slides his hands under my waistband over my ass, I try to commit every touch, every sight, every sensation to memory.

I'm going to fuck a man.

I'm going to fuck Damiano Andropolis, and I don't care that he's a man, or maybe I do care because he's *this* man. The one that I want.

Naked and breathing heavy from drugging kisses and the sensation of our bodies against each other's, we stare. His hard cock is pressing into the juncture of my hip, mine against his stomach. I can feel our heartbeats in every place we're connected. It's in the air in my room like a pulsing sound wave.

"Ready?" he whispers.

All I can do is nod. He climbs onto my bed, getting on all fours, his ass hiked in the air. Looking over at me, he licks his lips. It is the most erotic and wondrous sight I've ever seen, him offering his body to me, him waiting for me to pleasure him in the most intimate way possible.

Sidling up behind him, I can barely breathe while everything in me wants to dive into him body and soul. Staring down at his hole, glistening in the moonlight that's seeping in through my bedroom window, I can think of only one thing.

"Lube," I utter, cursing myself when it comes out like a bossy robot.

Dami seems unphased, because his lithe body stretches and reaches into his backpack on the floor. A second later, he hands me his mega bottle of liquid. I don't know how he found it that quick. He's got so much shit in there it's like a woman's purse.

Putting on the condom, I coat myself, my fingers, and even dribble some in his seam. I feel like I'm over-basting a fucking turkey and taking forever, but he's not complaining, and I don't want to hurt him.

I don't know how long he was playing with his ass on my couch, but I'm not taking my chances, so I breach his ring with my index finger and work as much lube inside as I can. Gently, I work in another, a rush of heat stirring in my belly when his groans turn deeper.

"Please, Graham," he whines.

I have to give my cock a squeeze hearing him beg. Why is that so freaking hot?

With trembling hands, I line myself up an inch away. Staring at the back of his bowed head, my stomach churns. Something isn't right.

Jen and I screwed in this position plenty of times over the years, but it never crossed my mind until now that it makes your partner faceless.

Without being able to look at him, Dami is just an ass at my disposal. The word *disposable* makes me nauseated.

He nudges his hips back impatiently, bumping the tip of my cock. Gripping his sides, I hold him in place and back off.

"I can't," I whisper.

"What?"

He's probably fed up with me. I've made him wait longer than he's likely ever had to, but all I can think of are all the ways he's seen me. He's seen past the prickly exterior everyone has labeled me with. He's not intimidated or put off by me when I'm frustrated. He never makes fun of my cat phobia, and he's the first person who looked like he understood the peace I find just sitting on my dock fishing. He sees me. I can't stuff my cock into him for the first time without seeing him.

CHAPTER 33

Ass hiked precariously, lube applied, the tip of his cock brushing the seam of my ass, and he says, he *can't?* He's trying to kill me. I swear.

"What?" I gasp, hoping I didn't hear him correctly.

"This isn't right."

His words are a sledgehammer to my heart. Stomach roiling, I let out a defeated noise and collapse onto my side. Rolling onto my back, I throw my forearm over my eyes, so I won't have to see the conflict on his face. The universe must really not want me to be with this man. I might actually cry.

Graham shifts. His heat covers my body, giving me a start. Pulling my arm away when he slides a hand into my hair, I open my eyes to his lips hovering over mine.

"Need to look at you," he murmurs, kissing me.

My lips don't even reciprocate. I'm too stunned when I feel his palm graze down my hip. He's still in this?

He must realize I'm lying here like a mannequin because he pulls back to look down at me. His expression is remorseful, making me guess he knows I'm completely flummoxed.

"It doesn't feel right to not see your face," he explains.

That was the problem? That's so…odd. I've never been with a guy who *needed* that from me. The knowledge that I'll be able to look into his eyes while he's inside of me makes me shudder in nervous anticipation. Is that a kink of mine too now?

"Oh," I blurt, forcing myself to swallow the lump in my throat. "You…want to look at me while we…"

"Why wouldn't I?" His expression as he says that, the beautiful confusion of it steals my breath. "But…does it work okay…like this?" he asks, glancing down between us.

I stop the delirious laugh bubble, clambering up my windpipe. Nothing is funny about this.

Smiling, I draw my legs up on either side of him and run my hands across his shoulders. "Yeah. Yeah, it works just fine."

He lets out a shaky breath and smiles, settling his hips between my legs. He's so nervous, it sends a rush of guilt through me.

"I don't mean to send mixed signals," I caution, running my hands up and down his arms, "because, clearly, I want this, but this is a pretty big favor, Graham. It's a big deal for you. I hope my eagerness isn't influencing your decision. I really don't expect you to, if you're not ready."

He frowns like I offended him. "I want to. It's not a favor."

"Oh." I chuckle in relief. "Well, it's a pretty fun lesson. I think you'll enjoy it."

I was trying to lighten the mood. Why is he frowning again?

"Does it have to be a lesson?"

When I stare stupidly at him, he adds, "I mean…can't we just do this because we want to? I'd rather do it because I want to, and you do it because you want to…with me."

I've never deliberated this much in bed. This deliberation, however, feels incredibly paramount. He doesn't want lessons. He just wants to *want* me. My heart thrums at his confession, tripping over the part where also wants *me* to want *him* back.

Wish granted, Teddy Graham. Wish granted.

"Alright." I nod.

"So…you really want to?"

"I do…*with you*," I assure him, hearing my voice shake.

Thank goodness for kissing. My heart was about to burst out through my throat. Our exchange has my body feeling like it's transforming as the words sink into my bones, and his tongue sweeps against mine. I'm melting into him, into a sense of completion I've never felt before. This feels like so much more than a crush.

His tip presses against my entrance. I bear down as he presses forward. Just as he starts to stretch me, he grunts and backs off.

"It won't fit," he rasps.

"It will. Trust me. Just push when I push."

"That makes no sense. Two objects pushing together equals something getting smashed, not insertion," he says, looking down between us with a scowl.

Is he seriously going to go all *Frustrated Graham* on me right now with a physics explanation?

"I thought this wasn't a lesson."

"It's not, but it's nerve-wracking."

Grabbing his face, I force him to look at me. "Graham, you think too much. Kiss me."

I can feel him relax as our tongues tangle. Every moaning breath he makes fuels the combustion in my abdomen. As much as I want this, I could honestly just inhale him and kiss him forever, and I think it might be because it feels like he's mine.

When I feel his cockhead press against my ring again, I draw my lips away and bear down as I look in his eyes. Slinging my legs around his hips, I nod and draw him in, tightening my hold around his body.

The metamorphosis of his expression turning from concentration to shocked pleasure as he passes through the first rings of muscles will be etched forever in my mind. A round of hard choppy breaths ghost my face as he pants. I bite my cheek to keep from groaning at the burn of the stretch.

"Oh, God," he chokes out.

"K-keep going," I pant, skimming his back anxiously.

His hips shift a fraction. My body draws him deeper, expanding around him. We both groan, and then he kisses me desperately, breathlessly.

As my body acclimates to the hot intrusion, I feel his muscles relax, and then he moves. His eyes lock on my face, gauging my every expression. Combined with the intimacy of the overwhelming fullness I feel from him, the sweet attentiveness makes me whimper. This doesn't feel like just sex. He's consuming me. It's a transfer of beings.

"You…good?" he pants.

I moan and nod, arching up to meet his little thrusts, making his cockhead pass over my prostate. "Oh, my gosh. Oh, my gosh," I chant, an icy static charge spiraling through me, tethered to my nuts.

His brows lift in surprise when I shudder. "Dami," he croaks, all throaty and captures my mouth, picking up the pace, diving deeper.

I'm clawing at him with one hand, trying to hold my leg to my chest with the other. I want every inch, every thrust. I'm mindless and full in a way I've never experienced before. For someone who was so uncertain, I sigh in relief when Graham draws my knees over his shoulders, sensing my maddening need.

"Yeah!" I cry out when he delves home, hitting all the right places, feeding on my neck like my body is his life force. That first slap of his skin against mine is like a boxing match bell, shattering any amount of vocal reserve between us.

"So good," he pants in my ear. "It's…fucking unbearable."

Grabbing his face, my lips tremble in front of his mouth, desperate to tell him secrets I didn't even know I had. "I never thought you'd be mine."

His arms clamp around me, saving me from the freefall of my imi-passioned honesty. His hips go wild as he seals his lips to mine. He comes up panting and breathes one word, "Yours," before devouring my mouth again.

Yours. The word brands my heart and my soul. There is no better *yours* in the world than the one Graham just gave to me. The intensity behind it, the conviction, shatter me. My balls explode, forcing pressure up my cock, blooming across my abdomen and around my spine. My freaking toes go numb and curl as my release pulses between us.

Graham yells as my ass clenches around him. His thrusts turn erratic, and he cries out against my cheek, his cock pulsing inside me, battling against my own spasms like a war between us for who has the better orgasm.

My body tremors with each of his strained, breathless moans in my ear, each little after shock of his cock inside me. I just shared the best orgasm of my life with my boss, my obsession, a man who I never dared truly believe would do this with me. Usually, I'd get up and clean up, but the thought of him pulling out makes me feel empty deep in my soul.

We lay still, tangled, trying to regain the strength to breathe. Whatever I've been doing or dreaming of my entire life seems inconsequential, because when he raises his head and kisses me tenderly, I tremble, learning another secret I didn't know I had. My soul has been carved out, and this kiss is the final act of serving it up to him on a platter. He can have whatever he wants from me.

As he smiles at me, I'm speechless and raw, yet put together in a way I never have been. I know we said no more lessons, but I just learned a life-altering one. I think Graham is my forever guy, my Mr. Right. I'm no longer worried about the details of my plan as long as it includes him.

CHAPTER 34

Graham

When I find the strength and will to ease off Dami, a pang of loss hits me as I withdraw from his body to dispose of the condom. I am changed, forever changed. People say sex doesn't garner feelings, that you need them without it. I believe that to be true, but sex can definitely make a terrified heart see what it was hiding from.

I could never do what we just did or feel the way I do right now with another person. How is it possible to feel alive for the first time and also like you could perish peacefully at the same time?

The smile he gives me as he lies spread out, bare naked, chest still heaving, warms me to my toes. Leaning over the bed, I press a kiss to his lips. Seeing him bared reminds me how this started, when I went into the hallway to put his clothes in the dryer.

"Be right back," I tell him and pad out of the room.

When I return, he's picked the clothes I lent him up off the floor and has his lube in his other hand, standing over his backpack. If he heads back to the jerk-off couch, my heart might actually break.

"You leaving?" I ask, handing him a cloth I retrieved from the bathroom.

"No, just picking up my mess."

Crouching down, he tugs his sketchpad out to stow the bottle at the bottom of his backpack. There's an outline of what has the potential to be an attractive nude man on the open page. Sprawling onto my stomach with my head toward the foot of the bed, I have the urge to see what his face would look like if he drew me like that, to see what I look like in this moment.

I'm not jealous of his nudes. I've seen nothing but concentration on his face when he draws, not even a flicker of the desire I witnessed in his eyes when he was under me just minutes ago. I want to remember this evening in every way possible but busting out a camera seems lewd.

"Would you sketch me?"

"Now?" he laughs.

Shrugging, I smirk. "I'm young. I have needs."

Chuckling, he glances behind him at the leather ottoman next to my dresser and nods. "Yeah. I'd be happy to satisfy your needy ass."

Tugging the sleep pants on, he tucks his legs underneath him on the ottoman and sets his sketchpad in his lap. When he looks up at me, my body tingles at the way he drinks me in, licking his lips. I don't prowl around my house naked, so my self-consciousness bubbles under the surface.

"Did you…want to put some clothes on or…" he trails off, reminding me of the way Leonardo DiCaprio looked at Kate Winslet in *Titanic* an hour ago on my TV.

"No. Hashtag draw-me-like-one-of-your-French-girls, *Jack*."

I wonder if I got the whole hashtag thing wrong because he gapes at me for a second, but then he cracks up. "Alright. You got it."

I realize I may have assumed too much and discredited his and Johnny's work. There's probably more to this than just flopping down on a bed with your ass bared.

"Um, how do you want me?"

Perusing my body as I lay with my head propped on one arm, he smiles, and whispers, "Just like that."

An hour later, when he takes my breath away with the most moving picture of myself that I've ever seen, and a kiss as he curls up next to me in bed, the memory of those words lulls me to sleep. He wants me just like this, just as I am. I drift off, telling myself he really means it.

CHAPTER 35

"I'll cook you anything, if you keep doing that," I whisper as Graham's lips trail down my neck where he stands behind me at the stove. "Or… burn anything," I amend as his hands move around the front of my hips and into my pockets.

"You burn it, I'm going to stop touching you," he murmurs, sucking on the skin below my ear.

"Your lessons suck," I inform him on a tremor.

Withdrawing from my pockets, he chuckles and pats my ass. "Why don't you go get a shower. I got this."

This is day-three of the best sex of my life, morning snuggles, lunch break blow jobs—yeah, I may have broken the no-messing-around-on-the-job rule—and now he's offering to make me dinner? He doesn't have to tell me twice.

Heaving a breath, I try to act disappointed. "If you insist."

"Go on, smart ass, before I change my mind," he laughs, poking my ribs.

When I get out of the shower, I preen down the hallway in my towel. Let's see what's more tempting, me or dinner. Except, he's not in the kitchen. The burner on the stove is off and so is the television.

"Graham?" I call out, but there's no answer.

The sound of voices outside draws my eyes to the living room window. Graham's sitting on his swing with an arm around a blonde-haired woman, a woman who's crying.

Something tells me it might be his ex, but I grow more certain when she reaches up and cups his cheek. Her thumb rubs across his lower lip, and he's…letting her. He's just sitting there, letting her. There's no sign of the nervousness he had with me at first as he holds her gaze and murmurs something I can't hear.

Leaning forward, her lips press to his. What really has my gut wanting to heave though is that his eyes close and his hand wraps over hers like a lover's.

I'm going to be sick.

I've just been reduced to a happy scene trapped inside a snow globe, unable to alter the world beyond the glass, beyond that window. The sex-cocoon I've been living in the last three days is just that, apparently—sex. Whatever emotion or attachment I thought was growing between us was just a smoke screen, a fog cloud distracting Graham from the person he really wants, the woman on the porch, not the man in his house.

I think I'm kind of tired of life lessons.

CHAPTER 36

Graham

"Jen? What's wrong?" I scramble out the door as soon as I open it and see the tears streaming down her face.

She buries her face in my chest and clutches my sleeves, sobbing without a word.

Dami's in the shower. I don't know who would be more shocked by the other's presence. Knowing Dami, he'll strut out in a towel. Knowing Jen, she might actually be happy for me, but…that was before she showed up crying. Why is she here?

"Come here. Sit down." I guide her to the porch swing. "What happened?"

"David and I…h-had a fight," she sniffles, and I see red.

Cupping her chin, I tilt her face in either direction in search of marks. "Did he hurt you? I'll fucking kill him!"

"What?" Her puffy eyes go wide with shock. How could she not think I'd defend her even though we're divorced? "No!" she blurts out. "He'd never hurt me."

"Then what happened? What did he do to upset you?"

Shaking her head, she chews on her bottom lip the way Dami does. "Nothing. He didn't do anything. That's what's so bad about it."

"I…you lost me," I tell her, rubbing her back. "Are you just not getting along?"

"No. Everything is great or *was* great until I ruined it. He asked me to move in with him last week."

"And you…don't want to?" I venture, trying to understand.

"I do. I…I said *yes*."

"Then what's the problem? Did you change your mind?"

It occurs to me, I'm lending an ear to my ex about her new relationship, when just a couple of weeks ago, I tried making an effort to win her back. As I sit here, I earnestly want to help Jen, but another part of me is itching to get back inside and finish making the dinner I promised a fluffy-haired artist.

"No," she mopes. "I want to move in with him. He's so good to me. I…really love him," she adds, giving me a guilty look.

I already figured she loved him, considering they've been dating for six months. I think I've known that for a while and tried to ignore it, hoping that if her heart was still mine it meant my life hadn't fallen apart. For the first time in a long while though, it doesn't feel like my life is falling apart. It feels like it finally started, and I desperately wish Jen could find that feeling too.

"Are you…asking for my permission?"

"No," she laughs humorlessly. "I, well, yes, maybe?" She blinks at me, her face constricted in worry. I've never seen her this distraught.

Chuckling, I squeeze her shoulder. "Jen, you don't need my permission. I'm okay."

She stares at me for a beat, and then blurts, "I'm pregnant."

My head rears back, stunned. It's the last thing I expected her to say. I still don't understand the worry on her face, or why she's looking at me like she's waiting for my reaction.

"Congratulations."

Her lips sputter. "What if I'm a terrible mother like mine was?"

"Did David say that?"

"No! No, I…I didn't tell him."

I wait, expecting further explanation. This isn't my show. I don't know what to say and get the impression she just needs someone to listen.

"I'm scared, Graham," she says in this small voice that reminds me of when we were kids.

"Scared of being a mom?"

"Of everything! I…I'm so happy it terrifies me. Everything is perfect."

"And that's a bad thing?" I ask softly.

"No," she warbles, swiping at her nose. "But what if he doesn't want a baby? What if he pretends to be happy just because he thinks it's the right thing to do? Or what if he actually will be happy, but I end up being a terrible mother and that ruins everything? I don't want to raise a baby in a divorced home like I had. I want him or her to have two parents who love each other and them."

"Jen, you won't know any of that until you tell him, and if he asked you to move in with him, he must be serious about you. Don't you think?"

Sniffling, she looks over at me and quirks the corner of her mouth. "I think he wants to marry me."

It's surreal to think of her marrying someone else, but not in the way I expect. There's a brief sense of loss, the kind of losing a friend, but there's also shame. I was a fool to hold onto her for so long. Did I make her feel guilty? Because while my heart soars knowing she's found happiness, an ugly selfishness in me is grateful that I'm free to find my own joy, the joy that's inside my house right now.

"That's great, Jen, but why are you so sad?" I finally say.

"When I found out I was pregnant, I started asking him if he was sure that it was a good idea to move in together so soon. He was positive about it, but I kept pushing, trying to find some kind of doubt so I could know…know if a baby would change everything. He started getting frustrated, and I think it was just because he thought *I* had doubts, but I told myself it was because he wasn't really certain. I told him he mustn't really mean it, and that he was jumping into things," she breaks off, choking on a sob. "God, I've made such a mess. What's wrong with me?"

"Nothing," I insist, squeezing her hand. "It's a big deal. I'd probably be a little scared too, but if he loves you, he'll understand, and you guys can work it out."

She blinks up at me, her mouth bowing in a frown. "That's the other thing," she prefaces. "When I found out…the first thing I thought of was you."

"Me?" I parrot, completely bewildered. "But we haven't been together…like *that* in over a year."

Sputtering, she wipes her eyes with a hint of a smile. "No, I know. I just mean…we always wanted to have kids, and now…I'm having one, but it's not yours."

My throat closes up. Is she still harboring feelings for me? "Jen, I…"

"Stop, Graham," she says, her face going serious. "That's not what I meant. Ugh. I'm sorry. I'm such a disaster today." Sighing, she sits up straighter and cups my cheek. "I just meant, my whole life, I thought it'd be *us*. That's the only picture of parenthood I had in my mind, you and me. So, as soon as I found out, it was instinct to think of you. Then I felt guilty for David for thinking of you."

"I get that, but, um, maybe you don't have to tell him that part," I say with a chuckle.

Smiling, she lets out a breathy laugh, but then her eyes search mine. "You're not…upset?"

I hesitate because I'm just a man in front of an emotional woman, and I don't know what the right answer is—the right answer being the one that won't make her cry more.

"No. I'm happy for you. We didn't work, Jen. You know that. I'm just sorry it took me so long to figure out, that I wasted so much of your time."

"You weren't a waste of time, Graham. You're the best part of my past. I guess…maybe that's why I was sad. I thought we'd kind of said goodbye last time, but this felt like another goodbye, one more final and harsher."

Scoffing, I cup her hand where it rests on my cheek. "I'd like to think I'm a little tougher than that. Are you saying, I'll never get to meet your baby?"

"No," she snorts. "You can be weird Uncle Graham."

"*Weird?* Gee, thanks."

"No. Weird as in when they're older, they'll probably find out you're my ex-husband."

"Yeah, but at least I'm a cool ex-husband," I joke.

"Cool?" she chuffs. "Who have you been hanging out with?"

My face heats. Geez, I even sound like Dami now. My heart rate quickens, wondering if he'll come looking for me.

"There's a young guy that started at work. I think I'm picking up his lingo."

Smiling, she grazes her thumb across my cheek. "You are cool. The coolest." Resting her forehead against mine, she whispers, "I'll always love you, Graham. Thank you for the life we had."

My heart trips in my chest as she presses her lips to mine. It's chaste, the kind of kisses I place on my mother's cheek, but gratitude wells up in me, and even a bit of sadness for the final demise of the dream for us she spoke of a moment ago. It's bittersweet, and now I know what she means about feeling guilty for David. Every fiber in my being wants to go inside and seek comfort for this ache in Dami's arms and to be held by my future, whatever it may bring for me and him.

"Love you too, babe," I whisper. "Now, go get your man."

Chuckling, she sucks in a breath and flashes a wary smile. "He's called me three times."

"Sounds like he wants to talk," I hedge.

Grimacing, her cheeks flush as she stands. "Yeah. I'm more worried about finding the right words to undue my stupidity."

Squeezing her shoulder, I brush a lock of hair from her face. "It'll be fine."

She heads for the steps and stops, looking out at the driveway. "Oh!" she gasps, covering her mouth. "Do you have company? I'm so sorry."

"No. It's…uh, yeah. It's that new guy I work with."

"Yeah?"

"Yeah," I say casually, kicking at nothing on the deck.

"Hanging out after work? Isn't Schmitty's Bar more your scene?" she ventures.

Fuck. Rubbing my goatee, I shrug. "We're just having dinner."

She eyes me conspiratorially, making my throat constrict. When her eyebrows raise and a huge grin overtakes her face, I know I'm screwed.

"Can I meet him?"

"No," I scoff with finality.

"Oh, come on! I won't tell anyone or say anything to embarrass you."

"That's…comforting, but I'd rather you didn't. It's…it's new."

"Oh, you're no fun." She pouts, kicking her hip out, leaning on the handrail.

When I catch her careening her head to peek at the window, I distract her by joking, "Hey, I thought I was cool."

"Oh, my word, now I really do need to meet him," she enthuses, ascending one of the steps.

"No," I warn, pointing at her car even as I let out a nervous laugh. "Go on. Get out of here."

Grinning like an imp, she gives me a fake pout. "Fine. Next time though."

"Yeah. We'll see."

Walking to her car, I shake my head as she scopes out Dami's *SMART* and casts me a devious smile. "Have a good night, Graham," she coos, opening her door.

Shaking my head, I wave, but can't fight the smile on my face. I am having a good night, and it'll only get better now.

CHAPTER 37

"Are you sure, you're alright?" Graham asks with a concerned look on his face as we head to the work site. "You can take the day off, if you're still not feeling well."

Returning my gaze to the passing scenery, I shrug, my head resting in my hand, feeling like it's taking all my effort to keep it propped up. Heartache is heavy.

"Yeah, I'll be fine. Just some kind of stomach bug, I think. I'm sure it'll pass."

The knots in my belly feel like a sickness, but not the kind that require fluids or medicine. Remembering that caress and that kiss from last night, my stomach twists tighter. He didn't even tell me.

I went back into the bathroom and got dressed. When I came back out, he was at the stove, making dinner, flashing me a smile as though nothing amiss had just occurred. Waiting to see if he'd mention his visitor proved unhelpful. The more time that passed without him saying a word about it just made me more determined to not let on that I knew. He never planned to tell me. I can't believe it. I never pegged him for treachery.

By the time we get to the job site though, I can't take it anymore.

"Did somebody stop by when I was in the shower last night? I thought I heard a car."

"Yeah," he says without missing a beat. "Jen needed to talk about some things."

"Oh. Everything alright?"

"Yeah. Everything's fine."

Yeah, apparently it is, *for them*. Was I just a bump in the road?

"Well, everything's fine between us anyway," he adds. "She's pregnant. Don't say anything though. I don't know when she wants to tell people."

I bite back a humorless laugh as the brick I'm holding falls from my hand. How can he be so casual about this and even have the nerve to ask for my silence?

"Congratulations," I murmur, unsure of how I'm even managing to breathe.

"What?" he asks, stepping closer. I can't even look at his face. "It's not mine," he scoffs. "It's her boyfriend's."

The air floods back into my lungs as I fiddle with a joint on the scaffolding inside the house. "Oh. Right, but…are you okay with that?"

"It doesn't matter if I'm okay with it."

That answer tells me everything I need to know about that kiss.

"What's wrong?" he asks, bracing my arms. I want to cringe away and wrap them around me at the same time.

"I just…maybe we should stop this."

"*This?*"

"Whatever this is with you and me."

Releasing me, he sputters. "You want to quit the job or do you mean…"

"Not the job." I sigh, rubbing my eyes, hating how I can tell they're starting to glisten. "But with us working together it might get weird, if you and Jen still have feelings for each other or if you meet some man or woman and then act weird around me. I don't want things to ever get weird between us. It'll be easier this way, if we just quit now."

"I'm not going to meet someone and certainly not a woman."

"And what about Jen?"

"What about her? She was just upset about a fight with David and needed someone to listen. It wasn't anything. We don't love each other like that anymore." He sighs, resting his hands on his hips. "I don't know if we ever did."

I honestly can't tell if he's lying. I thought I knew him, but maybe I saw what I wanted to see. "I saw you, Graham. I saw you kissing her."

My face heats. I hate how naïve voicing it makes me sound.

His expression goes slack, his brows pinching together. "She kissed *me*. It…it was like a goodbye kiss. I can't explain it. We were together for so long. It was just comfort or closure, not something I want to do again. I'm sorry I didn't tell you. You looked like you weren't feeling well when you came out of the bathroom, and I was more worried about if you were okay."

I want to believe him, and think I actually do, but can't help wondering if this is a good wake-up call for what we dove precariously into.

"Yeah, but I'm the only guy you've been with, Graham. You're bound to want to explore with other people, and you should. The plan was just to show you the ropes anyway. Right?"

His expression contorts. His hand goes to his stomach like he feels as ill as I do at the prospect.

"Are you serious? Is that how you really feel?"

The answer I should give him is one lie my stupid heart won't let me tell, so I just shrug. I never really imagined how it would feel putting myself out there for anyone. The thought of having that offer turned down now that I want to make it is excruciating.

"I don't want to explore," he rumbles. "I just want to be with you."

"For now," I force out even as his declaration swirls a tempting hope inside me.

"So, what's your plan?" he scoffs. "Just sow more wild oats? Are you…sick of me already?"

"No. I…it's not that. I'm done with oats. I just…think we should be honest with each other. I'm just some horny kid you've been messing around with. I mean, what did you even want out of this?"

As he stares at me in the dim daylight casting in from the unfinished windows, I brace myself. His hesitation tells me he's seeing the logic to my argument. How did I let this happen? It was just a crush. Whoever named it that, wasn't kidding. I am crushed.

CHAPTER 38

Graham

I have no idea what I wanted a few weeks ago, but I know without a doubt what I want now. I want that happiness I felt when Jen left my house, knowing Dami was inside to be the same way he feels about me.

I would have told him. I honestly didn't even think of it when he came out of the bathroom looking so wary. Now I understand why, but the whole just a horny kid part? I want to believe that isn't true, at least not in the way he's implying.

He wants us to be honest? I'll never know if he's being honest, if I'm not.

"I don't want to explore or kiss my ex-wife. I'm falling for you," I rush out. "Actually, that's not true. I've already fallen for you…hard."

Judging by how he finally makes eye contact, I've shocked him. Is it a good shocked or a bad shocked?

"If that's not something you want, I need to know so I can try to stop it," I get out through the tightness in my chest. "I honestly don't know how that'll be possible, but I'll try if you don't want me."

Lips parted, he blinks at me in silence. Has it been seconds or minutes?

"Is that something you want? Not lessons, not convenience, just… you and me?"

Stepping forward, he nods. "Yes. I want you hard."

Can he ever not think about sex, or am I just that bad at explaining myself? "I'm serious, Dami. I mean it, a real you and me."

"I'm serious too. I want you hard for me. I think I'm in hard for you too. So hard," he replies desperately, sliding his hands up my chest.

My heart does a hopeful flip. Capturing his hands in mine, I can only hope his definition of *hard* right now is the definition I want it to be.

"You *think?* Because I don't *think.* I *know.* It's nothing I ever expected, but I know. You…changed the way I breathe. I don't take a breath without knowing it marks the seconds I get to be with you or the time I'm counting until I can see you again. I didn't know somebody could do that to a person. I don't know what you've done to me, but I don't want it to stop."

"For real?" He smiles on a puff of air.

Stroking his cheek, I find myself laughing in relief at his delight and surprise. "For real."

Exhaling, he wraps his arms around me tight and buries his face in my neck. Hugging him back, I realize he hasn't exactly answered my question.

"Is that a *yes?*"

Drawing back, he beams up at me. "You want me to be your boyfriend?"

My next breath practically chokes me. I didn't consider that's the word I just described. Jesus, I'll have a boyfriend.

Grinning, he cups my face and nips at my lower lip, easing my fears. "You *do*," he challenges. "Say *yes.* "

His giddiness makes my answer easy to give. "Yeah. I do."

"Oh, my gosh," he exclaims with a little bounce, wrapping his arms around my neck. "I'm going to be the best boyfriend ever!"

"Because you'll have been the only one." I chuckle.

"Yeah, that too, but still."

And then *my boyfriend* kisses me until my lips are raw.

CHAPTER 39

Graham

Having a boyfriend is exhausting. If I thought Dami was high-energy before we started dating, I'm not sure what to call him now. To think I'm the cause of his boundless energy and joy is humbling. His smiles and laughter feed me every day like a drug I can't get enough of.

Since our "hard" conversation, I've slept like a rock the last two weeks. Each night I pass out after making love, making out, or just lying there talking, afraid to close my eyes in fear of missing a moment with him. And then it starts all over in the morning with kisses and laughter over breakfast as we get ready for work. It's the best kind of exhaustion.

I can't say how many times I've stopped just to look at him with the wondrous thought on the tip of my tongue—*so this is what dating really is?*

"What are you so excited about?" I ask the grinning fool in my passenger seat.

"I get to kind of officially meet your family. It's my first Brandt cookout. This feels sort of huge."

For once, his optimism deflates me. Does he have expectations for this dinner? It's bad enough that Aiden was the one who invited him, not me. *I'd* like to have been the one extending the first invitation to one of my family's dinners, just…not this soon, and definitely not while I have to pretend that I'm not crazy about him.

"Um, you know I haven't told them anything. Right?"

"Yeah, but I still get to see them in their natural habitat, where you grew up, and see you interact with them for the first time since we've been dating. It's like this will be their first impression of me in my mind."

"Right." I chuckle nervously.

Do I want to know what their impression will be? The possibility of them not liking him makes me ill.

"Well, I'm sure they'll like you," I add, mostly to reassure myself.

"You think so?"

The fact that he cares about my family accepting him both warms my heart and tilts me off-balance. How many times seeing us together will it take before they suspect something? I don't know how to have that conversation. How will they react to me switching teams after all these years? Jen is like another daughter to my parents.

"What's not to like?" I counter.

The terrified part of me shouts in my head, *the fact that he's a guy!* Dami grins at my compliment. Why do I feel like I don't deserve it?

When we pull up to Mom and Dad's place, I don't get a chance to wrangle my nerves one last time or lay conversation ground rules with Dami. He barrels out of the truck as soon as Johnny and Aiden wave to him like this is a carnival and he's got unlimited tickets.

I follow them through the fence gate to the back yard, grateful Dami isn't lingering at my side and offended that he isn't. This sucks already, especially seeing Johnny and Aiden hand in hand. It's not fair they can do that while Dami and I can't just because I didn't know what I wanted fifteen years ago, and his parents have unwittingly placed expectations on him.

"Dami!" Maxie coos from near one of the patio tables. "Welcome to the weekly Brandt-o-rama."

Veronique gives Dami a warm welcome, helping me relax. The woman is a saint, so I know he's in good hands even though instinct tells me to give Maxie a stink eye to deter her from bad mouthing me.

"There you are, stranger," my mother says, wrapping me in a hug.

Bending down, I reciprocate, my chin bumping the top of her sandy brown hair. I don't understand how my brothers and I came from this petite woman.

"I was starting to wonder if we wouldn't see you until the wedding," Mom jests, but it throttles me with guilt.

I skipped the last three cookouts to spend time with Dami. I'm surprised I got away with it for that long.

"Sorry. I've been busy."

"Is your suit ready to go for the ceremony?"

Sighing, I nod. "Yup. Still ready for the wedding of the century."

Giggling, she glances over toward Maxie and Veronique. "It is. I worry she's been so excited she'll be sad when it's finally over like a crash after a high."

"Yeah, well, that's called marriage," I snort, but want to bite my tongue as soon as the words are out when she frowns at me.

"Oh, Graham. I'm sorry. This must be hard for you."

I don't even know why I said that. It's like it was a remnant of the auto pilot attitude my brain had been stuck in the last few years.

Shaking my head, I squeeze her shoulder. "Nah. I'm good. I'm actually excited because as soon as it's done with then I won't have to hear about it at work anymore."

"Jen's bringing David, I guess," she informs me with a sullen expression. "Have you two…had anymore dinners?"

Fucking perfect. "No. We, uh, talked the other day though. She's doing good. I think they might be moving in together."

"Oh!" Her face lights with surprise as she studies me.

I can't take the scrutiny or the reminder that my entire life story consists of a life I no longer have. How can I possibly reprogram my family when all they know of me is Jen and Graham? I nip it in the bud before she can barrage me with questions.

"It's fine, Mom. Really. Bound to happen sooner or later."

Smiling sadly, she rubs my arm. "Yes. I suppose. So, are you…bringing anyone to the wedding?"

It takes everything in me to not look at Dami. He'll be helping his father in the kitchen at the reception hall. I was comforted by the knowledge that he'll be close by, but now that I have to tell my mother I'm going stag, it feels like the person I want by my side is a scarlet letter I'll have to avoid.

"No," I let out with a scoff. "Weddings aren't an ideal date night, if you ask me."

She lets out this sigh like I'm a sad, hopeless case. Across the yard, Skyler's twin boys are beating the shit out of Dami with plastic light sabers. Laughing, he deflects a blow to his perky ass and snatches one of the boys up around the waist as he tries to defend himself from the other one. Snickering at the scene, my heart warms at the natural glee on his face, hinting at what a good father he'd be.

Fatherhood, that's one of the things he said he wanted. How is he going to get from not being out to being a married father in Olympus?

"Aiden and Maxie say that Dami is turning out to be quite the worker," Mom comments as she smiles on the scene. "He seems like such a nice boy."

"He's twenty-three, Mom. Not exactly a kid," I reply with more heat than necessary.

"Well, twenty-three is a kid to me," she laughs with a shrug, saving me from the flush in my cheeks betraying me, but not pacifying my ire over her age gap comment.

Will she think I'm lewd for being attracted to a younger man?

Skyler and his wife Ashley stroll over, laughing, their arms around each other's waists. They pause to whisper something and share a kiss.

Skyler tilts his beer to me and nods. "Hey, glad you made it."

I haven't seen him looking this relaxed in years. "What are you so happy about?"

Tilting his head to where my father is sitting with their twin girls on his lap, not far from where one of the boys is now riding Dami's back like he's a pack mule, he says, "Two babysitters. I don't have to have my *dad radar* on."

"I wouldn't be so sure about that." I grimace even as Ashley departs to go save Dami from a beating. "One of the boys is making Dami eat grass."

Sighing, he shakes his head. "Well, at least it's not dirt."

"Which one is that anyway? Luke or Maddox?"

His face goes blank as he stares at the boys while Dami laughs, sputtering blades of grass out of his mouth. "Um, I'm not entirely sure."

"They're five. You still can't tell them apart?"

"She just got them haircuts," he snaps. "I told her not to do matching haircuts again, but they think it's funny so they can get away with more shit and blame the other one."

Shaking my head, I don't convey the sympathy I feel. Remembering Jen's freak out, I have to wonder how I'd handle twins let alone one child at the age of thirty. Am I too old to have kids now? Is my patience too trained to be short fused? Everyone says I'm a hothead. Maybe I'd be a terrible father.

"It's okay though," Skyler adds. "I put a mark on the back of Luke's neck when he's not looking?"

"You what?"

"With a sharpie," he clarifies, then looks at me like I'm the one with issues. "If you put it on his hand, he'll wash it off right away, or Maddox'll draw one on his hand."

"You fucking draw on your kid with permanent marker?"

"Hey, zip it. Ashley's coming. She doesn't know."

Pinching my eyes shut, I feel a headache coming on.

"So, Graham, Rosanna Muir was asking about you the other day," Ashley says.

"Ye-ah. What about?"

"Well, you know, since you're available."

"Oh! She's a beautiful girl," my mother pipes in. "And she's divorced too."

The headache is now real along with a bout of nausea. I volunteer to go get more paper plates when my mother declares the food is almost done on the grill. As I head into the house, my head is swimming with new conundrums.

My father is in grandbaby heaven since retirement, something I don't even know how I could contribute to. My family thinks Dami is a babysitting kid, that I should be upset over Jen and want to bring a woman to the wedding, and if I ever do have children, Skyler will brand them with toxic chemicals. They're fucking nuts. Dami will definitely rethink dating me if he sticks around any longer.

Staring blankly at all the shit in the pantry, my head wants to implode. Everything went from perfect to impossible in the course of an hour.

"Oh, hey! There you are," Dami's voice says from the pantry doorway. "Can you show me where the bathroom is?"

Turning around, the conflict in me expands, a painful ball of anguish in my chest. He's so fucking perfect. How do I let perfect go even if I can't imagine being able to hold onto it much longer.

"Graham? You okay?"

Grabbing him by the shoulders, I tug him into the pantry and up against my chest. I can't breathe, and he's the air I need. Crushing my lips to his, I'm a thief, taking things I don't deserve, things I was never meant to have, things I don't know how I ever existed without. He responds how he always responds, melting into me like he's filling cracks and making me whole. His arms slink around me. His soft lips part, welcoming me, pulling me in deeper to the world I want to never leave. Moaning, he pulls my hips tighter to his. *This need*, this fucking need is so cruel. Why does it ravage us only to force us to stay in the shadows?

Pivoting, I back him up against one of the walls of shelves, determined to get and give every taste I can before we have to go back outside. His mouth moves to my neck. The sound of his deep inhale like he's taking a hit of me makes my eyes want to roll back in my head.

"Wish I could see your old room," he whispers. "And make out on your bed like teenagers."

My hips tell him what I think of that alternate reality, grinding him into the canned goods. "You'd have been a bad influence," I rasp.

"It would have been all your fault," he whimpers when my teeth nip his earlobe.

"Graham! Where the hell are you with the plates?" Maxie's voice calls, sounding close. "I need to eat. I'm not one of those brides who starves herself before the wedding."

Spinning Dami around, I move him to the back of the pantry in an effort to keep him out of sight, but in my haste the momentum makes him lose his footing. He trips over a case of soda and stumbles into the back wall, grappling for one of the shelves to right himself as he makes an *oof* noise.

"Got 'em," I call, shuffling to the door and thrusting a package of plates at Maxie just as she nears the door.

"If you're this slow at my wedding, you're not going to be in the photos," she deadpans.

"I'll try to live with that."

Scoffing, she yanks the plates out of my hand and sneers, "Is it physically painful for you to be happy?"

Sighing, I turn around and find Dami straightening his shirt with an impish look on his face. When the door to the house slams shut behind Maxie, I finally breathe.

"Sorry. I got a little carried away. You alright?"

"Yeah." He chuckles. "Man, you and Maxie really don't like each other. Huh?"

"She likes to point out all my flaws, all the time," I reason. "And she's good at it, so I won't be surprised if your image of me changes after talking to her enough times."

Frowning, he steps forward. "Dark secrets?"

"No. No secrets." I shake my head and tug at the hem of his shirt. "Just the one I told you."

He smiles but it's halfhearted at best. "I know why I haven't told my parents, but have you considered telling your family?"

"No," I scoff, instantly hating the way he frowns at my quick reply. "I mean, yeah, I've thought about it, but thinking about it makes me not want to tell them."

"I don't get it. Aiden's bi, Maxie's a lesbian. What are you afraid of?"

Everything, I think as I stare into his concerned blue eyes. What if my family treats me like an alien for the rest of my life if I tell them I like a man? What if Dami stops looking at me like I'm *fire?* What would be the point then? How do I act around town? My entire life, everyone in my bubble has thought I was straight.

"They have this idea of me, and I don't know how to break it or what will happen if I do."

"It's okay, Graham. I'll be there for you."

That sounds like a window to close the conversation, so I close it with an appreciative smile. "Thanks."

For the first time in my life, I actually agree with Maxie on something. It is physically painful to be happy.

CHAPTER 40

I am the worst employee ever, but it's not my fault. We didn't have sex last night, so I am fully re-charged today, and the way Graham has been looking at me all day with those hood-eyed, heated little smiles is at the top of my kink list this week. It's almost our afternoon break. It's not like I'll be cutting into work hours too much, if I make the first move. I'm just speeding things along.

"Phew," I declare, fanning myself with my Henley, leaning against a half wall we finished yesterday. "I'm getting sweaty."

"Maybe you're hormonal," Graham snarks, applying mud to the window frame he's finishing off.

Tugging the bottom of my shirt over my head, I make a show of stretching out my abs in slow motion. I have to bite my cheek when I hear the sound of his trowel stop scraping. Dragging my shirt down my chest, I throw my head back and sigh, and then fan myself.

"What are you doing?"

"I'm getting hot. Aren't you hot?" I toss my shirt over the half wall and hook my thumb into the waist of my jeans, pulling them away from my waistline just enough to see the band of my underwear.

Graham shoots me a doubtful look. "It's fucking fifty degrees out. It's not hot."

"Yeah, but I worked up a sweat," I explain, trailing my fingertips down my abs to my happy trail.

His gaze follows their path. When his eyes return to mine, I wet my lips tortuously slow.

His nostrils flare, and he grits out, "Dami."

Resting my hands on the wall behind me, I lean back and spread my feet, jutting my hips out just a fraction. "So hot," I whine.

His trowel clatters to the floor. My pulse kicks as he stalks over to me like a predator and rests his hands on the island counter on either side of my hips, effectively caging me in.

"You're full of shit," he whispers at my lips.

My head rattles back and forth as I stare at his lips. "I'm not. I swear."

"You know how I know?"

Narrowing my eyes, I study his face. Is he seriously going to turn me down? "How?"

Tilting his chin to my side, he says, "Because you brought your sex backpack inside and," he dips his head and laps his tongue over one of my nipples, making me suck in a breath when he blows on it, "your nipples are hard."

Gripping his hair before he can get away, I drag his head up. "Well, now I'm cold," I complain. "So, you'd better warm me up, boss."

Scoffing, he kisses me, but pulls back to add, "I'm not your boss."

"That's too bad," I moan when he kneads my ass. Rocking my hips into him, I reach for the button of his jeans as I pepper his neck with kisses. "Because if I had a boss, I'd be so good to him."

"Yeah? Good how?" he breathes, working my belt open like it's an emergency.

Heck, yeah. I have the best ideas.

Grabbing his shoulders and maneuvering him around so we've changed positions, I push him back to sit on the island cabinet we paved around. His ass scoots back onto the plywood covering it that we've been using to set our supplies on.

Smirking, I hike my leg up and quickly work off one of my boots as I nuzzle the growing bulge in his jeans. We've never screwed on the job before, and I'm not about to let the chance of living that fantasy pass me by. Graham gasps and delves his fingers into my hair.

I shove my jeans and underwear down, kicking them off my freed foot, and snag a condom and lube packet out of my pocket—yeah, so I did grab it out of the sex backpack a few minutes ago. Sue me, Graham.

Climbing onto his lap, I drink up the arousal and surprise in his eyes as I straddle him. "I'd let him know how much I appreciate him by showing off all my skills," I purr, trying not to wince as the plywood scrapes my knees.

"What kind of skills?" he breathes at my collarbone, then traces it with his tongue.

"I should probably just show you." Reaching between us, I tug him out of the opening of his boxer briefs, enjoying the way his hiss says how sensitized he is right now.

When he reaches to remove his hard hat, I get a visual that I can't unsee and grab his wrist. "Leave it on?" I practically beg.

Snickering, he shakes his head and snags the lube packet out of my hand. I feast on his neck, the musk of his soap mixed with a light sheen of pure Graham sweat going to my head. With the cool air ghosting my ass and his denim covered thighs rubbing against mine, all my senses are on overdrive as his fingers slicken my entrance.

"Yeah, boss. Just like that," I moan.

"Such a distraction to the job site," he rumbles, his fingers working me open. "These better be some good skills."

"They are, but I need your help," I gasp, working the condom onto him, grinning when his hand and breath stutter. Rising to my knees, I guide him to my hole. "Need you to just…sit still so I can…give you a demonstration," I pant, working myself down his shaft.

Gripping my hip, he makes a strangled noise. My gosh, the way he bares his teeth as he fills me will never get old. Moaning shamelessly, I grip two handfuls of his flannel shirt, my dick growing harder at the sight of his hooded eyes under his hard hat as I take a slide up and then down on the best tool in this place.

"Oh, God," he grits, his eyes flickering between mine and where we're connected. He snares my neck and tugs me to his mouth, lassoing his tongue around mine, rocking his hips up into me. "You look so good on my cock," he rasps. "Not gonna share you with the boss."

"Yeah?" I whine, shoving him down so his back hits the plywood. "Then I'd better give you the private demonstration I've been…saving just for you."

Resting my palms on his chest, I undulate. Graham's head falls back against the wood with a *thunk*, forcing his hard hat down over his eyes. His mouth falls open, his fingers kneading my hips with every rocking motion. Work-sex is officially the best sex ever.

Picking up my pace, I can't hold back the urge to instigate more of his dirty talk. He lets it go like it was the first dollar he ever earned; the kind people frame on a wall in a bar.

"Maybe I need a new boss then. Think you can…fill the position?"

Choking on a laugh, he thrusts his hips up into me, making my eyes roll back. "You're gonna…pay for this," he gasps. "I'll fucking fill it," he growls, showing off the strength in his arms, slamming me onto his cock in rapid succession.

All of a sudden, his hands tighten harder around my hips, holding me suspended at the tip of his cock. I try desperately to make the sweet descent, but he goes rigid, holding me aloft. Something slams in the distance. I hear voices.

"Shit!" he whispers, knocking the hard hat off his head.

I take the opportunity to drop back down onto his shaft. I'm so close, he'll have to fight me to stop.

"What are you doing?" he grunts.

"Finishing," I pant, going for another slide.

Gripping my hips, he battles against me. "Dami, damn it! Get off my dick," he seethes, hoisting me off him and scrambling to his side.

My leg grazes the side of the plywood, scraping the inside of my thigh. When Graham barrel rolls off the other side, my weight lifts the board, dumping me and several tools onto the floor.

I yelp but catch myself on all fours on the floor. My knee throbs from the impact of landing on a hard crumb of mortar.

"Fuck! It's Aiden and Maxie," Graham curses.

I hear a zipper and the shuffling of clothes. "Get dressed, I'll distract them," he whispers, then the stomp of his boots against the floor make their way through the outside exit.

Geesh. He didn't even check on me. As I finagle my pants back up over my hips, and locate my other boot, the sting in my knee fades to the background. Does he seriously still have a condom on his dick inside his jeans? I get the not coming out thing to an extent, but these are his siblings and that seemed a bit over the top. I could have cracked my head open. I can't help but feel bitter at the way his words sounded like an order. Clothe myself post-haste like I'm something to be ashamed of. Maxie and Aiden have gay sex all the time. I'm starting to think Graham not coming out has more to do with Graham than his family.

Aiden and Maxie stay for about forty-five minutes, a very awkward forty-five minutes of them perusing our work while Graham makes very little eye contact with me, and I try not to limp. Each minute that passes burns the dirty brand of *secret* deeper into my skin. We've been dating for almost a month. I don't even remember what Johnny's swing bed feels like because I've spent every night at Graham's. He's come over to my apartment a few times, but never to spend the night. When I imagined my forever guy, I kind of imagined him not being ashamed to be seen with me.

"Hey, you alright?" he asks, sauntering back into the building when Aiden and Maxie drive away.

"Um, yeah. Sort of."

Closing the distance, he cups my face. His hands have become an extension of my own body that I need on me far too often. "I'm sorry. Did you get hurt?"

Chewing my lip, I stare at one of the buttons on his shirt. "Mostly on the inside?" I venture.

"What?"

Sighing, I force my gaze up to his face. "That…didn't feel good, Graham. You shucked me off like I was diseased."

"I'm not going to let me brother and sister see me fucking someone," he scoffs.

"I…honestly don't think that they'd care."

He sputters for more air. "Maybe you're fine being that indiscreet, but I'm not. I don't want to see them screwing their partners."

The word indiscreet gnaws at me. I have a feeling it doesn't just apply to the sex. "I just meant that we could have stopped a little more calmly and buttoned up casually like we weren't committing a crime."

"Yeah," he finally concedes. "I just…I wasn't expecting them."

"What'll happen if they do catch us some day?"

Why does he keep scoffing? I really hate that I've just found something about him that annoys me.

"You say that like you're planning for it to happen."

"You say that like you think getting caught might never happen," I counter, my stomach clenching in knots. "You never stay at my place, Graham. I'm not trying to push you into anything, but we should talk about it. Do you think you'd ever come out?"

Sucking in a breath, he shoves his hands in his pockets. "Dami, you don't know what it's like."

"Yes, I do."

"Yeah, and you're not out either. What about you? When are you going to come out to your parents?"

"I want to," I reason.

"Well, wanting to and doing it are two different things," he grumbles, returning to his work on the window. What's the point in me coming out if you aren't out?"

"So, I'm holding up the show?"

Sighing, he jabs at the mortar on his board. "I never said that. You're the one making a big deal out of this."

A big deal? How is us not being able to be together whenever we want not a big deal. Feeling defiant, I lift my chin. "Fine. I will."

"What?" he turns around and blinks at me.

"I'll tell them."

"I wasn't asking you to. You don't have to do that."

"No. I want to. I've been meaning to. I'm not ashamed of who I am. I can't keep hiding it."

"I'm not ashamed of you," he mumbles. It lacks so much conviction though, I think my heart might split in two.

We don't exchange a word for the rest of the afternoon with the exception of the bare minimum required for work. By the time we get back to the warehouse, it feels like every organ in my body is experiencing a slow death.

"Are you…stopping by tonight? I don't know when the rehearsal dinner will be over." His voice is low as he gazes out the window of the truck.

Someone who wasn't ashamed of me might look at me when they ask that, a voice in my head tells me. He's scared. I get it, but I'm scared too. We should at least be able to have a conversation about it, but Graham's never been the best at conversations. Maybe action is what he needs.

"No. My parents asked me to help them, so I'd better stick around afterward and help get things ready for the wedding tomorrow."

"I'm sorry. I hate that you have to work it instead of being a guest at it. I fucking hate weddings," he grumbles, running his palms down his face.

Maybe I'm being sensitive right now, but I kind of hoped my forever guy would be excited about one wedding in particular. The thought of marrying Graham is such a shot in the dark considering where we're at right now. I know we've only been dating for about a month, but it's something to assess. Where would he even see us going, especially if he can't come out?

My head is a mess. I know I'm being a hypocrite. Maybe a night apart is a good way to work on our individual issues.

"It's alright. I'd have helped Ma and Pop anyway."

He flashes me a tortured smile and squeezes my arm. "Alright. I'll call you later?"

Nodding, I force a cheery expression and get out of the truck. Why does this feel like the beginning of the end?

CHAPTER 41

Graham

Do you know how awkward it is to sit on your ass at a table full of people while you're being served by your boyfriend like he's some third-rate worker? I fucking hate this. I've barely gotten used to the word boyfriend and Dami wants us to go in all guns loaded.

I let him down. I could see it on his face. He cornered me, and I choked. I don't even remember what I said to him, but I can tell by his sullen expression it wasn't well received. Now he's not spending the night at my house. That's a red flag right there. I can't give him what he needs just because I'm new at this.

I mean, what does he expect? How many times do I have to tell him that I'm thirty years old and let the world think I was in love with a woman my entire life? It's not fucking simple. What's wrong with the way things have been going? I hate it. I fucking hate it, but it's not terrible.

Maxie shoves more food in front of me that I don't want to eat. I can't touch a bite of it knowing Dami had some part in serving it, while he's right. He should be sitting here next to me. This sweater collar is choking the shit out of me. Choking the guilt, the frustration, the doubts, and the worry, funneling them off at the base of my throat.

What's so bad about our quiet nights together? Can't we just enjoy those a little bit longer? I knew he'd get bored of me. He's so young and impulsive. He can't just stop to appreciate things. No. He's got to have the whole ball of wax all at once. A husband, kids, a freaking gay pride parade down main street where we bare our souls to the world.

"Thank you, Dami," Mom says, taking a plate from him. "Are you going to have one of these dinners anytime soon? Bob set up a great family benefits package with the business before he retired."

Oh, Jesus. Kill me now.

"Uh, no. Probably not," he laughs nervously.

"Oh, a handsome young man like you. I bet it'll happen sooner than you think."

Dami's mother smiles at Mom, collecting empty plates. "Dami had all the girls chasing after him in school," Donetta Andropolis boasts, making me feel smaller with each word. "He had dated one for a long time, but they broke up last year. I had hoped they would get married."

"Oh, I'm sorry," Mom tells Dami, patting his hand. "But you never know. Maybe you'll get back together."

"Uh, no. I don't think so," Dami replies. "We're not really compatible."

I want to throw him a lifeline, but all I can do is sit here like a statue. I can see my future in front of my eyes, my mother asking me the same questions for all eternity. This is hell. Why does everyone assume everyone is straight anyway? Maybe they're the problem, not us.

"Oh, nonsense," Donetta *tisks* her tongue. "You were the perfect couple. I bet if you sit down and have a nice talk, you two can work it out again."

I watch my lover's cheeks flush as his hand freezes where he's reaching for a plate. Imagining him with some age-appropriate woman seems laughable when I know the things that he's done with me. The absurdity in the air is so thick, I could cut it. My skin prickles, telling me we're being traitorous by letting our families believe these lies, but I can't move a muscle, hanging on Dami's response.

Straightening up, his gaze is aimed at the salt and pepper shakers on the table but seems a thousand yards away. I want to go to him and wrap him in my arms. I want to whisper in his ear to forget about all these people and only worry about what we think of each other. But I do none of those things when he blurts out, "I'm gay."

There's a few clanking of utensils against porcelain until all of my family realizes the rest have gone quiet. It's so silent you could hear a pin drop.

Dami's mother lets out an awkward laugh. "*Tesoro,* what?" she calls to him.

I catch his father standing at the end of the table behind my own father. His face is an eerie mask of what looks like understanding, as though he's bracing for the inevitable. My fucking pulse is pounding in my skull.

"I…I'm gay, Mama," he repeats, looking her in the eye. "Angelica and I won't ever get back together…because I'm gay."

How many times does he have to say the word *gay* before someone else decides to say something? He's fucking drowning and I'm just sitting here, petrified he'll look at me and aching that he won't.

"That's great, Dami. So, are you seeing anyone?" Maxie asks, folding her hands under her chin and smiling like she's having a casual conversation.

I want to kiss her for being normal for once in her life, but my lungs are locked up from the question she chose. This is it.

"No," he says with one of his nervous laughs, but it feels like a knife, especially when he adds, "there's nobody."

"Aw, well, you should come out with me and Veronique when we get back from our honeymoon. We can introduce you to some people," Maxie adds, earning her a throat punch from me in the near future. Except I can't throat punch a girl, so my brain feels like it's going to explode knowing I'll get no satisfaction.

Dami just chuckles and nods. Fucking nods. Then he scurries away to the kitchen, face red, and I swear his eyes search for me in his peripheral. A few seconds later after my family has gone back to talking like nothing just occurred, his mother excuses herself.

I want to jump out of my chair and track him down to tell him I'm proud of him, to make sure he's okay, to make sure his parents don't roast him over a pit, but the clip of her heels is swift as she heads toward the kitchen. So, I sit in my seat…where I'm nobody. Fucking nobody.

That's all this was, wasn't it? Him proving a point to me while I sat here like a coward, like the guy that can't give him what he needs. Because if I can't give him what he needs, I'm nobody.

CHAPTER 42

I might pass out my heart is hammering so fast. I did it. I ripped off the bandage. More like a freaking coat of arms, but I did it.

Bracing the edge of the sink, I stare out my window. The night suddenly looks so very different as though there's endless possibility under the moonlit sky. This window is no longer a prison. It's my freedom.

The clip of my mother's heels grows louder. The door swings, creaking on its hinges. The dishes rattle on the loose shelf behind me when it shuts. Silence. Nothing but silence.

A second later, the door creaks again, I know it's my father. How is it possible to distinguish two different people's silence?

"Why didn't you tell us?" my mother whispers.

I don't miss the sense of betrayal in her hushed voice. The fact that it's hushed also makes me bold. I refuse to be a secret any longer. Even as her "straight" son, I lived in silence.

"I can't tell you anything," I say to the glass, refusing to let go of the sight of freedom.

"What do you mean? You can tell us whatever you want. We are always here. You never once said anything all those years with Angelica."

"Mama, I pretended to date her for you," I confess, turning around. "You…you wanted so much for me. You want me to run the restaurant, but you guys won't let me do anything. You want me to get married and have kids, but you wouldn't let me earn an income on my own. You want me to be responsible, but you guard my bank account like I'm a kid and it's my piggy bank I can't be trusted with. You still buy my underwear. I'm twenty-three years old and my mother still buys my underwear. I've never gotten my own paycheck and all you guys let me do is the dishes. Did you know how much I like to draw?"

A puff of breath leaves her lips. I feel like a horrible son, but I can't stop the dam overflowing inside me. My father stands like a mute behind her, his gaze to the floor, shoulders slumped in defeat for me fighting the battle he could never win.

"Of course, we know you like to draw. What does that have to do with…with *this?* And when you need money, I give it to you."

"Yes, but I shouldn't have to ask. It's humiliating always having to ask. What if I wanted to buy condoms? I'd have to ask my mother for condom money. And *this*…this has a name. It's *gay.* I'm gay, and I always have been, but I was so scared to tell you because…" I have to say it. If I don't say it now, I never will. "Because I know how much it hurt you to lose Stefano, but I can't live for him. I'm a different person than him. I can't do all the things you wished for him. He's gone, and it was awful, but I'm still here. I won't break if you don't keep me under a glass. I won't disappear from your life if I don't live in your house anymore. I'll always be your son. You just…you just need to let me be the one that I am." Shaking my head, I falter, suddenly very exhausted now that I've spewed out my burden. "I'll probably not always be what you want me to be, and for that I'm sorry, but I love you the way you are. I just…I just wish you'd love me the way that I am."

As her eyes fill with tears, I want to take it all back and return to being her complacent puppet. When she inches slowly toward me, I brace myself. Her hands come up and grip the sides of my face in a classic Italian mother hold as her gaze bores into mine. Sniffling, she nods ever so slightly and presses a hard kiss to my forehead. Then, without a word, she turns and walks out of the room toward the back office.

Closing my eyes, I suck in a breath. When I hear my father's feet shuffle, I open my eyes to find him steering toward the office.

"Pop," I call out. He stops and turns back to look at me. Shaking my head, I caution softly, "Don't."

If he goes after her now, he'll always be chasing after her just as he always has each time she's fallen apart and thrown a fit. Exhaling, he presses the heels of his palms to his eyes. When he draws them away, he walks like a broken man over to the counter where he keeps a stock of his favorite liquor. My feet move without thinking.

Catching his wrist gently, my hand trembling, I shake my head when his confused gaze meets mine. Shaking my head, I tell him softly, "Don't do that either, Pop. No more, please."

His body racks with a tremulous breath, nostrils flaring like a painful demon has just been exorcised from his soul. It sends a chill up my spine. Eyes going glassy, he wrenches me into a hug and pats my back hard.

"*Endaxi. Endaxi*," he repeats. "*Olo einai endaxi*," he chokes out more Greek.

Everything is all right.

For the first time in my life, I believe it. I just thought that everything would be alright in my personal life first before, if ever, that happened with my parents.

Because Graham doesn't call me later or answer when I call him. Everything is most certainly not alright with me and Mr. Right.

CHAPTER 43

Graham

As Aiden makes a toast to Maxie and Veronique, I blink numbly through the flares of camera flashes pointed at us, where I'm trapped on display at the wedding party table. The dim glow of fairy lights strung throughout the reception hall leaves the sea of wedding guest faces in amber shadows like blurry, faceless ghouls that have come to feed on the happiness of others. I am the only one who will survive the carnage, and the only photo that won't be worth framing.

Somewhere out there is my pregnant ex-wife and her boyfriend, whom I'll need to smile at so no one thinks my misery is because I'm a bitter divorcé. Somewhere beyond that kitchen door is a guy with dreams bigger than I could ever dare to fathom, whom I'd have to hold back my smiles for if anyone saw us together.

He called, and I couldn't answer. I couldn't bear to hear a polite explanation of when or how I got put in the nobody category of his life.

He came out. He fucking came out like a lone reed in a tsunami, and he did it like a champion. Every champion has its adversary though, the other guy who gets trampled in defeat.

He came out because I wouldn't. He succeeded because I was failing him. Now the whole world is at his fingertips, and I'm left behind. We agreed to no more lessons, but he had one more up his sleeve. I wasn't enough. I can't give him enough, just like I couldn't give Jen enough.

All that's left is for him to say it. I've been blindsided twice in relationships already. At least I know it's coming this time. I didn't walk into that kitchen after him to console and commend him on his victory I had no part of, so I lost any hope I had that *nobody* was just lip service for our families.

My phone buzzes again in my pocket. With my luck, it's my mother reminding me again to smile. Slipping it out of my pocket, I check it underneath the table, so I won't look like I'm surfing on my phone and get yelled at by Maxie.

DAMI: 911. Please come to the kitchen.

DAMI: I'm sorry to bother you, but it's really an emergency.

What kind of emergency? Knowing Dami it could be anything from him being horny to…fuck, I have no idea, but I certainly don't want to hear his *Dear John* conversation here, tonight.

Grinding my teeth together for a minute, I reread his cries for help. He is a flame, and I'm still a freezing cold moth.

"Fuck," I mutter under my breath and scoot my chair back.

Maxie looks over and arches a scrutinizing brow at me. She said my wedding job was to put out fires.

Shit. What if Dami started a fire?

"I have to check on something in the kitchen. Be right back."

Slinking along the wall past the serving tables, I duck into the massive commercial kitchen. The change from darkness to bright industrial lighting takes my eyes a moment to adjust.

"Hey, thanks for coming," Dami says, rounding a steel rack of pots and pans.

The guy standing in front of me looks like a stranger compared to the one I've made love to over the last few weeks. Wounded and averse to my gaze, he rubs his wrist and looks toward a row of commercial fryers.

"What's the emergency?"

"My mom's running the restaurant tonight. It's just me and my dad, but he had to run back to Tapas because he forgot the take home boxes for the cake. He asked me to fry up the *tomatokeftedes*."

I wait to hear his segue into something about us, but it doesn't arrive. Fidgeting, his features are pinched. He looks like hell. Dami never looks like hell. Rubbing his wrist again, he glances at the fryer like it's a herd of ravenous alley cats.

"I…the fryer. It's just like the one at culinary school but…with more dials," he explains, his blue eyes filled with fright. "I don't know how to work it, but Pop gave me a pat on the back and said he had faith in me. He's never done that," he pauses, looking at me with this bewildered expression that yanks on my heartstrings. "I don't want to let him down. Is it like when we pan fry bacon at your house? Can I pour water in it, so it won't pop and burn me?"

The vulnerability pouring off him is so thick I can taste it. I wanted to be mad at him for being fickle along with all the other ugly things I've thought in the past twenty-four hours, but hearing that he needs me, that I'm the one he called for help unravels some of my bitterness.

Discarding my suit jacket, I hang it on a wall hook and roll up the sleeves to my dress shirt. From the corner of my eye, I watch him shuffle past me to the ovens. He checks on pans of roast chicken, and then stirs a pot of pasta on the stove. He has smatters of humus and tzatziki on his black Tapas t-shirt, a fine sheen of sweat dampening his hair at his temples. He's been hard at work and clearly knows what he's doing aside from his fear of the fryers.

Once I get the fryers to the right temperature, I start dropping the *tomatokeftedes* in. Dami's apprehension fades from his face when he realizes he won't be maimed after he sees me shake out a basket of the fried appetizers. His artist fingers work quickly, collecting them in one of the buffet pans and sprinkling them with freshly chopped oregano. When he starts running food out the door, I can't find it in me to leave yet, so I make myself useful, setting the next pans he'll need on the counter by the doorway. His look of surprise when he returns for the first one makes an ache cut through me. He clearly doesn't expect kindness from me tonight. That can't be a good sign.

I've dallied about as long as I should, since everyone will be eating soon. Refastening my cuffs and donning my suit jacket, I take my time until Dami returns for the last time. Wiping his brow with a rag, he blows out a breath and gives me a stilted smile.

"Thank you. I would have felt awful if I'd screwed those up for Maxie," he says.

I don't fucking want to talk about food. I can't pussy foot around this, so I just blurt it out. "So, how did it go last night?"

Taking a breath, he folds his arms and looks off thoughtfully at some point in the room. "Weird but good. We said things I think we needed to say for a long time."

The relief I feel for him is tainted by the agony of knowing I may not be there to share in his *good new life*. "And they…were okay with it?"

"They weren't *not* okay with it, but I don't care. I'm glad I told them."

The way he says it so confidently is salt to my open wounds. It feels like he's rubbing it in. *This is what freedom and honesty look like, Graham. This is what I have that you don't and couldn't give me.*

"Good," I quip. "Now you're free to work on your plan to find your rich guy."

"What's that supposed to mean?"

"You tell me. You told the world you weren't seeing anyone, that I'm nobody."

"I was protecting you. What was I supposed to do? If I said I was seeing someone, then they would have wanted to know who or meet him."

"So, are you embarrassed of me or just bored? Which is it?" I huff, hating what a child I feel like and that the words keep coming out of my mouth.

Dami must think so too because he scoffs. "Are you serious? I should ask you the same thing. I didn't hear you volunteering any information or answering my phone call last night. You're the one who jumps away anytime someone might see us together."

My face heats as I look away. Dami's never run away from me or hidden. He would have been fine letting Aiden and Johnny discover us. That's not the behavior of someone who's embarrassed by their partner. My entire body is tense from this debate, but I have to admit it's not because of him entirely.

He wanted more, more of me. I should be flattered, not pouting because I don't have the balls to take the leap with him. I'm only mad at one man in this room and it isn't Dami.

"It's not easy for me," I mumble pathetically.

"Do you think that was easy for me?" he counters, but there's no haughtiness to it, just Dami's ever-compassionate tone.

"No," I sigh, my feet moving me toward him. My heart is done torturing the both of us.

I can hear the music and hum of voices just outside the kitchen door. The backdoor has a window with a view to the rear parking lot. I'm not ashamed of him, but I'm not having this conversation interrupted once I start it.

Placing my hand on the small of his back, I guide him to the walk-in cooler, leaving the door cracked so we won't get locked in and freeze to death. He's looking at me like he doesn't know what's going on inside my head, and I'm grateful that he doesn't.

Resting my hands on a shelf on either side of his shoulders, my lungs shout in relief as soon as I feel the heat of his body and get a hit of his freshly showered scent. Resting my forehead to his, I cup his biceps.

"I'm sorry," I whisper to his lips. I wanted to be there for you. I just felt so fucking helpless, and then when you said there was no one, it made me feel like I'm no one to you, and my head went to a bad place. I should have answered your call, but I thought…I thought maybe you were calling it quits because I didn't…say or do anything. I just fucking sat there. I'm sorry. I'm so fucking proud of you."

"You're not *no one*, Graham," he murmurs, running his fingers down my cheek. "You're the *only* one."

"I'm sorry," I choke out against the ache in my lungs, brushing my lips against his. "I'm sorry," I whisper to his cheek, then repeat it at his neck, crushing his body against mine.

I want to cry when he holds me back just as tightly. I keep whispering my apologies down his neck and drop to my knees. I don't know how long we've been in here, but the world can wait for me to let him know what a fool I was.

CHAPTER 44

"Graham, what are you doing?" I gasp, shuddering from the chill of the cooler and the brush of his fingertips as he undoes my fly.

Pressing his mouth against the fabric of my underwear, he murmurs, "Making it up to you."

"N-now? You don't have t-to d-do it right now," I stammer as his hot mouth wraps around the head of my cock and doesn't stop until his lips hit the base of my shaft.

Moaning, I let my head fall back against the cooler shelf and brace myself with one hand. I'm dying to run the other through his freshly cut, combed back hair. He looks so freaking good tonight.

His beige suit compliments his sun-streaked hair like the color was made for him. All dapper, his crisp sleeves hugging the muscles in his forearms, down on one knee, his tie tack glimmering under the cooler lights, I feel like I'm getting a blow job from royalty, like I'm royalty. No matter that I smell like a kitchen and am in my sneakers.

He may look like a million dollars right now, but he's working me like a beggar who's desperate for a meal of cock. Peeking through the crack in the doorway, what I catch of the kitchen is empty and silent, so I stop fighting letting my eyes roll back in my head and buck my hips. He's moaning and growling around my dick and gripping my thigh like he has no intention of letting me go until I lose my mind and hand over my soul. His other hand works its way up my shirt and thumbs my nipple, making my balls tighten and tingle. My heart is hammering, knowing Pop could be back at any moment.

Something creaks. The darkness behind my eyelids brightens. I hear a gasp amidst Graham's growls and suction sounds. I open my eyes to a bright white dress, surrounded in ethereal light, like the vision of an angel, a very shocked Maxine-Brandt-looking angel.

"What the…" Maxie gapes, staring down at where her brother is attached to my cock.

Ohmymotherfreakinggosh!

Just as I yank my hips back to jerk away, Graham must hear her too, because his hands fall from my chest. He draws his mouth off and turns his head.

"Fuck, Max," he gasps like he just saw a ghost.

Maxie's gaze goes from where I just shoved my drenched cock back into my jeans, to my face, and then to Graham's as he stands and swipes at his abused lips.

"What the hell?" she squawks, accentuating each word.

"It's not what it looks like," Graham reasons, both of his hands up.

"You had his dick in your mouth. What else is it supposed to look like?"

"No one else saw. I swear. No one was supposed to see us," he assures her, taking a step forward.

"You fucking hypocrite!" she yells, backing away.

Inching toward her, he reaches for her shoulders. "Max, just calm down. Let me explain."

"No! Don't touch me!" she seethes, batting his hands away. "Don't fucking touch me! All your bullshit for all these years and then this?" she scoffs, gathering up her dress. "On *my wedding day?* I can't believe you."

"Maxie, it's got nothing to do with you. Just forget about it."

"Ugh. Shut it. Just, shut it! I can't even look at you!"

Her dress is a whir of white as she spins around and storms out of view. A second later, I hear the kitchen door rocking on its hinges. What in the heck was that all about? What bullshit is she talking about, and why was she so harsh?

Graham looks suspended in time. I don't even know if he's breathing, his ribcage is still. I can barely move myself. Pushing off the shelf, I take a step toward him, reaching out to place a comforting hand on his back.

He flinches. Why did he flinch?

Turning back to look at me, his mouth hangs open. "I…" he utters, his expression completely traumatized. Raising his hand toward the kitchen door, his face crumples into pure frustration or maybe it's rage. "Do you see? Do you fucking see now what I'd have to deal with?"

Turning on his heel, he dashes out of the room without looking back, without another word.

The portion of time between watching his shoulders push through that door and when my father enters through the back entrance, is nothing but a daze. Pop congratulates me on frying up the appetizers and getting all the food out to the buffet table, but it's an award I can't cherish right now.

Something is off. This feels like more than just a bad coming-out experience for Graham. It feels like an omen. I haven't heard shouting or bawling from the other room, so I can only hope our little tryst either hasn't made the gossip rounds or is being done so with propriety. I need to see him. I need to know if he's okay.

When Pop ducks out back for a cigarette after we get the dishes washed and loaded into Tapas' catering van, I creep to the banquet hall door in the kitchen. I can feel the vibrations of the music through the walls. Nudging the door open a crack, I peer through, trying to locate the beige suits of the men in the wedding party. The sandy-haired one is easy to spot.

He's on the dance floor with Jen in his arms. They're dancing and…smiling. He's…smiling.

I want him to smile, but why is he smiling now…after what just happened? If everything's alright, why didn't he come back in to tell me?

Searching the room, I locate Maxie who's entwined with Veronique on the dance floor. Her expression is somber, but content. Her gaze lifts and connects with mine, making my breath catch. I can't believe she had to see what she did on her wedding day. I should have stopped it.

She holds my gaze for a beat, and I can see sadness in her eyes like one of my drawings, but then the corners of her mouth lift and she gives me a what looks to be an accepting smile. I don't understand. I don't understand a bit of it, while at the same time my stomach tells me I understand everything.

My gut roils as Graham who said he wasn't much of a dancer, slow dances effortlessly with his ex-wife, his eyes crinkling as he chuckles. It looks forced, not the kind of belly laugh I've made him make. When his gaze meets mine, the laughter falls off his face, and he looks away back at Jen. I might vomit.

The picture is as clear as one of my sketches. He can be with a woman he doesn't love, but not with me. He can hold, and dance and laugh with a woman, but not me. The bitch of it is that he doesn't even realize the difference in how he looks when he's pretending versus when he's feeling wonderful. That I know the difference is my curse.

Maybe I'm just kidding myself. Maybe if it was wonderful enough, he wouldn't want to pretend. I can't even be mad at him because he was right. Being nothing to your someone hurts. Being something that no one is supposed to see feels just like being nothing.

"Pop," I call, barely recognizing my own voice as I make my way out the back door. "I'm not feeling very well. I think I'm going to head home."

CHAPTER 45

Graham

Panting, I reach the top step to Dami's apartment, tugging my stupid tie loose. Three hours of the evil eye from Maxie, playing the role of congenial ex-husband by congratulating Jen and David on the baby and their engagement, and hugging every relative my mother said I had to bid farewell to have made this the night from hell.

Maxie didn't say a word to anyone from what I gathered. I have no idea why. She hates me. She always has. This would be the perfect ammunition to destroy me emotionally. While that paranoia was in the back of my mind, I had to pretend to smile all night, while I fought every urge to sneak out back to meet Dami.

When I finally got my chance, his father said he'd gone home sick. Sick, my ass. We're not doing the whole making assumptions and not talking thing again. I learned that lesson last night.

He finally opens the door on my seventh knock. *Seventh.* What the fuck?

There's no way he was asleep. I always pass out before he does. Did he go home to jerk off?

Crap. I hadn't even considered that. Maybe I'm freaking out for nothing.

"Hey," I greet, taking in his bare feet, t-shirt, and sleep pants. "Are you alright?"

"Are *you?*" he counters, giving me a wary once-over.

Scoffing, I yank my tie off and shove it in my pocket. "No."

Chewing on his lip, he blanches. "Did we ruin Maxie's wedding?"

"No. She's always hated me," I assure him, trying to calm my tone to ease his concerns. "Can I come in?"

I thought that was a polite way of asking him to move out of the doorway, but he doesn't. Instead, he says, "I don't think that's a good idea."

The words hit me like a bucket of ice water. There are certain things you grow to expect to hear from your lover. *I don't think that's a good idea* is not a phrase I imagined being in his vocabulary for me.

"What? Why? We need to talk."

"About what?" he says on an exhausted stream of breath, running his hand through his hair. "I'm not going to be the guy who forces another one to come out, Graham because if you did, I still don't see you being cool with all this. I get it. You're not comfortable with us unless it's private, but I can't do that. I don't want to be something that can't be seen. I can't be nothing. You were right. It hurts. I've been nothing my whole life, and…it's not good for me. I like you, but I don't want to be nothing anymore. I don't want to hide."

"You're not nothing." The words fall out, sounding as inadequate as they feel.

His gaze locks onto mine and holds it like he's patiently waiting for me to understand his silence. My heart clenches when I remember what I said to Maxie.

"I *had to* tell her no one saw us. She was freaking out," I reason, but realize that just dug the hole I'm sinking into deeper. "It just came out. Okay?"

Wincing, he straightens up, hugging his arms around himself. "Graham, it's alright. Someday, maybe you'll meet someone you want more than hiding. You know?"

How can he be saying this? I don't want anyone else.

"I'm right," he adds, shifting his feet. "I'm not right often, but you know I'm right about this. You're not ready, and probably won't be for a long time, if ever. I've been ready for years."

"So…what? What do we… Do you not want to see me at all anymore? Are you going to quit and go model again?"

"No. I…if it's alright, I thought I'd take Aiden up on his offer. I can go on other jobs, so we don't have to work together. I think it'll be easier that way."

"*Easier*," I scoff. *Easier* is officially the dumbest word I've ever heard.

His eyes glisten as he presses his lips together. For a second, I almost wish a tear would spill over because maybe it would mean he'd rethink giving up.

"I'm really tired," he says, clutching the door with his hand, a harsh indicator he wants to close it.

I've just fucking lost him. Finally, I nod, but only to let him know I heard sounds, horrible sounds that I don't agree with.

Stretching up on his toes, he presses a soft kiss to my cheek, killing any shred of hope I had left. I just got a fucking kiss of death, and then he shuts the door.

CHAPTER 46

Graham

The only thing worse than a wedding is extending the wedding celebration by having a completely asinine event called brunch the next day, where you have to *ooh* and *ah* over the bridal couple forty-three more times. I think I may actually want to get married again, if only to make Maxie be my maid-of-honor and give her a list a mile long of every cockamamie activity I can come up with as payback.

She's sitting at the end of the table with Veronique, glowing like any bride should be, except for the occasional hell-spawn glare she flashes my way. I bet she's waiting to blurt out her discovery at any moment. She'd love that, so I'm sitting here, ignoring her, looking as miserable as I possibly can. Maybe if she sees that I'm already as low as I can possibly be, she'll realize she won't enjoy her victory. Unfortunately, I wish I actually had to pretend to feel this miserable.

Another spoon tapping against my mother's water glasses chimes. How many fucking toasts do we have to make? We're a blue-collar family who curses at football games on the television. Who the fuck are they trying to kid?

Aiden stands and reaches his hand out to Johnny, who smiles and rises next to him. A double-toast? This won't be awkward.

"We talked this over with Maxie and Veronique. We didn't want to home in on their sunshine this weekend, but we wanted to do this when you were all here. Johnny and I have an announcement," Aiden prefaces, but stops to clear his throat and blush at his boyfriend.

Johnny looks like his breath hitches, and are his…eyes getting watery? Oh, shit. If either one of them is terminal with something, I'm giving up on life after this weekend. It's the wedding curse. I'm telling you.

"We're engaged," Aiden beams. "We're getting married."

My entire family erupts into a fit of squeals and cheers. They're all a blur, shifting out of their chairs to hug Aiden and Johnny. I feel like one of those flies you find in the house in the middle of winter, the kind that you don't know how they got there. They just bump aimlessly off the walls with no sense of direction.

When it quiets down, my senses begin to return. I can feel the pull of Aiden's eyes on me like a strange brotherly beaconing system.

"Graham?" he calls, his elation still on his face.

"What?"

"Well?" He lets out a disbelieving sound. "How about congratulations?"

"Congratulations," I tell him somberly with as much enthusiasm as I can muster.

He met and is going to marry the man that he loves. He paved that path years ago by knowing what he wanted, while I floundered around making a perfectly good woman miserable along with myself, and apparently everyone around me.

"Really?" he scoffs. "That's all you've got to say? What's your problem?"

"Yeah, Graham Cracker," Maxie quips, leaning back against her chair like a gunfighter in an old Western movie. "Nothing to say about your brother marrying a man?"

Aiden's face blanches before my brain can even speed up enough to function. The look of hurt on his face is evident.

"Knock it off," I grumble, but I don't have the energy to put any heat behind the warning.

"Don't you two start," Dad warns. "Not today."

"You're my brother," Aiden sputters, clutching Johnny's hand, who looks stricken over Aiden's reaction. "Can't you be happy for us?"

"I *am* happy for you," I tell him sagely, trying to put more emphasis on the compassion that I feel deep down.

"Oh, yeah. You look ecstatic," Maxie drawls. "What's the matter? Should they just keep it quiet? Elope? Hole up in Aiden's house and not go anywhere in public together because it might embarrass you?"

"Enough!" Dad raises his voice.

"That's not what I said," I warn Maxie and turn my attention to my new brother-in-law, forcing a smile. "Johnny, congratulations. I'm proud to have you as part of the family."

Maxie lets out a dramatic sigh and picks up a doughnut off a serving platter. "Yeah. Just don't expect him to ever admit it to anyone."

Here we fucking go. I glare at her, hoping it will persuade her to shut her trap and stop ruining this moment for them, but of course, she doesn't.

A sickening smile takes over her face. She arches a brow and croons, "Oh? Nothing to say?"

Fuck her. Fuck hiding. Fuck feeling like I'm going to explode. Fuck everyone who ever thought I was straight.

If I have to put up with her crap for the rest of my life because of it, I don't give a shit anymore. I'd have to put up with her bullshit anyway. At least it'd be new bullshit.

"Yeah. I have something to say," my voice comes out on autopilot.

"O-kay," my mother coos in her classic Brandt-sibling-brawl-de-escalation tone. "Everyone just *calm down*."

"I'm gay."

The words hang in the air as I sit trembling with my fists on either side of my plate. A soothing voice that sounds like my own inside my head tells me to *breathe in, breathe out* like I forgot how. It's calming. It's working to ease the tremors, but the silence is sliced in two by a loud bark of laughter.

Maxie whoops out another eerie cackle. Poor Aiden is still standing there, oblivious as to why we're ruining his announcement.

Frowning, he glances from our sister to me. "You think this is a joke?"

Perfect. I was so fucking straight my entire life that he thinks I'm mocking him. Digging my fingers into my eyes, I rest my head in my hands and murmur, "No. I'm gay."

"Unfucking believable!" Maxie snaps.

It's followed by the scrape of my father's chair and deep, booming voice, "Alright. *You two*. With me."

All I see is the look Dami gave me last night when he said without saying how I let him down, how I'd continue to let him down if we stayed together. Maxie's feet stomp against the hardwood floor ahead of me angrily. The next thing I know, my father's hand is on my shoulder, guiding me into the pantry…wait, with Maxie? Turning around, I watch the door slide shut, and then I hear an audible *click*.

Maxie shoves past me without any grace and slams her fist against the door. "Dad! Seriously?"

When she's greeted with silence, she lets out a growl. Spinning around, she leans back against the door, folds her arms over her chest, and glares at me. If there was milk in here, she'd have just curdled it.

"This has nothing to do with you," I tell her, my voice comes out as exhausted as I feel. "I don't get why you're pissed off at me."

Eyes wild, hands flying to her hips, she starts in on me. "You don't *get it?* How can you not get it? *You* don't *get to be* gay. You have no right to be."

"What the fuck is that supposed to mean?"

"All the shit you've given me over the years for being a lesbian and turning your nose up at me, and then you have the balls to sneak around and mess around with some kid at my wedding? Are you just mental or that fucking sadistic?"

I've spent my life defending her and Aiden's right to love whoever they want. All through high school, at bars, even at the fucking grocery store when I've heard people saying, *oh, he's one of those Brandts. His brother and his sister are, you know…*

"What in the hell are you talking about? I *never* gave you shit! You're the one always giving me shit! You've fucking hated me for years!"

"Do you blame me?"

Did all the wedding planning mess with her head? Is she hung over? What is happening?

"Who else am I supposed to blame? What did I ever do to you?"

Scoffing, her head bobs. "Are you shitting me? Whenever I talked about my wedding you got pissy."

"Because it's all you've freaking talked about for a year. It got fucking annoying, and, hello! I'm freaking divorced. Weddings aren't my favorite subject."

The way she sputters and folds her arms tells me at least that point got through her thick head. "It's not just about the wedding. It's everything. You're like a completely different person with me. You hang out with Johnny and Aiden, you help Aiden with projects at his house, and you never avoid Skyler and Ashley. Whenever we have dinner at anybody's house, you make something fancy to bring over, but you rarely ever come to my house. When you do, you don't bring anything or act like you want to be there. I don't get the same Graham everyone else does. I'm your sister. It hurts."

I never thought for a second Maxie cared about a thing I say or do. "I didn't think you wanted me around. You're always sniping at me and insulting the way I do everything."

"Because it feels like you're punishing me or ashamed of me. Every year since childhood, whenever I talked about my girlfriends, you got all embarrassed."

"Not because I was ashamed of you, because I don't want to hear about my sister making out with *anyone*. I don't talk about that shit. Did you ever hear me talk about what Jen and I did in private? No! Because it was *private*! I don't flaunt stuff the way you do. I don't care that you do it, but it doesn't mean I want to hear about it, or that I know what to add to the conversation."

Snorting, she shakes her head and rolls her eyes. "You're such a prude."

"I'm *not* a *prude*. I just like *privacy*," I emphasize like one of those assholes on tacky infomercials who over-stresses everything, so the viewer remembers it. How can I give her the same Graham as everyone else when her only mood is hostile?

"Ha! What about *my* privacy?"

"Like you have any," I mutter, running my hand down my face, hating how this room is getting smaller by the second.

"Clearly, not, especially when you had no problem telling Derek Gunther that I wouldn't put out for him."

Her outburst jars my thoughts. Is she seriously bringing up that shit from high school? God, why couldn't I have had all brothers? Brothers don't hold grudges for fifteen years.

"Would you have?" I challenge, trying to get her to see how ludicrous she's being.

"No, but that's not the point! You were a jerk. You freaking yelled it right in the hallway when he was at my locker. You humiliated me in front of everyone." She waves her arms. "And then you got in that *stupid* fight, and he wouldn't take me to prom after that."

My jaw comes unhinged. "You're pissed off at me because you didn't go to the fucking prom?"

"No, moron! It's not about the prom. It's about you being too much of a coward to go because you can't dance, and you couldn't stand the embarrassment that your out-lesbian sister was going to go with a straight guy because you're hateful."

"I'm not hateful!" I grab my skull, feeling like I need to hold it together to keep from exploding, and whirl around toward the back of the pantry so I don't have to look at her anymore. Something fucking stinks like chemicals in here, giving me a headache, and I have other things to worry about than Maxie's class yearbook. "You have no clue what you're talking about," I grumble.

"Don't I?"

She's not going to quit, and Dad's whole be calm mantra since his heart attack tells me we're not getting let out of here as long as he can still hear Maxie running her mouth. Heaving a breath, I rest my forearms on a shelf and drop my forehead onto them, suddenly done with carrying the weight of the world. I fucked everything up that mattered already, what's one more black mark?

"Jen's mom got arrested, and we used all the money we had to bail her out. We weren't about to ask Mom and Dad to buy us shit for a stupid dance."

For the first time in ten minutes, Maxie doesn't come back with a scathing retort. "I didn't know."

"Because I never said anything because it was *private*."

I shouldn't have gone all infomercial again. I can practically feel her stewing.

"That still doesn't explain anything about what you did to me and Derek," she snaps. "You got kicked off the football team for picking that fight with him, and then you acted like it was *my* fault."

"I did not."

"You did too! Do you have freaking selective memory loss?"

Whirling around, I can't take it anymore. If she wants to hash up stupid shit from when we were kids, so be it. "How could I act like it was your fault when I quit? I never got kicked off."

Her body sways back like my words doused her in ice. "You got kicked off. I remember it perfectly. Everybody was talking about how Coach Rutledge went off on you."

The mention of another name of a long list that I don't want to hear about, has me seeing red. I can still hear every homophobic slur he used to yell at me and my teammates. Jabbing my index finger toward the floor, I've cast off Infomercial Man and gone for drill instructor instead. "Fuck coach Rutledge, and fuck everybody! Did you ever ask *me?*"

"You…quit?" she stammers, all the angry lines in her face finally dissipating. "Why did you quit? You loved football."

"Because Rutledge was a bigoted prick who was always on my ass for having an "abnormal family"," I rage in air quotes, "and I knew as soon as he found out what the fight was about, he'd blame me, so I didn't want to give him the satisfaction of booting me."

Huffing, she frowns. "But that still doesn't explain anything about why you started that stupid fight."

And there's the one bit she isn't getting from me. I turn back toward the wall, chanting my father's words from years ago, *look out for your sister.*

"Don't worry about it. It's none of your business."

"It was too my business! You had no right to start shit with him!"

Maybe I'm just too raw right now from losing Dami or from shooting my sexuality out like vomit at the dinner table. I have one thread left, and Maxie's nearly sliced through it.

"No right? Really?" I challenge, hoping she'll get pissed off enough, she'll just demand that Dad let us out.

"You just wanted to ruin things for me just like you tried to do at my wedding!"

The sting of Dami and I being compared to ruination of anything is too much. Spinning around, the weight, this fucking weight unleashes on my sister.

"Derek-fucking-Gunther was bragging in the locker room that there was no way the *hottest girl in school* could be *a lesbian* and bet his buddies that you just hadn't met a *real man* yet, and that he'd get you to put out! I kicked his fucking ass and told him if he so much as looked at you I'd kill him! I wasn't sorry I did it, and I'm still not. So, fucking hate me as much as you want."

My body sags against the shelves, crunching something under my ass that feels like a bag of potato chips because it pops. Relinquishing weight should bring relief, not make you feel heavier.

A tiny voice squeaks, "Are you serious?"

Great. I made her cry. Sighing, I rotate around to drop my head back on the shelf so I don't have to see the way her eyes are glistening.

"Yes," I say, softly, hoping it'll ease the blow of me crushing whatever fairytale idea she had about that stupid prom and that jackass. "I didn't want to tell you. I didn't want you to ever find out. You had a hard enough time as it was."

"You…got in a few more fights that year. Were they because of me too?"

No more. I can't take anymore today. Veronique is probably worried out of her mind.

"It was a long time ago, Max. Just let it go."

It's quiet for a beat. I take a breath, hoping that means she heeded my advice, but then she sniffles.

"I hate you," she whispers.

Nope. Not finished. Of course, she still does.

"What else is new?" I mutter on a puff of breath.

Turning around, I have every intention of crying uncle and pounding on the door until someone lets us out, but Maxie holds up a hand. "I wasn't finished, Graham Cracker! Gosh! You're so frustrating!" she grumbles, pinching her eyes closed, her hands curling into balls at her sides. I stagger, bracing for more ways I've disappointed her, while my heart pangs remembering all the times that Dami said *gosh*.

Sucking in a breath, Maxie's watery eyes pin me. "I hate you for letting me hate you all these years. I didn't *want* to hate you," her voice wavers. "You should have told me."

Jesus. When I'm wrong, I'm wrong.

"I thought it was better you didn't know what people say. I thought…I was protecting you."

"I don't give a shit what *people* say, but I care what *you* think. You're my brother."

I shrug helplessly, staring at the result of one more thing I held in because I thought it was the right thing to do. "I…didn't think you did."

She growls, and I flinch, expecting now to be the moment she finally decides to kill me. Her hands grab two fistfuls of my sweater and tug once like she's emphasizing something. She stares up at me, lips pursed together like I'm the most frustrating being on the planet. Maybe I am.

I grimace apologetically, and she sighs. The next thing I know, her arms are wrapped around me.

My sister hasn't hugged me in over a decade. I hadn't even realized it until now. It's like holding a long-lost friend I forgot I had.

"So," she murmurs into my chest after a while, "Dami…he's a nice kid."

Christ, how old do people think he is? Don't they have eyes?

Pulling back, I let out a guttural noise. "He's not a kid."

Smirking, she sing songs, "Sensitive silver fox."

"Oh, shut up."

"So…how long have you…been gay?"

Ye-ah. I almost forgot that happened. Here we go.

"Two weeks." I shrug, picking at a soup can label. "Always. I don't know."

I'm saved by a soft knock on the door. Veronique's muffled voice filters through, asking if we're okay.

"Yeah," Maxie calls out. "You can tell dad to spring us now!"

The lock mechanism clicks instantly, and the pocketed door slides open, revealing a very unintimidating pair of my father's steely eyes. Folding his arms, he must know we've grown immune to his death glare because he narrows his eyes for added effect. All it does is make him look older than he is.

"Really, Dad?" Maxie huffs. "Locking us in the pantry?"

"Well, it's not like I can ground you."

"It's like the size of a closet in here." Maxie gestures. "And I think the oranges are going bad."

Sniffing the toxic stench again, I locate a bag of the fruit on the bottom shelf. "Is that what that smell is?"

"Yeah," she says like she still wants to include the word moron after it. "They smell like nail polish remover when they start to rot. Duh."

Dad frowns and disappears down the hallway, his voice booming out, "Margie, we need more oranges!"

"But I just bought some!"

Pinching the bridge of my nose, I don't know if I'm relieved to hear the return of Brandt household normalcy. When I look up, Veronique's worried gaze flits from Maxie to me as my sister takes her hands in hers.

Stepping forward, I cup my sister-in-law's cheek and place a kiss on her head. "Congratulations again. Sorry, if I ruined your brunch."

"Nothing is ruined. We still have to open all the presents." She smiles.

"I'll be right there," Maxie promises, sending her off with a quick kiss.

Glancing over at me, she hugs her waist, giving me a once over like maybe she's seeing me with new eyes too. Flashing me a little smile that's surreal to witness, she starts down the hall toward the dining room. She only makes it two paces when she stops and glances back at me.

"Tell me something," she prefaces, "did he cry?"

The only image I can conjure is of Dami's sullen expression when he delivered his decree last night at his apartment. Forcing my heart back down my throat, I croak, "Who?"

"Derek Gunther," she says in her you're-a-moron tone.

Chuckling sardonically, I give her a smirk. "Like a fucking baby."

Her pleased smile lights up her face, and she nods. I think I'm officially forgiven.

"Go on." I gesture toward the dining room. "Go open all your toaster ovens."

"Pfft. No way. I asked for cool shit like knife sets."

There are only a few things besides Dami that can give me a hard-on. Kitchenware is one of them.

"*Chicago Cutlery?*" I venture hopefully.

Winking, she shoots me with a handgun gesture.

"You know it."

"If you get duplicate presents, I'll take a set."

"No freaking way! Get your own."

The greedy punk. She walks off but stops again at the end of the hallway.

Tugging her phone out of her pocket, she points to the pantry. "Hey, do you want to go back inside real quick and pop out?"

"Why?"

"So, I can take your picture coming out of the closet."

Closing the distance between us, I spin her around as she cackles and give her ass a light shove with the sole of my boot. "I liked you better when you hated me."

Laughing, she saunters into the dining room to reunite with Veronique. Leaning on the doorway, I take in my family, chattering and sorting through gifts, Skyler's kids running around screeching. Everything is normal. Nothing has changed except me, and it has nothing to do with admitting anything about myself or the past. I think it only has to do with trust.

A hand and something cold brushes the back of my arm. Glancing down, my mother smiles hesitantly and hands me a beer. What a travesty I made of her shindig for Maxie.

"Mom, I…I'm sorry I sprang that on you guys like that."

"Why are you sorry?" she asks like I'm a moron but in a much sweeter tone than Maxie does.

"You're always asking about me and Jen. Dad's always talking about grandkids. I…didn't want to disappoint you guys, but…I just…nothing's felt right for years to be honest. I don't even know if I still know who I am yet. I…"

"Graham, honey." She rests her hands on my arms. "We love all of you. I never worried about you as much as the others because you always took care of everything on your own. I thought you never needed my advice because you always knew and did what you wanted, but I can see how hard this was for you. You can ask your father if you want. He'll tell you the same thing—we don't need grandkids. We'd love them, sure, but we don't *need* them. If you don't want kids that's fine with us, as long as you're happy."

"I do," I confess. "I always have."

"Then have some." She shrugs, making me choke at her easy approval.

"With…a man?"

"With whoever you want, sweetie."

Just like that. It rolls off her tongue just like that.

"Jen's pregnant," I blurt out. "She and David are getting married."

Nodding, her eyes twinkle knowingly as though she's happy about the news. "I wondered."

"But you…just asked me about her a couple weeks ago."

Straightening some non-existent wrinkle on my sweater, she frowns at my chest. "I always ask about her because I thought you wanted her back."

"I don't," I admit, letting this cleanse of honesty sweep through me.

"We want whatever *you* want, Graham. So, go find what you want, but promise me something."

"What?"

"Quit worrying about taking care of everyone else all the time. We love you for it, but shut it off now and then. Okay? It's alright to be a little selfish sometimes and think about what you want."

Most of my life I figured my parents didn't really know me. It's quite possible they've known me better than I knew myself.

Hugging her, I don't have to try too hard to think about what I want. I know exactly what I want.

CHAPTER 47

Graham

How the fuck do you go after what you want, when what you want won't talk to you? I get censured *hellos* in the mornings, and that's it before Aiden takes Dami off to a different work site for the day. At least Maxie is off on her honeymoon, so I don't have to find out if she'd bring up the cooler debacle in front of us and my brothers. Something tells me she won't. The ball is in my court.

I've called a few times, but Dami doesn't answer, and I refuse to leave some rambling message. What would I say? I'm not having a heart-to-heart with voice mail or through a text message. No, I will not think about how old that makes me sound.

It's been almost two weeks since Maxie and Roni's wedding. Every day he clearly avoids me adds another pound of depression to my soul. I wanted to tell him my news to see if that would make a difference, but I realized I'd sound like I was bragging or seeking a reward for something he did first without being cornered. Every morning, I hope for just one look, a smile, something to give me a clue as to if I have a chance left, or if he's changed his mind about us. A smug voice in my head repeats, *why would he?* Coming out doesn't mean that I check off all the boxes on his forever guy checklist.

It's Friday night. I can't take one more evening of sitting alone on my couch. Every freaking movie that's aired lately has something to do with the ocean, making me think of Dami and his love of oceanic films.

"Hey, wait up," I shout to Aiden when I see him walking to his motorcycle as I pull back into the warehouse lot at the end of the day.

Killing the engine, I hop out and meet him halfway. "You and Johnny want to go out for a drink?"

I'd really love one-on-one time with just my brother, but I've been making an effort to reassure him how happy I am about his engagement.

The lying bastard part of me also knows that Johnny might have information about what Dami's been up to. I am a glutton for punishment.

Frowning, Aiden scratches his temple. "Uh, well, we kind of are already."

"What? You don't want a third wheel?" I joke.

"No, I mean, we've got Dami's birthday party at Tapas tonight. Didn't he tell you?"

"It's his birthday?"

I realize my brother is scanning my face when the fog of realizing Dami neither told me about his birthday nor invited me to his party clears. Why would he want to include me in special occasions where he thinks I'd pretend he's nothing to me? I know it's my fault, but it still hurts.

"Did you guys have it out again or something?" Aiden asks. "Haven't seen you two talk much since he said he was ready to go on other jobs."

If Aiden knows or suspects something intimate occurred between us, he doesn't let on, and for that I'm grateful. I don't feel like telling my brother what an idiot I was or insulting him by asking how to find courage after the course of a month to be someone he had the balls to be his entire life.

"Something like that," I concede, raking through my hair, but it only reminds me of how Dami used to card his fingers through it. "He didn't do anything wrong," I add, my obligation to protect him still at the forefront.

Aiden studies me for a moment and nods. "Alright, but, uh, remember what I said last week. If you ever want to talk about what you told us at Maxie's brunch, I'm here," he intones with a cuff to my shoulder.

I do remember the way he casually dropped that when he stopped by my work site last Monday with the blatant ruse of checking on my work again. Aiden never pushes. It might be why it took him so long to find his own happily-ever-after. Hell, for years he was pretty much like what I thought of Dami a month ago, landing in whatever bed called to him, but look at him now. He's only got smiling eyes for one person. These Andropolis men know how to bring us to our knees.

"Yeah, thanks. I appreciate that."

His phone pings. When he checks it, a big grin forms on his face, but he clears his throat and shoves it back in his pocket. Judging by his blush, I can only imagine it was Johnny.

"Sorry," he says, clearing his throat.

"Nah, I'm good. You guys have a good weekend."

"You too."

Watching him walk back to his motorcycle, I remember how he up and hopped on a plane to Greece a few months ago for Johnny without any certainty of where they stood. I've learned I'm shit at communicating my emotions, but I'm leery about whether I know which actions speak louder than words.

Mom told me to be a little selfish and to stop worrying about everyone else. Do I have a hero complex that makes me want to take care of everyone? Because as I chase my brother down, the only thing I can think of that I selfishly want is to make Dami's life better.

"Hey, Aiden! Hold up," I call after him. "I need a favor."

CHAPTER 48

Graham

Rolling through town, the trendy business fronts that litter downtown Olympus' ever-growing tourist-speckled streets are an obscene backdrop. *Beans On Banner, The Cheesehead House,* and the most absurd, *Big Head Adult Entertainment* named after nearby Big Head Lake.

I've been casting my sinkers into a lake named after a part of a cock my entire life. How did I not know I was gay?

Shaking my head, I snort as I roll to a stop. It's Monday afternoon, the start of one more week of being on Dami's stranger list. He's twenty-four now. The number has been tumbling around in my head all day. Our age gap has effectively been reduced to only six years.

I don't think I ever really cared about the difference, if I'm honest with myself. He certainly knows a hell of a lot more about life than I do. How to have fun, how to be happy, how to go after what you want, and how to distance yourself from things that infringe on your happiness. My phone rings, and I smile for the first time in two weeks when I see that it's my buddy Thor. The fact that he knows nothing about the epic high of my life or the following shit show it became over the past two months is comforting.

"Hey, Master Chief," I call over the line. "Don't you ever fucking work, or is it all desk job shit now that you're so important?"

His deep voice rumbles through my truck speakers, filling my cab with the soothing memories of friendship. "Man, I wish. It's a painful mix of both."

"Can you go out on a mission anytime soon to scratch the itch?"

It's silent for a beat, and I wonder if the connection got cut, but his commanding voice comes through subdued. "No. I think, uh, I've had enough missions to last me a lifetime. Not really my thing anymore to tell you the truth."

I really must have a hero complex because something tells me instantly that there's more to that admission. "You alright, brother?"

"I don't know." He sighs. "Maybe. Yeah. Just got some shit to work through."

It's a sad thing to imagine how the mighty Thor might have fallen. He has no one but the military, and if that's lost its appeal, I can't picture my buddy doing anything else.

"You still getting out?" I inquire.

"Yeah, I think so. I'm just done, man. You know?"

In an effort to infuse positivity into his mood, I ask about his girlfriend. "I bet Neeva's excited about that. You going to take her on a vacation?"

"Um, Neeva's gone, man. We split up."

"Shit. I…I'm sorry," I stammer. My hero skills are off par today.

"It is what it is. It's for the best, but I didn't call to unload shit on you. How was the wedding of the century?" he jokes, sounding more like his old self, so I go with it if it'll help distract him.

"It was…effective. Two people got married, so it worked."

Snickering, his baritone chuckle floods my cab. "Don't ever apply to be one of those wedding columnists for the newspaper. Okay?"

"That won't be a problem," I say sagely.

"Did Jen go?" he asks, bursting the bubble of laughter in the air.

It feels like there's an endless list of people I have to inform that I'm no longer foolishly pining for my ex-wife. Maxie always calls me a hermit. I never stopped to consider how many people might actually care about the state of my life.

"Yeah, she brought her fiancé, David. They're having a baby."

"Oh, shit. Man, I'm sorry. I didn't know."

"No, it's fine. We're good. I'm happy for them. I…I mean, that ship sailed a long time ago to be honest. I don't know why I thought I had to fix things. We were just married for so long, you know? But it's good. We're good."

Can I say *good* five more times? Wait until I try to tell him I'm gay now. Not having that conversation in traffic.

"Well, shit. You sound…adjusted. I'm glad I called. Sorry I haven't kept up with you. I've just been swamped and trying to look for jobs for when I get out."

"Oh, yeah? Which type of careers are you looking at?" I ask, finally approaching the office building Aiden's been working on. "Wedding columnist? Underwater basket weaver?" I venture.

"Fuck off, smart ass," he chuckles. "No. I've been getting a lot of requests from private security companies."

"What? Like black ops or guarding oil fields?" I squawk in disbelief as I pull into the lot and spot the work truck Dami's been using, but no sign of Aiden's. "Isn't that kind of like missions?"

"No. They're mostly companies that provide bodyguard services for rich people and celebrities. The pay is stupid crazy."

"Yeah?" I ask idly, my stomach making a flip, realizing this is the closest I've come to being alone with Dami since the wedding.

"Yeah, so maybe I can buy a pair of shades and stand there looking pissed off and intimidating to protect some pampered prat or diva. How hard can it be?"

I'm being a shitty friend because I'm not exactly sure what he said, but Mom's request for me to be selfish has me slipping on my hard hat and hurrying out of my truck. "Hey, man. I've got to let you go. Sorry, I'm at work."

"No problem. Let me know if you're up for a visit at the end of the year when I get out."

"Sure. Of course."

My pulse kicks as I walk into the unfinished building. I have no idea what to say to Dami, but the thought of spending every night of my life alone with only family cookouts, where I see my siblings' families and happiness grow and occasional text messages from Thor make my feet move forward.

I finished our house today. Well, not *our house*, the Hodges place that we worked on, although I'll forever think of it as *our house*. I must have sat there for an hour just staring at every spot that held a memory of Dami before I forced myself to leave. I need to know. Even if I can't have him, I need to know if he still cares at all. I can die a happy hermit, if I know the kindest man on the planet thought something of me for a flicker in time.

The sound of music echoes in the empty spaces of the open room, along with the scrape of Dami's trowel. He's working on a window ledge, something I only ever coached him through, and it's turning out nicely. I'm proud of him and also sad how it marks he's moving on without me.

"It looks good," I call out, cringing at how his back stiffens.

"Thanks," he says without turning around. "I still need to cut a few more bricks for the last corner."

I don't want to talk about work or him doing work without me. My mother will be proud of how selfish I'm being right now because all I want is to hear about him even if he doesn't want to tell me.

"How was your birthday?"

"Okay."

"Just *okay?* What? No big camping party?" I joke, but flinch at the same time he does when I realize how judgmental that probably sounded.

He says nothing, just drops his head and rubs the pad of his index finger over one of the seams. I'm pushing him even further away when it's the last thing I want to do.

"Where's Aiden?" I ask just to break the painful silence.

"He went to go do an estimate for someone. I thought I'd stay here and keep at it." Glancing out the window hole, he adds, "He'll be gone for a while, if that's what you're worried about."

Ouch. Hello, *douche-baggery* reminder. I can't imagine how he felt the night Jen stopped by or when Maxie and Aiden dropped by the work site, and then after my freakout in the cooler at the wedding. I'm a fucking prize.

The announcer on the radio introduces an Eddie Money song, and I realize it's the second eighties tune they've played since I got here. Doesn't he shake his ass when he works anymore? I'll feel like a total jerk if he still believes that crap that I said about the radio being broken.

"I thought you didn't like old music?"

"Some of it's okay."

Is he ever going to turn around? Did I hurt him so bad he can't stand the sight of me?

"You don't even look at me anymore," I whisper unable to hold back the complaint a minute longer.

Dipping his head again, his speech sounds low and fragile. "It hurts, Graham. Okay?"

How can someone else's pain give you hope? I don't want him to hurt, but it has me stepping forward to get closer to it, to find out if it's really mine. "Why does it hurt?"

His finger stops tracing the seams of the bricks, and he says nothing. During his apartment confessional, he said I'd never be ready. If I'm not ready now, I don't know what to call it.

"So, I have this plan," I preface. "It has three steps."

His head raises, but he doesn't turn back. "Yeah?"

"Yeah. First, I meet this man who I think is way too young for me, who couldn't possibly want anything to do with an older, grumpy guy who pretended to be straight his entire life, and I fall hard for him."

His chest expands, and he turns his head to the side, making my breath hitch. "Then what?"

"Then I think maybe he falls for me too, but I fuck it all up by being too scared to give him what he deserves."

I can see him chew on his lip from his profile, hands on his hips. "This plan kind of sucks to be honest," he murmurs.

"Yeah. I know," I rasp, inching forward, afraid one wrong move will shatter what I think might be an opening.

"What's part-three?"

"Part-three—I go find him because he's so hurt that he's avoiding me and won't even talk to me. When I find him, I ask him out on a date."

Squinting in thought, he picks at a crumble of mortar on the side of the window opening. "What kind of date?"

"The kind where we go anywhere that he wants to go, and if I'm lucky, he lets me hold his hand."

He turns around and gapes at me in surprise, letting all the air back into my lungs. I don't wait for him to shoot me down or accept, I just keep going.

"The kind…that leads to a second date, and a third. The kind where he lets me introduce him to my family as my boyfriend."

His eyes flare a fraction, and then he dips his head. If someone didn't know his face as well as I do, they might miss it, but I see it. The corner of his mouth hitches up on one side. I have to tell the warmth blooming in my chest to hold off until I'm certain I have a right to hope.

"Is the fourth date the kind where there's dancing?" He asks, glancing up at me, that little smile growing.

I don't need Christmas or birthday presents the rest of my life. I don't need to catch another fish. Big Head Lake could dry up for all I care. I'll spend the rest of my days being thankful for this chance.

Smirking, I inform him, "Really terrible dancing."

"Oh, yeah? Can I get a preview? I'm kind of an expert."

Instinct tells me to remind him he already had a preview, but I can be foolish for a few seconds if it gets me Dami. Stepping over to where the radio is resting on a bucket, I turn up the dial. "Nothing's Gonna Stop Us Now" by Jefferson Starship. I can handle that. Tossing my hard hat at him, I proceed to make a fool of myself for the man I'm a fool for.

CHAPTER 49

He's actually here. He's here, talking about dates in public, and now he's…shaking his ass. He's shaking it very badly like a robot, but he's still shaking his ass…for me.

I've been kicking myself a little more each day since that night he came to my apartment. Part of me kept shouting that he was worth waiting for, that I'd live under a rock with him the rest of my life. The part of me that wanted to act like the responsible adult Graham seemed to want to see when he first met me, along with my wounded heart, kept telling me to be strong, that I made the right decision. The responsible part of me can take a hike, because I'm just now realizing I haven't been horny in two weeks. My decision broke my cock along with my heart.

I imagine he's going to have a difficult time coming out, but I believe him about the dates. I can see it in his eyes. I'll wait. However long it takes, I'll wait.

Adjusting my junk, I plop my ass down on the pallet of bricks behind me as Graham peels his sweatshirt torturously slow over his head, stretching his abs in the process. The smile he flashes me, a sweet mix of remorse and gratitude, as he tosses his sweatshirt at me has my heart fluttering.

"Just a piece of advice," I caution, wetting my lips, "you should probably do this on every date."

Snickering, he steps closer, leans down, and reunites me with the feather duster I have missed with my entire being. "That can be arranged," he assures me tenderly, straightening up and reaching for his sweatshirt in my hands.

I know he's out of his comfort zone, but what the heck? This is like the romcom moment of my life. Dami needs more.

"Whoa!" I warn, holding his shirt out of reach. "What about the pants?"

Frowning, it's cute how he honestly looks clueless. "What *about* my pants?"

"It's still technically my birthday week. I deserve a *proper* strip tease, one that includes pants."

A puff of air bursts from his lips, so I do what any responsible grown man would do. I fold my arms and pout. Sighing, he grimaces and glances around like he's planning on doing cartwheels, and I'm asking the world of him.

Stepping back, he starts jerking his hips back and forth again, looking like the grumpiest stripper on the planet, but I don't care. I get to see Graham's abs in action. I show my appreciation with a giant grin. Snickering, he shakes his head and closes his eyes.

Ohmymotherfreakinggosh! He just whipped his head back with a naughty face and is trailing his fingertips down his chest…down his happy trail. The man wants to kill me. I swear.

"Yes," I hiss like a leaky tire.

Pivoting around, his hands disappear. Oh, yeah. The waistline of his jeans just went loose and is dropping. His thumbs slink around to his hips and shove the fabric down. I need to play old man music for him more often because he looks like he's actually getting into it now. That perfect compact ass of his is shifting more smoothly in time with the song.

Bare, hair-speckled, sexy, muscular Graham legs reveal themselves. His jeans are just a memory around his ankles. *Uhn.* He spread his knees and dipped low. I think he just grunted, and that *pop* noise might have been a joint cracking, but I'll let him know in a minute that it was worth the pain.

Shuffling around to face me, he inches forward, and sends those fingers idly down toward his navel again. There is a giant present come to life waiting for me underneath the blue fabric of his boxer briefs, and I am happy to unwrap it. Reaching out, I barely get my fingertips in his waistband and face nuzzled next to his cock, when he eases me back.

"Hey, hands off the merchandise," he teases. "Eyes up top. I'm a person."

"No way." I shake my head, grabbing onto his thighs and tugging him forward before he can back away. "I want the end of date-four right now."

"So needy." He chuckles, but it gets cut off when I circle his belly button with my tongue and squeeze his ass.

His fingers graze through my hair. I've missed those fingers. I don't care if they're opening a beer bottle or clicking the TV remote. I just want to see them.

Bending down, I unlace one of his boots at the speed of light and tug it off. Checking on him, he looks equal parts self-conscious and turned on, but then he smiles and kicks his foot out of his pant leg. Guiding his thigh, I help him straddle me. This will be the birthday I remember above all birthdays for the rest of my life. Wait…

Snagging up his hard hat, I hand it to him. He stares at it for a second and just chuckles. Shaking his head, he shoves it on and settles his ass down onto my lap. Cupping my face, he leans in and whispers, "Such a distracting employee."

I've had all kinds of kisses, but I've never had the desperate I'll-never-leave-you-again kind. As hard as I am, I was just messing around to get a delightful visual out of Graham. I don't need the sex right now. I just need him, to know that he's mine. As my hands rediscover every inch of warm flesh on his back, and his anguish-filled pants and moans fill my mouth, I know he's mine and that I'm his. No lesson or delusional sense of responsibility is going to change that.

"I told them," he whispers, coming up for air. "I told all of them. I…came out."

"When?"

"The day after the wedding."

"That long ago? Why didn't you tell me?"

"You…wouldn't talk to me. I didn't know what to do, and it's something I needed to do anyway."

Half-naked birthday presents aren't supposed to make you cry. Holy crap. He did it. He did it, and I wasn't there for him. No one told me. Well, why would they tell me? No one knew about us.

"How did it go?"

"Fine. Awkward, but fine."

"Yeah?"

"Yeah." He nods, tracing my lower lip with his thumb. "And worth it. I wanted you more than I wanted to hide."

My head collapses against his chest, my heart spasming. I expected him to do something based on a decision he only made a few weeks ago compared to one I've known my entire life. Nobody should have that pressure placed on them.

"I'm sorry," I murmur against his skin as he strokes my hair. "I shouldn't have pushed you."

"I'm glad you did. I almost lost you," he says, tilting my jaw so I have to look up at him.

"No," I tell those kind eyes staring back at me. "You never really did."

His face softens with a light I don't think I deserve. He leans down and brushes his lips over mine.

"I have a present for you."

Maybe I *am* immature, or maybe it's because his warm cock is still pressed against my stomach, but I tug on the band of his underwear and wriggle my eyebrows. "I'll say!"

Laughing, he wiggles his hips. "You can have *that* after your present."

"Whoa!" Aiden's voice booms from the doorway. "Did not need to see that!"

Graham flinches, and I try to extricate myself from underneath him, but stop when I realize he isn't moving other than to grab his sweatshirt. I watch mesmerized as he sighs and slowly gets off my lap, slipping his foot back through his pant leg.

Covering my junk, I stand and hide myself behind him. It's broad daylight in downtown Olympus and Aiden is more or less my real boss. Some situations feel a little different when you're twenty-four, I guess.

Peeking back around, Aiden turns to face us as Graham slides his sweatshirt over his head. "Um…the client had to reschedule. I can…I'll just come back later."

"What's the matter?" Graham asks lazily, tugging the hem of his shirt over his waistline. "Aren't you happy for us?"

Aiden scoffs. "You and Dami? Yeah, sure, but…I don't need to see… that." He waves his hand at us as he glances in the other direction.

Why is Graham snickering? Who is he, and what has he done with my boyfriend?

"Sorry, boss," I call from over Graham's shoulder, feeling caught red-handed with the bulge poking my jeans. "He, um, distracted me. Won't happen again."

"Why are you hiding behind me?" Graham whispers. "You weren't the one without clothes on."

"Because I have a problem," I scathe back.

Chuckling, he wraps his arm around me and squeezes as he drops a kiss on the top of my head. "You're going to have a problem for a long time, if I have anything to say about it."

CHAPTER 50

Graham

If I'd known how happy art supplies make Dami, I'd have filled my truck up with them weeks ago. Filing away how he's jabbering and brimming with astonishment over my gift, I catch his hand when he makes to head up the stairs to his apartment with an armload of his art booty.

"No, in here first. I need to show you the rest of your present." I motion to the hallway that leads to Johnny's studio.

"*The rest?* You bought out like half of the sketching supply section at Olympus Crafts."

"Always complaining," I tease, flipping on the lights.

I watch him blink, his face scrunching up as he looks around the studio. He's probably expecting something with a giant bow on it. I should have segued about this gift with a little less mystery and hype. It's not technically a gift after all.

"Over here," I tell him, leading him to the waiting area at the front of the building. His face lights up, and he lets out a little gasp. "It took some finagling on Johnny's part, but he managed to sneak a few of your drawings out of your apartment and frame them to hang up here while you were at work. He texted me earlier and said you sold one already. He'll get you the money," I inform him as he gapes at his sketches like he's never seen them before.

"Wh-why did you do this for me?"

"Because I believe in you. Because you're amazing, and I want everyone to know how amazing you are."

Frowning, he turns to me. "You don't want me to work with you anymore?"

"What? No! You do whatever you want to do. I love working with you. I just…wanted you to know you have more options than you thought."

"Even if I break a few of *Osha's* rules now and then?"

He grins, but I can't share his humor this time. Reaching out, I stroke his jaw, still grateful that I can. "I was such an idiot."

"Come on. I was teasing. I love it when you get *Osha* boners."

Fucking Dami. "I *was* an idiot though."

Running his hands up my arms, he squeezes them. "You had a lot to process, so maybe don't be too hard on yourself." I return his smile this time as he tugs at the flap of my flannel pocket. "I do have one question though."

"What?"

"Did you really hate me at first?" Chuckling he adds, "Well, I *know* you hated me, but what changed and when?"

If I could go back, I think as I drink him in. I can't do my life over. All I can do is try to make sure I don't want to do over what's left of it. "I never hated you. It was me."

"What do you mean?"

Does he really not know? When will I ever get it right?

Looking into his eyes, I cup the back of his neck. "Maybe one day you wake up and realize weeks of trying not to fall in love with someone you thought you shouldn't want were actually more difficult than years of trying to convince yourself that you loved someone you thought you were supposed to love, and maybe…you realize what a damn fool that makes you."

His puff of breath wafts my face. "You fell in love with me?"

Smirking, I rub my thumb across his pulse, thankful for all the life there that I'll get to be a part of. "Hard. So hard."

Beaming, he yanks my head toward his and holds his mouth to mine until he comes up panting. "I'm hard for you too!"

"You're always hard," I tease, stroking his cheek while my heart reverberates.

"No. Like part-three of my plan *hard*."

"But I'm not rich," I remind him.

Shrugging, he slinks his arms around my neck. "Nobody's perfect."

CHAPTER 51

I probably should have spread my dates out a bit more. Friday night and date number-four is in the books. Graham always teases me that I'm needy, so I guess that explains why we knocked them all out in one week.

I couldn't help it. I have a boyfriend. Correction. I have *the* boyfriend I want for the rest of my life. Now after an evening of terrible, sexy dancing, at a club north of town with Johnny and Aiden, he's going to spend the night at my place.

"You sure you don't mind staying here?"

"Why would I mind?" Graham says, unslinging his bag from his shoulder. "You saw me pack this cool sex backpack and everything."

"Oh, good. I can retire mine."

"Never. That thing is like an extension of your body in my mind," he says, hanging his coat up and then working on his boots.

"Are you sure your fish will be okay until tomorrow morning? I think they might be starting to get jealous of me, monopolizing all of your time."

Rolling his eyes, he helps me out of my coat. "Fish don't get jealous."

"I don't know. I think Cetus was giving me the evil eye last night when you were rimming me over your couch," I tease.

His hands still with my coat in them, his tone going suspicious. "Why would you think I named one of them Cetus?"

"I *may have* found your *Fish Files* notebook while you were in the shower. They're adorable by the way."

"You snoop," he grumps, jabbing me in the ribs.

That blush doesn't get old. It's laughable that he's sensitive about me finding his *Fish Files* and not the mention of the epic rimming he delivered. He's certainly come a long way, and I like to believe it wasn't because of lessons, but rather because of his affection for me.

Deflecting him with a laugh, I head to my studio room. "You've been spoiling me all week, so I made you something."

With butterflies in my stomach, I return to the living room and hand over the special sketchpad I've been working on for him. Each slow flip of pages he makes crushes my excitement. It's such a juvenile gift, drawing all his fish. What was I thinking?

"I've never drawn fish before," I concede. "Do they look okay?"

"Dami," he murmurs wistfully, "they're phenomenal. Thank you. When did you do this?"

"Lunch breaks…after you passed out last night."

"I'm old. You know this," he warns, his gaze flickering to mine for a second and then back to my work like he can't take his eyes off it. "And satisfying you is a full-time job."

"You can have the night off."

His eyes narrow like I suggested we adopt a cat. Setting the sketch-book down, he snags up his backpack and steps forward.

"Whoa!" I yelp, finding myself hoisted over his shoulder. Laughing as he heads us toward my room, I explore his ass. "That wasn't a challenge, Graham. We seriously don't have to. I do have *some* self-control."

"No, you don't," he chides. "Besides, you can't draw a guy's fish, and say things like that, and not expect to get tackled."

"I'll remember that."

When he stops just inside my room, I wonder what's taking him so long to put me down. He's just standing still.

"What's wrong?"

Setting me on my feet, he frowns in the direction past my shoulder. "I forgot about the swing bed."

"What? It's fine. Seriously, I haven't fallen out once."

"*Yet*," he emphasizes gravely, but starts unbuttoning his shirt.

"Come on. You'll love it. It'll be like having sex on a ship. I bet it reminds you of the Navy," I say, shimmying out of my pants.

Giving the platform a nudge so it starts swinging, I wriggle my brows at him. He gives me that skeptical look of his that's not in the least bit disconcerting.

"*One*," he prefaces, shucking his jeans, "I never had sex when I was underway. Two—the Navy wasn't exactly sunshine and roses. Are you *trying* to turn me off?"

"No, but I think *you're* trying to turn *me* off," I tease as he glowers at me and climbs onto the end of the bed in just his boxer briefs.

Crawling rigidly on all fours, he makes his way up toward my pillows and settles on his knees facing me. The bed rocks into the wall-mounted headboard bumper a foot away, sending it on a slow glide forward. He flinches dramatically and scowls. Reaching his arm out, he grips the headboard until he and the bed stop moving.

He must spot the amusement on my face because he smirks and crooks his finger. "Alright, smart ass. Get over here."

I take my time peeling out of my boxer briefs, enjoying the lust taking over his expression. When I strut toward the bed, he holds up a hand.

"Wait. Sex backpack." He nods his chin to his bag on the floor.

"I thought you were joking. Did you really buy supplies? All by yourself?"

"I know how to buy condoms and lube. It's not like scoring a drug deal."

"So prepared," I coo, unzipping his bag. "Just like you are at work when you get your *Osha* boners."

"I don't get OSHA boners, but this one's going to go away if you keep talking shit," he says, stroking himself over his underwear.

"Fine." I snort, rifling through his backpack until I find a bag from the local pharmacy. "Ooh, what'd you get? Oh! No way! *Kin-ky!*"

"What's so kinky about me buying lube and condoms?"

"Uh, it's kinky when Graham Brandt buys *glow-in-the-dark* condoms," I declare, holding up the box.

His face sags. He frowns at the box as I waltz over to the bed.

"What the fuck?" he mutters, snatching it out of my hand to read the label.

Snickering, I climb onto the bed, joining him on my knees. He gives a jolt when the platform shifts and clutches a hand onto my waist.

Running my hands down his back, planting kisses on his torso as I go, I venture, "So, I take it you didn't mean to light up my world?"

"I just…grabbed the first thing I saw," he confesses. "Do you have any?"

"No way! We're not using mine. I wanna see your dick glow."

Tugging down his underwear, I take him into my mouth, cutting off his laughter. He gasps, but then I hear the tearing of a condom wrapper. Operation Light Up My World is a go.

No matter how much he initially protests about something, whether it be which movie we'll watch or what we eat for dinner, he always ends up laughing with me. He says people think he's grumpy, but I know he really just has a selective sense of humor. I love that about him. I love everything about him actually.

Popping off his cock, I wipe the slobber from my chin. I imagined I'd look a bit more romantic when I found the nerve to get what I want to tell him off my chest. In a roundabout way, we confessed our feelings downstairs on Monday, but sometimes I feel like he thinks I'm joking when I'm not. I have this need to clarify the extent of what this man does to me.

"Um, I have a confession."

"What?"

When he tenses, I rub his shoulders to reassure him. The fact that he fears losing or disappointing me in any way only reinforces what I'm about to tell him.

"You asked me once if I'd ever been in love before."

"Yeah?" he asks, cautiously, scanning my face.

"I haven't. I know that now. I know because of you."

His chest rises like it's painful for him to breathe. Cupping my face, he gives me a long chaste kiss, holding his lips to mine. When he releases me, he crushes me in his arms, making my heart clench. How lucky am I that the first person I love loves me back? Not everybody gets to experience that.

His feather duster brushes my jugular with a murmur. "Love you so much. Never wanted anything the way I want you."

Moments like these are my favorite, when all the laughter is set aside for slow, silent worshipping. Graham paints his way up my neck with his lips, across my jaw, over my face. His hands glide all over my back like he's smoothing out wrinkles in a bed sheet. They detour downward, skimming over the curve of my ass as he finally reunites our mouths.

"Gotta make up for that day at the site," he says all husky, kicking off his underwear and widening his stance on his knees.

"You made up for everything already. It's not like I didn't make mistakes too. Ooh, wait. Do you mean—"

I get cut off when he tugs me forward onto his lap, reminding me of when I straddled him on that unfinished counter at the Hodges house. The way his lovemaking has grown in confidence blows me away. It's such an abstract from when I fooled myself into thinking we were just experiencing lessons.

Bracing a hand behind himself on the mattress, he gives a cursory glance to the sway of the bed, but then his heated gaze is back on me. Straightening up, he captures my lips one at a time, savoring, teasing.

I hear the snick of the lube bottle cap as he whispers, "Can't believe I ever tried to talk myself out of wanting you."

"Eh, I'm a lot to handle," I concede even as little fireworks burst inside me at the compliment.

"I can handle you. I've had lessons." He smiles, running his slickened fingers through my crease.

He slips one through my ring, and I groan when he hits my honesty button inside. "Couldn't…talk myself out of wanting you either."

"Thank God for that," he rumbles, kneading my ass and stroking my prostate, his mouth, dragging wickedly against my throat.

I rock shamelessly onto his finger and then another, snarling his hair into my favorite style—*Pleasured by Dami*. I still can't believe he's mine. Now all his laughter and smiles are mine. His moans and sexy declarations are mine. His passion is mine.

"Ready. Put it in, put it in, put it in," I chant mindlessly.

He chuckles, slipping his fingers free from my channel. Watching him grab his impressive rigidity, I rise up on my knees. Something's wrong.

"Wait. You're not glowing. Why aren't you glowing?"

"You usually need to activate glow-in-the-dark stuff."

"Oh, right."

Wrapping my hand around his shaft, I stroke a few times, but nothing happens other than Graham sucking in a breath. What the hell? Maybe that pack of condoms was on the shelf too long.

Tightening my grip, I quicken my strokes, getting frustrated when I still don't see a spec of light other than the dim glow of the moonlight filtering in through my bedroom window.

"Dami, it's not…a glow stick," Graham rasps, grabbing ahold of my wrist. He lets out a choked breath when I release him and shakes his head.

"Well, they're not working! You got defective condoms or something."

"They're not defective. You probably just have to keep them under a light for a little bit to get them to glow. That's how you activate the glow shit."

Scrambling to my nightstand, Graham yelps and clutches onto my thigh as the bed rocks. "What are you doing?"

"Getting a flashlight."

"A flashlight?" He scoffs. "You do realize this thing will still work even if it's not glowing."

Nonsense. My man is talking nonsense. I'm on a mission.

I feel like one of those explorers who goes on expeditions in the jungle as I fumble around in my drawer for the little flashlight Johnny left in there. When I find it, I resituate myself on Graham's lap. Grabbing a hold of the base of his shaft, I click on the light and take aim. The pale green latex just looks…*latexy* as I move the light to cast its beam down from the tip of Graham's cock. Nothing's happening. How come nothing's happening?

"How long?" I ask, impatient for the show.

"How long until my erection goes away?"

"No," I chuckle. "How long until you start glowing?"

"I'm starting to worry about you."

"Why?" I glance up to a comical expression on his face.

"Am I going to have to make my cock glow from now on to get you to want it?"

"No, but I've never used one of these. I'm not wasting a perfectly good light show."

"I'll buy you a disco ball. Come on. That light's getting hot. You're gonna burn a hole in my dick."

"Fine." I sigh, clicking off the flashlight. This is so disappointing. What's the point of having glow-in-the-dark condoms if they don't— *ohmygosh!* It's glowing!

"Yes! Look at that!" I exclaim, punching my fists in the air. "Your cock works!"

"It worked just fine before," he snarks, tugging my hips forward and positioning his shaft.

"Yeah, but now it's like cock two-point-oh. Like a magical sex wand," I elaborate, tilting my head down to get another view.

I realize after a minute of my gawking that Graham is still and has gone quiet. When I look at him, he's staring up at me, brow arched.

"What?"

"Do you want my magical sex wand, or did you just want to stare at it a bit longer?"

"No. Yeah. Go ahead." I grin, gripping his shoulders and lowering my hips. "Firefly me, baby!"

Graham snorts, rubbing his tip back and forth against my hole with a grimace on his face. "It looks more like one of those forensic crime scene light bars where you can see all the stains in the room."

"Ew! That's not sexy. You realize Johnny and your brother used to have sex in here. Right?"

He lets go of his sex wand, eyes flaring up at me. "Oh, my God! Why did you have to say that?"

"*You're* the one who planted the image in my brain first! Now can you please firefly me before I have to get the flashlight out again?"

Sighing, he grabs his shaft and lines up again, muttering, "I hope your ass glows for a week from this thing."

"No way! Do you really think it—uhn! Oh, yeah! Nevermind," I pant, as his hips rock up into me, filling me so good I can't think.

"You were saying, Firefly?" he purrs at my lips, but it's all grunty as heck like the sensation of me is getting to him too.

I reply with a carnal moan into his mouth as he guides my hips up and down. His heat pumps into mine like he was made for me. The bed starts swaying back and forth, making me have to cling tighter to him.

Wrenching his mouth away from mine, he curses. "This stupid fucking bed."

No. Not now. He can't call this off now.

"Sorry," I whine defensively. "I didn't think it'd be that bad. We could—"

"Wrap your legs around me," he orders, cutting me off.

I'm flexible, and if it keeps his sex wand in me, I'm game. When I snake my legs around his ass, he adds, "Hold on."

Swinging his legs over the side, he stands, hoisting me up with him. With his hands gripping my thighs, he lumbers across the room, shifting inside me. Maybe I'm not as much of a sex expert as I thought.

Groaning, I confess, "Never…been carried before."

"Neither have I."

"I'll get you back, I promise," I assure him, craning my head to kiss his neck.

"No way," he cracks up. "You'll drop me."

"I will not. How do you—*oof!*" I moan when my back hits the drywall. Wall sex. Yes! We're going to have wall sex.

"You okay?" he whispers.

Glancing over my shoulder, I nod. "I'd feel better if you built it, but yeah. This is super hot."

"You won't be…saying that when my…back goes out," he gasps, thrusting his hips.

"It'll be worth it," I whisper, my head falling back with a *thunk* as my eyes roll back into my head.

Graham is a sight, arms flexed, holding me up. Hips moving, skin slapping, through the owning feel of fill, release. Fill, release. All I can do is hang on and moan, watching his beautiful expressions.

"Dami. Dami," he chants. "Crazy for you."

His face holds the truth behind his words, his eyes half-lidded. The static he's pumping into me compounds until it's unbearable. I need to come, but I'm afraid if I let go to touch my cock, I'll fall.

Grunting, I whimper. "Can't touch my…cock. Need to come."

Nipping my lip, he picks up the pace. "Always…in a hurry."

Groaning, my head thrashes back and forth against the wall like I'm being exorcised. The delayed release is torture. I've never made sounds like this in my life, but Graham must like them because his voice goes all dirty.

"Yeah. Fuck, babe. Listen to you. Gonna make you…wait from now on if…you sound like that."

Whimpering, my head spins. How am I sweating if all I'm doing is being pinned to a wall like a butterfly specimen?

"Please! Need to c-come," I beg like it's his fault I can't stroke myself.

Technically, it is. He's going to have to get over the fear of my bed. My nuts can't handle this much pressure.

Readjusting me with a hoist, he slams to the hilt. Leaning in, he rests his head against mine, his lips to my ear.

"Then come for me, sweetheart," he rasps.

His hips do an erotic roll over and over. I listen to my boss' sultry order, shooting between us.

"G-graham! Ah!"

He lets out a war cry that I vow to make him produce again someday, so I can record it. The skin on my back stretches with each of his erratic jerks, shifting me against the wall.

His hot breath vents against my neck for a few moments. My ass is still twitching around his cock. I can feel the trembles from his legs reverberating up through him.

Slipping free from me, he eases me to the floor and collapses against my chest. Who needs a gym when you can do that?

Wrapping my arms around him, I let out a contented sigh into the crook of his neck. "We don't need a disco ball," I inform him. "Your glow stick works just fine."

CHAPTER 52

Graham

My nephews fly toward Dami and I, where we're leaning against the wall in my parents' living room. Maddox…or Luke—I honestly can't tell them apart—twirls an unstrung yo-yo by the string like a medieval morning star weapon as he goes by. The circular reel dings Dami in the nuts, the khaki slacks he wore to my family's Thanksgiving dinner, offering little protection. He flinches, doubling over, grabbing his junk.

"Hey!" I shout after the boys. "That's enough! Slow down!"

At the same time, my mother yells, "If you kids are going to fight, go outside, so you don't break anything!"

It's the same pearl of wisdom she gave me and my siblings when we were kids. I still don't understand it. There is nothing in this house worthy of a museum and leaving children unsupervised to murder each other is probably as unsafe today as it was when I was young.

"Ah!" Dami winces. "Geez, they're fast. Like ninja reflex fast."

Rubbing his back, I wince in sympathy. "You alright? I told you that we shouldn't have come until dinner was ready."

"Yeah. You can rub them later."

Glancing around the room, we seem to be a backdrop in the chaos. Dami's mom is fawning over the entrees in the kitchen with my mother, while his father is shouting at the football game with my father in the living room. Maxie and Veronique are giggling by the front window of the dining room, probably looking at their honeymoon photos again. Skyler is sleeping with one of his girls on his chest on the couch, while Ashley feeds the other one. Johnny and Aiden are deep into a game of chess at the side table in the corner of the living room. Judging by their expressions, it looks to be sexual innuendo chess. Disgusting, but more to the point, we won't be missed.

Tugging Dami by the hand, I duck down the hallway into the pantry and slide the door closed. When I back him up to the far wall of shelves and circle his waist, he makes a confused expression.

"What's this all about?"

"I've got time to rub them now," I murmur, capturing his lips and grazing my palm over his package.

"Mm. Such an efficient use of time. You should really be in management."

"Speaking of time management, we always take the day after Thanksgiving off. Mind if I come over to your place, while you sketch tomorrow?" I ask, referring to the mandatory one day a week I insisted on him using to work on his drawings to fill his orders.

He is now a Brandt and Sons employee only Mondays through Thursdays, and his artwork has been flying off his website and Johnny's lobby walls these past few weeks. I see a bright future for him in it someday, but for now, my stubborn boyfriend refuses to give up his brick mason career entirely. Not that I mind having him there to distract me all that much. After all, he's a damn good brick mason, and it's a bonus that he's become adept at shooing away feral cats for his "boss".

"Hm. I don't know. You might be a distraction, but," he lets out on a sigh, "*I suppose*. If I put you to work, you wouldn't get in my way."

"Oh, yeah? What did you have in mind?"

"Well, it'd be nice to have a live model, a hot-blooded, sexy model to keep me company in case I get needy. Did I say *needy?* I meant lonely."

Snickering, I nip his lower lip and press my hips into him. "That can be arranged."

Drawing his head back, he adds, "But bring your hard hat."

"Seriously?"

"Yeah."

"What? Do you want to draw me in my jeans and work boots too? Don't you have enough of those already?"

"I didn't say anything about clothes."

I bury my face in his neck and squeeze his perky ass, pressing him harder against me. "I take it back. You're not needy, you're just a deviant."

The pantry door slides open with a rumble right as Dami moans in my ear. "Dad!" Maxie yells. "Graham's back in the closet!"

Pinching my eyes closed, I rest my forehead on Dami's shoulder. My sister's newfound affection for me still includes her razor-sharp wit.

"It's okay," she amends for all to hear. "Dami's in here with him."

"Thank you, Maxine," I grate out as Dami chuckles, clutching my sides.

"Stay away from my oranges!" my father's voice resounds.

"Hey, Mom needs another can of cranberry sauce," Maxie throws out like this is a public diner and not an invasion of an intimate moment.

"Um, here you go," Dami says, his hand fumbling a can off the shelf and tossing it to her.

"Dinner's in ten," she informs us, shutting the door when she goes.

Sighing, I lift my head, preparing to give him one chaste kiss before we have to make the walk of shame. "Well, this was a bad idea anyway. Raincheck?"

Tugging me back to him, he squeezes my ass. "No way! She said we have ten minutes."

"Your parents are right outside the door."

"Well…" he hesitates. "They've seen my artwork and hang it up in the restaurant now. They're adjusting."

"Dami," I chuckle, "Your mom had you draw pictures of her home village in Italy for the restaurant, not men in their underwear."

"Speaking of that. Are we still on for a Friday night date at Tapas or are we taking it off tomorrow because of the holiday?"

Smiling, I graze his chin with my thumb, my heart warming at the reminder of what I think will happily become a tradition for us. We've spent every Friday night washing dishes at Tapas for the last few weeks, followed by dinner with his parents. Well, a few times, his mother shooed us from the kitchen and sat us down by ourselves at a candlelit table in the restaurant, but it still feels like a family affair.

"You don't like our dates at Tapas?"

"I love our *dish dates*," he exclaims. "I just feel bad that you spend half of them elbow deep in dishwater."

"I don't care. It doesn't matter what we're doing as long as I'm with you, and besides, I think your mom likes me. She always gives me extra cannoli."

"She better not make you so fat you can't do that thing I like," he warns with a wry smile.

"Which thing?"

Grinning, he wraps his arms around my neck and kisses me. "All the things."

Parking my truck behind his apartment four hours later, I grab my sex backpack and glance over at Dami. Groaning, he rubs his stomach.

"Why did you let me eat so much?"

"It's not my fault you have no self-control."

"Hey, that pumpkin pie was better than sex. I couldn't help myself."

"Thanks a lot."

Laughing, he opens his door. "Not all sex. Like it can't top glow stick sex for sure."

"I'll let my mother know," I inform him.

As we head into his apartment, I recall a bit of news Skyler gave me. Given Dami's past record of couch activities, I was wary to share it with him in my parents' living room.

"So, Skyler said he got the payment for the Hodges job we did."

"Yeah? Can I promote you to rich boyfriend yet?" he jokes, kicking off his shoes.

"Not quite, but if you're in the market for one, you'll know where to find him."

His scrunched-up face will never get old. I can't wait to see his reaction.

"So, you know that singer you're obsessed with?" I preface.

"Which one?"

"There's more than one?"

What the fuck? How many celebrity fantasies does he have?

Chuckling, he strides over and kisses my cheek. "Well, sure, but Vin Stoller is on the top of my stalker list."

Frowning, I study his face. Now that he used the word *stalker*, I'm not so sure I want to tell him.

"How big of a stalker are we talking?" I ask, gripping his hips, so I can lean back to scrutinize him.

"I just had his poster in my room and subscribe to his fan newsletter on his website." He laughs. "Why?"

"Well, Skyler said the job was for Stoller Industries, and he didn't think anything of it until he got a personal email from Vin Stoller, thanking us for the good work after Skyler sent photos to the industries email."

"What?" he gasps, his eyes bugging out. "Shut the back door! Vin Stoller? *The* Vin Stoller?"

"Yeah." I laugh.

"*I* built Vin Stoller a house?"

"I think I helped a little too," I remind him.

"Oh, my gosh!" He wrenches out of my arms, gripping his head. "What if my crappy mortar falls apart? What if something collapses and kills him? I'd be responsible for killing the god of pop music. You'll be sued!"

"Which part of that concerns you more, crushing a pop star or your boyfriend losing his livelihood?"

Laughing breathlessly, he shakes his head, snapping out of his daze. Cupping my face, he smiles. "Well, I'd still love you if you were poor."

"That doesn't exactly answer the question, but thank you."

Wrapping his arms around my neck, he chuckles. "He's great, but he's no Graham Brandt."

"I like that answer better," I murmur at his lips.

When our kiss breaks, he gets that excited twinkle in his eyes again and pats my chest. "Hey, you realize we had sex on his kitchen counter. Right? Every time he makes something to eat, he'll literally be eating over the memory of our hard hat sex."

"I doubt Skyler put that in the house plan notes that he sent him."

"Aw, bummer."

"I'll re-enact it for you someday. Hard hat and all."

"Really?" he chuckles.

Shrugging, I snake my arm around him and head toward his room. "You seem to make me do stupid shit that I end up not minding at all."

As I strip down for the night, I notice it's gone quiet, too quiet, considering Dami's excitement a moment ago. When I get to just my boxer briefs, I turn around to find him leaning against the doorframe, staring at me.

"What?"

Shaking his head, he lets out a quiet laugh, but then his face grows more serious than I've ever seen it. "Nothing, just…I love you."

We've said it dozens of times, but this feels different, deeper, prophetic. It warms me from head to toe, making my heart gallop away.

"I love you too."

Straightening up, he stuffs his hands in his pockets and inches toward me. Why does he look so nervous?

"Um, feel free to say no. I won't be offended or hold it against you. It's not a deal breaker for me, by any means. I'm more than happy with the way we do things."

"Dami, what?" I interrupt, the anticipation combined with his jitters getting to my nerves.

Biting his lip, he runs his eyes over my body. "I know we've never really talked about it, but if you…ever wanted to try bottoming, that… that'd be something I'd be up for…with you."

The thought of feeling more than his tongue or fingers inside me has my cock bucking in my shorts. I remember what he once said about how he feels about topping, like he's giving more of himself, taking more of the other person. He said *maybe* with his *forever guy*. He's let me know I'm his forever in more ways than one already, but a part of me was worried I didn't check every single box in his heart since he'd never asked this of me before. It wasn't something I couldn't bring myself to broach, to request a gift like that from him. I wanted to know I'd earned it.

"You'd really want to do that…with *me?*"

Reaching for my waist, he lets out a breathy sound of disbelief. "Only you, Graham."

Trembling, I cup his face and thank him with a soft kiss. I used to worry if I would be good at sex with him when we first started messing around. I'm nervous as hell, but performance is the last thing I'm worried about right now. Pain? Maybe. Guilt? Of course, considering how many times I've done this to Dami. My nerves are askew because I wonder just how far you can fall for someone. How much love is it possible to feel? I used to think I didn't know who I was, but now I know I'm me. I'm me because of him. He can have however much of me he wants.

CHAPTER 53

My heart is threatening to hammer out of my chest. Graham turns and stares at the bed, letting out a breath.

"Are you still scared of my bed or is it the sex? Because we don't have to do this."

"I've thought about it…a lot, actually," he confesses with a small smile.

He's thought about it? Oh, my gosh. My heart might burst along with my balls.

"Yeah?"

"Yeah." He shrugs, sheepishly. "I just didn't want to ask. I figured that was something you needed to decide without any pressure from me because of what you said it means to you."

He remembered. I've never been with a guy who remembers everything I say, especially since I say a lot.

"Everything with you means a lot to me. I'll be both gentle and rock your world. I promise," I assure him, but he frowns and glances at the bed again.

"I know you say your bed is like being on a ship, but I never had anything jabbing me in the ass when I was out to sea. Exactly, how much rocking are you planning on?"

Laughing, I snake my arms around his waist. "Graham, I don't plan on *jabbing* you, and if you don't want to *jab*, I really don't mind. I told—"

"I do," he cuts me off, running his hands up my back. "I can't wait… to feel you like that, actually."

Oh, my gosh. Now, I want to jab the shit out of him.

"Okay," I let out breathlessly, and tug off my sweatshirt.

When I slide down his boxer briefs, my hands tremble in anticipation over what we want to give each other. I'm unwrapping a precious gift. I never realized how much we chatter until we're both stripped completely naked without having exchanged a word.

I feel as bare as one of the blank pages in my sketchbooks, waiting for Graham and me to draw this next picture of our love for each other. We kiss like shy virgins for a few minutes until the headiness of his arousal brushing against my stomach overtakes my nerves. Guiding his shoulders, I turn us around, so his back is facing the end of the bed. He sits down, and the bed frame shifts. Grimacing at it, he scoots himself back toward my pillows, and waits.

It is a sight. My man, bared, legs spread, waiting for me to claim him. Sliding a knee carefully onto the mattress, I settle between his legs and press a kiss over his heart.

Running my hands down his thighs, I rest them on his knees. "I have another confession."

"What?"

"Maybe it's not a confession. You probably figured it out already, but…you're just…you're my everything. I used to dream about you looking through my window over the sink, but now…now I'm outside that window *with you*. I'm living my dream. You came true."

He makes a choked sound. When he reaches for me, I go to him, kissing him into the pillows.

"Make love to me, sweetheart," he rasps.

Sweetheart. Gah! Graham Brandt calling me sweetheart and begging me to make love to him? My heart just burst. If they want to find the pieces, they'll have to ask him for the map. I don't want them back.

Reaching into my nightstand, I grab the things I need. Graham's eyes track my every move. I'd better not screw this up. It has to be good for him.

I take my time, slickening and massaging his hole and cock, absorbing every moan and breath that leaves his lips as his gaze grows hazy and hooded. Working him open, I kiss him the way I know he likes, a complete devouring, until he's panting, and his hips are rocking onto my fingers.

"Dami, now," he pleads. "Need you now."

Nodding, I roll on the condom with shaking fingers. I've only fingered him a few times. He either has no idea how much *more* a cock feels like, or he's being brave and getting lost in the pleasure.

Drawing his thighs over top of my knees, so his legs are extended and relaxed, I make slow, soothing circles on his stomach as I line myself up. His thumbs rub my kneecaps anxiously, his gaze flitting back and forth from my hands to my eyes.

"Okay," I warn. "Your favorite part. Push when I push."

With an amused puff of air, he nods. My emotions creep up on me, mounting pressure in my chest, as I ease past the constriction on his ring. He's giving himself to me, this man who took a brave leap late in life and could have had anyone, this man that I draw in my mind every day.

His eyes flare, and he gasps when the head of my cock slips inside. I feel some of the tension leave him as he stares at me and exhales like a woman giving birth. He's still wound up like a spring, and I'm trembling at the feel of his tight heat, hugging me. Leaning down, I kiss him softly and stroke his softening shaft back to life. Within seconds, it's rock hard again, and he's whimpering, relaxing around me, allowing my cock to settle in deeper.

"It's okay?" I pant between little kisses around his lips.

"Full, so full," he rasps even as he reaches to clutch my hips and urge me deeper.

Diving into his mouth, my tongue dances with his. There's nothing robotic about the way Graham's tongue dances. It moves with sensual fluidity, taking and accepting with all his heart. Drawing back, I ease forward slowly until I'm fully seated inside him, surrounded by the quivering warmth of my forever.

Breaths strangled, we stare at the wonder in each other's eyes. I don't know where either of us begins or ends. I'm every other beat of his heart, and he's mine. When he smiles at me, I know why true love is described as a fairytale. Nothing in existence has the ability to describe it adequately.

"You ready to be jabbed?" I joke on a shaky breath, not sure how much longer I can hold back the pressure in my heart or my balls.

Scoffing, he smirks. "Don't say *jabbed*."

"But it'll be a love jab, baby," I tease, stroking his cheek with my thumb.

Chuckling, he grabs my face and kisses me as he raises his knees. Easing back, I delve into him carefully, feeling his prostate brush the head of my cock.

"Uh! Dami," he cries, quivering with pleasure so hard it feels like he's vibrating.

I do it again, biting my cheek to stave off the building need that's being packed like a cannon barrel in the pit of my navel.

"Uhn! Fuck! Oh, better. That's better," he gasps, grabbing the back of his thighs to hold them in place as he watches our connection with wide, bliss-filled eyes.

"Yeah," I agree, picking up the pace as the bed rocks, thumping against the headboard bumper on the wall.

It adds an erotic jolt each time I plunge home, that Graham seems to appreciate as much as me. Sitting back, I draw his legs down over mine, latching onto his hips and using them for leverage, changing the angle.

Arching, his mouth falls open. He lets out a throaty wail that goes on so long, my eyes want to roll back in my head. In and out, I guide my thrusts in time with the motion of this ship of ecstasy that I never want to dock, driving my man and myself wild.

"Oh, gosh! *Ohmyfreakinggosh*, Graham! You don't know how sexy you look."

Something brushes my shoulder. If there's a freaking bug in here that's going to ruin this for us, I will hunt it and its entire family down. Getting back into my lust-filled headspace, I focus on the rhythm that's producing the most carnal sounds I've ever heard as I plunge back and forth into Graham's maddeningly, hot, tight heat.

Something makes a creaking noise amidst the *thump, thump, thump* of our soundtrack. A chunk of something white tumbles onto the edge of the bed. Graham must hear it too because when I meet his gaze, he looks confused. He glances up, and I revel in seeing his eyes go wide, so I undulate my hips again, watching his cock bob and slap against his stomach.

"Oh, shit," he whispers, tensing.

He must have liked that move. I'm grateful that he's about to come because I can't hold back much longer. He's so freaking beautiful, pouring all of himself into this the way he always gives everything. My heart still remembers the ache of how much I missed him for those two weeks. Never again. I'm not letting anything ever keep us apart.

The bed jolts awkwardly. There's a creaking noise. I grip Graham's hips tighter, instinctively. Grainy dust rains down from above. Graham covers his eyes with his forearm, a death grip on my knee with his other hand.

It happens in a matter of seconds. The cracking, the *snap* of the tension on the ropes of the swing bed, the jarring descent of the mattress as we crash to the floor. I bend forward over Graham instinctively, trying to shield him from the drywall debris toppling down from the ceiling. We land hard, jolting my cock deeper into him. He lets out a sound that's part unholy, part orgasm-inspiring.

I freeze, panting as I swipe the dust from his face. "Crap! Are you okay?"

When he opens his eyes, I'm amazed at how much his shocked expression resembles arousal, but then he tugs my neck down and kisses me, grinding himself on my cock.

Wow! My man *likes* being jabbed by a falling bed. A dinner plate-sized chunk of drywall knocks me in the head, making me flinch.

Graham draws his knees up, planting his feet on the mattress. Apparently, he's done with this. I don't blame him, but my heart weeps that this is how his first time bottoming is ending.

"Roll over," he whispers, canting one hip up.

Whoa. Does he want to—

I get my answer when he topples us off the mattress onto the carpeted floor, inching us away from the wreckage. Smiling, he straddles my hips and chews his lip as he guides me back into him with a look of concentration I will remember until I die. Taking me until he's fully seated, he lets out this hearty satisfied sigh.

Gosh. Yes. *That*. I'll remember that too.

Leaning forward, dusting drywall crumbs from my hair, he whispers, "You alright?"

I blink dumbly at his controlled inquiry. He just slid himself onto my cock and the first thing he thought to do instead of riding me was to check on my wellbeing? It's like he just needed me back inside him.

"Yeah," I assure him, "but I think we should stay at your place tomorrow."

"So needy," he teases, but then rocks back onto my shaft and groans.

It's still surreal to see this mighty man giving himself to me, taking me on a level I've never been taken. "You sound pretty needy right now too," I joke.

Chuckling, he rocks on me again as he kisses me. "I wanted you from the second I saw you, I'm just sorry it took me so long to give into it. I wish I'd looked in that window a year ago."

Nuzzling his neck with my lips for a hit of my favorite scent, I tell myself all men cry when their forever says things like that. Wrapping my hand around his steely length, I stroke a groan out of him. Watching him rise, he plants his hand on my chest, starting to ride me in earnest.

"Dami, is it always this good?"

"I don't know," I gasp. "I've never done it like this."

Barking out a laugh, he rises and wraps his other hand around mine over his cock. "Close. I'm close," he grits, his face a picture of beautiful anguish as his channel suffocates my cock with every shift of his hips.

With his mouth hanging open and that need in his eyes, I can't take not feeling his expression. Reaching up, I trace his lips. He sucks my fingertip into his mouth and moans. His tongue sweeps around it, suckling me in deeper like he needs me everywhere.

A moment ago, I assumed the pinnacle memory of tonight would be how my bed fell apart, but as Graham repeatedly takes me to his depths and whimpers around my finger, I know that watching the way he's falling apart will be the memory I keep on recall. My balls cinch up. Erotic static pummels my mid-section, shooting all the way down my legs, and I fall apart with him.

"Dami!" he shouts, eyes flaring at the sensation of me pulsing inside him. He spills over the top of my fist, head bowed, jaw hanging open, pressing my palm to his cheek.

"Graham," I gasp, my favorite word.

Moaning, he collapses on my chest like a ton of the best bricks. The rise and fall of his chest against mine, lulls me into a sex coma as I stroke the warm skin on his back.

"Dami," he murmurs after a moment. "That was…that…I love you."

My fog clears from those words said in that exhausted sated voice. Squeezing my arms around him, I press a kiss to his neck.

"I love you so hard." Sighing, I murmur without even thinking, "forever."

Turning his head, he smiles sleepily at me. "Forever, huh?"

My face heats, realizing my filter has shut off, but it's not a lie, so I shrug. "Tough love, sweetheart," I mock him. "You're stuck with me."

Grinning, he presses his lips to mine. Delving his fingers into my hair, he whispers, "So needy."

Seven months later

"I hate weddings," Graham grumbles as I fasten his tie for him guided by the morning light coming through the window of his old spare room that he let me turn into a studio at our house.

"Really? Or are you still just hung over from the bachelor party?"

Glaring at me, he mutters, "I'm still finding glitter in places no one should have glitter."

"Hm. Yeah, Fontaine was getting pretty handsy at the end there," I remark airily, remembering visions of his lap dance at the drag club we went to last night for Johnny and Aiden's bachelor party.

"I don't want to talk about it," he says, his cheeks turning crimson.

"She rode you pretty hard. If Thor and Vin hadn't stepped in, I was going to break it up."

"Was that before or after you let the dancers yank my pants off? But thanks for letting a pop star and his bodyguard do your dirty work." He huffs, turning away to check his tie in the mirror above my drawing table as I bite my cheek to hold back a snicker.

"Well, Brennan and Will were kind of indisposed, or I'd have asked them."

"It's disgusting how often those two are indisposed. I still can't be-lieve they're a couple for how much they hated each other."

Arching a brow, I give him a provoking look. "I don't know. They're working relationship at first kind of reminded me of ours."

"I never hated you," he concedes. Craning his neck as he looks in the mirror, he swipes at something shiny just below his ear. "Damn it. Is that more glitter? It was a strip club. Aren't *the dancers* supposed to be the ones stripping, not their customers?"

I smooth my hands over the fabric of his suit jacket, giving his shoulders a squeeze. "You're just that hot, babe. Get used to it."

Snorting, he turns around and gives me a peck on the lips. "Only when you do it."

"Oh, if I must." I sigh, straightening his handkerchief.

His hand reaches around and slaps my ass, producing a mild sting through my suit slacks. "Thanks a lot. You about ready?"

"Yeah. I've just got to wrap these." Heading over to my workbench, I unroll the wedding wrapping paper I picked out for the two sketches I did of Johnny and Aiden.

"That is so disturbing," Graham mutters, coming up behind me and grimacing down at the framed drawings.

"You've called my work many things, but never disturbing. Please don't add that to your *Yelp* review of Gallery Andro. Bitsy will hunt you down and destroy you," I threaten, imagining Johnny's friend doing as much. She takes a lot of pride in helping run my art studio above Johnny's photography business. And to think, the shoppers may never know they're viewing my work where a swing bed once hung from the ceiling.

Shooting me a challenging look, Graham retorts, "That's because none of your work was of my brother and brother-in-law in jock straps."

He sighs when I laugh at him then checks his watch. Planting a kiss on my cheek, he informs me, "I'm gonna go feed the boys."

"They're fish. How do you even know if they're all boys?" I call out as he heads for the living room.

"I'm gay!" he yells back. "Why would I have girl fish?"

When the sound of his footsteps stops where I imagine the fish tank to be, my stomach does a double flip. I hope I didn't underestimate just how much he hates weddings. Sucking in a breath, I force my shaky knees to move until I reach where the hallway meets the living room.

He found it, judging by that frown he gets when he's confused. Digging his thumb and index finger into the can of fish food, he pulls out the ring box I placed in there earlier this morning and opens it.

"Dami, what…"

Swallowing, I step forward and drop to a knee in front of him, feeling lightheaded. I'm going to sweat through my suit at this rate and ruin all the wedding photos. Gosh, I have the worst ideas.

I have to clear my throat to speak. "So, it's kind of freaking me out right now, seeing just how much you hate weddings, so if you say *no*, it's okay. I'm happy however I get you, but, um, I had this plan…"

"What kind of plan?" he says all breathy, but there's a hint of a smile that feels like a life preserver.

"The kind where I made all these other stupid plans first and then realized that love is tougher than that, and you can't really make any plans. Maybe you find the person who's perfect for you and makes you smile even before you open your eyes in the morning because you know they're there." Reaching for his hand, I squeeze it and pause for a breath. "So, you decide you should at least ask them if they want to suffer through hating yet another wedding just so they know how much they mean to you."

"I won't hate it," he whispers, tugging me up by my shoulders and wrapping his arms around me. "It might actually make me like weddings."

"Yeah?"

"Yeah."

EXTENDED EPILOGUE

Graham

He wants to marry me. I already planned on forever with Dami a long time ago. I was going to ask him the same question after a big show he has coming up at his art studio, but I won't steal his thunder right now. The fact that he asked me, that he wanted to also ask me, makes my cup runneth over as my mother says.

Covering his mouth with mine, we grip each other like our lives depend upon it. It's fitting really. The way I view life now is the direct result of him. I was nothing but a thick suit of hollow armor before he came along, a shell of a man afraid of his own shadows. He saw past the armor and loved me out of my shell.

Pulling back, I trace his face, visioning memories to come. Our wedding, holidays, lazy afternoons by the lake, and maybe even children running around our front yard.

"There's an inscription on it," he says, guiding my hand up between us.

Pulling the silver band from the box, I rotate it between my fingers, eager to read what message my man wrote for me. The scrolled script reads, *my love is thicker than my morter and forever yours.*

Mortar is spelled *m-o-r-t-e-r*.

He fucking spelled it wrong.

"Do you like it?" he whispers anxiously.

Choking on my tears, I laugh and hug him to me. "Yeah. It's perfect."

Just like Dami.

DEAR READER

Thank you for discovering and supporting my work. You allow me to be able to do what I love. I say that often, but I'll keep saying it. It is such a gift that you give to me.

I hope you enjoyed Dami and Graham's story as much as I enjoyed writing it.

Random facts:

- The "three kidneys" joke was intentional, just FYI. I know how many kidneys one should have. And I am aware that "salty" isn't a four-letter word.

- My brother-in-law used to keep saltwater fish tanks and documented fish activity and pH levels in his *Fish Files* notebook, complete with very archaic, but amusing drawings, along with his fish' names, such as "Fat Bastard". I still have his *Fish Files* and miss him dearly. He passed away in a fishing accident, doing what he loved.

- My entire basic training unit came down with pink eye when I was in the Army. It was awful and very much like a zombie apocalypse.

- Most of the names in my books are a nod to my ARC readers and book friends.

- I used to sleep in a hammock on a hammock stand when I was a teenager. Thus, the swing bed inspiration, but nothing risqué happened in my hammock.

- I have stories planned for Vin and Thor and for Brennan and Will but have no idea how I can make them nearly as funny as this one. I'll be in my Smut Cave, plotting.

- I finger-type all my drafts on a Word .doc on my cell phone because family life keeps me away from my home office. That is a lot of finger-typing! When I'm finished, I retire to the Smut Cave and do the edits on the computer.

If you'd like to connect with me you can find me here:

www.diannaroman.com

ACKNOWLEDGEMENTS

Christie, you were my muse for so many things in this story. Your humor is bar none, so I want to let the world know they have you to thank for: firefly, cat phobias, loving someone out of their shell, "draw me like one of your French girls", and probably much more that I forgot because I'm a terrible friend.

To my fabulously fun and loyal beta reader team—I love you guys so much. Thanks for sticking with me, your enthusiasm for all of our she-nanigans and my work, and for being all around wonderful to each other by building a quirky reader family from what we started.

Bob aka Uhura, what would I do without your kindred misanthropeness and funny bone? I feel so spoiled because not everyone in this world gets a "Bob". I wish you more happiness than a quokka.

Kassandra and Emma, much appreciation for proofreading. You're both lifesavers!

Special thanks to Jen & Maxie for the last-minute life savers--and for your friendship that means so much to me.

Alexa at The Fiction Fix, I can't do without all of your sound advice. You are such a dear to me.

Katie & Brey PA—my ARC reader hunters—thank you for introducing new readers to my work and riding my ass. To the Possum Posse, your moral support for life in general always gets me through; I'm so grateful to have you in my corner.

Much appreciation to the big sweetheart Christopher Jensen for giving us the face of Graham. To David Carrion for the perfect photo to portray Damiano. And to the talented photographers Rafa Catala and Michelle Lancaster, so glad I found your wonderful work to help bring my book to life.

David Farquhar, you have such an incomparable talent, which I am so grateful to have witnessed. Thank you for allowing me to share your work.

Stephanie Henigin, I can't tell you how much I appreciate our continued collaborations with your bookboyfriend characters, giving an extra bit of fun and flare to my paperbacks and special edition covers. You are such a talent and lovely human being.

TOUGH
Love
NARRATED BY
LIAM DICOSIMO
AND
TIM PAIGE
DIANNA ROMAN

WORKS BY DIANNA

M/M ROMANCE

The Shutout

Men of Olympus Series
You Again (Book 1)
Tough Love (Book 2)

M/F ROMANCE

Grand Valley Series
A Fair Warning